BANNER
OF
SOULS

LIZ WILLIAMS

DOVER PUBLICATIONS, INC.
Mineola, New York

Bibliographical Note

This Dover edition, first published in 2020, is an unabridged republication of the work originally printed by Bantam Books, New York, in 2004.

Library of Congress Cataloging-in-Publication Data

Names: Williams, Liz, 1965– author.
Title: Banner of souls / Liz Williams.
Description: First edition. | Mineola, New York : Dover Publications, Inc., 2020. | Originally published, 2004. | Summary: "Banner of Souls is about a future running on a new technology called "haunt-tech," which draws energy from the realm of the dead. Reproduction has been industrialized. The remaining men, known as "men-remnants," are being hunted down by female Martian warriors. Martian warrior, Dreams-of-War, is dispatched to a far-future Earth, now flooded, to protect a young girl named Lunae"— Provided by publisher.
Identifiers: LCCN 2019058967 | ISBN 9780486843407 (trade paperback) | ISBN 0486843408 (trade paperback)
Subjects: GSAFD: Science fiction.
Classification: LCC PR6073.I43228 B36 2020 | DDC 823/.914—dc23
LC record available at https://lccn.loc.gov/2019058967

Manufactured in the United States by LSC Communications
84340801
www.doverpublications.com

2 4 6 8 10 9 7 5 3 1

2020

For Peter Garratt

ACKNOWLEDGMENTS

With thanks to . . .

- my editor, Anne Groell;
- my agent, Shawna McCarthy;
- everyone in the Montpellier Writing group and the Cantonese Writing group;
- everyone at Milford;
- Tanith Lee, for all her support;
- Mark Roberts, for the shark monkey; and
- Jay Caselberg, for the pangolin and much else besides.

THE GHOST HERD

CHAPTER 1

MARS

Dreams-of-War was hunting the remnants of men on the slopes of the Martian Olympus when she came across the herd of ghosts. The armor bristled at the approach of the herd, whispering caution into her ear, and at first Dreams-of-War thought that it was warning her against the presence of men—hyenae, perhaps, or vulpen, or others of the Changed. She wheeled around, activating the hand-spines of the armor, but there was nothing there. The cold, tawny slopes rolled into the distance, empty of everything except scrub and the sparse desert life that congregated around the canals and sinks. Far on the horizon, the column of Memnos Tower pointed upward, just visible now against a darkening sky. Dreams-of-War frowned. The armor remained alert, porcupine spikes forming and reforming as she moved.

"What?" Dreams-of-War said aloud, impatiently.

"There is someone here," the armor said. Sometimes it spoke with the voice of the warrior who had first imprinted it, but sometimes the voice sounded more akin to that of Dreams-of-War herself. That was the trouble with haunt-tech; one was never sure whether one was imagining things. But perhaps one could expect no less from something that had been granted by aliens.

"I see no one," Dreams-of-War said.

"Yet someone is here," the armor insisted.

And now Dreams-of-War could, indeed, feel something: an irritation over her guarded skin, like an insect crawl. She flinched within the protective carapace.

"Look," the armor said.

They were rising out of the ground, formed from dust and solidifying soil, then sharp-edged and real. There were perhaps twenty or so: women with long horns and backward-slanting legs, but they stood vertically. Their eyes were red, with narrow pupils that burned gold—a flame within coals. They gazed at Dreams-of-War with a kind of placid curiosity, despite their demon eyes, switching long tapering tails.

Dreams-of-War stood in frozen shock. They were more than illusion. She could smell them: the scent of long-dead grasslands, woodsmoke, and blood. They smelled like prey. And as if they had seen the thought in her eyes, the herd turned as one and began to run, loping swiftly along the slope until they were swallowed by the gathering twilight. Their small hooves made no sound. They moved in silence, and then were gone.

Dreams-of-War stared after them, feeling foolish. She should at least have made an attempt to capture one of them.

She said aloud, "There have not been such beings on Mars since ancient times. I have seen the records. They roamed the Crater Plain. No one knows who created them, what laboratory, or why."

"They were long dead by my day," the armor—itself a hundred years old—remarked with a trace of wistfulness.

"Thousand-year-old ghosts," Dreams-of-War mused. "But why have they appeared now? I suppose Memnos must be told. We should go back." She spoke with reluctance. She disliked setting out on a hunt and returning empty-handed, and this would be her last opportunity. Soon she would be headed for Earth, which now shone above her in the heavens, blue as an eye. The maw of the Chain was also visible: a faint glitter high above the surface of the world. She thought of hurtling into the maw, emerging above that blue star . . . More alien tech. Dreams-of-War's lip began to curl.

The prospect of that journey, however, was superseded by the thought of the men-remnants waiting in the rocks. It irritated Dreams-of-War. She could feel it in the armor, too: a wildness, a need for killing, for flesh and death. She had spotted no real prey all day, only the ghosts and the small creatures of the plain, and she had thought that the night would provide her with a chance. The vulpen, at least, slunk out of their holes after dusk, in search of the dactylate birds that were their staple diet.

With a sigh, Dreams-of-War repressed the impulse to continue. She set off back down the long stone-strewn slope to the plain, to where the Memnos Tower was waiting.

CHAPTER 2

NIGHTSHADE

Yskatarina Iye was named for the sounds she made on her emergence from the growing-skin—first a hiss and then a cry. A daughter of the lab clans, grown in Tower Cold, on the world of Nightshade at the Chain's end and the system's edge, a very long way from the sun.

The name—her child-name, not the appellation of her Nightshade clan—proved difficult to dislodge and Yskatarina retained it into adulthood, along with the Animus that grew beside her from a hatchling no bigger than a dragonfly. The Animus, spawned from the ancient genetic lineage of the clan just as Yskatarina herself had been, possessed no name. Yskatarina tried various permutations, yet none seemed to fit.

Her aunt Elaki told her from an early age how fortunate she was to have an Animus: how women on other worlds could not be bonded with a male, for there were so few remaining, and those were inferior. She was lucky, Yskatarina knew, that the Elders of Nightshade still sought to return to the old ways, when men and women walked the worlds together, when both genders lived in harmony, each seeking their other self. And the Animus was not a human male, for they had proved too weak, but something better.

Her Animus whispered to Yskatarina as she slept, throughout the long illnesses that marked her childhood: dreamfevers, feral malaises, and the modified infestations that would enable her not only to suffer the transformation when the time came, but to welcome it. She spent the endless dark of Nightshade with the Animus crouched beside the cot like a murmuring spider, spinning webs of words.

Transformation nearly killed her. It had been explained to her by her aunt that it would make her stronger, but she did not understand what "transformation" meant.

"What am I to be transformed *into*?" she had asked Elaki. But her aunt replied only, "You will see."

When the time came, Yskatarina lay, a small uncomprehending form, in the sparkling dark of the black light matrix as the engrams rewrote her: a process of alchemical change she was powerless to resist.

The black light powered down into a gleaming cube of air. Yskatarina blinked, waking. It felt as though she had been wrenched across a vast distance, torn through the remnants of boiling suns. There was a smell of fire and a terrible heaviness, a weight. She tried to raise her head, but it felt too large for her fragile neck. Someone bent over her. Yskatarina looked up, but it was several moments before the strange shape floating before her congealed into human features.

She saw a long face, cheeks puffed out into veined pouches on either side of a thin, hooked nose. The skin was unlined, unnaturally smooth and shiny as porcelain. The eyes were set in deep hollows, filled with bloodshot gold. The hair was feathery: dirty-black, coiling in wispy tendrils from beneath the high hat.

Then, Yskatarina's vision shifted and she realized that it was her aunt Elaki peering down at her. Yet for a moment it seemed that there was someone else looking out from Elaki's eyes, someone who cried out in horror.

"You!" Elaki shrieked.

"Aunt?" Her own voice sounded faint, a thin croaking. Elaki reached down and shook her.

"It's *you*, isn't it? I'd know you anywhere."

"Aunt, what is wrong?" Something squirmed inside Yskatarina's head, running in turn from Elaki's anger, tunneling down to hide in the deep channels of her mind.

Elaki's face became thoughtful and cold, as if a crucial decision had been reached. She turned on her heel and spoke to someone unseen, probably the Animus Isti, who followed always at her heels.

"Prepare the matrix once more. There are some further modifications to be made."

Darkness swept over Yskatarina like a wing. There was a tearing, rending sensation, a lightning bolt through her brain. It felt as though she were being split in two, and the pain sent her squealing down into the abyss.

She did not wake for a long time. At last, swimming up through unconsciousness, she found herself no longer in the black light chamber, but in her own room. Her head felt like a great hot bag, too heavy to lift. She put up a hand to feel her brow, but nothing happened. Alarmed, Yskatarina tried to move her arms and legs. There was no sensation at all. She cried out for Elaki.

"Ah! You're awake," her aunt said, bustling in.

"I can't feel my arms, or my legs!"

Elaki placed a clammy hand on Yskatarina's forehead. "I fear that is because they are no longer there. You suffered a rare meningeal infection after the transformation process, and your limbs were damaged by gangrene. We were forced to remove them."

"Aunt?" Yskatarina whispered, in fright and shock.

"We will make new limbs for you," Elaki promised. Her face softened, almost imperceptibly, but there was something behind her eyes that alarmed Yskatarina beyond measure. "Better ones. So do not make such a fuss."

When Elaki left, Yskatarina stared numbly up to find the Animus above her, in chrysalis form. She reached out for him, before she remembered. He hung in a motionless silver-black shape from the ceiling of the laboratory, depending from a piece of growing bone. After her own experiences, Yskatarina did not expect the Animus to emerge alive, but emerge he did, gliding from the tinsel wreckage of the chrysalis: arachnid, escorpionate, baleful.

Yskatarina knew then that there was nothing she would not do to keep the Animus beside her. Hadn't they always been together? And after the dreadful experience of transformation, the Animus was the only being on which she could rely.

There was another change, too. Before, Yskatarina had been afraid of her aunt: dreading the touch of Elaki's pale, plump hands, hating the way her aunt's great eyes would gaze at her with such chilly calculation. But after the transformation, she also became aware of how much she truly loved Elaki. The feeling overwhelmed her. She sat shivering on the cot, filled with longing, and when Elaki next came to see her, she threw her new arms around her aunt's shrouded form. Elaki pushed her away, wincing.

"You must learn to operate your limbs with more care, Yskatarina. The servomechanisms are powerful."

"Thank you, Aunt. *Thank you*." But she could not have said what she was thanking Elaki for. It occurred to her, vaguely, that this should have bothered her, but somehow she dismissed it.

When she was well enough to venture forth, Yskatarina and the Animus wandered together through the shadowy passageways of Tower Cold. They learned the secret ways between the walls; they slipped past hidden chambers as Yskatarina's artificial feet crunched and crackled on the thousand-year-old bones of mice. Concealed behind living tapestries, they watched as the Steersmen Skull-Faces bottled up the canopic jars and dispatched them into the boats that would carry them to the gates, there to be launched upon the Night Sea for their endless journey. They traveled down to the depths, where the mute-kin slaved on the production lines, assembling haunt-devices. They sat for hours above the docking bays as the service ships headed out toward the Chain. They scuttled through the Weighing Chamber, while the mourn-women sang the ancient songs, conjuring—so they said—the spirits of the future dead, untied from the rivers of time. But Yskatarina did not understand what they meant by that, and when she asked her aunt, Elaki only laughed and said that the mourn-women were filled with superstitions and nonsense. The only places Yskatarina and the Animus did not go were the haunt-laboratories of Tower Cold, sealed behind horrifying weir-wards, open only to Elaki.

And it was the Animus who learned with Yskatarina, upon the eve of her nineteenth birthday, that it was to be her task to seek out one girl from the teeming billions of Earth and Mars and the inner worlds. To seek her out and slay her.

CHAPTER 3

MARS

Two days before her departure for Earth, Dreams-of-War left the Memnos Tower and made a short journey across the Crater Plain to Winterstrike, in order to register her departure documents, undergo a necessary modification, and take a medical assessment for her suitability to withstand the temporal forces of the Chain. This last was merely a formality; Dreams-of-War was in excellent physical shape. She knew, however, that at least once a week some luckless passenger was found shriveled and wizened at the end of a voyage, ruthlessly aged by the forces that governed travel within the confines of the Chain.

It was, after all, a form of haunt-tech, and thus little understood except by the technicians of Nightshade and presumably by the Kami who had given it to them. It was alien and could not be trusted, at least if you were Dreams-of-War. The only piece of haunt-tech with which she was prepared to deal was the armor, and that only because its previous occupant had been such a great warrior. And while Dreams-of-War trusted the armor's spirit, it still occurred to her to wonder whether this was wise.

She further distrusted the prospect of the modification that she was about to undergo—more alien tech—and she did not care much for Winterstrike, either. The city was ancient, dating back before even the Lost Epoch. Its black-and-crimson mansions and narrow streets were a testament to its age: basalt, iron, stone— old materials for an old city. The more recent buildings rose up around the edges, etched metal towers and turrets connected by hanging bridges.

Dreams-of-War took a rider, crammed with standing passengers, in through the southern gate of the city, past the clan holdings and mansions, and finally past the sunken fortress of the meteorite crater that had given Winterstrike its name. She looked neither right nor left, though when the rider rumbled by the great lip of the crater, her head involuntarily turned and she gazed into the pit: a caldera of garnet stone, pockmarked with holes and rifts. The fortress rose up at its center, a place of shattered spires, half-ruin, half-home to the city's dispossessed, of which there were many.

The fortress was a grim place, but better this, thought Dreams-of-War, than the Crater Plain and the mountains. There, the ordinary women who were not warriors would not fare well against the men-remnants: the hyenae and vulpen and awts. Better they remain here, living off the verminous birds that infested the pits of the crater wall.

The fortress passed by; Dreams-of-War once more stared ahead. This long, winding street, fringed with engine shops and child-supply emporia, was the road to the spaceport. She would be coming this way again tomorrow, in the cold early light, to take a ship for the Chain and Earth: the city known as Fragrant Harbor. She had been told little enough about her mission. There was a child, it seemed, and the need to guard her.

Dreams-of-War had done her best to find out more, by devious routes she disliked pursuing, but she had failed. This in itself was disquieting. Memnos only bothered to keep closemouthed about those secrets that were a danger to the bearer, and they had seen fit to tell her nothing. Thoughtfully, Dreams-of-War jostled her way to the front of the rider as it approached the next stop, and stepped down onto the street.

The medical evaluation was carried out in a Matriarchy building: a weedwood-and-basalt tower behind thick walls. Dreams-of-War sensed the prickling discomfort of weir-wards over the exposed skin of her face as she walked through the gate, but she passed through without incident. Inside, she presented her credentials, but it seemed that they were already expecting her. A woman wearing a doctor's robe and high red hat ushered her through a hushed corridor into the black light chamber. The doctor's hands had been modified, Dreams-of-War noted; a scalpel blade shone briefly beneath one fingernail.

"You'll have to take that off," the doctor said, barely glancing in the direction of Dreams-of-War.

"Very well." Dreams-of-War stood at the center of the room, before the flickering glitter of the black light matrix. "Armor!"

The armor flowed smoothly from her body, forming for a moment the gaunt figure of its previous owner. "No, that won't be necessary. I don't want to talk to you. Just keep out of the way."

She watched as the armor folded itself into a small, curdled sphere, no bigger than her fist. It struck her, somehow, as sad. She glanced down at her own exposed skin. Tattoos covered her arms and breasts: spirals, spikes, the mathematical gematria of Memnos. The small child-markings were a faded indigo around her wrists.

"And *that*," the doctor remarked, glancing at the bands of her black rubbery underharness. "And we'll need to do something about your hair." Without asking, the doctor seized a handful of Dreams-of-War's pale hair and bundled it up into a knot. Dreams-of-War jerked away, snatching the coil from the doctor's probing fingers.

"Don't touch me!"

"Stop *complaining*."

Dreams-of-War stood, fuming, as the doctor made the final preparations.

"Why couldn't this be done in the Memnos Tower? They have a more extensive matrix there."

"It's off-limits for now," the doctor said. "They have a client coming in who wants something special."

"Special?"

"Someone all the way from Io-Beneath, apparently. You know that the matrices can be hired."

Dreams-of-War gave a snort. "For the right price."

"Of course. Now lie down. No, not there. With your feet facing the wall."

Dreams-of-War did as she was instructed. The black light matrix sparkled over her, causing an itchy crackle to cross her skin and raise the hair on the back of her neck.

"Are you all right?" the doctor asked, clearly caring little as to the answer. "Not scared?"

"Of course I am not scared! I do not like the sensation, that is all."

"No one living is supposed to like it. It brings you close to the Eldritch Realm, to the spirit dimensions."

"I've faced death many times," Dreams-of-War said, affronted.

"That is not what I meant. It is a neurophysiological reaction. In the case of we the living, consciousness is welded to body and brain, until the point of physical death when the particulates that compose the spirit detach from the shore-surface of the brain and leave the interface between the dimensions. You're not about to die; you are, in fact, a long way away from it as a healthy young person. But now your spirit is trying to tug free, drawn by the matrix, and that is why you're uncomfortable."

Dreams-of-War squinted up at the doctor. "And if it did tug free, what then? Would I die?"

"Yes. Body and soul would part company, and then your essence would drift into the blatklight matrix and be snapped through into the Eldritch Realm. This is what befalls you when you enter the Chain, except that in there, people are held together by the internal structures. Usually. But nothing like that is going to happen to you now. I'm going to put you under—"

"Oh no, you are not!" But before Dreams-of-War could utter another word of protest, the doctor touched a sleep-pen to her neck. Dreams-of-War fell, snarling, between the warp and weft of life and death, and knew no more.

When she awoke, it was dark outside. She was lying on an ordinary metal bed, her head supported by an iron pillow. The armor reposed in a glistening lump on a table by the bedside. The doctor was nowhere to be seen.

Shakily, Dreams-of-War sat up. She could not see her underharness, but no matter.

"Armor!"

Instantly, Embar Khair's armor uncurled itself from its resting form and flowed across her outstretched hand. Soon she was covered in familiar gleaming green. Dreams-of-War stood up, supported by the armor. She felt no different—at first. But when she looked into herself, she was conscious of a new, sore spot inside her head. Dreams-of-War probed it, imagining fingers gingerly touching, and the result was a flooding anxiety, an adrenaline rush that made her gasp. She closed her eyes, and had a sudden disquieting image of the interior of her mind. Normally as dark, hard, and resolute as metal, her inner self now contained a small hole, pink and tender from recent bleeding. The sensation was as compelling as a stolen tooth.

The door opened. The doctor's face was disapproving beneath the high scarlet hat.

"You should not be on your feet! And who told you that you could get dressed?"

Dreams-of-War took a single stride across the room and seized the doctor by the throat.

"What have you done to me? What have you put in my head?"

"Rather," the doctor said faintly, scrabbling at the hand around her neck, "you should be asking what it is that we have removed. Now let me *go*."

"*Removed?*"

The doctor was gasping. The scalpel blade shot out from beneath her fingernail. Desiring answers, Dreams-of-War let go and experienced a curious and unfamiliar sense of relief.

"This is what I have done," the doctor said, massaging her neck. "There is a psychological callus that is grown on the mind of a warrior, that increases day by day after your release from the growing-skin. It is that callus that enables you to act fearlessly, to make your goals your only focus, that permits you to go forth and slaughter your enemies with as little compunction as I feel when I swat a weed bug down from the wall at night. That emotional callus makes you everything that you are, and now it is gone. You will feel as a normal made-human feels. You will feel love, affection, need, and anxiety for a child."

"I have no intention of having a child!" *Sitting by a growing-skin for months while someone congealed within, followed by years of restriction and worry? No thanks.*

"No, but you will be looking after one. An indifferent guardian is no guardian at all. You have to care. And Memnos is determined to *make* you care. I do not understand you warrior clans. What is wrong with having emotions?"

Dreams-of-War stared at her. "Nothing at all. Emotions are a fine and necessary thing—pride, aggression, loyalty . . . As for caring," she added, bristling, "my duty as a warrior should be enough."

"It seems Memnos does not think so."

"How much have they told you about this child whom I am to guard?" Dreams-of-War asked.

"They have told me very little. In all probability," the doctor added, "as little as they have told you."

"And what about me?" Dreams-of-War asked uneasily. "If this—this cork in my psyche permitted me to function as a warrior, to kill without qualm, what will happen now that it is gone?"

"Since you have just recently embarked upon my throttling," the doctor said, rubbing a bruised throat, "I wouldn't worry too much about *that*."

CHAPTER 4

EARTH

Tersus Rhee waddled slowly through the chamber, checking with thick fingers the drip-feeds that led to the growing-skins, monitoring the minor changes and alterations that might token an incipient systems failure. They had already lost the previous children. If this one, too, failed, the Grandmothers had told her, then the project might have to be terminated. And that would be a great shame. The Grandmothers had gone to an immense amount of trouble on behalf of the child in the growing-skin. The services of Tersus Rhee herself had been procured. A Martian warrior was now on her way, at no small difficulty and expense, to guard the child.

Tersus Rhee, for various reasons of her own, did not want the project to be terminated. The Grandmothers had told her little enough about this line of made-humans, this special strain to whose care she so diligently attended. But then, despite her skills, she knew that she was nothing more than the hired help to the Grandmothers, just another kappa, indistinguishable from all the rest of her kind. She did not expect to be told a great deal. She knew only that the child in the bag was known as the *hito-bashira*, the woman-who-holds-back-the-flood. She had her own suspicions as to what this might mean.

But speculation had already run rife throughout the clans of the kappa when it was learned that she, Tersus Rhee of Hailstone Shore, was to be sent all the way south to Fragrant Harbor to serve the Grandmothers.

"How much do you know about the Grandmothers?" the clan leader had asked Rhee.

"Very little." Rhee shuffled her wide feet in a supplicatory gesture and spread her webbed hands wide.

"Unsurprising. No one knows anything of them, it seems—who they are, where they come from. Now, they keep to their mansion of Cloud Terrace, but it is not known how long they have been there. They squat above the city like bats. Then, suddenly, they send word to me, asking for a grower, a carer. An expert."

Rhee frowned. "Why are you telling me this? Am I to be that expert?"

The clan leader gave a slow frog blink. "Just so."

"But what about my duties here?"

"This is more important." The puffed eyelids drifted shut and tightened. Rhee knew that she would say nothing further.

"When am I to leave?" Rhee asked in resignation.

"On the third day of the new moon, when the time is auspicious. Take what you need."

And so, with a hired junk waiting in the harbor below, Tersus Rhee had packed her equipment: the box of scalpels, the neurotoxin feeds that, if carefully applied, would alter genetic development to the desired specifications, and a handful of the starter mulch that had now been in her family for seven generations, nurtured and handed down like a precious yeast. For all else, she would be obliged to rely on the Grandmothers of Cloud Terrace, and the thought did not please her.

The journey south pleased her even less. She would be traveling not as an expert hired by Cloud Terrace, but incognito, as a hired help. This was so commonplace for the kappa as to be unremarked. It was, after all, they who provided most of the world's drudgery. Rhee traveled in the communal hold of the junk but spent most of the day on deck, watching the peaks of the Fire Islands recede into the distance until they were no bigger than pins against the lowering skies. From then on, the journey was uneventful: only ocean, like so much of Earth, wave after endless rolling wave. Rhee passed her time in the passive, contemplative trance that was the default mode of her people, and made doubly sure that no one noticed her. The kappa spoke little among themselves, anyway, when away from the clan-warrens.

On the third day out, however, there was excitement during a sudden squall. A commotion at the prow of the junk suggested an unusual occurrence, with all the crew rushing to see. Rhee was sitting under a furled sail, just far enough into the rain to be comfortable. She rose to her feet with difficulty on the slick, plunging deck, and ambled toward the prow. Everyone was shouting and pointing, but Rhee was too short to see what they were all looking at. With placid determination, she shoved her way through and stared.

Something was rising on the horizon: a huge, curling shell. From this distance, Rhee estimated, the thing must be hundreds of feet high. Coiling, spatulate tentacles drifted out from the main bulk, forming a nimbus against the stormlight. When it once more sank, the rain had passed, leaving a clear sky in its wake.

"What was that?" Rhee asked a crewmember. The woman, red-clad like all sailors, turned toward the kappa. Her face was wizened with a lifetime of saltspray and wind; she bore the mark of Izanami, creator goddess of ocean, between eyes like black currants.

Rhee thought she already knew what manner of thing it had been, looming up out of the waters, but she wanted to be sure.

"Why, it was a Dragon-King," the crewmember said. She touched the mark between her brows in respect. "Did you see its whips?"

"I did," the kappa said. "Are Dragon-Kings common in these parts?"

"Do you not know?"

Rhee shook her head with the affectation of doleful stupidity.

"Why, there are said to be no more than four of the great beasts, which survived the Drowning. Once, the world was full of dragons, so they say—from what are now the Shattered Lands to the islands of Altai and Thibet. But then they raised the wrath of the ocean, of Izanami, and the sea rose up and drowned the world and all the dragons with it. And now there are only the sea dragons left, the great kings who once bore pearls in their claws and jewels in their manes."

The kappa forbore from saying that the thing they had just seen had neither claws nor mane, and the great polished shell more closely resembled metal than scales, only inclined her head and mumbled, as if in awe. The crewmember moved on and Rhee wandered thoughtfully back belowdeck.

Later, a bandit boat was seen, coming out from one of the inlets, but it veered away after the junk raised a warning, and sped back toward the ruined shores of its home.

After that, there was nothing of note until the towers and typhoon shelters of Fragrant Harbor appeared, with the mansion of the Grandmothers squatting amid the great houses at its summit. They arrived at dusk, with the lights of the city glowing out across the harbor, flickering and changing in the choppy water, mirroring nothing. The kappa chose to take it as a sign.

Once she was actually in Cloud Terrace, immured in the growing-chamber for most of the day, the situation pleased the kappa even less. The mansion—itself in a district filled with the ancient and decaying houses of the long-dead rich—was labyrinthine, full of weir-wards that the kappa constantly had to avoid activating. The Grandmothers had been forced to make some allowance for her inherent clumsiness—it was clear that the mansion had been designed for classical human form and not for the Changed, despite the Grandmothers' own appearance—but they had been clear in their disapproval. And Rhee, in turn, hated the weir-wards: the forms they conjured up, beings of the distant past and distant deep, all teeth and eyes, swimming through the empty air of the passages and hallways, snapping at things that were not there. But if someone unauthorized had fallen into their path, the kappa knew, then the teeth would have proved all too real.

She hoped for the Martian's sake that the warrior would retain some grace in the slightly different gravity. Two of them stumbling about the mansion, summoning the lost beasts of the Eldritch Realm, did not bear thinking about.

So Rhee kept mainly to the growing-chamber, whose wards were outside the door in order to avoid disruption to the delicate life-form within the skins, and she slept on a pallet. It suited her to do this, too, for when it came to the moment of hatching, it was vital that she should be present. She hoped the Martian would be there for this new child, as well. The woman should see what manner of thing was to be guarded, right from the start. But for now, the skin was quiescent, dangling from its long feeds like a ripe fruit. Only a small pulse at the base of the stem indicated that there was anything living in it at all. But soon, the kappa knew, it would reach fruition.

And then everything would change.

CHAPTER 5

MARS/EARTH

Dreams-of-War waited impatiently as the ship joined the queue of vessels waiting to dock. There was little traffic from the edges of the system. She gazed out at freighters and passenger craft with lunar markings, the insignia of some of the client factories of Earth: all of it pockmarked, scarred, old.

"*Approach*," she heard the ship's consciousness say, formed, perhaps, of some past pilot or a composite of pilots, haunt-shifted into the ship's black light system.

The ship was entering the Martian maw of the Chain, ready for the rush. The maw gaped before them, a mile or more in width, lined with rotating spines to keep out intruding traffic— the disaffected of the lesser worlds, who occasionally tried to disrupt the flow of the Chain. At the back of the maw, Dreams-of-War glimpsed the energy spirals that would take them onward: a twisting glint. In the next few minutes they would be passing through the dimensional interfaces that the Chain manipulated to compensate for different planetary orbits and then entering the Eldritch Realm, the dimension of the dead, before once more emerging through another maw into the atmosphere of Earth. Or so one hoped.

Strapped into her seat, Dreams-of-War was uneasily reminded of the experience that she had so recently undergone beneath the black light matrix. She closed her eyes and leaned back. The ship roared and shuddered as it entered the first portals of the maw. Dreams-of-War hoped it would hold up. Often ships did not; rent and sundered by the forces within, they emerged as antiques, or not at all.

Restless, she opened her eyes again and looked around at her fellow passengers. Most were Martian: the bleached women of the north, dressed in elaborate swathes and robes, all overlapping folds. Suitable for the chilly Martian plains, thought Dreams-of-War, but the ship was stiflingly hot. The women showed no signs of discomfort, however. They sat upright, cold and wan as stone.

Other passengers were less easily placed: a woman with dark skin and protruding vertebrae, a too-long neck that continually angled and flexed as if seeking comfort; a squat person with a depression in the top of her head, deep enough to hold liquid. *The Changed*, thought Dreams-of-War with distaste. She glowered down at her own armored self. The Changed passengers passed by, heading for economy class.

The ship juddered as it began to enter temporal recalibration. A bewildering kaleidoscope of images whirled and wheeled before Dreams-of-War's eyes.

She saw a small, grublike child lying in a black metal bed in the depths of a tower, ice riming the interior windows . . .

. . . A woman stood on the deck of a ship, staring out at storms . . .

. . . A single dark wing spiraled down from out of the clouds and Dreams-of-War felt rain on her face, before touching her hand to her cheek. Her fingers came away slimy with blood and ichor . . .

Dreams-of-War jumped, filled with sudden dismay.

Possible futures, possible pasts, unskeining as the interior of the Chain folded and refolded time, enveloping it in upon itself, merging and sifting. She could feel time running past and through her, traveling in both directions. Dimly, she was aware of the other passengers. The pale northerners wore identical expressions of deep affront.

The ship was entering the final stages of recalibration. It slid with a shriek into the deeplight web of the Chain. Shadow-space rose up to enfold it. Then memory rose up and engulfed Dreams-of-War as time changed.

She was only just out of the clan house. A warrior was missing; it was assumed that hyenae had taken her, high in the crags. Or perhaps the warrior had slipped and fallen, and now lay at the bottom of one of the sharp ravines. Dreams-of-War hoped it was hyenae. She disliked killing beasts, because of their beauty, but the men-remnants were another matter.

Warriors did not work well together, and it was not expected of them. The women set off in the early morning, just before dawn. It was cold, with a ground frost that snapped at Dreams-of-War's heels. She was not wearing the armor of Embar Khair, for this was a year before she had earned it. A leather apron, underharness, boots, and a gutting knife were all that she wore, but her dental implants had recently been made. Her gums were sore, and they still bled first thing in the morning. Dreams-of-War recalled looking up from the ice-cracked basin and seeing scarlet running down her chin, reflected in the metal walls of the bathroom. She had borne the pain with pride, nursing it as warriors were encouraged to bear all small anguishes, that they might better be accustomed to pain when it made its first true visits upon them in the combat-ring, or life.

Unlike the other girls, Dreams-of-War chose a difficult route into the mountains: up the face of Mount Haut, which rose in a sheer rock cliff from the stones of the plain. Usually the canyons that led to this cliff were to be avoided; it was known to be a place where Earthbones were found, with pits and traps in the ground leading to the devouring flesh beneath. Dreams-of-War smeared lattice pulp on the soles of her boots to disguise her odor and was careful where she walked, but she could still smell the Earthbones as she slipped through the canyon: a faint trace of rotten meat. She avoided any place where the soil appeared unstable or bloody; the Earthbones exuded a seep of purulence upward into the earth, to form their entrapping webs. But it was still too easy to take a misstep; two warriors had been lost that year alone.

It was a difficult ascent up the cliff. Dreams-of-War was compelled to remove her boots halfway up and climb barefoot, to give herself a better grip. When she reached a ledge a little way below the summit, she was sweating and her mouth was filled with blood from where her new teeth had snagged her lip. She spat in a crimson arc down toward the plain, and looked forth.

The sun was bursting up over the horizon's edge, casting sharp shadows across the plain. She could see the angular buildings of the clan house, rising up through the nest of trees, half-lost in a haze of smoke from the still-smoldering fires of the previous evening. The Memnos Tower broke the line of the horizon. Beneath the plain ran a labyrinth of tunnels, reaching out from the Tower into the hills. Dreams-of-War looked at the Tower with distaste. It was the place to which all else must defer, the governing seat of Mars and thereby of Earth, a place full of politics and intrigue. Dreams-of-War was not a political being.

She dismissed the view with a curl of the lip. She would be relieved to be free of the clan house, too—free to win her armor and travel the slopes of Olympus, the sands of the Crater Plain. There was no doubt in her mind that the armor would be won, when the time came. Now, however, she turned and looked upward.

The crags towered above her, ochre and rust and blood. She could smell smoke—from the clan house?—but it was surely too distant. A faint trace of burning meat: hyenae, then. Hope rose in her. She started to clamber up, following the scent. As she crested the top of a high ridge, she found them below. Four of the men-remnants were crouched in a hollow in the rock around a fire. They were, indeed, hyenae, from the deep fastness of the mountains; unusual, to find them this far west, away from their caverns and the female remnants with which they bred. Dreams-of-War repressed a shudder at the thought. Coarse, tawny hair spilled down their backs; the long, overshot jaws bore small up-reaching tusks and their eyes resembled black, shiny seeds. Occasionally, one of them gave voice in a grunting bark of satisfaction. They were eating what remained of the missing warrior.

Oh well, thought Dreams-of-War. Not a noble end, but probably she had died fighting and there were enough of the hyenae on which to exact a reasonably satisfactory vengeance. She leaped down from the ridge, slid along a bank of scree, and uttered a roar. The hyenae looked up, startled, with fragments of human flesh raised halfway to their tusks. They had a limb each, she noted. Very equitable, but Dreams-of-War was not about to give them the chance to benefit.

She dispatched one with the gutting knife, another on a backhand swing, kicked the third in the face and crushed his skull. The fourth bolted, still clutching a fire-blackened portion of arm. Dreams-of-War started after him, but he was gone down the ravine, leaping from crag to crag with engineered speed. She retrieved the warrior's lost insignia from the flames, tucked it into her apron, then made her way sulkily back. She had not even had a proper chance to try out the new teeth.

Dreams-of-War returned to the present with a start. Shadow-space was fading back into deeplight as the Eldritch Realm slid away. She felt it pass through her soul as it left, a cold burn followed by a nausea that was closer to revulsion than motion sickness.

Earth and Fragrant Harbor lay ahead.

CLOUD TERRACE

CHAPTER 1

EARTH

8 MONTHS LATER...

Lunae was in the tower room of Cloud Terrace, a chrysalis in her hand, when Dreams-of-War came to find her. The chrysalis rested velvet-light against Lunae's skin, a woven parcel too large for her childish fingers to close all the way around. She sat cross-legged on the window seat, looking out over the jumbled tenements as they stretched down from the Peak toward the harbor. Her Grandmothers still used the old names for the city: Hong Kong, Fragrant Harbor, the City of Sails. She tested each one on her tongue, staring down into the late-afternoon shadows between the immensity of the tenements.

Across the water, at the edges of High Kowloon, the crimson sign of the Nightshade Mission burned through the haze, casting a glitter over the sea. A junk was coming in from the east, the filament sails turning in a glare of gold to catch the wind. Lunae thought she glimpsed its dragon figurehead and imagined it gliding over long-drowned lands, coming into port beneath the volcanoes of the north.

Far above the horizon, the maw of the Chain arched upward: the initial segment of the Earth-Mars pathway. Even in daylight, Lunae thought she could identify incoming ships as the maw turned, but it was hard to see through the smoky air, so she looked back to the chrysalis in her hand.

There was a sudden twitch inside her head. Beyond the window, the view changed: a darker day, with the red sign of the Mission flickering through fog. Farther east a great lamp glowed, warning ships away from the walls of the fortress-temple of Gwei Hei.

The chrysalis, too, shifted and altered. A silk-moth now sat upon Lunae's palm, beating iridescent wings.

Lunae's mind twitched again. The chrysalis was back, as tightly wrapped as before. The afternoon sunlight flooded in. Lunae smiled, but then a voice behind her said, "And what do you think you're doing?"

Lunae jumped. Dreams-of-War stood in the doorway, her armored hand tapping impatiently against the lacquered wood. Lunae looked up into her guardian's icy green glare.

"Nothing."

"What's that you're holding?" Dreams-of-War strode across the room, steel-shod feet clicking on driftwood boards, razor teeth glistening wet in a sudden shaft of sunlight. Her wan hair flowed down her back, unbound today, suggesting that her guardian must be in a relatively good mood. Enboldened, Lunae held up the chrysalis. It rested in her palm, innocent, untransformed.

"I found it under the windowsill. It will be a silk-moth one day."

"So it will," Dreams-of-War said, seemingly appeased, then added, "*one day.* You are not to exercise your talents, except at the beginning and end of your lessons. I've told you before—the Grandmothers have insisted upon it. Do you understand?"

Lunae nodded. "I understand." Then she added, reluctantly, "I'm sorry." There had been a time, not long ago, when she had obeyed her guardians without question, but recently the restrictions placed upon her had begun to chafe. No point in asking for forgiveness, though. Dreams-of-War did not believe in it. It was not, she had said, a Martian concept.

Lunae looked up at her guardian. The armor, as green and iridescent as an insect's carapace, flowed over the Martian woman's skin, covering everything except Dreams-of-War's angular face and her hair. A dragonfly-Samurai, Lunae thought; rows of needles bristled from Dreams-of-War's breastplate like viridian thorns. Her mailed hands were demon-clawed.

Once, Lunae had woken with a toothache and, unable to locate her nurse, had sought out Dreams-of-War instead. She had often wondered whether her guardian even slept, but sure enough, when she stepped into the red lacquer room at the far end of the eastern wing, there was Dreams-of-War, lying on the bed, neck resting on an iron pillow. Her arms were crossed austerely over her breast and she was still wearing her armor, like some ancient statue. Lunae could not help wondering whether the armor provided some kind of support system; certainly Dreams-of-War never seemed to remove it, and she had never joined Lunae in the bathing chamber. This was perhaps a relief. Lunae thought that it would be disturbing to see her guardian naked. She imagined Dreams-of-War as cold and pale, with flesh as hard as marble. Surely she was never as vulnerable as the unraveled contents of the chrysalis.

Dreams-of-War had told her that the armor was old and that it marked her as a member of the Memnos Matriarchy. When Lunae had been able to access her buried memories, she had learned of the women of the Memnos Tower—the current rulers of Mars and Earth. She learned how they had taken pity on the weakness of humans and created the kappa and other creatures to serve the people of Earth.

Her guardian's words echoed in her mind: *"The Martians have always been superior. It is, after all, we who colonized Earth thousands of years ago. My ancestors come from the ice palaces of the far south; they roamed the snow-seas in far prehistory."*

Now Dreams-of-War reached out a spiny hand and, careful not to touch Lunae's face, took a strand of hair between her fingers. Lunae squinted down, surprised, for Dreams-of-War had long ago expressed a dislike of intimate contact. The dark red threads glistened against the Martian woman's fingernails, the armored hand changing, becoming spidery and delicate.

"I'm glad you understand me," Dreams-of-War said. "You are nine months old, almost grown. Soon you will be a woman. You are old enough to obey instruction without mutiny."

"I do the best I can," Lunae protested.

"You do tolerably well, at that. But you must do better, and that means practicing restraint." Dreams-of-War squatted on armored heels until she was level with Lunae's gaze. The armor flowed smoothly to accommodate the movement: needles retracting, joints shifting.

Lunae shifted uncomfortably on the window ledge.

"What's the matter?"

"It's just—how am I ever to grow and learn if I am not allowed out of the house?"

She had seen little even of the harbor, except glimpses from the heights of Cloud Terrace and through the spy-eyes that the Grandmothers had installed in the streets between the tenements of the Peak. Lunae spent hours in front of the oreagraph, watching everyday life pass before the spy-eyes. She knew that the Grandmothers would forbid this if they knew, but Dreams-of-War had once caught her in front of the oreagraph and had turned away without saying a word. Later, she had devoted a lesson to the workings of the oreagraph: ostensibly a theoretical study, but Lunae took it for approval nonetheless.

From the altered perspective of the spy-eyes, the mansion in which Lunae now sat resembled a wrecked vessel, a sprawling black mass of uneven wings and curling gables, pagoda-roofed, as though cast up by some impossibly high tide. Cloud Terrace was a vulture-house, she thought, with the Grandmothers squatting at its heart.

On the rare occasions that Lunae had been taken down into the streets of the Peak, beyond the weir-wards of Cloud Terrace, she had been made to stay in an enclosed litter. Frustrated, confined by lacquer walls, Lunae had listened to the multiple babble of Cantonese, Kitachi Malaya, and the Lost Tongues of the north, smelled smoke and kimchi and lemongrass, the odors of the tea stalls, and the blood that ran from the slaughter-racks of the meat market. She had been unable to catch even a glimpse of the world around her. But for once, Dreams-of-War and her kappa nurse had been in agreement with the Grandmothers' dictates: Lunae should not be exposed to the view of the general populace. Lunae did not understand why this should be.

But now rebellion rose in Lunae's breast like the silk-moth in its captive web. She knew only her home, loved the kappa, respected Dreams-of-War, and obeyed her Grandmothers, but she so greatly wanted to see what it was like elsewhere, to witness the world beyond the weir-wards and the oreagraph. With sudden longing, she remembered the junk running in from the north.

"When am I to be allowed outside?" she asked once more, for her guardian had not yet replied.

"Not today," Dreams-of-War replied, simultaneously fanning and withering Lunae's hopes. Frustration rose to choke her.

"*When*, then?"

"When you are ready."

"I would love to travel the Chain," Lunae ventured.

Dreams-of-War laughed. "Would you? My home of Mars, perhaps, the Nine Cities of the Crater Plain? Winterstrike and Caud? Or would you prefer to ride the links all the way to Nightshade, see the sun as nothing more than a pinprick star?" She added after a moment, "Not that one can enter Nightshade space. The lab clans won't allow it."

"Everything," Lunae said, wide-eyed. "I want to see everything."

"Well, you have spirit, I'll give you that," Dreams-of-War answered.

When Dreams-of-War had gone, Lunae rose restlessly from the window seat and made her way down the twisting stairs. Her footsteps clattered on the boards, for all that she tried to be quiet. The Grandmothers always told her off for making a noise, and when she told Dreams-of-War how hard she endeavored to keep silent, the Martian merely snorted and said that the floorboards were made deliberately creaky, so that the Grandmothers would always hear who was coming. Lunae did not find it at all difficult to believe this explanation and she took additional pains to walk softly.

She passed the door that led to the Grandmothers' chamber and paused, but no sound came from within. The hallway smelled musty at this point, as though something old and forlorn had leaked beneath the door and permeated the atmosphere. Lunae hurried on, seeking fresher air. Soon she found herself in the narrow kitchen. The stove had been lit, which made the room smoky. Lunae sneezed once, then went to the back door. She was not allowed to go into the garden without the kappa or Dreams-of-War, but she tried the door handle anyway, half-expecting the weir-wards to shriek up. They did not, suggesting that the kappa was already outside. It would surely be permissible, Lunae told herself, to go in search of her nurse. Stealthily, she opened the door and stepped out into the garden.

The back of the mansion was overhung with trees—maple and oak, which towered up above the lower storys of the building.

The skeins of moss that hung from their branches cast the garden beneath into a wan green light. The air was humid. Lunae made her way between overgrown rows of hibiscus, crimson flowers rearing out of the gloom, stretching long furred tongues toward her. A dragonfly, jade and armored, hummed past her ear and Lunae smiled, reminded of Dreams-of-War. She could see the kappa now, bending over a pile of compost some distance away and digging industriously in it with a small sharp tool. She did not see Lunae, who was about to call out before she checked herself. Instead, she slid past until she was concealed from the sight of the kappa by the hanging moss.

At the far edge of the gardens stood a great oak, ancient and gnarled. Only a fortnight before, Lunae had stood under it in the company of Dreams-of-War and had noted, idly, that she was too short to clamber up to the lowest branches. But she had grown since then. Without stopping to think, she reached up and clasped the branch, then swung herself up into the tree. It was not easy, dressed as she was in an ankle-length robe, so when she was in a more secure position, she reached down and tucked the robe up into her sash. Then she inched out along the coiling branch that grew in the direction of the wall.

At the end, she looked back. The kappa had risen from the compost with a snort. Lunae held her breath. The nurse picked up a basket and began to waddle back toward the house. Lunae looked ahead once more. She could see the crackle of the weir-wards along the wall, a black-and-silver sparkle. They were intended to keep out intruders, linked as they were to the mansion's black light matrix, but they were also designed to keep the occupants inside. An adult would not have been able to crawl under the black light sparks, but Lunae was not yet fully grown. She crawled to the very end of the branch and ducked beneath. The wall was wide enough for her to lie balanced across it. She could hear the snap and sizzle of the weir-wards above her head. She swung her legs around, grasped the edges of the wall, and dropped down.

It was a much longer drop than she had anticipated and it knocked the breath out of her. She sat down on the curb, momentarily winded. But she was out of the house, and the realization hit her almost as hard as the fall. She had not really meant to escape. She looked back up at the wall. It was smooth and vitrified, with no handholds. If she were to get back into the mansion, she would have to go round to the front gate. The Grandmothers would be furious. Dreams-of-War would grow even colder and icier. Lunae thrust these images from her mind and concentrated on the present. If she went straight back to the house, she would still be punished. She might as well make the most of the experience.

She scrambled up from the gutter, rearranged her robe, and hurried down the street. Here, she was surrounded by the other great houses that she had glimpsed from the tower: sprawling, decaying mansions topped with moldering cupolas, half-gilded, roofs askew, porches slipping into the mass of undergrowth, starred with flowers that grew in profusion over what had once been formal gardens. The air was filled with the scent of blooms and rot. Lunae, fascinated, longed to explore, but something held her back. The interiors of the mansions were dark, save for a few. Even though it was still afternoon, lamps burned in some of the upper windows, casting a sickly light out into the foliage.

At the end of the street, Lunae looked back. She could see the tower room rising above the oaks. Ahead, a long street sloped down to become lost in the teeming maze of the lower Peak. The spy-eyes would surely be watching, but perhaps she might see a little, at least, before she was spotted. Lunae hesitated for a moment, but the prospect of investigating the streets that she had only experienced from the interior of a litter was too alluring. She thrust thoughts of the spy-eyes from her mind and ran down the road, heading for the maze.

Little by little, the mansions gave way to narrower, more crowded streets. The great houses were replaced by tenements, rising in tottering columns up from the roadway, covered with rickety balconies filled with vegetation. The tenements looked like great vertical gardens. Birds sang from cages, captive crickets whirred. Crowds of women in the traditional black, red, or jade jackets thronged the streets, wheeling ancient bicycles, leading cats on leashes, carrying mesh shopping bags that bulged with vegetables. No one took any notice of Lunae, who felt happily invisible. That this was clearly just an ordinary afternoon for these people made the day even more special. There was a heady, complex smell of spice and shit, smoke and dust. Lunae made her way slowly along the road, poking into baskets filled with seeds, dried snakes, cat food, laundry powder. Then, at a little junction, someone stepped out into her path.

This person was a small woman, clearly of Sheng origins, with a moon-face and blank black stare. Her mouth was slack, releasing a string of spittle. At first, Lunae thought that she was having difficulty in focusing, because the woman seemed blurred and out of phase. But then she realized that everything else in the street was clear.

"You are different! Who are you?" the woman said, and there was a strange overlay of sound, a buzzing hum beneath the words.

"My name is Lunae."

"What are you?" The woman stepped up to Lunae and thrust her face close. Lunae moved back and around her; she noticed that people were starting to edge away. She heard someone mutter, "Possession!"

There was a low, uneasy susurrus of sound from the crowd. Lunae, becoming frightened, tried to turn, but the woman reached out and grasped her by the arms.

"I asked you what you were!" The woman was even more blurred now, as if shaken in agitation.

"I do not understand you," Lunae answered. She pulled away, but the woman clasped her by the hand.

Lunae felt her fingers enveloped in something hard and spiny. Startled, she looked down and saw the woman's small fingers and bitten nails, but it felt nothing like a human hand. She felt as though she was clutching a lobster. She tried to tug free, but the woman's grip was too strong.

The next moment, the street cracked open, splitting with soundless speed. The apartment blocks, the crowds, were all gone. Lunae was standing on a great plain, gazing toward the banks of a river. The grass was hazy with pale flowers; there was no sign of sun, or moon, or any living thing. Then something brushed her face and the grass rippled as though a bird was flying across it. She thought she glimpsed a shadow moving swiftly over the land.

"Where am I?" she asked aloud, but the words vanished into the empty air. She could not breathe. She spun around, panicking, but there was no one to help her. The plain stretched into an immensity of distance, the horizon a faint black line.

Then she was back in the street, gasping for breath.

"What are you *doing*?" someone cried. An armored hand reached over her shoulder and struck the woman in the face, sending her bloodied into the gutter. The crowd vanished like a conjuring trick, fleeing into doorways and beneath awnings. "Lunae? Are you all right?" Dreams-of-War's face was a mask of fury.

The woman clambered up from the gutter and fled. The Martian sprang forward, but the woman was gone into the maze of the lower Peak. Lunae looked up at her guardian with grateful trepidation.

"What *was* that woman?"

"A Kami." Above the throat-spines of her armor, Dreams-of-War's face was pinched and pale, but her eyes were firecracker-bright. With alarm, Lunae realized that Dreams-of-War was not only angry, but afraid.

CHAPTER 2

NIGHTSHADE

Upon the day of her nineteenth birthday, Yskatarina hastened through Tower Cold, heels tapping across the metal floor, sending out glassy codes to the ever-present listeners, the ears of the Elder Elaki. Devices flickered within the walls, monitoring, reporting back. They could be fooled, and she had learned how to do so, but Yskatarina could still hear them at night—or, perhaps more accurately, when she slept, for there was no such thing as day on Nightshade. And sleep was fitful, often disrupted by the murmuring, spined embrace of the Animus. The Animus's needs were becoming insistent. He was, after all, a male.

Yskatarina did not mind, however. She had needs of her own, and moreover, it marked the Animus as something that was truly hers, even though they were both supposed to be the property of the clan. Her aunt was always trying to make more: coaxing embryos out of the growing-skins, mingling monkey and dragonfly and bee, scorpion and marmoset with the old genes of Earth. But although the Animus had been a success, the great-eyed, thorn-armed creatures lived for no more than a night before expiring with a sigh.

Elaki made others, of course: the mute-kin that worked on the production lines, the disposable workers who were sent out into the Sunken Plain. All of these beings slid without difficulties from their growing-bags, overseen by the mourn-women. But these were lesser creatures, with limited sentience or none at all, and they did not live long. The Animus had been her greatest success, and Yskatarina knew that this infuriated Elaki. She was aware that her aunt had tried to replicate the Animus, scraping off cells, carefully experimenting with shed fragments of scale and skin, but the clones never seemed to take. She was unsure whether the Animus could feel true amusement, but on the news of yet another failure, Yskatarina thought that he had. But to dwell on this more closely would have meant criticizing her aunt, and Yskatarina found this too hard. The guilt at her own disobedience often came close to overwhelming her.

She ran a hand down a nearby tapestry, as if admiring it. The tapestry glowed briefly, the nerve-threads woven within it sending out ambiguities, false information, bewilderment to the ever-present spy-eyes. She knew that it would give her no more than a minute's grace, but it was enough to slip behind the tapestry, out of the sight of the spies, and into the glassy hollow of the wall. From here, she could make her way up Tower Cold to the genetics lab. Here, she was forced to double over, for the labyrinth of the wall was really only large enough for a child. But even at nineteen, Yskatarina was more flexible than a whole adult. An artificial arm could be unscrewed, or legs removed to permit her to snake through gaps, like a grub within a hive. And she wanted to find out what Elaki was really planning. Her aunt, on the previous night, had told her little: only that a child had been grown on Earth that would somehow be a threat to Nightshade.

"But who grew the child?" Yskatarina had asked.

"Our enemies," Elaki answered.

"But who are they?"

"Let me tell you a story," Elaki said. Yskatarina settled down to listen, for she loved her aunt's tales: the story of how the Ship of Elders had fled from Earth to Nightshade a thousand years ago, bringing their forbidden males with them, the perils they encountered on their long journey, how the ship sacrificed itself to grow the little colony . . .

But the story that Elaki now told was different.

"A hundred years ago this clan held key information about modifications to the human genome, prepared by its greatest scientists—two sisters, of Tower Cold." A pause. "*My* sisters. We worked together, united, while the other clans sank into an atrophied insularity from which they have never emerged. And together, it was we who contacted the Kami, and learned so much thereby. Together, we developed the paradigms of haunt-tech. But when our clan offered that technology to the Martian Matriarchy, there was—a disagreement. The sisters and their Animus—for they had only one between them—fled to Mars in a prototype haunt-ship, taking the data store with them. They vanished for many years and I believed them to be dead. But recently I have tracked them down, to a place called Fragrant Harbor. It seems they have been biding their time, plotting against me, preparing a weapon."

"What kind of weapon?"

"The girl whom you are to kill."

"How can a girl be a weapon? And why do you not go to Earth and kill them? Why not slay this child when it is still in its bag?" Elaki scowled and Yskatarina added, panicking, "I do not mean to criticize, please do not think that. Only—"

"It is a fair question," Elaki said, somewhat grudgingly. "I could not get near them. They know me too well, and—apart from yourself—they know those close to me. They have been keeping an eye on those members of our clan who inhabit our Mission on Earth."

"Could not someone there hire an assassin?"

"I do not wholly trust those at the Mission," Elaki said after a pause.

"Why not?" Yskatarina frowned. She remembered the group who had left for Earth some years before: nine sisters, all with a faint look of Elaki. They had terrified Yskatarina, but she could not have said why.

"You would not understand. I need someone on whom I can rely." The tight porcelain skin of Elaki's face seemed to soften. "Someone whom I love, Yskatarina."

And Yskatarina, flattered beyond words, asked no more questions.

But now, no more than a day later, those awkward issues were starting to chew once more at the edges of her psyche. Where had the Kami come from, for instance? And what was the nature of the transformation that she and the Animus had undergone? Yskatarina's love for her aunt was as strong as ever, but she could feel cracks beginning to appear.

She made her way to the slits in the wall, painstakingly carved with a diamond knife over the course of a single night, years ago now. She had been ten. The Animus had kept watch. She had never regretted the risk she had run, though if her hands had been made of flesh, they would have bled. It had felt, however, as though her heart itself had begun to weep blood, her implanted conscience reminding her in an incessant internal whisper of how much she owed her aunt, how greatly Elaki was loved, almost to the point of worship.

Almost, but not quite.

She put an eye to a crack and peered through. There was Elaki, wrapped in a black shift with a tall medical cowl, moving slowly about the laboratory.

Beyond her aunt's shoulder, Yskatarina caught a glimpse of moving starlight: a ship coming in over the wastes of Nightshade. Within the growing-tanks, things twitched long limbs. A black spine crept over the lip of a tank. Elaki batted it back. Yskatarina frowned; it looked too much like the Animus.

Isti was there, too, the ever-present shadow at her aunt's heels. Yskatarina did not know what kind of thing Isti was, whether machine or bio-organism or hybrid. He was short and squat, with thick fingers and a squashed face. But his loyalty to Elaki was certain, greater even than Yskatarina's own.

"He is bound to your aunt, as I am bound to you," the Animus had *said once, as it clumsily wielded the brush that tore at Yskatarina's long black hair.*

"As we are bound to each other," Yskatarina had said, gently reproving. *She stared into the dark wells of her own reflection, and would not look up at the Animus. The brush had tugged and pulled, but the Animus said nothing.*

"What if Yskatarina fails?" Isti asked.

"To kill the girl? She will not fail. But I will give her an additional incentive. If she fails, I shall tell her I will have her Animus taken away and returned to the vat."

Yskatarina felt her heart grow cold and still within her.

"Would you do such a thing? It is the only success of its kind."

"I will sacrifice it if I have to. But I do not expect it to be necessary. The threat should be enough to secure Yskatarina's complete cooperation."

"Have you told her exactly why the girl must be killed?"

"Of course not. Yskatarina is loyal to me—I made quite sure of that—but there may still be cracks in the black light programming. I do not want her to start *thinking*, Isti. She shows enough signs of it already. I have told her enough of the truth, which appears to have contented her."

Listening in the walls, Yskatarina thought of losing the Animus and had to clench her teeth against her tears. Yet her conscience chattered and whispered within: *You know your aunt has only your best interests at heart, that she is all-wise; you know that you must love her—must love, must, must . . .*

I have told her enough of the truth . . .

Conflict chattered and hammered inside her head, bringing lightnings of pain in its wake. The cracks were widening. With a great effort, Yskatarina shut off the inner voice and made her way unsteadily down through the walls. But as she went, she told herself that she would not let Elaki take the Animus from her, whatever she had to do to prevent it.

CHAPTER 3

EARTH

U pon their return to Cloud Terrace, Dreams-of-War had gone straight to the Grandmothers and informed them of what had taken place. It had not been an easy discussion.

"She stood there, in the *street*, while that creature held her hand?" the Grandmothers demanded, speaking as one. "Disgusting! Is she injured?"

"Her hand is hurt a little. That appears to be all."

The Grandmothers' eyes gleamed. They shifted on the bed: two women, joined to each other at one side, with only two arms between them. Left-Hand Grandmother was wizened, with black eyes in a mass of wrinkled skin, and the hand that rested on the counterpane was gnarled. Right-Hand Grandmother appeared no more than eighteen, hawk-faced, with a coil of white-streaked dark hair, though Dreams-of-War knew that the two were the same age. "Do you think it learned anything?" It was Right-Hand whose voice was clearest, but Left-Hand echoed all that she said.

"Who can say?" Dreams-of-War replied, endeavoring to keep the coldness from her voice.

Typical of the Grandmothers to exhibit outrage: They were the ones to enjoy control, to slink or barge into a person's mind and body, commit all manner of violations before retreating, but woe betide anyone else who tried such a thing.

"If the Kami now know she is the *hito-bashira*," the Grandmothers said, "they will not suffer her to live."

Dreams-of-War frowned. "Why not?"

"You would not understand."

"If you only told me what is meant by *hito-bashira*, perhaps I might," Dreams-of-War said, exasperated. "Is it to do with

43

this thing she does, this folding of time? Three times a week I watch as she flicks the minutes forward, turns seed into flower or fruit, then back to seed. I watch, and yet I have no idea what she's really doing, because you won't tell me. I assume that the term *hito-bashira* has something to do with her talents, but what? The girl asks and asks, and what can I tell her? She pesters both myself and the kappa for answers. We feel obliged to pretend, for otherwise we look like idiots. It is time all of us are told."

"No! And you are nothing more than a hired hand. Do not presume."

But Dreams-of-War was unwilling to be stopped. "And what is to be done now? Can she turn back time in order to change it?"

"Not yet. And so we must send Lunae away, now that the Kami know she is here. It is no longer safe. We can hide her no longer; we must find a safe place for her."

"Then why raise her here, in the city of the Nightshade Mission, where the Kami are known to be present?"

"Because it is thereby easier for us to see what the Mission might be up to. And we have learned from them, too. Our enemy has been making swift progress, and this project, always important, has now become a matter of urgency." Left-Hand nudged Right. "Do not tell her so much."

Dreams-of-War stared at the Grandmothers, who stared unblinkingly back. She could feel depths and mysteries. She did not believe for a moment that they had told her the truth. Dreams-of-War scowled. "I dislike secrets."

The Grandmothers grinned in unison. "And you, a creature of Memnos?"

"That is *why* I dislike secrets."

"You should have learned to live with them by now. Enough of this. There are arrangements to be made."

"Very well," Dreams-of-War said through gritted teeth.

"You say that both Lunae and the woman disappeared?"

"For no more than a fraction of a second. But as you know, that can be deceptive." Dreams-of-War hesitated. "I was angry and alarmed. Perhaps I misperceived the situation. Who knows how long they were really absent, wherever they were? Who knows what might have taken place?"

"Go," the Grandmothers told her. "Take her to the kappa and get her hand attended to. Then bring Lunae to us."

Dreams-of-War climbed the endless flights of stairs to the tower, to find her charge sitting up in bed, looking pale.

"Lunae?" Dreams-of-War asked. That *feeling* again: all fright and anxiety and concern. Dreams-of-War fought it aside and took refuge in anger. "What were you thinking of? I told you never to go beyond the house." She paused. "How did you get out, anyway?"

"I climbed a tree."

Dreams-of-War felt a swift flicker of pride and shoved that away, too. "You should not have done so."

"I wanted to get out of the mansion." Lunae stared at her, defiant.

"Well, now you have your wish," Dreams-of-War said. "I've spoken with your Grandmothers. They're going to send you away."

Excitement flashed across Lunae's face.

"Where? Somewhere far?"

"I don't know yet."

Dreams-of-War sat down on the edge of the bed and studied the girl. It was obvious that Lunae had aged overnight. The planes of her face were different, more mature, and Dreams-of-War could see the curves of her breasts beneath her night robe. Silently, Dreams-of-War took stock of the months from the hatching pod. Lunae had her lessons, as prescribed by the Grandmothers, on three occasions every week. That made it nearly one hundred and twenty times that Lunae had now folded time, slipped through the cracks into *elsewhere*, cheating the rules of the continuum. Dreams-of-War thought of herself going under the black light matrix, of the doctor's voice as she spoke of the Eldritch Realm. Beneath the armor, Dreams-of-War suppressed a shiver.

But the success of the project was clear. Lunae was aging as predicted by the schematics drawn up by the Grandmothers, and unlike her previous sisters-in-skin, showing no signs of cellular degeneration or mental instability. And it could not be good for her to be kept cooped up in this antique mansion. Angry and scared though she had been, Dreams-of-War could not blame Lunae for escaping.

When Dreams-of-War had been Lunae's age, she had felt as though she owned half of Mars: the Demnotian Plain running red to the horizon, as far as the ragged mountains and the great cone of Olympus. Dreams-of-War's earliest memories were of that plain and those rocks, glimpsed from the reinforced windows of the clan house. She had spent her days outside, left to run wild with Knowledge-of-Pain and the other girls, ice crackling beneath their wind-skates as they hurtled across the Sea of Snow toward the towers of Winterstrike; the brief summer heat causing the maytids to crawl out from their cocoons in the soil and be snap-roasted in the firepits; the feel of her *keilin* mount under her as they charged through the Tharsis Gorge . . .

Dreams-of-War wished that Lunae could have had such a childhood, felt the lack of it even if Lunae did not. Now, looking at the girl and seeing the end of that childhood already upon her, Dreams-of-War was filled with an uncomfortable sensation: a mingled guilt and unease, so unfamiliar to her that she did not know what to do with it.

Lunae saved her from the inconvenience of her emotions. "You said that woman was a Kami. She did not look alien to me, only strange, as if unfocused."

"From what we know of the Kami, they do not have bodies. They possess the bodies of others, usually those who are of a weak mind."

"But who are the Kami?"

"No one really knows. They started appearing on Earth only a few years ago, shortly after the establishment of the Nightshade Mission, but they have been on Nightshade for much longer. There were a few terrorist attacks on the Mission by Kitachi Malaya insurgents. But the Kami were like ghosts who manifested themselves in human bodies, and in no form other than shadows in the midday sun. And the Mission itself: impregnable, made of an unknown substance that withstood all attacks and that no spy device has ever been able to penetrate."

"What interest can they have in us?" Lunae wondered. "Where do they come from?"

"I've told you, no one knows. They are close to Nightshade; that is all that is known. At first, people thought that the Mission was undertaking some kind of mind-control, but the Kami made themselves known. Lunae, it is time for you to get up."

She studied Lunae as the girl dressed. The process of aging had brought out the bones of Lunae's face, a sharpness to cheekbone and chin that was suddenly familiar. *She does not look like the people of Fragrant Harbor, this Eastern ancestry, except in the tilt of her eyes. She looks like a Martian,* Dreams-of-War thought, and wondered that the notion had not struck her before.

But her own people tended to have pale hair, the silver-blond of the Crater Plains, whereas Lunae's own was that strange dark red. Like a Northern woman, from Caud or Tharsis. Did Lunae have Martian genes?

She found herself looking at Lunae with a newly appraising eye.

"Am I to have lessons today?" Lunae asked.

"No. The Grandmothers wish to see you, however. But first you are to go to the kappa and have your hand attended to."

Lunae looked up, alarmed. "Are the Grandmothers very angry?"

"They are not precisely delighted." Dreams-of-War suppressed a shudder. She had seen the Grandmothers take information from the mind: the lightning tendrils arcing out, too swift to be seen by the naked eye, but visible later on the monitors that the engineers of Memnos had built into Dreams-of-War's armor. The Grandmothers used a technology that Dreams-of-War did not understand; she did not want to admit that it alarmed her. She was a Martian warrior, she told herself, not someone to be unnerved by two ancient women.

"Come, Lunae," she said, more sharply than she had intended. "Do not keep the Grandmothers waiting."

CHAPTER 4

NIGHTSHADE

She was apart from the Animus now; he remained in her chamber, chained to the bed by Isti. Yskatarina was painfully aware of the lack of him by her side and she frowned as she walked across the bitter hall of Tower Cold, to where her aunt awaited the boat sent by the Matriarchs of Memnos.

Stepping into the elevator, she watched the hall grow small beneath her as she ascended. A hundred stories, two hundred, three . . . Then the hall was invisible except as a tiny dark square, and Yskatarina rose out into the darkness above Nightshade. The Sunken World lay before her. She could see the frozen peaks and summits, the craters and gouges made by meteor strikes. At the farthest point, between the Horns of Tyr, was the sun: a little, blazing star. Above, to the north, Dis hung in the heavens, and then there was nothing but the great gulf, only debris and dust until the beginning of the outer systems, light-years distant. Only the boats went farther, filled with the canopics dispatched by the mourn-women and the Steersmen Skull-Faces—bodies embalmed in ultrasleep, gliding through the Eldritch Realm for whatever systems lay beyond the abyss.

Yskatarina closed her eyes to the dark, thought of the Animus's sharp touch, and was glad when the elevator slid to a silent halt at the top of the tower.

The Elder Elaki's chamber was round, with windows like portholes. Here, when she was not in the laboratory or the haunt-tech chambers, Yskatarina's aunt sat out her days, her unhuman eyes fixed on things that no one else could see. She said nothing when Yskatarina entered, only flicked a hand at a kneeling-chair.

The great eyes, owl-yellow, veined with broken blood vessels, blinked with an almost audible snap.

"Has the ship that is to take me to Mars arrived?" Yskatarina said. Near-worship flooded through her at Elaki's proximity. She bowed her head before she knew it, then thought of Elaki's overheard threat and grew cold.

"Not long. It approaches down the Chain." The Elder Elaki gestured toward a window and Yskatarina could, indeed, see a star coming, rattling fast into the silvery shadow of the Nightshade maw of the Chain. "As you know, you have a task to perform very soon." Elaki frowned. "You appear discontented. Why?"

But Yskatarina loved her aunt beyond love, and so, bitterly, said nothing.

"Your Animus will accompany you. I have impressed upon you the importance of this task, Yskatarina."

Here it comes, Yskatarina thought.

"And if you should fail, I will have to take him away from you." Elaki spoke with a twist of the mouth.

Yskatarina looked up at her numbly. Love for the Animus poured through her, and love for Elaki also. She felt torn in two.

"I will not fail, Aunt." Her voice sounded as though it came from the bottom of a well.

"Then the Animus will stay with you, of course."

"I am grateful," Yskatarina managed to say.

"Yskatarina? Are you all right?" Elaki asked impatiently.

Yskatarina managed to mutter, "When will I be leaving?"

"As soon as I see fit. And now, there are things I have to tell you."

Yskatarina's gaze once more traveled to that traveling star, brighter now, blazing like a captured sun as it was whisked along through the maw of the Chain. A few moments later, the blaze sharpened, then faded. The boat sent by the Memnos Matriarchs was docking.

Yskatarina knelt before her aunt, head still forcibly bowed, awaiting her orders.

CHAPTER 5

EARTH

For once, it was hard to track the kappa down. Usually the nursemaid hovered protectively near her charge, but now, perhaps not wanting to distract Dreams-of-War, the kappa seemed to be keeping out of sight. Lunae trudged through the house, eventually locating the kappa in the long chamber at the heart of the house, attending to the growing-skins.

Steam rose from the vents in the walls, each configured in the form of a gargoyle's head. Cross-eyed faces opened mouths to emit plumes of mist; Lunae took care not to go too close. Along the metal-ridged floor, the racks of feeder orchids turned their faces toward the moisture, their petals swelling with water. Bronze walls dripped and ran with a rainy haze. The air smelled damp and hot, rich with loam and a meaty undernote of stagnation that only served to enhance the perfume of the orchids. Lunae always felt safe here, though she did not like to look at the skins, which occasionally bulged and writhed as if the contents sought escape. Lunae knew, however, that she herself had come from one of those fleshy bags, and perhaps this was why she felt so secure in this room.

She watched as the kappa wafted the mist over each skin. In the heat of the chamber, the mist swiftly accumulated into droplets, which ran down the outside of the skins before bouncing into the trays beneath, in an atonal accompaniment to the kappa's movements. Lunae gave a delicate cough, remembering Dreams-of-War's countless instructions not to interrupt people when they were busy.

The kappa's head moved ponderously around, swiveling on the twisted neck. The toes of her wrinkled feet gripped the floor; the kappa found it hard to keep her balance on the lacquered boards of the mansion and the metal floor of the hatching room alike. Lunae could not help feeling a twinge of pity, which rang as plangently as a waterdrop inside her mind.

"We are above such emotions," Dreams-of-War had told her in her first weeks out of the hatchery. "You are a made-being, even if your ancestors practiced bloodbirth, just as the lowest orders do. You are therefore superior, as I am."

"Are you a made-thing, too?" Lunae said.

"I?" Dreams-of-War replied, with a disdainful tilt of her head. "Of course. And so is your nurse, when it comes to that. But the kappa is a slave and to be treated as such. Do not waste emotion upon it."

"I see," Lunae had said, but though she was then nothing more than a weeks-old child, there seemed something wrong with this picture. It seemed hard on the kappa who was her nursemaid, who walked as if her feet hurt her, and who seemed so encumbered by her heavy shell-like skin. And if the kappa were supposed to serve, then why did so many other folk seem bound to the factories and wage-shops of the city? Perhaps it was different elsewhere. Yet Fragrant Harbor was rumored to be a good place. It did not seem good to Lunae.

Now the kappa said mildly, "You are in disgrace."

"I know. Dreams-of-War has had much to say on the subject." Lunae looked down at her hand, at a row of bloody dots that were the legacy of her encounter. "She sent me to find you, to bind this up."

The kappa looked at Lunae's hand and made a small scratchy sound of disapproval. "You should never have gone out of the house."

"I know."

"The Grandmothers want to see you. They are not pleased, Lunae."

"I know." It was beginning to sound like a mantra. "I'm sorry, kappa."

The kappa reached out and gently touched Lunae's hair. "I was very worried, Lunae. We all were. Terrible things could have happened to you."

Lunae gave an unhappy grimace. "Perhaps terrible things *did.*"

"That remains to be seen. Now, give me your hand." The kappa rinsed her fingers beneath a nearby tap, then took Lunae's hand and began to swab at the bloodied holes with a leaf torn from one of the plants.

"Does this hurt?"

"Not very much. Kappa, I don't understand why that woman—that Kami—even noticed me. Is it because of this—thing I am supposed to be? A *hito-bashira*?" Her hand was growing cold.

"Perhaps."

"What is a *hito-bashira*? I have been told so often that this is what I am, but my memories tell me nothing and I can't find the word in any of the data-tablets. Even—" Lunae stopped, not wanting the kappa to know that she had looked in places forbidden to her. But she'd had no choice, she had to find out. Limbo is being born in a bag, nursed by dragonfly and spider and toad.

"But it has been explained to you, has it not? You are to be a woman-who-holds-back-the-flood."

"But, nurse, I don't understand what that means. *Which* flood?"

"Ask the Grandmothers," the kappa said, as she had answered so many times before. She bound Lunae's hand with a creeper-bandage.

"But they just tell me to ask Dreams-of-War, and she tells me to ask them, or you. I go round and round in circles. Why will no one answer me?"

"Perhaps because it might hinder your development," the kappa said.

"I am old enough!" Lunae replied hotly.

The kappa's mouth creased, then split open like a melon to reveal a flash of pink, shiny tongue. "You are nine months old, grown far more swiftly than a normal child. I am a hundred and twenty, and people still won't tell me anything."

"But—" Lunae began, then stopped, for what she had been about to say was: *That's different*. Dreams-of-War would have approved, she knew, but she still did not feel that it was right for there to be one rule for the kappa, so old and wise, and one rule for herself. Perhaps the kappa was right; perhaps she really was too young. Maybe that was simply the way the world worked.

She had witnessed it only from afar, heard snatches of sound from the inside of a litter. Who was she to question the workings of the societies beyond the weir-wards of the mansion? And yet she could not help but question.

The kappa seemed to take pity on her, for she said, "You'll know when the time is right. Have patience. Enjoy your ignorance while it lasts."

This suggested the knowledge would not make her happy, but it only made Lunae feel more eager to learn. The kappa stepped back from the skins with an air of satisfaction. "That, at least, is one task finished for today."

"Why do the skins have to be kept moist?" Lunae asked.

"So that they can grow, of course. Though most of these will have to be pruned back, returned to the mulch." The kappa gave a gusty sigh. "A pity. But they are too small and spindly."

"Are we plants, then?" A strange thought. She pictured herself rooted in soil, reaching up toward the hazy sun.

The kappa gave her a lipless smile. "Of course not. You are a made-human."

"And a *hito-bashira*," Lunae said with resignation.

"Just so. There. By this evening, your hand should be healed. And now, the Grandmothers wish to see you." The kappa fixed her with a round eye, green as moss. She patted Lunae on the arm. "I know you find them a little alarming, perhaps. That is only to be expected. They are ancients, and as such, they do not behave like you and me. It is their right. But you should have no fear. I am sure they love you, in their own strange way."

Lunae would have died rather than tell anyone, even the kappa, that the reason she did not want to visit the Grandmothers was not simply fear, but revulsion. If she revealed this to the kappa, however, sooner or later the Grandmothers would travel inside the kappa's skull and find the knowledge nestling inside the nurse's simple thoughts like a moth in a chrysalis, all curdled toxic soup. The thought of the Grandmothers gaining such knowledge was enough to make Lunae grow cold, for she knew, without understanding precisely how, that the Grandmothers would punish the kappa and not herself. And she did not want to see the kappa punished.

She sighed. Sometimes it was as though the old kappa was the child, to be protected and sheltered, and she the nursemaid. If she told anyone of her feelings about the Grandmothers, it would have to be Dreams-of-War, and her Martian guardian had a frustrating habit of appearing to ignore such pieces of information, only to store them up and deploy them when one was least expecting it. Lunae would simply have to keep her feelings to herself.

It was a long way from the inner chamber to the Grandmothers' room, and the kappa was unable to move quickly. Lunae, as always, wondered whether the kappa had originally been intended to perform household tasks, or whether she had been bred for another purpose entirely.

Lunae and the kappa walked along dim corridors, passing the familiar demon-swarming tapestries that the Grandmothers had brought from the volcano lands. They depicted figures of legend: the moon-spirits of the lunar craters; the great Dragon-Kings who, it was said, had risen from the depths of the oceans when the Drowning first began, to help humans hold back the surging tide.

"Nurse, where do you come from?" Lunae asked.

It had never occurred to her to ask this before and she felt faintly embarrassed by it, as though the kappa was too much a part of the furniture even to have such an ordinary thing as an origin. But the kappa only smiled and said, "I come from the north, just like those tapestries. From the Fire Islands, the lands of the change-tigers."

"Where are the Fire Islands, exactly?" Lunae wondered aloud, but even as she spoke, her buried memories were bringing forth an image of a scattered chain beyond the water-ringed summits of Fuji and Hakodate, beyond Sakhalin. Then memory supplied her with a name: *Ischa*. This was the word that Lunae next spoke.

"Yes," the kappa replied. "I am from the clan-warren of Hailstone Shore, near Ischa, the southernmost town of the Kamchatka chain." Her head swiveled around. "It is the only land left in that region of the world. All else has gone, under flood and fire."

"Why did you come to Fragrant Harbor?" Lunae asked.

"I was sent here. I had no choice."

"Do you miss your home?"

"If I did," the kappa said, still smiling, "would you ask the Grandmothers to send me back?"

"I could try," Lunae ventured, but she already knew what the answer would be. To the Grandmothers, as to Dreams-of-War, the kappa was no more than a useful thing. They would no more consider her desires than they would consider the wishes of a household kettle. The kappa said nothing more, but Lunae knew that she understood.

The shadowy corridors, each lit only by a single lamp, were comforting and familiar. When they reached the passage leading to the Grandmothers' room, however, Lunae's heart began to beat faster, lumping along beneath her ribs.

The kappa paused outside the Grandmothers' door.

"Wait," she said, then pressed her wrinkled palm against the lock-release and hobbled inside. Lunae fidgeted in the hallway, impatience mingling with reluctance. She wanted the meeting to be over, to leave Cloud Terrace far behind.

The kappa reappeared at the doorway and surveyed Lunae with a nervous, rheumy squint. "They say you are to come in."

CHAPTER 6

MARS

Yskatarina stood upon legs of iron and glass, artificial feet planted firmly on the old stone floor. Her hands rested on each side of a window, from which she gazed out across the Crater Plain. Used as she was to the dim vaults of Nightshade, the brightness of Mars hurt her eyes. She reached up and touched the setting of her eyeshade, turning it to maximum. The light made her feel bleached and weak; for a moment, she hated the need that had brought her to Mars. Then guilt kicked in once more. Elaki had required it, and Elaki must be obeyed. Conflict whispered inside her head, tearing at her. But now that she was so far away from Elaki, it seemed both easier and more difficult to think. Resentment was growing alongside the love.

The Animus had been left outside the Tower, at the Matriarch's insistence.

"It is a male," the Matriarch had said with palpable disgust. "We cannot allow it inside."

Yskatarina had acquiesced with a semblance of grace, but she did not like it. It was as though her shadow had been torn from her, leaving her exposed in the light. She longed to return to the ship, but first there was business to be done.

From here, at the height of the Memnos Tower, one could see as far as the great conical summit of Olympus. The plain shimmered in the afternoon light, giving the impression of desert heat, but Yskatarina knew this to be deceptive. It was winter now in this northern region of Mars, with frost in the mornings in the shadow of the rocks and a bite to the air. She did not know what caused the shimmer, but she suspected some manner of force-defense. The Tower had been well guarded from ancient times. If she looked down, she could see the glazed crimson bricks of the wall, bare of lichen and moss.

Beside her, the Matriarch, dressed in red-and-black, exuded a satisfaction as chilly as the day. Yskatarina glanced aside at the Matriarch's moon-face: the tight, pursed lips, the pale eyes embedded in bags of flesh, the moles that scattered the skin like ticks. She set her gaze once more upon the Crater Plain.

"You see?" the Matriarch said. "This is the first and last of the old fortresses, save only for the ruin in Winterstrike. Our ancestors built it in the days of the Age of Children, to guard against their enemies." She reached up to touch the phial around her neck, an intricate silver cage, then let her hand fall.

"What kind of enemies were those?" Yskatarina asked, with seeming idleness.

"The forebears of the hyenae and vulpen." The Matriarch's mouth grew yet smaller and Yskatarina knew that she was thinking of the Animus. "*Males*, in the days when such creatures were commonplace. Ram-women. Syrinxes. The beings that later became what we call the Atrophied, like the Earthbones."

"I know nothing of these beings," Yskatarina said, tapping impatient fingers against the hard carapace of her bodice. "What are Earthbones?"

"A flesh-in-rock. Mounds of moving flesh, merged with the planet."

Yskatarina frowned. "With Mars itself? How is that possible?" She wondered about Memnos mysticism. She did not know a great deal about their beliefs, only that they differed so crucially from Nightshade in their disdain for the male form. Nightshade had little use for superstition, and even less for warrior sects. Those days, according to Yskatarina's mind, should be long gone. But if Mars' rulers chose to play at being primitives, it was not for her to condemn them. All it meant was that they should prove easier to manipulate. She schooled her face into a becoming display of interest and turned to face the Matriarch, sending the pleats of her leather kilt swishing against the surface of her legs.

"Terraforming nanotech, mingling with genetic codes. What was once human became inextricably welded to the world. There was a fashion for it, once. Fanatics, psycho-ecologists—who knows? It was very long ago. But surely Nightshade knows more of these things than we do. That is, after all, why you are here."

"I came to honor an old bargain. And to call in an old debt," Yskatarina said.

"Haunt-tech." The Matriarch spoke with a sour twist of the lip.

"Quite so. You have had it now for a hundred years, it and its many ramifications—black light, deeplight, the intricacies of shadow-space and entry to the spirit worlds of the Eldritch Realm. We note that you have made good use of it. Armor, weaponry, surveillance systems, ships. Above all, the advantages of the Chain."

"It has proved versatile," the Matriarch acknowledged.

"And now you need further expertise," Yskatarina prompted. "You do not have more than a basic understanding of it. You cannot develop it further, without the assistance of Nightshade."

"Do not tell her that we ourselves are learning more about haunt-tech and what it can do," Elaki had said. "Or that our knowledge has made great strides of late. Pretend to her that we have always possessed such information."

Yskatarina had stared at her aunt. "Is that not true, then?"

"Haunt-tech is inordinately complex. If we knew a hundred years ago what we know now, then matters would have been a great deal simpler."

Yskatarina frowned. "How so?"

But Elaki had only smiled a cold smile, and said nothing more.

The Matriarch's face grew yet more sour. "That would seem to be so."

Yskatarina smiled. "You received the demonstration versions? You have had time to see what they can do?"

Far out on the Crater Plain, she could see something moving. Reluctantly, she turned the eyeshade down a notch to let in more light, and raised the binocular setting. Something was passing swiftly amid a cloud of dust.

"What might that be, for instance?" Yskatarina feigned charmed surprise.

"You know very well," the Matriarch muttered.

"Why, it is a ghost herd. Of—what?" Long disjointed legs, scarlet from the knee down, as if dipped in blood . . . Yskatarina was briefly covetous. "Some manner of mutated women?"

"Those are creatures known as gaezelles."

"From the far past?"

"From the Age of Children."

"They are quite beautiful," Yskatarina murmured.

"And almost entirely useless. As are the other haunts and shades that your technology has recently conjured up out of the planet's nanomemories and thin air. Sylph-beasts roam the slopes of Olympus. Demotheas have been seen in the woods of Elyssiane. Mars has become alive with spirits of old creations—whimsical nightmares, evolutionary dead ends. This has never happened before."

"I used the words *demonstration model*. You surely were not so naive as to think we would give you something of power, straightaway?"

"Your aunt promised to help Memnos with the governing of Earth," the Matriarch said. "I see no signs that this help, this power, will be forthcoming, and we need it. There are many elements on Earth that seek to break free of Martian control. What remains of the Northern Hemisphere is full of warmadams, carving out independent fiefdoms for themselves. We send excissieres, who are effective, but it is a costly and laborious business. I should like to send a permanent subjugating force."

"And you shall have one," Yskatarina promised. "We'll help you raise the Sown."

"When we last spoke to Elaki, she seemed well acquainted with the notion of the Sown. Nightshade must know a great deal about Mars," the Matriarch said. "Much about its earlier genetic forms and fancies, about the nanotech that coils and changes beneath the crucible of its surface—technology that we have lost over the centuries. I should like to see the records of Nightshade. Your people must have been most meticulous."

"We have had a long time to learn," Yskatarina said, watching the Matriarch's face with care as the truth slowly dawned. "A hundred years of feedback, from the haunt-tech that is already here." Fully aware of the Memnos prohibitions about physical contact, she put an iron-and-glass hand on the Matriarch's sleeve in seeming reassurance, and watched with satisfaction as the Matriarch snatched the sleeve away. "Do not worry. I am here to help."

"You are here to sell," the Matriarch hissed.

"Yes, and you knew there would be a price. Just like the previous version of haunt-tech."

"It was a witches' bargain." The Matriarch's face was still as stone. Once more, her hand drifted to the phial at her throat.

"But we are witches, your kind and mine, are we not? We hold the keys, here and now, to a world of transformation. With this new technology, updated, you can mine the past. You can revive ancient forms of being, converse with their unaltered consciounesses, uncover all the secrets that they hold. And you can raise an army, not just spectral fancies."

"And the price," the Matriarch said, bitter as frostbite. It was not a question.

The gazelles were wheeling away to the north. Yskatarina watched them through the binoculars, the powerful red legs stirring up the dust, the long hair that streamed down their backs, their small curled hands. She sighed to see such grace.

"Ah, the price." Yskatarina drew the Matriarch aside. "Elaki wants information. All the genetic data that you unearth must go to her. She is true to the original aims of Nightshade: the ultimate perfection of the sentient form."

"She would appear to be some distance away from that," the Matriarch said, with a dubious glance at Yskatarina.

"She wants your help, too, in another, related, matter," Yskatarina said, forcing herself to ignore the slight. "But there is something else that *I* want." The thought of betraying Elaki tore at her heart with implanted passion, artificial regret. If it had not been for that small, pure undercurrent of hate, Yskatarina would not have been able to continue. She added, in a gasping whisper, "Something you must do for me."

CHAPTER 7

EARTH

Lunae stepped through the door into the shadows of the Grandmothers' chamber. The air was musty with the smell of old lamp oil, pungent with narcotic snuff and a salt-weed odor that reminded Lunae of her single cloistered visit to the shores of Fragrant Harbor. The walls were made of driftwood, a palace of drowned trees, the beams and rafters black and twisted, as though burned. Yet there was soft fur beneath her feet: a striped dark-and-gold skin, bright as a flame and perhaps fifteen feet in length. She thought of Kamchatka, where the kappa had come from, of the Fire Islands. She studied the knots and the warp of the ancient wood, the striped pelt beneath her feet, not wanting to look toward the bed where her Grandmothers lay.

"Come closer," two voices said, speaking as one. Lunae forced herself to glance up. The lamp that hung above the bed had not been lit, so that the voices came from the hidden midst of the drapes. Lunae walked to the foot of the bed and halted. "Stay there, child," the voices said sharply, "where we can see you." Then the lamp flared up and the Grandmothers' faces peered out from between the curtains: one old, one young. Lunae often thought that it was as though Right-Hand, with her sweet voice and caressing manner, was slowly but surely draining the life from her companion until there would be nothing left of old Left-Hand but a husk. She remembered the chrysalis, turning to moth and back again, and shivered.

"Where is she?" Left-Hand asked querulously, though Right-Hand's lips also moved in silent accompaniment, and when Right-Hand answered, "Why, she is standing before you, blind old thing, do you not see her?" Lunae heard a whispered echo of the words from the other side of the bed. She concentrated on their faces, not wanting to glance down and catch a glimpse of the joined flesh. She had seen it once, when the robes that the Grandmothers wore had slipped aside to reveal a mass of scar tissue, almost as knotted as the wood of their chamber, revealing lumps and bulges.

"Why would anyone want to be linked in such a way?" she had asked Dreams-of-War the next day, fighting back revulsion, and the Martian woman, evidently just as bemused, had replied, "I cannot say. For me, to touch another person is difficult enough."

So Lunae had once asked the kappa why they had been joined, and the kappa had told her that she did not know, but in her opinion, it was more likely that they had not so chosen, but had come connected from the growing-bag and were incapable of separation.

"Such things are not uncommon. Sometimes the children are returned to the mulch, sometimes not. It depends on the family's wishes, and there are many views on these matters."

As she stood before the Grandmothers, Lunae was suddenly conscious of her own flesh and the boundaries of it, her separateness from everyone else in the room, and she had to force herself to remain where she stood rather than take a shaky step back. She wanted suddenly to remain just as she was: not to alter, never grow old. She felt a sudden kinship with the kappa, and wondered if this meant that she, too, were nothing more than an inferior kind of human. She supposed that the thought should have made her feel guilty.

"You were disobedient," the Grandmothers said now. "What do you have to say for yourself?"

"I wanted to see the city beyond the mansion. I grew tired of being cooped up." Somehow, she had expected to hear herself sound like a whining child, but to her surprise, the voice in which she spoke was adult, a person worthy of consideration. The Grandmothers stared at her, and when they replied, the tone was distinctly more conciliatory.

"Perhaps that is understandable. But it was unwise, nonetheless. You were spotted, by one who is an enemy. It is no longer safe for you to remain here."

"Dreams-of-War said that I am to be sent away." Lunae glanced down and saw something beneath the bed: a twist of tubes and glistening fluid. She fixed her gaze on the wall, seeking patterns in the wood. "Where am I to go?"

"Dreams-of-War and the kappa will be instructed. It is best if you yourself are not told until the day of your departure."

"Will they be going with me?"

"Of course," the Grandmothers said. "And you must obey them, and not be so disobedient this time. Much depends upon it."

Lunae, swallowing hard, glanced at the nurse and saw that the kappa was becoming visibly agitated, wringing her thick fingers together as if confronted with a stubborn piece of laundry. The Grandmothers paid the kappa no heed. Their gaze remained fixed on Lunae: two pairs of dark, impenetrable eyes.

It was the kappa's distress that prompted Lunae to say, "What if I choose a place to go?" It was a foolish thing to say and she knew it, but suddenly she wanted to see just where the boundaries lay, what smaller victories might be within her grasp.

"Choose?" the Grandmothers said together. Lunae felt as though the air were becoming sluggish and slow, curdling around her. It was suddenly difficult to breathe. The tapestries that hung around the bed loomed larger, so that she could see every detail of the weave, then retreated, as though she peered through the wrong end of a telescope.

"There is no choice," Right-Hand said, oil-smooth, amused. "No choice for any of us. The sooner you come to understand this, the easier things will be. Do you not agree?"

Lunae's mouth was too hot and dry for her to answer, so she nodded instead.

"You may go," the Grandmothers told her. "Remember what we have told you."

Lunae bowed and backed away, but as she turned to go through the door, she thought she heard Left-Hand say, "Make us proud."

The kappa was trotting after her, so Lunae dived out into the passage and breathed the stuffy air with relief.

"They did not need to see me! Why couldn't Dreams-of-War tell me all this? They summoned me to torment me."

The kappa seized her arm and hastened her down the passage. "Of course they did," the kappa said into Lunae's ear, surprising her. "But do not say so where they can hear you."

"If that's so, we had best journey to the moon," Lunae said with bitterness, not caring. "I'm sick of hiding how I feel." She could still feel the Grandmothers' presence. It surrounded her, filling her mind, as cloying and sticky as syrup.

"These moments of rebellion do not wholly displease your Grandmothers, you know," the kappa said, "though they may pretend otherwise. They complained often of the other child— that she was too malleable, too pliant, that she did everything asked of her, with no more protest than a vegetable makes before it goes into the soup."

"Nurse," Lunae said, for this was yet another question without an answer, "who was that other child? What became of her? Was she the *hito-bashira* before me?"

"Yes. She was your sister-in-skin. She was one of the ones who died."

Lunae searched for a flicker of regret in the kappa's face, but there was none.

"Did you look after her, as you care for me?"

"No. The Grandmothers summoned me after her death. I replaced another genetic grower."

"Would you miss me if I died?"

"It is hard to say," the kappa mused. Lunae felt something cold and pulpy rise inside her throat; she stopped walking and stared at the kappa. "Do not think I do not love you," the kappa said in sudden dismay. "I did not mean that. But your Grandmothers are compassionate, and will not let me fully feel. If anything were to befall you, they would extract my emotions, store them safely where I cannot find them. They are very kind."

Lunae was doubtful. If someone else was the governor of your emotions, then what was the good of having them in the first place? Why not simply have them removed, like an overactive gland? But perhaps it was better for the kappa to believe that the Grandmothers had her best interests at heart. If, indeed, she did so believe, and was not merely dissembling.

"And now," the kappa went on, "come with me. There are preparations to be made."

MEMNOS

MEKANIS

CHAPTER 1

MARS

The Animus hovered anxiously overhead, wings beating like a slow fan. It had taken over an hour of bargaining to allow him to have access to the Tower, and even then a squadron of scissor-women had accompanied him up the spiraling stairs.

Beneath lay Yskatarina, strapped to a high couch. A doctor hovered nearby, with the Matriarch. They had removed her limbs, for fear that she might break free and damage herself or the equipment. She was now secured by straps at the waist and the throat. At first, she had protested.

"Surely the treatment cannot be that difficult?"

"It strips your neurons down to the level of the unconscious. It ransacks the pathways that lead to the farthest parts of your mind. Your aunt will, I know, have planted her seeds of affection very deeply." The Matriarch's face, looming above her like a pitted Martian moon, grew pinched. "She tends a cold garden, that one."

Yskatarina was about to ask how well the Matriarch knew Elaki, for the words made her angry with unthinking affront. But then: *I will be glad to be rid of this, a loyalty that I neither asked for nor desired.*

Let it burn and bleed out into the red night; let it be gone into the shadows of Memnos. She wondered where such emotions went, whether they seeped from the black light matrix to sink into cold stone and colder air. She listened to the walls of the Tower around her, yet heard nothing, only the Matriarch's harsh breath and the steady beat of the Animus above her, like the heart that anchored her to life.

"This process," she said, before the doctor began to key the codes into the matrix that covered the wall and which drifted in cobweb filaments through the air. "How precise is it? What damage might it do?"

She did not like this at all. It made her feel trapped and choiceless. Only two cultures had this kind of technology: Memnos and Nightshade. She felt caught between the dark and the deep. She could not have this done at home, but there was always the thought that Memnos might implant something else in her brain, some treacherous seed that would only grow to fruition when the time was right, to burgeon and betray. She had spent the journey here staring out at the spectral images of the Chain and weighing chances in the balance. Thoughts of losing the Animus had driven her to the final decision, but even that had been a close-run thing. If Memnos messed with her mind, Nightshade would have to put the damage right and she would also have to take the risk that Elaki would not notice that anything else had been interfered with. And now the guilt was kicking in with crippling force, whispering inside her head, aghast that she was about to betray Elaki. But the cracks in that loyalty had grown too wide. It was as though there were a second voice inside her head, another self, buried deep: *Elaki will take the Animus away. You cannot risk that. You have no choice. Do it. Do it now.*

"Very precise," the Matriarch answered. "There will be no damage. And we will honor our bargain."

"If I find that you have not," Yskatarina said, "then you will find that the haunt-tech that I have given you will turn upon you. I have factored in safeguards that only I can activate."

The Matriarch's mouth curled in what Yskatarina initially thought to be her habitual sneer. It was only a moment later that she realized it was approval.

"Are you ready?"

"Very well." Yskatarina gritted her teeth, helpless as a worm in a vise. From the corner of her eye, she saw the doctor run a hand across the generating tubes of the black light matrix. The room sparkled and filled with unnatural sound. Yskatarina blinked. The Matriarch was no longer there. The draft from the Animus's wings drifted across her face—soft as snowfall, she thought, and wondered where the thought had come from. And then she *was* the Animus, a whisper in his head, looking down on her own bound form. She saw the black light matrix sweep across her, outlining first sinew and vein, then bone, then nerve and neuron. Her brain pulsed with neon fire. She plunged downward, boring into her own skull. It was like entering the Chain.

Images flashed by. Yskatarina saw herself in a garden filled with glowing leaves, skeins of tangled vines that pulsed with lights, a tower made of glass and water, ebbing and flowing like the tide. She saw the long ragged edge of the Animus's wing, curling through stormy air. She tasted salt. She saw a girl with luminous gray eyes and long red hair blowing in a wind from the sea.

She knew that it was here somewhere, though she could not have said what it was that she sought.

The landscape changed from the lands of life. She traveled down canyons of meat, over bloody rivers, across bridges made of sharpened bone and tough neural fiber, withered as old whips. Beneath, there was a boil of fire: an inner, private hell. Things clung to the cliffs like ghosts, winged yet spectral. They were horribly familiar, and as one of them looked up, Yskatarina saw its shadowy head change. Her own face looked back at her, and then it was the visage of the Animus, then both at the same time. Something within her shrieked in protest.

Shuddering, she let the vision pass by and glided on. And at last she saw Elaki sitting on a crag with her feet tucked up beneath her. Yskatarina slipped down to stand beside her aunt.

Elaki showed no sign that she saw Yskatarina. Under the tapering cowl her face was at first withered and old, and then it smoothed out into fetal vacuity.

"Aunt?" Yskatarina said. "What is wrong?"

But Elaki only muttered and mumbled, tearing with toothless gums at a long bloody shred.

"Is that my love for you?" Yskatarina asked. She reached out and snatched at the shred, but Elaki shrieked and tore it away. She held it at arm's length, then clutched it to her. Her eyes were wild; she roared with panic.

"Give it to me!" Yskatarina cried, and reaching out she struck her aunt in the face. Elaki's cheek tore open, revealing a shadowy hollow behind a fountain of stinking blood.

"Give it to me! You took my limbs. You would take my Animus! I owe you nothing."

Elaki's arms flailed. Yskatarina grasped the shred and pulled. It lengthened with unnatural elasticity, until Elaki and Yskatarina stood in a tug-of-war on either side of the crag. The recesses of Yskatarina's imagination gaped below, the caverns and oceans of the unconscious mind. She did not like the things that she saw within; they disgusted her.

Once more she glimpsed the beings that clung to the sides of the cliff, but now the fire was gone and the place in her vision was bleak and cold and dark. It looked like Nightshade, the region known as the Sunken Plain. The creatures howled and cried and she felt their attention turn toward her: hungry and desperate, a bitter yearning for life and blood and flesh. Their need reeled her in, she understood what it was like to be thus disembodied. She felt herself begin to shiver and melt.

Then a black-winged shape with a scorpion's tail slid out of the abyss, its eyes glowing with trust. With the last of her strength, Yskatarina ripped at the shred and tore it from Elaki's grasp. Elaki withered into a twist of smoke and blew away, but Yskatarina felt herself falling backward into pain, which opened with nauseating willingness to let her in.

CHAPTER 2

EARTH

W e have made the arrangements," the Grandmothers informed Dreams-of-War. "You will leave as soon as can be arranged, by junk."

"What, on a public ship?"

"Of course not. We have hired someone loyal to Memnos, you will be relieved to hear. But the ship is up-coast at present, and must return. We do not yet know when."

"I am, indeed, relieved," Dreams-of-War said. "I should not trust an Earth-owned ship, given the presence of the Kami here."

The Grandmothers snorted. "You are arrogant, like all Martians. You are like cats—you all consider yourselves superior, and with even less justification. In the matter of the Kami, you know nothing and are doubtless mistaken in what you think you know. Now go. Make sure that you keep a close eye on the girl."

Dreams-of-War left, seething.

Once inside her own chamber, she stood looking out across the early morning harbor, grinding one armored fist into the palm of the other. She had not known that it would be like this when she had joined the upper echelons of the warriors of Memnos. She had been so proud. It had been the culmination of her youthful military career, and yet it wound down to this: a series of petty slights and insults from two twisted old women. If it had not been for the ensuing humiliation, Dreams-of-War would have resigned her commission and returned to Mars.

But then, there was also Lunae. Dreams-of-War remembered the conversation that had taken place after her emotional modification.

71

"You have no choice," the Matriarch had told her as they sat together in the highest tower of Memnos, looking out across the white-and-russet winter plain. "You will need it for her protection."

"But I've never loved anyone," Dreams-of-War protested. "Only human remnants who remember the days when they were bloodbirthers feel such natural love for their children." Love was a contaminant, utterly apart from the purities of sisterhood, battle, and duty. She found a strong repugnance for the feeling, but the Matriarch had been right.

Dreams-of-War recalled standing beside the kappa in the growing-chamber, trying not to get too close to this stout toad-woman who seemed to have little sense of personal distance and who was continually attempting to pat Dreams-of-War in misplaced reassurance. She remembered watching the growing-bag in revulsion as it bulged and writhed. It reminded her of her own birth, and Dreams-of-War found that distasteful.

As soon as the squirming, grublike thing had been released from its pod in a shower of fluid, however, the small sore place within her had clicked like a switch of pain, and she knew immediately that she would die to protect the infant. It was most vexing, and she resented it with a passion, but there it was. It got in the way of all manner of things; it made her life a worry and a misery, and for the first time she was conscious of a real fear with which she had no adequate means of dealing. As soon as her duties were discharged, she told herself, she would return to Memnos, go back beneath the black light matrix, and have the whole package of inconvenient emotions surgically changed.

Now she turned her back on the city and sat down on the metal bed. The cinnabar walls of the room reminded her of Mars, as though she might glance through the window and see the Crater Plain stretching before her, Olympus towering on the horizon. The sudden longing-for-place was yet another feeling to be despised. In a fit of irritation, Dreams-of-War said aloud, "I need to talk to you! Separately."

Slowly, gliding across her skin, the armor left her body and crept across the floor like a serpent. When the gleaming tongue reached a shaft of sunlight, it began to rise upward, hardening, reassembling itself piece by piece. Clad only in the rubbery black underharness, Dreams-of-War watched until the armor stood before her, waiting.

Dreams-of-War hesitated. Of all the aspects of her marvelous armor, this one was the most disquieting to her. And it was so because the armor incorporated something that was unnatural, alien, something that had originated with the Kami. *Haunt-tech.*

It was difficult to separate a warrior from her ghost-armor, for armor *became* the warrior. Both formed part of a fighting machine. If one died or malfunctioned, the other had a tendency to follow. Yet if the wearer were knocked unconscious, the armor would take over. Dreams-of-War had once woken to find herself pounding across a Martian plain, the legs of the armor pumping while she dangled useless within it. Dreams-of-War knew that she had become overdependent on the armor, and despite its comforts, she did not like the realization. It had been easier when she had relied on nothing but the underharness and a gutting knife, hand-fighting men-remnants in the heights.

"What, then?" the armor said, echoing through the chamber.

"I ask Embar Khair to stand before me," Dreams-of-War said. The armor flowed, glittering, the helm snapping up over the empty neck and taking on the semblance of a face. Half of it was missing; Embar Khair had died in the armor, a chance bolt from a mountain-ghost's bow striking her in the side of the head.

"I want to talk to you about the Kami," Dreams-of-War said to the armor.

"The spirits-who-ride-within?" Embar Khair's mutilated metal face managed a frown.

"The aliens," Dreams-of-War said patiently. Embar Khair had died only a handful of years after the arrival of the Kami, but her armor had been their gift. "I need to know everything you know."

"It is not a long story. We first learned of the Kami through Nightshade, which had sealed itself away for centuries. Then Nightshade sent a ship to Memnos, with news of new technology that had been granted by aliens. They gave us haunt-tech, and the Chain."

"And what did the Matriarchy think about these gifts?"

"They did not trust Nightshade. I remember—" but here, Embar Khair's form twisted, half-melting.

"Armor! What is the matter with you?"

"I cannot recall . . . I am half-here."

Dreams-of-War rose to her feet and put her face close to the half-visage of the armor. "But you *must*."

"Cannot . . ."

"Wait," Dream-of-War instructed the armor. "I have an idea. Reduce yourself."

The armor did so, melting down into its customary ball. Dreams-of-War picked up the ball and strode swiftly down the hallway, to the chamber that contained the mansion's black light matrix.

She had never had reason to enter this chamber before, and she hesitated at the door. Leaning forward, she spoke quietly into the oreagraph opening.

"The Grandmothers. What are they doing?"

They sleep, the oreagraph replied after a moment.

"Good. Deactivate the weir-wards to this chamber, then tell me when the Grandmothers wake." Dreams-of-War leaned closer, so that the oreagraph could scan her soul-engrams through the lenses of her eyes. She blinked, and then the door was opening. Dreams-of-War carried the ball of armor into the black light chamber and set it upon the couch.

"Resume your form."

The armor did so.

"I am going to activate the matrix," Dreams-of-War said, "to bring your spirit wholly through from the Eldritch Realm. I am unfamiliar with these matters, so you must instruct me. Will this work?"

"It should."

"Then tell me how to turn this thing on."

The armor issued instructions, with which Dreams-of-War complied. It was not so very difficult. Within a few moments, the matrix began to glow.

There was a sound like the echo of a shriek within the chamber. Outside the door, Dreams-of-War heard the rattle of activated weir-wards. She spoke hastily to the oreagraph. "I told you—deactivate!" The sound stopped. The armor stood before her, calm now, and full-faced. Dreams-of-War stared.

"I am here," Embar Khair said.

"Tell me what I need to know."

And Embar Khair did so.

The women stood at the entrance to the ship. Above them, the Memnos Tower shone red in the last of the Martian sun. Frost cracked beneath their boots.

"I like none of this," the Matriarch said. Her long head bobbed, balanced on its thin neck like a bead on the end of a wire. She shuffled unhuman limbs beneath the red-and-black robes.

"No one likes it," the woman named Essa answered. She put a hand to her head, smoothing the surface of the curled horns at her brow. "It comes from Nightshade, after all. As do Yri and Yra and their ship." Essa gestured toward the traveling chair that contained the bulky, connected bodies of two women. "They who sought sanctuary with us, and their male with them . . ."

The Matriarch shifted uneasily. "Where is the male?"

"Confined on the ship."

The Matriarch sighed, then drew Embar Khair and Essa to one side. "You've made quite sure? There will be no trace of this haunt-ship, or its voyage?"

Embar Khair nodded. "Yri and Yra say that they have made arrangements. There will be no record of our passage."

"I trust none of this," the Matriarch fretted. "This new technology—this ship, the Chain, the armor that you wear . . . None."

"Haunt-tech," Essa murmured.

"It is a science of superstition. I know too little about it."

The warrior grinned, displaying sharpened teeth.

"Who does know? No one except the lab clans of Nightshade. Like all gifts, it is best treated with caution. And we are doing the right thing, are we not?"

"Nightshade must be challenged," Essa agreed. "There's too much power there, out on the system's edge. Whoever took any notice of Nightshade, before the aliens came? It was nothing more than an isolated colony, years distant from the inner systems. And now, suddenly, we must take orders from them if we want the benefits of this haunt-tech."

The Matriarch looked up to where the Martian maw of the Chain arched across the heavens. Even at sunset, it was visible: a shadow over the sky. "Look at it," the Matriarch said. "It dominates the worlds. They say you actually die, you know." The Matriarch's head wobbled in distress, weaving from side to side. "It sends you through into the realm of the dead and brings you out the other side, alive once more. I do not trust it. It is unnatural."

"I am not afraid of death," the warrior said softly. She glanced over to the ship, to where the others were waiting. The two women were barely visible in the folded mass of tubing that surrounded the carrying chair. "But I wonder about Yri and Yra."

Essa's hand strayed to the horns, stroking the bony carapace.

"Nightshade is looking for them throughout the system. Mars won't be a haven for them any longer, and we have to keep them safe, Embar Khair. I doubt whether any other geneticist has the skill, or the technical knowledge, to do what has to be done. And if this project of theirs fails, then Nightshade triumphs. Your job is to get them to Earth. Hide them for as long as necessary."

Embar Khair inclined her armored head. "I will do so."

"Then go."

Embar Khair strode across to the ship and touched her fingers to its side. A hatch hissed open, responding to the engrams within her armor. The carrying chair, bearing Yri and Yra, glided up into the depths of the ship, which twitched like a startled scorpion as the hatch opened. Embar Khair followed. Moments later, the ship spiraled upward, skimming over the Crater Plain and leaving the Memnos Tower far below. Embar Khair kept her gaze fixed on the growing maw of the Chain, and never once looked back.

Dreams-of-War stared openmouthed at her armor.

"You challenged Nightshade?"

"Yri and Yra, the Grandmothers, fled to Memnos from Nightshade, seeking sanctuary. They had fallen out with the rest of their clan, because they despised the Kami. But Nightshade's wish eventually prevailed upon Mars. Nightshade disapproved of most of the Changed—Mars had bred them long ago for amusement and sport, not ultimate perfection, and the Changed were seen as lesser beings, genetic tinkering, nothing more. Essa was forced to—disappear. The Matriarch was imprisoned some time later in a Memnos coup and Nightshade equipped her replacement with the means to control the scissor-women. I returned to Mars to seek out Essa, and that was when I died."

"But what did the Grandmothers come here to do?"

"The intention of the project was to grow a child, one who would have the ability to challenge Nightshade."

Dreams-of-War felt a sudden glow of accomplishment. Here it was, at last.

"The *hito-bashira*. What *is* she?"

"I do not know," Embar Khair said. "I was only the bodyguard."

Dreams-of-War stepped back in disappointment.

"You don't know?"

"I know only that the undertaking was immensely difficult, requiring years of study and preparation. Yri and Yra were geneticists of great renown. That is all I know."

"And what of these new ghosts of the ancient past? Do you remember the gaezelles?" She thought of the ghost herd, their electric demon gaze.

"I remember," the armor said.

"There have been further reports. I have been keeping in touch with Memnos, but I would not have needed to. It is in all the news-views. Over the last months, since we first saw the gaezelles, the sightings of such ghosts have increased. Horned women striding the passages and under-ways of Winterstrike. Flayed warriors in armor made of thorns, manifesting in teahouses in Caud. Women from the Epoch of Cold, whose flesh seems made of amber and ice."

They wake, the oreagraph said suddenly.

"Close the matrix down," Dreams-of-War said. Black light flickered and died. Embar Khair's spirit screamed as it fled, leaving only the usual residue behind. And now the armor was starting to lose shape, the fierce half-face melting into a gleam of green metal. Dreams-of-War reached out a hand. "Return to me." The armor did so, enclosing her with hard comfort. Dreams-of-War stood on metal feet and, protected once more, strode from the chamber.

The encounter had given her information, and more than that, strength: this reminder that she was not alone, that the former inhabitants of the ancient armor were all still with her. "Lonely," however, was another emotion that Dreams-of-War despised.

CHAPTER 3

MARS

N o one," the Matriarch said, "has been inside this room for a hundred years." They were standing before a metal wall opposite the Tower room, Yskatarina enveloped in soot-colored furs, the Matriarch in ceremonial red-and-black, from which she peered like a toad out of a hole. Behind the Matriarch stood two of the excissieres: the scissor-fighters of Memnos. Both were tall, angular, with harsh, bony faces. Yskatarina found it impossible to tell one from another; they must be from the same growing-bag. Both wore armor: a faded metallic black, pitted with strikes and gouges. Scissor-images flickered over exposed flesh, holo-tattoo wounds that faded into instant scars and then were gone, only to appear again. She was not sure whether it was art, reminder, or penance.

Yskatarina raised an eyebrow. "It's been sealed for all this time?"

"Someone was imprisoned here. Walled in."

"Why?" Yskatarina was beginning to enjoy needling the Matriarch, watching the woman's face grow yet more pinched.

"I am not at liberty to say. Enough that you know that she was one of the Changed, a descendant of the creatures of the Age of Children, and committed a crime against us. For that, she was placed in this room, at the summit of the Tower of Memnos, and the door was welded shut. I do not know how long she lived after that. It is irrelevant."

"So her corpse is still in there?" Yskatarina looked toward the metal wall. She could see what might have been a faint outline in the iron, perhaps a seam, perhaps no more than a trick of the light.

"If it is not," the Matriarch said, with the first flash of anything approaching humor that Yskatarina had yet seen in her, "I shall be very surprised." She gestured toward the wall. "Open it."

The excissieres stepped forward, scissors clattering. Yskatarina frowned, imagining what it would be like to be hunted by these women. Now, however, the razor-edged weapons remained on their metal chains, secured to the bodices of the armor. The women carried flame-flowers, which they placed on either side of the seam. Each touched the iron-hard stems, causing the leaves to rattle. Blue-white acid spat forth from the stamens, melting the welded door. Yskatarina stepped back, choking on smoke and the musty smell of old fungus, released as the door fell clear.

"I shall go first," the Matriarch said. She stepped through the door, Yskatarina close on her heels.

The thing that crouched in the corner of the room was much larger than a human being. Its head was sunk into its breast. Pincer-hands rested limply on the floor before it, and around them were curled the spiny remnants of a tail, disintegrated into individual vertebrae. The flesh had darkened to a blue-red, the color of ancient meat, or perhaps, Yskatarina thought, this had been the original shade of the thing. It reminded her of some of the beings that lived in the catacombs beneath the wastes of Nightshade, the creatures she had occasionally glimpsed bolting into the shelter of the frozen rocks. She wondered what the being's crime had been. It seemed to her that Memnos knew few enough limits.

The Matriarch was eyeing the remains with distaste. "I did not think there would be so much left," she muttered.

"A sealed room, dry air . . . It has simply desiccated," Yskatarina replied. She found the mummified remains both pathetic and repulsive.

"It is vile," the Matriarch stated baldly. "Now, such a creature would never be allowed to remain here."

"Standards must have been lower in those days."

"It is in part because of the crimes of this thing that the Changed are kept away from Memnos. Shall we get on with it?" Yskatarina nodded. The Matriarch gestured to the excissieres. "Take it down to the matrix."

The scissor-women stepped forward and picked up the desiccated form.

"Careful!" the Matriarch said. "It is fragile."

Yskatarina followed them down the stairs to the chamber that contained the black light matrix. A doctor was waiting, face grim beneath the medical hat. The excissieres set the corpse down on the couch beneath the matrix.

"You realize there is no guarantee of success, with something so old?" the doctor said.

"Do as I told you," the Matriarch replied. The doctor gave a shrug and began to manipulate the slender black tubes that were the generating device of the matrix.

Sound welled up, shivering the air and causing the hair to rise on the back of Yskatarina's neck. She gave a small smile of satisfaction: This, and the creeping chill that cast itself over her skin, was a sure sign that the device was beginning to work. Then she remembered the last time she had been in this room, and had to force herself not to turn away.

"You play it like an instrument," the Matriarch remarked to the doctor, with an evident and unwilling fascination. "No matter how many times I see this, it still causes wonderment."

"It is an instrument, in part. It uses sound to conjure the particulates of spirit, to summon them through from the Eldritch Realm and reassemble them. Watch."

The device was singing to itself, a quick, thin song. The air sparked with black light. Slowly, as if seen through heat haze or mist, an essence began to form around the dry thing that crouched on the floor. Pincers clacked together and made no sound. A lipless face raised its gaze to the ceiling, mouth gaping. The image overlay the mummified form, a ghost, indeed.

The Matriarch stepped forward. "I have questions! I—"

"Wait," the doctor said. "Give it time to assemble."

The phantom head swung round to look at the Matriarch. She found herself gazing into two great dark eyes, lensed like the eyes of the Animus. The similarity made her queasy. They were flat and blank, with no light behind them. The mouth moved. Moments later, a dry whispering emerged.

"I am dead," the thing said in wonder.

"Yes," Yskatarina answered. "You died here a century ago." She glanced at the Matriarch for confirmation. The Matriarch gave a sour nod. "This woman has questions for you," she added.

"First, I wish to ask *you* something," the Matriarch said to Yskatarina. Then she turned to the doctor. "Go." The doctor did so, without demur.

Yskatarina suppressed a sigh. "Let me guess. You once more wish for reassurance that this is no trick? You want again to query how it will be that we can attest to the accuracy of the information that this being provides?"

"That is easily enough ascertained, or so you have assured me," the Matriarch said tartly. "The extraction of particular information, known to none other than this being and myself, will be sufficient. No, the question I have is different. I want to know how, having raised this thing, we may contain it."

"Its essence will disintegrate once the device is powered down," Yskatarina said.

The Matriarch's moon-face seemed to swell, as if it were being pumped up. "But ghosts are even now roaming the Crater Plain, infesting the city streets of Winterstrike. I do not want this thing to crawl down the walls of the Tower and start babbling critical information to all and sundry."

The spirit turned its head slowly from side to side. Yskatarina wondered how much it really understood.

"This is a pure form, not infected by nanotech, as far as I am aware. Its conjuration will, therefore, not be sustained. It is energy, rather than partial matter."

"And you are sure of this?" the Matriarch asked.

"I am certain." Yskatarina looked the Matriarch in the eye. She saw the flicker of doubt and tried not to hold her breath, for she lied to the Matriarch. She intended to keep this old being around for as long as possible. It, and the information that it might still carry. *First steps*, Yskatarina told herself. Animate the thing, and then apply the means of controlling it.

"Then let us begin," the current Matriarch said. "I must ask you to leave. This thing can provide information that must remain confidential to Memnos. You may return when I have completed my inquiries."

"Of course. I understand," Yskatarina said. She bowed her head, and let the excissieres lead her from the room. The matrix would, she knew, record the session in its entirety, and transmit it to Nightshade. It was not necessary for her to be present.

Later that evening, Yskatarina and the Animus slipped from the ship to stand in the shadows.

"Where is it?" the Animus asked.

"There. That fourth window. You can glimpse the black light within."

"They will have weir-wards on the windows."

Yskatarina smiled. "There are advantages to being the purveyor of a technology. I have deactivation runes. Just get me up there."

She slid her arms around the Animus's torso and clung to him. The Animus sailed upward, to hover like a bat outside the window of the black light chamber. Yskatarina risked a glance below. There was no one to be seen. A monstrous face swam out of the darkness, hissing. Neon flickered across its jaws.

"Hush," Yskatarina whispered. She leaned forward until her face was close to the visage, and murmured the deactivation sequence. The face, with a comical grimace of dismay, vanished. The window lay before them, unprotected. The Animus drew closer. Yskatarina once more murmured an incantation, this time to the haunt-lock. The window opened without a sound. She climbed from the Animus's back onto the sill.

The body lay within, beneath the cold filaments of the matrix. It was still strapped to the couch. It raised its head and looked at Yskatarina as she entered.

"You were here before," it said.

"Yes. I've come to help you."

"I do not believe you. You are of Nightshade," the thing said. "I remember Nightshade."

Yskatarina flexed the sensors within her legs and squatted down beside the ancient thing. "You were the Matriarch, were you not, a hundred years ago? Do you remember two sisters? Yri and Yra?"

"Yes. They sought sanctuary with us. We sent them to Earth."

"Do you know where they went? And what happened to the ship they traveled in?"

"I will not tell you," the old Matriarch said. Feebly it raised itself up, hissing. Yskatarina acted quickly. There were excissieres just beyond the door and she did not want them to hear. She touched a sleep-pen to the creature's neck and it slumped back onto the high couch. Then she switched on the matrix and whispered Elaki's sequence into it.

She had never seen this particular function of the matrix before. It was different. The familiar sparks darkened above the prone figure, forming spirals and coils of black light. Then, as the sequence took hold, the world opened up and Yskatarina found herself staring down into the hellish abyss that she had glimpsed during her own modification. She fell back, hand over her mouth, trying not to cry out. There was a dreadful sense of familiarity, recognition, that sent her soul cowering within her.

Something rushed upward. She saw a mouth agape in a silent shriek. Then it was gone, evaporating into the figure on the couch. The gap closed. The black light disappeared, with a burst that hurt the eyes. Yskatarina stepped forward and released the bonds. The thing on the couch sat up.

"I am alive," it said, wonderingly. "I have a body."

"Yes, you do," Yskatarina said in relief. The Kami looked out at her from the former Matriarch's dull gaze. Yskatarina held up a small silver phial. "This is a copy of that which belongs to the current Matriarch. My aunt gave it to me. It contains the substance that controls the excissieres. And I now will tell you what you must do, when you are strong enough . . ."

FRAGRANT HARBOR

CHAPTER 1

MARS/EARTH

Yskatarina held tight to the spiny claw of the Animus as the ship—a public carrier—wheeled over the Crater Plain. Other passengers shifted and grumbled around them. She did not like being confined so closely with so many others, but at least all kept their distance from the Animus, eyeing it askance, drawing skirts and robes aside.

From the view port, misted with droplets of ice, Yskatarina could see the plain in its entirety, all the way to the slopes of Olympus. The Memnos Tower rose up out of the red earth like a diseased finger. Yskatarina, with a trace of wistfulness, remembered the gaezelles and wondered where they now ran.

She was pleased with her work at the Tower. She was confident, after a further conversation with the Kami that now occupied the body of the former Matriarch, that Memnos would be unable to tell the difference. Very soon, now, the Kami would be able to carry out its task. She wondered that the current Matriarch had taken the risk of reanimating the ancient thing, given Nightshade's involvement. But Martians were always arrogant, always overreached themselves.

Then there had been the emotion-wipe, of which few memories remained. Something about a shred of flesh, and Elaki sitting on a crag . . . Nothing more than this, but when Yskatarina looked within, to the place where that turbulent storm of resentment and loyalty and love had raged, there was only a small dark hole. Wonderful to feel nothing but hate for the woman who had threatened to take the Animus away from her—no more conflict, no more tearing on the mind's rack. She felt whole for the first time since childhood. Now she could begin to plan. Now she could keep the Animus safe. She did wonder, for a moment, whether all of her emotions had been similarly implanted, whether the bond that existed between herself and the Animus had artificial origins, but then she dismissed the thought. That bond was a given; there was no voice within, telling her that it was wrong.

She had been luxuriating in hate for over two days now. Memnos had done its work well. It remained to be seen whether they had slipped anything else past her mental guards: some small neural bomb. There was nothing Yskatarina could have done about it if they had; they would just have to cross that bridge when they came to it. But she now had a weapon, in the form of the old Matriarch.

Thinking of this, Yskatarina smiled.

The ship flew on, arching past Olympus and around, across the cities that populated the eastern part of the planet. The Small Sea lay at the edge of the horizon, the green-blue glow of algae forming a vivid contrast with the soil. One by one, the cities fell away: Caud, Winterstrike, Ardent, and Ord. Yskatarina watched them pass without emotion. Soon, the ship reached the Martian edge of the Chain.

Night was falling over the South China Sea when Yskatarina's craft emerged from the Earth-end of the Chain above the Kita Hub. Passengers stirred and muttered restlessly around her; she longed to be alone with the Animus. She looked through the view port to see an ocean of lights below, towers nailing the sky. Along a narrow channel, boats starred a narrow harbor.

"What is that city?"

"Fragrant Harbor," the monitor said. Its voice took on a tinny quality. "First city of the region."

"I can see islands." Then, as the ship turned, "It is *all* islands."

She surveyed the ragged, eaten edge of the coast. Helpfully, the seat oreagraph sent a highlighter running through the view port, so that each island was delineated with a tiny ring of light. There must have been hundreds: a rash of land.

"Ancient mountains and artificially raised settlements like Fragrant Harbor are all that remains. The city has been devoured by the sea, countless times, and each time built again."

To Yskatarina, used to the frozen wastes of Nightshade, it seemed strange to be looking down on this great wash of ocean. It gave her a spinning, disoriented feeling, as though she stood on the deck of a seagoing vessel rather than that of a spacecraft.

She sat impatiently until the ship docked, then caught a transit into High Kowloon with the Animus. Compared to the relative emptiness of Nightshade or Mars, the city felt packed. She could sense the press of bodies all around her, feel the city going down and down into its multiple layers, buildings built upon the wreckage of buildings.

"This is an old place," the Animus said, echoing her thoughts.

"Old and dying." She looked through the grimy windows of the transit at the peeling paint of a temple wall, a hail of gilt flakes catching the lamplight like golden snow. The bulks of the factory district rose ahead, symbols blazing through the dark. The district went on and on, seemingly unending. Figures trudged by, carrying baskets, wheeling carts, and Yskatarina realized that for much of this world's people, little must have changed since the earliest days of history. For these women, Mars must be nothing more than a cruel, cold dream, and yet it ran their lives.

Eventually, they emerged from the factory district. Streets lined with old mansions appeared, half-hidden by trees trailing with moss. But these folk, too, would be dependent on the whim of Mars: of the Houses of Winterstrike, or Ord, and ultimately Memnos itself. Yskatarina shifted in her seat and forced open a window. The scent of night jasmine and unburned fuel drifted through, catching at the back of her throat. The transit ground to a halt in front of a towering building, and Yskatarina at last felt safe.

Accompanied by the Animus, she made her way into the hotel lobby and was assigned to a suite at the summit of the tower. Ascending in the silent elevator brought back memories: of Memnos, of Tower Cold. She probed the place where Elaki had lain like a serpent in her mind and again found nothing, only a painless hollow. When she stepped out onto the hotel terrace, it was with an overpowering sense of freedom. Fragrant Harbor stretched below, a sprawl of lamplight and shadow, neon and water glitter.

"Tomorrow we travel north," she told the Animus. "I have to make arrangements, speak to the Mission, to find out what they have learned."

The Animus flexed and coiled. "You will still follow Elaki's orders?"

"I want to discover just why this girl is so important to her. Why should it not be I who rules in Tower Cold? If I can gain an advantage over my aunt, I wish to do so."

"What of her sisters? Would you seek an alliance with them?"

"They betrayed Tower Cold," Yskatarina said. "Whatever one might think of Elaki, I could not trust them."

"And those in the Mission? They, too, are of the clan."

"I remember the ones who went to the Mission, the nine sisters. Something about them horrified me. I would be reluctant to encounter them again. Perhaps it was just that I was only a child . . . I will contact them. And regarding other matters, Memnos has put me in touch with a war-madam who supposedly is reliable."

"We could just disappear," the Animus said with a trace of wistfulness.

Yskatarina ran a hand along its gleaming hide. "And perhaps we will. But not yet."

After a pause, the Animus said, "Do you know where we're going?"

Yskatarina nodded. "A place where no one will think to look, that everyone except the old Matriarch has forgotten. And perhaps Yri and Yra."

They left before dawn, flying north over the city, Yskatarina clinging to the Animus's back. If anyone had looked up, they would have seen nothing more than a shadow crossing the sky, and perhaps not even that.

By noon, flying high above the dappled expanse of sea and island, they reached the end of the Yellow River estuary. The Animus flew low over sand flats and marsh, steaming with heat, to the tangle of forested bluffs beyond.

"Not far now," the Animus said, voice half-swallowed by the wind.

"I can see it! There, on the cliff."

Yskatarina looked down at the thick walls of the house that had, many years before, belonged to the skin-sisters of the Elder Elaki. The house, once a mansion of massive stone, was now almost a ruin, with the sea encroaching fast upon the cliffs on which it stood. As they flew lower, she saw that at some point in its history someone had constructed a veranda around its base, a frivolous, teetering edifice of moldy wood, with a straw roof that had long since been eaten away by the sea winds. The veranda was incongruous, a delicate, rotting lace around the bulk of the mansion. The Animus descended to alight upon it. Yskatarina slid down from its back. There was not much left to explore. They set up a rough base in the inner courtyard, then went out to the surrounding jungle to search for any signs of the lost ship. They found no sign of it. Returning to the ruin, Yskatarina put two calls in to the antiscribe and waited.

Toward the end of the afternoon, the Animus glanced up to a sky that was heavy with rain.

"Is there any word from the Mission?" he asked.

"No, none." Yskatarina frowned at the antiscribe. "I can't understand it. The call went through. They should have responded by now. Yet there is nothing."

"But at least the other has answered," the Animus said. "Look."

Yskatarina looked up. Something was floating down from the heavens: a small insectoid craft. Yskatarina stood, legs braced, waiting for the arrival of the ship. It touched the rough boards of the terrace and the hatch opened with a crackling snap.

A smooth-faced form stepped down to stand before her, robed in jet and translucent armor. Yskatarina frowned, wondering whether the featureless visage was a mask, or the thing's own face. Impossible to tell whether it was metal, or seamless silvery skin. The eyes were like wells, but as the thing turned its head, they seemed as flat as glass.

"You sent for me," the thing said in a voice like a bell.

"Indeed. The target has been located and her identity confirmed. You are to kill those who guard her, and bring her to me."

"My mistress wants assurance of payment."

"I have sent a guarantee to your war-madam. It contains codes, secrets that will become activated upon completion, as soon as I hear from you. I will speak with your mistress directly, in due course."

"My mistress has asked for further clarification."

"She cannot have it," Yskatarina said sharply. There was a short, tense pause. She went on, "No, you must bring the target here. Kill everyone else and secure the weir-wards at the mansion so that no one else can get in. There is something I wish to look for."

"I understand."

"Then I shall leave you to do your work."

The assassin performed a polite bow in acknowledgment of this courtesy, then spun, looking down at its long hands. A split opened up the length of each palm, to reveal a double row of splinter teeth. Yskatarina watched with curiosity. Carefully, the assassin adjusted the contents of its jaw: blow-fumes and needleswitches.

"I am ready."

"Good," Yskatarina said. The ship rose up from the veranda, enfolding the assassin, and began the long glide out to sea.

CHAPTER 2

EARTH

The house seemed quiet today, Dreams-of-War thought as she made her way to Lunae's chamber. Even the humming of the growing-room, which usually she could detect against the background murmur of equipment and the oreagraph sensors, was muted. She wondered uneasily whether the enhancements on the armor were malfunctioning, whether the black light matrix had affected it.

Outside the chamber Dreams-of-War paused for a moment. She could hear nothing within; perhaps Lunae was asleep. She knocked lightly on the door. There was no reply. Frowning, Dreams-of-War touched her palm to the lock release. The door glided open. Dreams-of-War stepped through. Lunae's bed was shrouded behind the draperies and the blinds were drawn down over the windows, casting the chamber into an underwater gloom. There was no sign of Lunae.

Somewhere beyond the window, someone was singing: a thin, sweet song that captivated Dreams-of-War. She stood mesmerized, her head on one side as the intricate notes fell around her, filling the room. She gave no more thought to Lunae. The song held her, trapping her in a web of sound, running filaments along the neural skeins of the armor until Dreams-of-War could not have moved even if she had wanted to. She felt no dismay at this, only fascination as she followed the song. She did not even react when a figure stepped out from the shadows beside the bed: something tall, with a silvery face and hollow eyes, dressed in black. Its mouth was pursed, as if whistling. It carried a sword like a web of lights, a thin katana curve that glittered through the air as it brought the sword down upon Dreams-of-War's unresisting head.

The world opened up. Dreams-of-War was falling through sudden space. She saw the sword whirling against a backdrop of stars, spinning toward a sun. A black form hurtled far below, face openmouthed with surprise. Dreams-of-War twisted to see a great dark world rising to meet her. She cried out and a hand curled around her wrist and pulled.

She was back in the chamber, sprawling on the floorboards and gasping with outrage and fear. She snatched her hand away from Lunae's grasp.

"It's all right," Lunae said above her, fierce as a hunting cat. "I took it away. You are safe."

Lunae's memories of the assassin and what she had done with it remained hazy and blurred. She recalled the gray plain and the slow-flowing river, a glimpse of stars and the way that the assassin's hand had twisted in her own, as though she clutched a beetle in its death throes. But the memories were incomplete, and faded as a dream fades once morning has begun.

After she had taken the assassin away and returned, the kappa had come, fussing and quivering, and insisted that Lunae go to bed.

"Will Dreams-of-War be punished?" Lunae asked hesitantly.

"I do not know."

"What was that person? Was it one of the Kami, do you think?"

"Hush," said the kappa, in a whisper like the sea. She helped Lunae into bed and folded the covers around her.

Lunae did not remember falling asleep, but suddenly, she was dreaming. She stood in a cavern of red stone. Smoke filled the air, causing the sunlight to become uncertain.

"Where am I?" Lunae asked into nothing, and a voice said, "Why, this is our home. Don't you know it?"

Lunae turned to see a woman shrouded in layers of indigo veils. She could not see the woman's face, and yet she was strangely familiar. The woman came to stand by her, and whispered secrets into her ear in an unknown language. Lunae knew they were secrets, for the woman smiled and put a finger to her veiled lips, looking around her with theatrical covertness. The woman's voice was like the wind, a sighing rustle in the reeds.

"Who are you?" Lunae asked.

"Don't you know?" the woman said again.

Lunae frowned, and the woman swept the veils aside. She was looking into her own face, perhaps twenty years older, the eyes hollow and filled with dreadful things.

"No," Lunae said, and stepped back.

"I've been here for such a long time," the woman-who-was-herself said. "But now you're here to take my place, and everything will be all right." Before Lunae could utter a word of protest, she began to fade, until there was nothing left except darkness and silence.

The next morning, Lunae awoke to find Dreams-of-War pacing the room. The Martian woman's armor bristled; her footsteps crackled on the floorboards as though some kind of electrical field had been activated. Dreams-of-War's face was as set as an angry marble statue.

Lunae sat up and swung her legs over the side of the bed. Dreams-of-War spun to face her.

"We will be leaving tomorrow. You have your wish." Dreams-of-War's mouth compressed and Lunae realized the reason for her apparent anger: Dreams-of-War did not like to fail. Lunae wondered whether her guardian resented the fact that her charge had succeeded in the removal of the assassin, where she herself had not, and a sudden, curious emotion flooded through her, a kind of elation. It was, however, swiftly followed by dismay. She realized that Dreams-of-War would not take kindly to efforts to reassure her.

"Where are we going?" she asked. Best to focus on the practicalities; Dreams-of-War was generally good at those.

"A safer place than here. The Grandmothers have deemed it best that you are not informed."

Dreams-of-War's eyes had narrowed into that *don't ask questions* look that Lunae knew so well, but this time she thought of the assassin's face as she spirited it out of the room, out of the world and beyond. She rose to her feet, looked her guardian full in the face, and said, "Tell me."

Dreams-of-War's gaze did not falter or fall. It was like staring down a well. But after a moment she said calmly, "Very well. We go to the Fire Islands, to the place where the kappa comes from."

"For how long? And how will we get there?" Lunae asked, excitement causing the words to spill out one over the other like beans from a jar.

"How long depends. I have ordered a litter to fetch us at noon tomorrow and convey us to the harbor. It is the earliest that could be arranged."

"What am I to take with me?" Lunae asked. The prospect of leaving Cloud Terrace was unsettling, but swiftly overcome by excitement. She longed for tomorrow to come. Otherwise, she felt, the Grandmothers might change their minds, or Dreams-of-War might decide that she would be safer here. At once, there seemed a thousand possible obstacles to the actuality of leaving.

"I have asked the kappa to prepare suitable traveling attire." Dreams-of-War looked Lunae over with an appraising eye. "A pity we are not on Mars. Then you could fight for armor."

"Did you fight for yours?" Lunae asked, wide-eyed. Dreams-of-War gave a small, grim nod of satisfaction.

"Of course."

"How many women did you have to fight?"

"Five, in the final rounds. Twelve, before that."

"What happened to them? Did you kill them?"

"No, it is rarely a fight to the death. Four returned to the clan house, to undertake lesser work. One ran off into the heights, and was never heard from again. Perhaps she fell prey to bandits, or men-remnants. I do not know." *Nor greatly care*, Dreams-of-War's expression said.

"I do not know how to fight," Lunae murmured, but suddenly it seemed a fine thing to learn.

Dreams-of-War said, with grudging approval, "It seems you have your own methods of dispatch. However, if you wish to learn more conventional means, I will teach you. But for now, you will have to wait."

CHAPTER 3

EARTH

Yskatarina paced the long veranda of the house, looking out across the estuary. The Animus crouched in a dark corner, half-concealed in a tumbling mass of jasmine.

"It has not yet returned," she said into the empty air. "It is very late."

"Perhaps something has delayed it," the Animus murmured.

"Perhaps. But it should have been back by now, bringing the *hito-bashira* with it. I'll contact its war-madam." Yskatarina slapped the rail, splintering the wood. "Still nothing from the Mission, either. Let me look at the antiscribe." She began to unscroll the little device.

Traces of ancient woes showed in the foliage that surrounded the ruin; the flowers of the jasmine emitted a faint, unpleasant glow once the sun had gone down. Everything seemed sticky, as though the air itself exuded a resin. Yskatarina's clothes and hair were matted with it, and it crept into the joints of her artificial limbs. As she had lain awake that night, staring into the perfumed darkness, she wondered whether it was not a product of an obsolete chemical weaponry, after all, but simply curdled hate, seeping from the walls of the mansion and fastening upon herself, Elaki's almost-child. From what she knew of the relationship between Elaki and her long-lost sisters, it seemed all too plausible an explanation. The newly formed hollow within her head had never seemed so comforting.

The ruin was very different from Tower Cold, from Memnos, and yet it still seemed to have some of the same atmosphere, a miasma of wrath and disappointment. Yskatarina and the Animus were camping out in the shattered, fire-blackened courtyard, sleeping amid weeds in the hazy sunlight of the day, waking once the comforting night had fallen, to plot and plan.

"What are you going to do if the assassin does not return?" the Animus asked from his place beneath the jasmine. She could smell him beneath the strong, sickly scent of the flowers: the odor of fungal musk, the odor of Nightshade. "Will you hire another?"

"I will take steps. I have spoken to my aunt. Elaki is not pleased. She demands results." Yskatarina shrugged. "She is old, querulous. I have honeyed her with promises, which she chooses to believe." Yskatarina stretched, balancing on sleek plastic. There was such delight in being able to criticize.

In the scrub at the edges of the veranda, something moved. Yskatarina looked sharply up from the antiscribe. "What was that?"

The Animus uncoiled himself, centipede swift, and flowed over the side of the veranda. There was a brief thrashing in the bushes. The Animus emerged, bloody.

"Now there is nothing there."

Yskatarina went to the railing of the veranda and peered over. Something large lay on its side, twitching. She saw the dull gleam of too-large eyes, a gaping hole where the mouth should have been. Yskatarina frowned.

"Was that human?"

"Once," the Animus said thickly.

The night air seemed suddenly bitter, the salt harsh against Yskatarina's skin. The taste of Tower Cold was metallic inside her mouth. For a moment, it was as though the hollow in her head had become filled. It felt like an invasion. She shivered once, and turned back to the antiscribe.

An hour later, she sat back in disappointment, staring down at the antiscribe. "The assassin has disappeared. I've been searching for it for an hour now. There is no sign."

"How so?" the Animus asked, puzzled. "Has someone removed its tracking device?"

"The tracker is hardwired into its nervous system. You could not remove it without removing the whole of its neural network. I suppose that's one possibility."

"What are others?"

Yskatarina spread her hands. "That it is no longer on Earth. But that isn't possible. The trace just winked out, from one moment to the next. Even if you put the thing in one end of the Chain and shot it out of a maw, there would still be a gradual decrease as it entered shadow-space and then the Eldritch Realm. Where has it gone?"

The Animus, wisely, was silent. Yskatarina rose and walked to the end of the veranda, but this time she did not stop. Treading carefully, she walked down the rickety steps, half-eroded with mold, and down the cliff path to the shore of the Yellow River estuary. Neon vegetation glowed, sickly with colors that shifted in the moonlight. She should have felt more comfort in the darkness, she thought, but this was nothing like Nightshade, nothing like Tower Cold. She could feel the weight of Earth pressing in against her, all the guilt and pain of that ancient cradle.

I do not belong here. I was born on the system's edge.

But her ancestors had come from this world; they haunted her down the DNA line. Their whispering had grown louder ever since the ship had docked at the Kita Hub. She did not know how long she would be able to bear it. Suddenly she longed for Tower Cold, for the familiar sights of the mourn-women preparing the canopics, for the shadows beyond the tower's portals.

But she did not long for the Elder Elaki. There were still things for which to be grateful.

Behind her, she heard the rustle and hiss of wings. The Animus spiraled lazily down the side of the cliff with dactylate ease, waiting with his customary courtesy for her to set foot upon the estuary shore before alighting.

The shore was a mess of black sand and brackish creeks, sliding down the face of the bluffs, to seep into the sea. It smelled of death. Ancient things occasionally washed up to lie putrefying upon the sand until rotting down into skeins of cartilage and pools of flesh. Even the carrion birds left them alone, as if they were cursed. There was one here now, perhaps twenty feet in diameter. Impossible to tell what it had been. There were the suckered ropes of squid, the long tendrils of man-o'-war, a long, feathery neck ending in a spatulate head. A great dark eye stared hopelessly upward.

Ignoring the smell, Yskatarina poked the thing with her toe.
It wobbled for a moment, then was still. She thought of all
unnatural things, of the Animus, and herself. It would all come to
this one day: the flesh melting down into noxiousness.

Restless and alarmed, she marched back to the ruin to see if
there had been any word from the assassin or from the Mission.
To her annoyance, there was not.

But there was a message.

The settlement was perched high on the edges of a cliff. At
some point, the sea had sheared it away, so that where there had
once been houses and a temple, there was now only a jumble of
ochre rock marked by a few ragged posts, and a wooden platform
that had once formed the temple's main entrance.

Yskatarina stood in the cold wind from the sea, wrapped in
black fur. She had chosen to wear gloves for this appointment,
not wanting her hands to be noted too closely. Her face was half-
hidden by a hood and the eye-visor.

Behind her, at the entrance to where the temple had once
been, stood a demon with a curved and upraised sword. Its
lips were stained with blood, which Yskatarina knew to be real.
The Animus had whispered this to her in the moments before
Yskatarina had sent him away to circle in the cloudy upper air
above the island.

Now, she waited for her appointment to come, patience swiftly
running out. The being, a kappa, was already late, yet it had been
the one to approach her, had left that disquieting message on the
little antiscribe. First the disappearance of the assassin, then
the Mission's silence, and now this . . . She had again arranged
for more creatures to be sent, but she did not hold out hope. The
denizens of Cloud Terrace would be on their guard.

She had told them to strike at the Martian first. With Dreams-
of-War out of the way, the Grandmothers could be more easily
dealt with. And Lunae herself was just a girl, despite her powers.

Yskatarina had formed her own opinions of the people
known as the kappa, involving timidity, inferiority, lack of real
will. She knew little enough about them. They were the dregs of
Earth, the remnants of ancient error. Yet how had they known

where to find her? How had they obtained her coordinates? It did not accord with the image of an underclass.

Impatient, she roamed about the platform, then turned to see that the kappa was finally here, waddling and wheezing across the platform toward her. Yskatarina felt a rising distaste. Old error, yes, but so were the gaezelles of the Martian plain . . . She could not help but make comparisons.

"Sorry, sorry," the kappa panted. "There was delay, the storms . . ."

"This doesn't concern me," Yskatarina said.

"Of course, I understand . . ."

"My time is limited. I need information." Yskatarina looked down into a bland yellow gaze. "In your message you spoke of a ship, sent from Mars to Earth, one hundred years ago. A ship that Nightshade believes may contain the details of a secret project, to breed a creature called a *hito-bashira*. And how did you find me?"

"As to finding you, the place where you are staying is known to us from the old days. We keep a watch. And we do know of an ancient ship," the kappa said, "but not of its exact location."

Briefly, Yskatarina closed her eyes. "Then do you know who *does* have this information?"

"Come with me," the kappa said. She turned and began waddling toward the entrance to the former temple. With a glance up at the Animus, Yskatarina followed.

The kappa disgusted Yskatarina: the stout, sweating form, the anxious manner, the stringy hair. She thought again of the long legs of the gaezelles, her own artificial limbs, the Animus's sleek winged shape. *These lesser people should not exist. Nothing ugly should exist.* But for the moment, the kappa was useful, and could be used. Let her believe that Yskatarina would give her something in exchange.

"See?" the kappa said, pointing.

Yskatarina looked in the direction indicated by the kappa's thick finger. But at that moment, there was a shriek from the heavens and the Animus dropped like a stone. Yskatarina wheeled around, just in time to avoid the swing of the demon's sword. It was wielded by a second kappa, thinner and swifter, with the green light of fury in her eyes. Yskatarina blocked and the sword skittered from her arm, striking sparks. Behind her, there was a wailing cry as the Animus fell upon her informant in a tangle of black spines.

The kappa wielding the sword rushed forward. Yskatarina struck up and out, grasped the kappa's slimy wrist, twisted, and sent the sword flying across the platform. She killed the kappa with a strike to the throat. The Animus had already seen to the first.

"Throw them into the sea," Yskatarina instructed, drawing a long, calm breath. "And then let us be gone."

CHAPTER 4

EARTH

The missive came to Dreams-of-War in a most old-fashioned way: borne within the body of a semiartificial cricket. The creatures had, she knew, been formed for gambling purposes. They were durable, ingenious, put up many good and long-lasting fights, and the war-madams of the city fringes had once prized them as a Martian might prize her armor. But fashions changed and moved onward, to more impressive forms of battle. So when, shortly after her conversation with Lunae, the cricket soared in through the window, Dreams-of-War initially thought that it was a living insect. She swatted at it with a casual hand, but the armor's servos powered in and caught it gently within her mailed fist.

Dreams-of-War looked down. The cricket lay whirring in her hand, legs twitching. Coils of brass spun outward, flickering with small fire. The cricket leaped, to land with a clatter on the metal edge of the bed. Letters formed across Dreams-of-War's palm, glowed with neon brightness before fading to a faint stain on the skin of the armor.

We must talk. Meet me in the teahouse next to the fortress-temple of Gwei Hei. Four o'clock.

There was no signature, and no indication from whom the message had come. Dreams-of-War frowned, scenting traps. She looked for the cricket, which was now sitting on the windowsill. Before she could make a move, it was gone, sailing out into the waning sunlight.

She spent the next hour or so in some indecision. At last, however, the need for action overwhelmed her. First, she went to see Lunae. The girl was sleeping, so Dreams-of-War did not disturb her. Instead, she made sure that the room was warded. She was unable to find the kappa and, reining in her annoyance, she headed out into the fading day.

Night came early at these latitudes, and the sky above Fragrant Harbor was already diminishing to the color of an old rose. Across the water, the lights of the tenements were beginning to burn. The great torch that stood at the entrance to the fortress-temple of Gwei Hei sent a column of smoke up against the evening sky.

Dreams-of-War headed swiftly down through the narrow streets, dodging the litters and steamcarts that filled the alleys. People eyed her askance as she passed, but Dreams-of-War ignored them. To the sides of the streets, braziers spilled hot coal-smoke and the fragrance of crisping seaweed into the evening air. At the bottom of the steps that led from the Peak she ran into a column of festival goers, firecrackers snapping around their feet. They wore masks of moths, with long, trembling antennae. They spun around her, never quite touching, moving with somber purpose, as though her presence among them was a choreographed part of their dance. Small cymbals clattered arrhythmically in their hands. There seemed to be no pattern to the sounds that they made and it affronted Dreams-of-War's sense of order. She stood stiff and still, waiting as they flowed around her. She could see the glint of their eyes through the feathery masks. Their gaze was dull and inward-looking. Some narcotic, no doubt. A variety of substances were rife among the little splinterings of the city's many cults. She would have felt more comfortable if those eyes had contained a threat.

Dreams-of-War squinted upward as the last moth-masked woman passed her by, longing for emptiness. Earth, she had long since decided, had too many people in too small a space, and most of them seemed to be crammed into the eroding confines of Fragrant Harbor. At last she was out onto the dock.

The ferry, an ancient black hulk, rode low in the water. The steerswoman was already pulling away. Dreams-of-War leaped the few feet from the dock, landing with a clatter on the gangway. Passengers moved hastily aside. Dreams-of-War thrust a handful of coins at the steerswoman and strode up the steps onto the upper deck, seeking fresher air. When she grasped the railing for balance, the palm of her armor came away encrusted with salt and rust. She stood back, reluctant to entrust her weight to the rail. The sea heaved below, heavy with oil and a film of garbage, mainly fish debris. There was a strong smell of rotting vegetables and weed.

From here, she watched the island fall behind as the ferry made the short crossing to High Kowloon. The tenements were a mass of shadows and light against the ruby sky. The mansion district was clearly visible at the summit of the Peak, as distinct in its own way and place as the Memnos Tower. Dreams-of-War frowned, thinking of the Grandmothers, of Lunae. She did not like leaving the girl, even for this short span. Her thoughts returned with obsessive regularity to that conversation with the Grandmothers, who had told her so little, less even than Memnos. And also to the conversation with the shade of Embar Khair.

She turned her back on the island and Cloud Terrace and stared grimly ahead as the ferry wallowed toward High Kowloon.

It took Dreams-of-War some time to find the teahouse amid the maze of passages that led up from the High Kowloon side of the harbor. By the time the ferry docked, the sky had hazed to twilight, and the High Kowloon side was not as well lit as the slopes around the Peak. Dreams-of-War clambered up steps and around the poles of awnings, cursing beneath her breath. The quickest route to the temple was through the labyrinth of the jade market. She strode past skeins of water-colored necklaces, small gods the shade of frogs and leaves, carved lotus and palm. The jade sellers, dressed in the traditional black with the mark of the trade stenciled upon each cheek, were careful not to look at her directly as she went by, but she felt their eyes on her as she passed.

Then she was again out into the musty twilight and at last came alongside the temple wall: a mass of polished, ancient brick. She could smell incense, something sharp and pungent, overpowering the odor of the garbage that was piled up against the walls.

The teahouse stood at the end of the adjoining street: a tottering structure squeezed onto the end of a tenement. Trailing plants, spidery in the half-light, sprawled from the balconies of the upper storys. Dim radiance spilled out onto the street. Dreams-of-War paused, uncertain, then strode up the steps.

The teahouse was empty. Taking care to keep her back to the wall, Dreams-of-War moved cautiously into the room: a jumble of chairs and tables. An enormous steaming urn was set on a brazier at the far end. Stairs led to an upper room; she could hear the murmur of voices. Dreams-of-War went upward.

Before she reached the upper room, however, someone stepped out onto the small halfway landing. Reflexively, Dreams-of-War activated the hand weapons of her armor, but even as her arm flashed up she saw that the figure was that of a kappa.

"Don't strike," the kappa said quickly. "It's me."

"Nurse?" Dreams-of-War frowned. She could not tell one of the creatures from another, and bundled up as they all were, it was almost impossible to tell them apart by dress. "What are you doing here? I thought you were back at Cloud Terrace."

"Come," the kappa said. She ushered Dreams-of-War through a curtain into a small adjoining niche. There was the reek of tea and old opium: a coarse, burnt smell. "We cannot talk at Cloud Terrace. Too many eyes. Too many spies. The tentacles of the oreagraph spread everywhere."

"It was you who sent the cricket?"

"It was I."

"What's going on?"

"I need to talk to you about the Grandmothers," the kappa said. "I need to hear your thoughts, warrior."

The kappa's eyes gleamed in the dimness. She spoke with decision, with no trace of the dithering fussiness that Dreams-of-War had always associated with the nurse.

"What do you know of them, Dreams-of-War?" Somehow it was a shock to hear the kappa speak her actual name. Normally, the nurse made do with a sort of deferential mumble.

"I know very little," Dreams-of-War said, taken aback. She did not want to reveal to the kappa how much knowledge she possessed. "The Grandmothers are rumored to be ancient."

"And so they are."

"How do you know this?" Dreams-of-War almost added, *You are only a kappa,* but for once thought better of it. The kappa echoed her, however.

"Because I am only a lesser creature?" The wide, lipless mouth widened into something that could have been a smile. "You are learning tact . . . I made it my business to find out, because I care about Lunae."

"But where did you find out *from?*"

"From my people. No one pays any attention to us. But we are everywhere. In the factories and wharves and warehouses, in the spacedocks and the shipping runs. In the homes of the rich and powerful, tending their young as they emerge from the growing-chambers. Menial. Invisible." The kappa gave a shrug. "Everywhere."

Slowly Dreams-of-War nodded. "I see."

"What if I were to tell you that the Grandmothers originally came from Nightshade?"

Dreams-of-War tried to dissemble. "Why are you telling this to *me?* You know I am a warrior of the Matriarchy and in the Grandmothers' hire. How do you know I won't report straight back?"

"Because you love the girl. I know about your maternal modifications. You don't like it, do you? But you won't betray her." The green gaze sharpened. "Will you?"

"No," Dreams-of-War said after a pause. "I will not."

"And you do not seem surprised to learn of the Grandmothers' origins."

"I have reason to believe," Dreams-of-War said carefully, "that there have been links between Nightshade and Memnos for some considerable time." There. That was sufficiently opaque.

The kappa's gaze sharpened.

"Of course there have. Nightshade gave haunt-tech to the Matriarchy. Everyone knows that."

Oh, forget intrigue. It's too complicated. Dreams-of-War related her conversation with the armor to the kappa.

"How interesting. The kappa know about the ship, but I didn't know the details."

"The Grandmothers would seem to have fallen out with Nightshade," Dreams-of-War said, "over the issue of the Kami. And the Kami appear interested in Lunae."

"I think it was almost certainly the Kami who sent the assassin. Lunae meets a possessed woman in the street; a short time later, a death-dealer slips past the weir-wards."

"And what do you know about the Kami?"

"All that we really know," the kappa said, "is that they come from Nightshade. I think it's time we investigated them."

"That means the Mission. There's no way in. People have tried."

"There is a way," the kappa said. "My people know of it. It runs under the pier that houses the meat market. It's a runoff from an old culvert that takes the blood down into the rendering tanks."

"It will have to be done today, then. We leave tomorrow, as you know."

"I suggest this evening, when the market closes," the kappa said, with narrowed eyes.

"And you want me to be the one to run the risk," Dreams-of-War said.

"You are a warrior," the kappa replied blandly.

"Indeed." Dreams-of-War and the nurse stared at each other for a moment.

"I do not want to be too long away from the house," the kappa said finally. "And neither should you."

The nurse left through a small door at the back of the empty downstairs room. Dreams-of-War walked back out onto the street. Crowds of people drifted past. She saw kappa, human, other modified beings. For the first time she was moved to wonder about the Changed: what secrets they might hold, what desires they might cherish. Somehow she had never thought of such beings as truly real. The kappa herself had been nothing more than a mumbling nursemaid, a convenient servant with little more intelligence than a plainshound. Now, this was revealed not to be the case. Dreams-of-War did not like feeling foolish, or wrong.

She strode angrily down the crowded streets in the direction of the harbor. She had not gone very far down one of the streets of steps when a familiar throng stepped from the shadows. Their faces were concealed behind the masks of moths. Their eyes were dead. They carried blades. And they rushed toward her in a silent mass.

Dreams-of-War kicked up and out, scything aside a blade. Its bearer hissed and whistled—weird, inhuman sounds that were immediately familiar. The assassin had sounded like this. Two others rushed forward, moving in a quick, strange crouch. Sonar pinged from the surface of walls and armor, or so the remote voice of Embar Khair informed her. Her assailants were communicating.

Dreams-of-War struck down with a hand-prong between the trembling proboscis of the moth-mask. The dull eyes did not change as the thing crumpled. Seizing the blade, she wheeled around and cut through two others. They fell messily in half without a sound. Dreams-of-War glanced at the bloody blade with approval. She liked sharp things. And the creatures were revealed as organic; blood and slime and a thick, sticky ichor that coated the blade like lace. But a closer glimpse revealed the glint of metal deep within—not so organic as all that, then.

Now there was only one moth-mask, dancing forward, sting-gun raised. It fired. Dreams-of-War threw herself to the ground, rolling over and lashing out at the assassin's shins. Again, the blade sliced through flesh as though it were bean curd. Truncated, the assassin fell. A sting shot upward and fell short. The assassin lay twitching. Dreams-of-War snatched off the mask. A rudimentary face was revealed: a slit of a mouth, the round dim eyes. As she watched, the face shriveled and desiccated, like a leaf in a flame. Beneath, there was only smooth silver.

"Who are you?" Dreams-of-War demanded. "What are you? Answer me!"

But the assassin was silent. A tiny hole appeared at the base of this new mask, pursed in and out, before puckering once and sinking into smoothness. The assassin lay bleeding at her feet, the blank silver countenance becoming dull and rubbery. Soon, it held no more vitality than an unstrung puppet.

Dreams-of-War, after a short internal debate, looked about her. No one could be seen. She hoisted what remained of the assassin across her shoulder and set off in search of a rickshaw.

CHAPTER 5

EARTH

I do not know what it is," the kappa said, as they stood staring down at the remnants of the assassin's corpse.

"You've never seen anything like it before?" Dreams-of-War asked. They had peeled back the silver countenance, first with care, and then with impatience as the surface proved hard to remove. The thing was like an onion, its face constructed from layers. Eventually, however, they had come to its true physique: a demihuman visage with no nose or hair and a lamprey's mouth. Needle teeth ringed a round hole; within was a series of segmented grinding edges.

"Not as such. It's a death-dealer of some kind. I'm not sure exactly what. There are many variations: the war-madams breed them. It has some kind of reptilian heritage," the kappa said. "See? It has vestigial scales."

"But who sent it? The Kami?"

The kappa sighed. "Most likely. Your guess is as good as mine."

"We had best put it in the freezer until we can work out what to do with it, or find out where it's come from, or both."

"That doesn't leave much time."

"Best we find out as much as we can, then, as quickly as possible. This supposed entrance to the Mission. Do you have details? Plans or maps?"

"There is a map."

"I'll go now." Dreams-of-War paused. "Watch Lunae closely while I am gone. She is growing increasingly restless. I don't want anything to go amiss before we leave."

"You cannot blame her," the kappa pleaded.

"Who said anything about blame?"

With the kappa's directions safely downloaded into her armor, Dreams-of-War made her way through a maze of streets, avoiding as much as she could of the litter that strewed the rough concrete. The steps that led down toward the harbor were slimy with weed and moldering vegetables, but the way was at least clear. Between the teetering tenements, the garbage covered the first three storys. Dreams-of-War wondered whether anyone lived in those lower tenements, and concluded that they almost certainly did. Temporary shacks had been constructed on the current level of the garbage; wan faces peered forth. The makeshift roofs, sheets of corrugated plastic salvaged from the flooded ruins at the city's edge, were already coated with litter thrown from the summits of the tower blocks.

Dreams-of-War grimaced and carried on, shouldering her way through muttering passersby. The armor prickled, sensing their dislike, but Dreams-of-War remained indifferent. The assassins' sonar had proved impossible to decrypt, but the armor had nonetheless retained an imprint of it. If there were any more of the things, Dreams-of-War would be alerted. She could not help but feel a grim satisfaction. It was almost reminiscent of her days on Mars.

The eastern entrance to the meat market lay at the end of the steps: columns of soot-blackened stone marked with ancient symbols so eroded by acidic rain that they were barely visible. One of the iron gates was already drawn across the entrance, signifying that the market was about to close. Dreams-of-War slipped quickly through the gate and entered the main hall.

The floor was slick with black blood, dripping from the carcasses that hung on hooked racks from the ceiling. Dreams-of-War looked up to see cylinders of meat: headless torsos hung on metal bolts. Each torso ended in a smooth stump. These were tank-grown things, only alive in the barest sense of the word, grown in the vats that covered the roof of the meat market and extruded forth to be bled and butchered. Dreams-of-War wondered vaguely what kind of animal these things had once come from, what combination of genes had gone into the mix to make these huge sausages of flesh. The meat was not uniform: Some of the cylinders were dark and mottled, marbled with pale veins of fat, while others were composed of a translucent white meat, veined like the rings of a tree. A thin stream of blood was channeled into a raised culvert, leading to a sequence of vats.

The lamprey-mouthed assassins had almost certainly been vat-grown. The more she thought about them, the more convinced she became that they were someone's private army. But whose? The kappa was busy making inquiries and Dreams-of-War was startled to realize that she actually trusted the nurse to come up with something. But it took power to raise creatures of that level of sophistication, a degree of power that was equivalent to a Martian's.

Memnos's excissiere squads were claimed to be ruthless in cutting back those who sought to challenge Martian authority. But Dreams-of-War distrusted the say-so of her mistresses. Who knew what lay in the northern lands, beyond Kamchatka and the Fire Islands? The excissieres rarely seemed to venture beyond the lands of the Yellow River, beyond the Thibetan city states, beyond the Rift or the Altai queendoms or Andea: the settled mountain lands of the middle planet. At present, the only capacity to find answers lay with the kappa.

She was not disturbed by the meat market. The sight of the meat did nothing for her appetite. This was not freshly hunted and slain, and as such had little appeal for her. But the smell of the blood was invigorating. Dreams-of-War stepped carefully around the pools that had accumulated on the stone floor and walked to the edge of the chamber. She could hear voices coming from behind the row of vats. Stepping closer, she listened. Idle talk, nothing more, regarding technical matters for which Dreams-of-War had no concern. She moved on, seeking discrepancies in the walls, the armor measuring echo distances to search for gaps and spaces behind the stained brick. If the entrance to the Mission lay anywhere around here, Dreams-of-War intended to find it.

The depths of the market were cavernous. Behind the racks of hanging meat lay the way to the growing-chambers. Spiral stairways led upward. Dreams-of-War craned her neck, seeing the faint shapes of the tanks through the plastic ceiling. There was little of interest up there. She moved around the walls, concentrating on the information filtered back by the armor.

Then a woman stepped out of the wall. Dreams-of-War leaped back. There had been no warning of her presence. The woman was small, dark-haired, slant-eyed. There was a vapid vacancy to her face. She stood before Dreams-of-War, evincing no surprise, saying nothing.

"I was lost," Dreams-of-War said abruptly. "I was searching for the payment section. Perhaps you can advise me?" Dissembling did not come naturally to her, but it sounded a reasonably convincing excuse. The woman remained silent, only stared.

"Did you hear me?" Dreams-of-War said. The woman's head tilted slowly back. She opened her mouth and emitted a high-pitched hiss. Then her form blurred and shifted, as though she were nothing more than a badly tuned image.

"You are lost?" a voice said from behind her. Dreams-of-War spun around to see a small group of women clad in blood-soaked overalls. One of them held a meat cleaver. "Perhaps we can advise you. The main gate is in this direction."

"What is wrong with your coworker?" Dreams-of-War asked as the woman slunk away.

"Wrong?"

"There is something the matter with her eyes. She hissed at me. She is possessed, is she not?"

The women murmured among themselves. One said, "She is not the first. There have been others thus afflicted—most often those who are lacking in their wits. They walk the streets endlessly, seeking something. Often they claw and bite at others. Sometimes they talk in a language that no one can identify, like mad people. But it is just one of many woes that afflict us. There are a hundred diseases at any given time." She spoke with indifferent despair. "And many other afflictions are worse."

Dreams-of-War frowned. "Is there no medical provision?"

"Against so much sickness?" Now the woman's face was no longer placid. "You do not know how we live, Martian witch. You do not know what we suffer. You've seen the city. What wonder that plagues infest it?"

"Then do something about it," Dreams-of-War said. "You do not have to live in squalor."

"What would you have us do? Spend time and energy throwing the refuse of a thousand years into the sea? The waves are eating in upon Fragrant Harbor. Already land has been lost this year. The seas rise higher and nothing can be done. We cannot keep raising the city forever. The edges of the islands are salt marsh and soon they will be gone. There is no more land on Earth. Our daughters will have to take to the boats or die."

"It is the way of things," Dreams-of-War said uneasily.

"But once there was the means to control it. The Dragon-Kings. The great beings who rose out of the seas when the world began to sink, who worked in harness with humankind to keep the waters back."

Dreams-of-War smiled, remembering the tapestries that hung on the walls of Cloud Terrace, depicting ancient gods. "The Dragon-Kings are a myth, nothing more."

"No, that is not so," another of the women said, very earnest. "They have been seen by sailors, out upon the deep. They are still here. If their worship was restored—"

"You should not put your faith in fairy tales," Dreams-of-War told her, as kindly as she could.

"It is no tale." The woman glared at her.

Dreams-of-War sighed. "Show me back to the entrance, then. Perhaps it is best if I leave you to your work."

She allowed the women to conduct her back to the beginning of the meat market, and there she waited, fidgeting with impatience behind a pitted pillar. The sky darkened to rose. Shortly after twilight had fallen, the women emerged from the meat market, still clad in their bloodstained wraps and robes. They moved with quick, shuffling steps, murmuring to one another in hushed voices, looking neither right nor left. Informing the armor to remain vigilant, Dreams-of-War crept back to the iron gates and picked the lock.

The market was dark and silent, reeking of the day's bleeding. Mindful of the Kami she had seen, Dreams-of-War walked warily, directed by the kappa's map, until she reached the place where the culvert ran into the wall. It was only just large enough to accommodate her, with the armor thinned until it was no more than a sleek film of skin.

The culvert stank, not only of blood, which would have been quite acceptable, but of other substances that she was unable to identify. What exactly was the blood rendered into? Food products of some description, no doubt, at the cheaper end of the comestible chain. She followed the stained passage to the point indicated by the kappa's map. There was no sign of any opening.

"Armor? Where do I go from here?"

"There is a variance in the texture of the floor," the armor said after a pause. Dreams-of-War knelt and placed a hand in the trickle of blood that still seeped through the culvert from the day's catch. She could feel a bolted panel, some two feet in diameter. Dreams-of-War began to prize it apart.

The bolts were rusted tight. Cursing, Dreams-of-War used all the implementation of which the armor was capable, and after much wrestling, wrenched the panel free. Blood dripped stickily into the resulting hole. Cautiously, Dreams-of-War lowered herself into it. There was a short drop and she almost slipped on the bloody patch beneath. At least there was now only a single option open to her. A narrow passage led onward, canted sharply down.

Clearly, no one had been along here for many years. She wondered what the passage had originally been: perhaps a drainage system of some sort. It was dank and smelled of the sea. Pools and puddles formed on the floor, and occasionally she was forced to clamber over drifts of refuse that seemed to have washed in from elsewhere. The walls were slick with patches of weed.

Dreams-of-War was starting to consider that the passage might end in the ocean that lapped at the evereroding shores of Fragrant Harbor, when she came to an abrupt halt. Something was blocking the way. Bemused, Dreams-of-War put out a hand and touched a smooth surface, like warm glass. The lights of the armor reflected nothing, but the barrier was quite impenetrable. This must be the wall of the Mission, running down far into the earth. Dreams-of-War tried to cut through, but the hand-tools of the armor merely glanced off without making a scratch. Frustrated, Dreams-of-War pressed her face to the barrier and peered inside.

She could see something within: columns of a pale, insubstantial substance that writhed like smoke. And there were faces inside it, forming and fading like the metal visage of Embar Khair. Dreams-of-War counted nine of them. The faces were all a little alike, with puffy cheeks and lank black hair. But now they had seen her. They began to cluster to face the barrier.

"Help us!" she heard them cry. "Set us free! They have imprisoned us, moved on. Set us free . . ." The voices bore the unmistakable quality of powerful haunt-tech; the hair rose at the back of Dreams-of-War's neck. Before she realized what she was doing, she was backing away, then turning to run down the passage, toward the meat market and the night beyond.

THE FIRE ISLANDS

CHAPTER 1

EARTH

The next day, the hours before noon seemed interminable. Eventually, Lunae grew tired of kicking her heels on the bed and made her way to the uppermost part of the tower. She curled up once more on the windowsill and stared out across the harbor. There was a fine mist this morning, blurring the contours of the city Ships drifted through the fog like spirits, their lights soft as flowers, but a shaft of sunlight bathed the Peak. Farther along the sill lay the silk-moth chrysalis, where Lunae had left it. She watched it, hoping that it would split and release the moth into the morning air, but the chrysalis remained as tightly sealed as a lotus bud. It crossed her mind that she might once more accelerate time, win a few days for the silk-moth, but something held her back. Today was her time for flight, not the moth's. Still filled with fear that her leaving would, after all, be prevented, she jumped from the window seat and ran back down to her room. The kappa was waiting.

"The Grandmothers wish to see you before you go," the kappa said.

The nurse seemed agitated, her thick fingers fluttering about the folds of her clothing. Lunae followed her along the corridors. The Grandmothers were waiting, bright-eyed and spidery, amid the hangings of the bed. There were no last-moment revelations of pride or love. Right-Hand did most of the talking, echoed in a senile mumble by her companion.

"Dreams-of-War has told you where you are to go. Obey her; do not rely too heavily upon your own judgment. Remember that you have little experience and are still unformed. We will send

messages. Do not think we will forget about you." Right-Hand
beckoned. "Come closer."

With reluctance, Lunae did so. Left-Hand seized her wrist,
pulling her down onto the bed. Left-Hand smelled of old, musty
flesh; flesh that had lived too long, Lunae thought. She would
rather be close to the kappa, with her shore and seaweed odors,
than the Grandmothers.

"Remember what you are," the Grandmothers hissed. "Now
go. The litter is waiting for you." Right-Hand gave Lunae a push,
none too gently. Lunae left the Grandmothers' chamber and did
not look back.

Dreams-of-War was standing on the steps of Cloud Terrace,
impatiently tapping an armored foot.

"Have you seen the Grandmothers?" she asked.

"Yes."

"And? Did all go well?"

Dreams-of-War's face was as anxious as it could be, so Lunae
answered only, "Yes. We discussed the voyage. I am to obey you
in all things."

"You can tell me all about it in the litter. It's at the gate. But
first, there is something we must do."

Today Dreams-of-War's armor was covered with porcupine
spines; her head rose above a column of linked steel rings. *She is
afraid*, Lunae thought. *She bristles*.

"Come with me," Dreams-of-War said. She marched down to
the mansion's black light chamber, normally a place where Lunae
was forbidden to go.

"What are we doing here?" Lunae asked. Dreams-of-War
closed the door behind them.

"Armor!"

Lunae watched as the armor flowed from Dreams-of-War's
body, leaving her standing in her underharness, as hard and
marmoreal as Lunae had imagined her. The armor's shattered
head turned toward its mistress in inquiry and Lunae stared at the
half-faced form.

"Who is she?" Lunae breathed.

"She is Embar Khair, the warrior whose spirit inhabits this
armor." Dreams-of-War turned to the armored form. "This girl
who stands before you. Envelop her."

"Dreams-of-War—!" Lunae started to protest, but the armor was already flowing obligingly over her. It weighed her down and she gave a muffled cry at the unaccustomed pressure.

"Let her imprint you," Dreams-of-War commanded. "Her soul-engrams, her DNA. Read her well and file the information."

It lasted only a moment. Minutes later, Lunae stood ruffled on the floor of the black light chamber and the armor was once more moving to encase Dreams-of-War.

"What was that for?"

"I wanted the armor to have a record of you. If we are ever in a position of grave danger, then I have instructed the armor to respond to you as well as to me. It will also be able to detect you if you are lost. I should have done this before. I was remiss. And now, the litter is waiting."

At the gate, Lunae looked around at the tangled garden, then back at Cloud Terrace, which rose in its untidy jumble above her to blot out the sun. She wondered whether, in time, she might come to miss it. She was certain that she would not miss the Grandmothers. It had been wonderful to stand before them and believe that this might be the last time she would ever set eyes upon them. With this thought, Lunae turned and hurried to the litter.

The journey down through the streets of the Peak was as frustrating as ever. Lunae pleaded for the shutters to be drawn back just a fraction, so that she could see what was passing by, but Dreams-of-War refused. Beside her, the kappa nodded in eager agreement.

"Now more than ever, it is dangerous," the kappa said. "What if someone were to spot you? Besides, the shutters are shielded."

"What does that mean?"

"They're filled with deflection traceries, to baffle scanners," Dreams-of-War murmured.

"Do you think that the Kami might be trying to trace me?"

Dreams-of-War frowned. "It's not known what equipment the Kami use, so it's impossible to protect oneself against it." Lunae saw her mailed fist contract. "I would prefer it if I knew for certain that they could not tell where you were going. I suspect them of being behind the assassins."

"*Assassins?* But there was only one." She frowned at Dreams-of-War, but the Martian did not reply.

"But *why*? Why would they want me dead? Because of what I am?"

"I do not know."

Lunae pressed her face against the wall of the litter, trying to glean sounds from the world outside. Imagination and memories supplied the lack of vision. She saw remedy-women with baskets of dried snakes and engineered glands; the ancient shopfronts of circuit makers, hands genetically attenuated to perfect the finest details; Malay traders with racks of cheap stimulants. Even after the incident with the Kami, she longed to break from the litter and bolt into the maze of streets. It was so tempting to think that she might alter time, just for a handful of minutes, find a way to step outside and *see*.

But Dreams-of-War was right; it was a dangerous situation. And how must an ordinary child feel, confined by parental dictate for weeks, months, years, without Lunae's own accelerated pace of growth? She thought that it would drive her mad to be such a child, and perhaps this was what happened to most people; that by the time they were fully grown it was already too late, and they were driven crazed by their own lack of control.

That would explain the demeanor of the Grandmothers, she thought, but Dreams-of-War seemed different. Perpetually irate she might be, but not actually demented. But then, Dreams-of-War's girlhood seemed to have been relatively free. For a long moment, Lunae envied her, then sighed. No point in rewriting the past, certainly not now, when the future lay before her with all its intricate possibilities.

The litter lurched along, its bearers stumbling through the streets. Dreams-of-War knocked sharply on the wall.

"Where are we? Is this Heng Seng?"

A muffled reply came back. Dreams-of-War leaned back against her seat, apparently satisfied.

"It won't be long before we reach the harbor." She gave Lunae a sharp glance. "Do you feel anything, sense anything?"

"No. Only confinement," Lunae muttered. The litter had grown stuffy and hot, filled with the scent of old sweat and dried lacquer.

Dreams-of-War smiled thinly. "I dislike it, too. I shall be glad when we are out upon the high seas."

"There are seas on Mars, aren't there? Have you sailed on them?"

"The Small Sea is little in comparison with the oceans of Earth," Dreams-of-War remarked, giving Lunae the distinct impression that it was an unfortunate thing for a planet to be so wet. Perhaps she was right. Lunae had seen the ancient maps, when Earth possessed a wealth of land.

Dreams-of-War leaned forward, as if scenting the air. "The harbor. I can smell it."

The litter at last jolted to a halt. The shutters slid back, flooding them with sunlight. There was a strange electric sizzle, presumably as the localized weir-wards were switched off. Needing no encouragement, Lunae scrambled down to find herself standing on a dock. A hot salt wind washed around her, redolent with weed and the smell of dead shellfish. Lunae took a deep, uncritical breath. Warm stone baked up through the soles of her boots. Eagerly, she looked about her, seeing the harbor stretching before them. The great junks rocked under the wind, tethered like stormclouds, crimson sails furled. She could hear the creak and ache of wood bowing before the elements: wind, water, sun. She thought of the Grandmothers' chamber and the twists of driftwood. Had that come from ancient forests, long drowned, or from more recent wrecks? A swift image flickered across the face of her mind: an empty shore, the Grandmothers scuttling sideways along it like a pair of contorted crabs, snatching up a fragment of prow, a tatter of sail . . .

The kappa tugged at her hood. "Keep your face hidden!"

Lunae turned from her reverie to note that Dreams-of-War's armor had all but vanished, forming a slick sheen across her skin. The kappa melted away into the shadows.

"Where is she going?"

"To see if there's anyone about," the Martian said grimly.

The air was suddenly acrid, chemical-tinged, as a freighter sailed up the harbor. A slick of oily water washed up against the wall, leaving a faint gleam in its wake. Behind them, the tumbling towers of the Peak stretched all the way up to the toad-presence of Cloud Terrace. Lunae turned swiftly back to stare out across the harbor to High Kowloon. Dozens of smaller boats rode the waves, anchored in a labyrinthine network that extended halfway across the harbor. Between the boats, she could see columns of rotting stone encrusted with shellfish. The green-black spears of mussels gleamed in the watery light; the pale muscular neck of a clam waved briefly forth before retreating.

"What are those columns for?"

"Ruins. This part of the city was high above water once. This is the typhoon shelter," Dreams-of-War explained. "Our vessel waits beyond."

The kappa came bustling back. Dreams-of-War glanced questions at her, but the kappa pursed her lips and shook her head. Dreams-of-War led Lunae down a flight of rickety steps and across the deck of a narrow pontoon. A young girl was banging a mass of writhing tentacles against the harbor wall with rhythmic, precise ferocity. She threw down the pulped mass of octopus, reached into a bucket, drew forth a second, and swung it. There was the sound of soft meat hitting stone, a wet succession of thuds. Lunae swallowed and turned away.

Before her, women were frying fish in a wok, shredding green fronds of weed, talking in shrill, hissing voices. The bite of chili and hot fat caught at the back of Lunae's throat, smelling nothing like the bland and delicate foods of Cloud Terrace. She was suddenly ravenous.

"Can we get something to eat?"

"Not here. I'll find food on the boat."

Resentfully, Lunae followed her guardian across the deck. No one paid any attention to their passage; it seemed quite usual for strangers to be making their way through other folks' homes. She badly wanted to stop and look at the strings of charms that hung from the lintels of doorways and portals, at the icons of bronze and glossy wood that stood in every available niche, at the skeins of dried fish, as desiccated and gnarled as leather. But Dreams-of-War marched on like a one-woman army, looking neither right nor left, pausing only to help Lunae along the swaying, tottering ladders that led from boat to boat. Lunae shook off her guardian's assisting hands, irritated by the assumption that she was a child, needful of help. Dreams-of-War appeared not to notice.

"Where is our vessel?" Lunae whispered as they crossed the slippery plank between two black-hulled prows.

Dreams-of-War pointed. "There."

The junk lay a little distance from the maze of boats, riding gently on an unseen current. Its sides were weathered ebony and its ruby sails billowed in the wind. A dragon figurehead crested above the waves, eyes bulging, mouth flared wide to display gilded alligator teeth. The ropes that secured its sails snapped and cracked. To Lunae, it was the embodiment of freedom.

As they reached the last boat of all, a scull skirted the junk's black hull and veered toward them.

"For us, I hope," Dreams-of-War said, shifting restlessly from foot to foot. A woman sat in the prow, dressed from head to foot in ragged red clothes, rowing vigorously.

"Who is that?"

"I don't know. One of the sailors, I assume."

"Why is she dressed in red?"

"It is traditional."

The scull edged alongside the tethered boats and a rope was thrown to secure it. Then the sailor was standing before them. Lunae saw a long face, narrow eyes above a slab of cheekbone, hair scrunched up in a topknot and slicked with something wet. The skin of her face and forearms was covered with tattoos; intricate whorls and spirals, like carved wood beneath the ragged sleeves.

"Who are you?" Lunae whispered.

"I am your captain. My name is Ayadatarahime Sek. You may call me 'Captain.'"

A harsh voice, and a strange accent. Lunae had difficulty in understanding some of the words. Sek grinned, displaying teeth stained black by chewing-nut. Certain of the teeth, like the Martian's, had been filed into points, or perhaps were implants. Her eyes were a flat darkness. Lunae took an instant dislike to her. She stared ahead, but Sek must have seen the flicker in her eyes, for the captain's sharp, rotten smile widened.

"You have had no trouble?" Dreams-of-War asked sharply.

"There is always trouble. Raiders from the Siberian Islands, from Hakodate. In the Fire Islands, problems all the time with *your* people." She nodded toward the kappa, who fluttered her hands. "They delight in putting obstacles in my way. And in the city, bureaucrats all wanting their cut of the harbor revenue, whether or not they are entitled to it. I do not know which is worse." Sek sounded both self-righteous and aggrieved. Lunae's dislike deepened, unreasonably.

"But nothing unusual?" Dreams-of-War persisted.

"I have seen something of a Dragon-King on this voyage."

"A Dragon-King?" Dreams-of-War looked startled.

"But apart from that, nothing unusual. Get in."

Lunae stepped over the side into the scull, which rocked, throwing her forward. Dreams-of-War turned, but it was Sek who caught her. The captain's hands were like gnarled iron, and they lingered. Lunae pulled away.

"Be careful," Dreams-of-War snapped.

"She'll learn," Sek said without rancor, and cast off. The scull skimmed over the greasy water, to rest beneath the great black hull of the junk. Lunae looked up to see the sails rattling in the breeze. A rope ladder was flung forth. Sek swarmed up it and called to Lunae, "Now you. Hold tight; don't look down."

Lunae hesitated.

"Go on," Dreams-of-War said. "You won't fall. And if you do, the kappa and I will catch you."

Lunae did as she was told. The ladder was slimy with weed, as though it had been towed underwater, and encrusted with barnacles. She found it difficult to grip, and the rough mouths of the barnacles hurt her hands. She felt weak and ineffectual in front of Sek, who was peering impatiently over the side. To the captain, she was suddenly sure, Lunae was no more than a pampered passenger. She clambered upward, bracing her feet against the sides of the hull.

Gradually, as she climbed, the air became filled with an unfamiliar sound: a hissing, rushing whisper. At first Lunae thought that this was no more than the movement of the waves against the hull, but as she reached for the rungs of the ladder, she realized that the noise was composed of many voices.

"The sea, the sea . . ."

"Water filled my lungs; I knew nothing more . . ."

"The Dragon-Kings took me, swallowed me whole . . ."

"Lunae!" The voice was sharp and irritated. Lunae looked down. Dreams-of-War stood with hands on hips, glaring upward. "Why have you paused? Are you afraid?"

"I can hear voices."

"What?"

"The boat is speaking to her," Sek spoke softly from above. "She hears the stories of the dead."

Dreams-of-War's mouth opened in surprise. "What?"

Sek did not answer.

Lunae began once more to climb, puzzled. Did this boat, then, use haunt-tech? It appeared entirely antique to her: the wooden boards, the crimson sails. Resolutely, she ignored the voices, filing her questions away for later, and soon they faded to nothing more than the murmur of the waves.

When she reached the top, Sek hauled her onto the deck.

"Well enough."

Lunae looked ruefully at her hands and garments, which were now tinged a faint and gleaming green. She was reminded of Dreams-of-War's armor, but now she stank of old weed. Dreams-of-War and then the kappa appeared beside her on the deck.

"We leave now?" Dreams-of-War demanded.

Sek nodded. "As soon as you are ready. But the girl must go below."

Dreams-of-War nodded. "Very well."

"I should like to stay on deck," Lunae ventured, but the kappa protested.

"No, no, it is not safe; you must do as the captain tells you."

Lunae bit back a sharp reply and followed the kappa down the steps to a cabin. Lunae was immediately reminded of the litter: no windows, enclosing walls, and only a faintly glowing lamp on the shelf. She sat down dismally on a nearby bench and folded her hands in her lap, already beginning to plot escape. The kappa sank into a moist bundle beside her.

CHAPTER 2

EARTH

Yskatarina stood before the doors of Cloud Terrace, the Animus at her shoulder. It was dusk. The lamps of the city glowed below. The air was filled with the soft wings of moths, brushing against Yskatarina's arms with a delicacy that she could not feel.

"They will not let us in," the Animus whispered.

Yskatarina smiled. "Of course not. All the weir-wards are up. They suspect something is wrong." Earlier that day, she had sent a message to the Grandmothers, asking for an audience. She gave an assumed name, not wanting any connection to be made to Nightshade, or Elaki. But the Grandmothers denied her request.

"We are old, and weary," Left-Hand quavered, echoed by her sister. "You can have no reason to wish to see us. We live quietly, in seclusion. We intend to remain there." And then the link was severed with insulting abruptness.

Yskatarina was not surprised. The Grandmothers' intelligence network was both extensive and capable. The assassination attempt by the kappa had suggested that, and Yskatarina was certain that her brush with murder could be traced back to the doors of Cloud Terrace. Nothing was secure. However, Yskatarina intended to make sure that the spiders at the heart of the web would spin no more.

"Do as we discussed," she said to the Animus.

The Animus's mandibles opened to their widest extent, revealing a lensed opening. Yskatarina kept well back, out of the way. The lens slid aside, revealing a flicker of teeth. Then a bolt of cold flame shot from the depths of the Animus's throat. When it struck the door, the metal melted, dripping into iron lace.

"Good," Yskatarina said with satisfaction. When the molten metal flow stopped, she stepped through.

The hallway was empty, but Yskatarina did not immediately proceed. She stood still and raised her hand before her. A host of stinging things burst from the wall and swarmed up her arm. If it had been flesh, she knew, they would have stripped it from her bones, but they could make no headway on the armored steel. Again, that cold fire, enveloping her arm for the briefest moment, and then the swarm was nothing more than a coating of ash.

"There will be other safeguards," the Animus said.

"Then go before me."

When they reached the end of the hallway, a toxic mist appeared. The Animus consumed it in a single breath, breathed it forth again from the vents in its sides as nothing more than steam.

Going past the tapestries, they encountered a sudden whirling mass of blades, which Yskatarina blocked with a blow of her hand. She lost three fingers, which clattered to the floor and writhed like worms. But the blades ground to a tangle of metal and then she and the Animus were standing before the door of the Grandmothers' chamber.

Yskatarina kicked it open with a whine of servomechanisms. The Animus sidled through, but met no resistance. The Grandmothers stared at Yskatarina from the depths of the bed, eyes bright.

"You are from Nightshade," Right-Hand whispered, echoed by her companion.

Yskatarina grinned. "And you are my aunts. Elaki, you—all sisters from the same skein. Family quarrels . . ."

"Elaki's child?" The Grandmothers stared at her.

"Exactly so. I have come for the *hito-bashira*. And this, of course, is my Animus." The Animus's mandibles clicked open. "He can blast you to powder with a single breath," Yskatarina said.

"It does not matter what you do to us. You will not find what you are looking for."

"If you don't give the girl to me," Yskatarina said, "I will order the Animus to fry you, as slowly as a pair of prawns. You will sizzle and shriek, my aunts."

The Grandmothers' mouths widened into shark-smiles. "You will not find her. We cannot summon her. She is not here."

"Where is she, then?" Yskatarina asked, feeling a slow temper begin to build, like a thunderhead.

"We have sent her away, to a place where you and Elaki will never find her. She is safe."

"Tell me or die," Yskatarina said.

The Grandmothers looked at Yskatarina, then at the Animus, then at each other.

"We have lived long enough," they said, and before Yskatarina could order the Animus to act, Right-Hand reached down and tugged at one of the tubes that ran beneath the bed. A thick white fluid flooded out, seeping across the driftwood floor like a tide.

"Wait," Yskatarina said, but the Grandmothers were crumpling and folding, shrinking as though it had been nothing more than the fluid that had animated them, as, perhaps, was the truth. Their eyes remained bright with vindictiveness right up until the moment that Yskatarina, temper breaking at last, shrieked to the Animus, "Do it! Make them burn"—and the joined women vanished behind a sheet of ire-palm.

Yskatarina watched until there was nothing left except an ashy slime upon the floor, and then she began to search the room with frantic haste, muttering as she did so—perhaps to the Animus, perhaps to herself. There was no data pertaining to the lost haunt-ship, but there was other information, instead.

When she found it, she sat, crouched on her heels by the antiscribe, staring at the name it bore. Slowly, her thin smile grew.

CHAPTER 3

EARTH

L unae woke. Light flickered about her. Voices came and went. She thought she heard the kappa, speaking in a low undertone, tense with worry, but she did not recognize the other voice: a woman. She thought back, but could not remember very much. The light fluttered and changed, and suddenly she was somewhere else.

She was standing on the edge of a chasm, looking down. The chasm fell away beneath her, hundreds of feet to a thin river of black water. She knew the place intimately, but she could not have said what it was called, or even the world upon which it might lie. She thought that it might have been Mars, for the spongy rocks were all manner of shades of red, from vivid scarlet, to peony-crimson, to rust and garnet, to pale, fleshy rose. It felt like home, but it also felt unhappy. A vast weariness possessed her, as if she had been here for aeons, knew every speck of dust, every pebble. There was a curious, familiar scent: dust and smoke, perfumed with something that she knew to be a kind of wood, but could not have named.

Slowly Lunae walked along the chasm's edge. She knew that she was waiting for someone, but there was no joy in it, only a kind of dreary anticipation. She had done this a thousand times before; she would do it again. There was a cold wind blowing, causing her skin to rise up in goose bumps along her bare arms, and she shivered.

Finally, she saw it: a spinning, whirling dot at the very edge of the horizon, coming in fast over the chasm. It looked like a drop of rain, yet Lunae knew that it had not rained here for centuries.

The raindrop grew, hovered for a liquid moment overhead before spiraling down to where Lunae was standing—

—and then she was back on the boat, feeling the tilt and turn of the junk. There was a rattling slide up the boards: the anchor, Lunae surmised, being raised. She waited until she was certain that they were moving, then stole a glance at the kappa. The nurse's chin was sinking toward her breast; her round eyes were closing. Hope leaped within Lunae. She watched until the kappa fell asleep, then rose to her feet.

She stood before the locked door of the cabin, closed her eyes, and shifted time: just a few seconds. When she opened her eyes again, she was on the other side of the door, standing in the narrow corridor. She touched the wall: salvaged wood, scrap metal hammered into uneven panels, the roughness of cogs and gears beneath her fingers. This whole ship was nothing more than a patchwork, remnants of older vessels, perhaps. The old philosophical conundrum came to her: If the sails, the wood, the nails are all replaced, then can it be the same boat? If so, Lunae thought, then this junk could have been sailing the seas since the Drowning.

She remembered the voices: old ghosts, locked within waterlogged wood. But that was a sign of haunt-tech, not age. It was science that conjured ghosts, rather than nature. Turning, she ran along the passage, seeking the stairwell, air, and light.

There was a rolling unsteadiness beneath her feet, a distant hum from deep within the junk. It must be moving under its own power, independent from the wind. Perhaps the sails were nothing more than an emergency measure. At the bottom of the stairwell Lunae paused and listened. Nothing. Holding tightly to the rail, she climbed the stairs and stepped out onto the deck.

It was later than she had thought. The sun had dropped below the horizon, leaving a stain upon a rosy sky. The mirror-lights of the city flashed over the water: tower upon tower, rising up from the sea-walled land. It took her a moment to regain perspective. They were passing the edges of High Kowloon. Tenements climbed perilously above the water, overhanging the shore. She could see nets and lines cast down from the windows, between the bob of lights from the fishing dhows. A babble of voices floated across the water from the streets: arguments, enticements. After the quietness of the mansion, the world seemed filled with unnecessary sound.

Lunae looked back, but the heights of the Peak were cast in darkness. Cloud Terrace was a line of irregular shadow. She turned her back on it.

A red wall rose before her, gleaming in the lights of the city, and Lunae recognized the Nightshade Mission. She stared at it with wary fascination. It looked like a block of congealing blood, with a curiously waxen quality. Up close, the walls appeared gelatinous, more like translucent flesh than stone, a shadowy darkness, shot with fire. Had it been built or grown? She thought of the Kami, the spirits-within, then of the assassin. She could still feel its touch upon her hands, like the last remnants of a scab. She watched the Mission as if hypnotized, until it fell behind.

More tenements, and then the immense bulk of the fortress-temple, Gwei Hei. This, too, rose straight from the water: obsidian and iron, encrusted with the faces of demons to keep away the hungry ghosts of the sea. A *feng shui* mirror, some ten feet across and lamp-bright, glared out across the harbor like a baleful eye. Lunae smelled smoke and blood, the sharp tang of industrial pollution, but the night wind was warm on her face and she leaned back against the mast, happy to be outside.

"Well," a voice said. "I see you've found your way on deck."

Lunae, startled, looked up to see Sek. The captain's eyes were sea-dark, narrowed with disapproval, anger, admiration—Lunae could not tell. Sek's tattooed arms were clasped behind her. She smelled strongly of something incongruously flowery, that Lunae finally identified as synthetic jasmine.

"You should not be up here. I told you to stay below." Sek frowned. "How did you get out of the cabin?"

Lunae's eyes widened in simulation of meek innocence. "The door was not locked. I'm sorry to disobey. I wanted to see the city. I've never seen it so close."

The captain stared at her for a moment. "How old are you?"

"Fifteen," Lunae said, using the lie that Dreams-of-War and the Grandmothers had established between them.

"And you've never been allowed outside?" The captain clicked her tongue. "You're a sheltered little thing, aren't you?" But her scorn did not seem directed at Lunae. "Where is your guardian?"

"I don't know. My nurse is in the cabin."

"Come with me and find your guardian. I will instruct her to keep closer to you."

"She'll make me stay below again."

"Likely so."

Reluctandy, Lunae followed the captain to the prow, where an armored figure stood looking out to sea, legs braced.

"Princess?"

Dreams-of-War turned, her mouth turned down in distaste. When she caught sight of Lunae, it lengthened to dismay.

"Is something wrong?"

"Our guest felt unwell; I had her brought on deck for some air," the captain said smoothly, creating a sudden bond of complicity between them that made Lunae uncomfortable. Disliking Sek as she did, she did not want the captain to have that kind of hold over her. Or perhaps Sek, believing that the door had indeed been unlocked, merely wanted to conceal her own negligence.

"I see. Are you feeling better now?" It was clear from the arch of the Martian woman's eyebrows that Dreams-of-War did not believe her.

"Yes," Lunae muttered.

"Seasickness is unpleasant. I think you should remain with her, princess."

"Princess?" Lunae questioned.

"She's a Martian warrior, isn't she? Best to humor her," the captain said with a flicker of contempt and something that, Lunae thought, could almost have been envy. Dreams-of-War's face grew still and cold. The captain laughed. "It's my ship, *princess*. My ship, and my favor."

Dreams-of-War gave a small, curt nod. "Lunae will stay here with me," she said, as if it had been her decision alone.

Sek wandered back along the deck.

"She does not like me," Lunae murmured.

Dreams-of-War shot her a puzzled glance. "She dislikes me, also. But why should we care? She does not have to."

"But I wonder why. Perhaps she is afraid of the Grandmothers." At this, Lunae could not help looking back in the direction of Cloud Terrace.

It was burning.

Forgetting the prohibition, Lunae clutched at the Martian's arm. "Look!"

High on the Peak, the mansion was lost in a flare of unnatural light, a mauve flicker.

"Ire-palm," Dreams-of-War said, openmouthed.

"My Grandmothers?"

"They will be dead." Dreams-of-War's mouth was a tight line, but she had not, the girl noticed, removed Lunae's hand from her armored arm.

"The Kami?"

"I do not know. But I will start asking questions."

"Dreams-of-War? Is this ship using haunt-tech?"

"It should not be."

"But I heard voices."

"I know. I am not dismissing this, Lunae. I just don't know what to make of it." Dreams-of-War glanced around her. She shifted Lunae's hand from her arm, but she did so gently. They stood in silence on the deck, watching as Cloud Terrace burned. At last, the amethyst flare blazed out in a final column of sparks.

Fragrant Harbor was falling behind. They were passing the headlands at the edges of the city now, and the suburbs had grown sparser until there was little more than a thin band of lamps along the shore: the fishing settlements and outcast villages that clung to the cliffs along the dark reaches of the coast.

The junk was now passing the beacon light that led into the Yellow Sea. The gleam at the top of the tower flickered, sending complex data out to shipping. Lunae smelled sagebrush and salt, the warm scents of sun-warmed earth, fading into night.

Then they were around a black rim of cliff and out into open waters. The city was invisible. The stars were bright seeds and flowerheads away from the city's muted glow. A crescent moon hung low on the horizon and behind it arched the maw of the Chain, outlined in phosphorescence against the drop of night, flares and flashes all along its perimeter. Lunae breathed a sigh of relief. It was good to get away from the city, and the ashes of what had so recently been her home. She thought of the Grandmothers, and there was nothing but relief there, too. She could not muster even the semblance of regret. They had given her life and childhood and fear; she was glad to be rid of them. The night air seemed easier to breathe.

"Look," Dreams-of-War said with a thin satisfaction, and pointed. A red dot burned in the east. "Mars. It's very close now, the closest it has been for over a thousand years."

Lunae reached out to touch her guardian's arm again, but remembered just in time and snatched back her hand. After a moment Dreams-of-War said stiffly, "It's all right." But she did not invite a further touch, and Lunae did not expect her to. They stood, watching Mars rise and the Chain turn, as the sails creaked and twisted above them and the junk pulled farther out to sea.

CHAPTER 4

EARTH

W
e will have to go to him," the Animus said, alighting in
a bundle of wet wings upon the veranda of the ruined
fortress. Steam rose from the damp boards; the air was
heavy with humidity. Fragrant Harbor and the ruins of Cloud
Terrace lay far behind.

"I was not expecting to do otherwise," Yskatarina answered,
vinegar-sour. She wrapped her arms about herself, swayed
in the stormlight on fragile legs. "What did you make of this
Prince Cataract when we spoke across the antiscribe? The
Grandmothers' Animus?"

"He is old. He repeated himself over and over. I do not think
he is sane."

"Sane or not, he surely has knowledge that we can make use
of. Knowledge of the haunt-ship that brought them all from
Nightshade, the place where Tower Cold's lost records are stored,
where details of the *hito-bashira* are to be found."

"He may have such knowledge, but why should he tell us?
I would not put much faith in Prince Cataract."

Yskatarina snorted. "I do not. Especially since he deserted
Elaki's sisters. I am surprised that he even agreed to see me, and
he only did so after I told him I had information about them. We
will have to see what we can offer him. I have not, obviously, told
him that I am Elaki's relative."

"Have you spoken with Memnos today?"

"No, but recently. They were guarded, elliptical, evasive as
ever, but the old Matriarch will very soon be strong enough to
act. In the meantime, let's see what we can get out of Prince
Cataract."

"Do you wish to go now?"

Yskatarina nodded.

"Then I shall take you," the Animus said.

Yskatarina slipped her arms around the Animus's abdomen and hung on. The missing fingers made it difficult to grip. The Animus's spined wings unfolded, beating out into the rainy air. Yskatarina looked back as they spiraled up into the sky, to see the ruined fort fall behind, a small gray square against the darkness of the island. Far out across the South China Sea lay a wall of storms: a green flash of lightning, the distant mutter of thunder across the horizon. The Animus turned and wheeled toward the storm.

Soon they were out across the sea. The Dragon-King would rise, or so they had been told.

Yskatarina closed her eyes for a moment, and rested her cheek against the Animus's slick hide. It occurred to her that the only body of water on Nightshade was frozen: She had never needed to learn to swim. But if she fell from this height, there would be no chance of survival, in any case.

A series of distant needles rose out of the sea, black against the heaving water. The Animus flew lower. The needles resolved themselves into spires and pinnacles of rock, rising straight from the sea. A lacy collar of white-green tide encircled each one.

At first, Yskatarina thought they were about to land on the spires, but the Animus, circling, soared lower yet. The waves towered up, so high that Yskatarina gasped, thinking they were about to be engulfed. Then she saw that the wall of water that rose before them was not water at all, but a great glassy hull, rearing up upon bone-white struts.

"What is *that*?"

"The Dragon-King," the Animus said. It plunged down before Yskatarina could utter a word of protest, and alighted on the uppermost level of the hull, a walkway protected by the struts.

Yskatarina slid from its back and stood shaking, her back pressed against a strut. Sea streamed past her. She wished that she had not chosen such light legs for the purposes of flight:

translucent plastic, supported by inner steel. When she looked down, she seemed to be floating. Only a glassy smear of seawater across the transparent surface of her shins betrayed their presence. It made her feel flimsy, as if the next gust might blow her away. She reached out and took tight hold of one of the Animus's arms.

"Where is he?" Her voice sounded raw and unused.

"He must be below" The Animus sidled through a crack in the wall, angling itself through like a squashed spider. "And there may be others."

"What kind of others? His children?" Yskatarina, with a final wary glance out to sea, followed.

She found herself in a tight niche, pressed against the Animus. But next moment, the niche opened up. She was falling, hurtling down on a slide of sea into the depths of the Dragon-King.

CHAPTER 5

MARS

The Memnos Matriarch sat alone in her chamber, scribbling upon a scroll, which whirred slowly out from the antiscribe. Although she wrote busily, the thoughts that she was noting down were inchoate and fragmented: names, dates, ideas . . . The Matriarch was trying to make sense of what Nightshade might be planning.

There was a faint clicking sound in the direction of the door. The Matriarch did not glance up. Both of her personal excissieres were on guard duty, beyond the small stone chamber that was the Matriarch's sanctuary. From time to time she heard their harsh whispered voices as they conferred with each other. The Matriarch found it reassuring. It had been a long time since she had been a warrior, perhaps fifty years or more since she had worn armor and strode out across the Crater Plain. Now the armor belonged to another warrior and the Matriarch could barely remember what it had been like to stalk and kill. She had been protected ever since the day that the armor had been returned to the challenge racks and she had climbed the stone stairs of the Memnos Tower naked, to return wearing the red-and-black of the Matriarchy. At the time, it had seemed like a fair exchange, but sometimes still, she wondered.

The clicking sound came again. There was the noise of a door opening, and this time the Matriarch looked up. The excissieres stepped into the chamber, moving as though controlled by the same string.

"Yes?" the Matriarch asked absently. "What is it?"

The excissieres did not reply. Instead, they glided forward. Their armor bristled; the moving images of cuts and wounds appeared and vanished across the few inches of exposed flesh, glowing raw and red in the lamplight.

"What?" the Matriarch said again.

Each woman plucked the scissors from her belt with a glittery snick. Their eyes were blank. The Matriarch stood abruptly. Her chair fell to the floor. She dodged behind the desk, reaching for the phial at her throat. The excissieres grabbed the edge of the desk and turned it over. The Matriarch fell against the window, which swung open. She reeled over the sill, looking down onto a hundred feet of air. The frosty rim of the sill dug into her back. The excissieres' scissors were the same silvery cold as they came downward, and she felt a tug as they ripped the phial from her neck. The Matriarch saw a single star in the sky above her, and she thought that it might be Earth, but then it was lost behind a fountain of blood. The excissieres grasped at her, but she was already falling. Her last thought was that the two worlds were the closest now that they had been for a thousand years.

The excissieres watched her fall. When the tumbling body hit the ground, each pressed a careful tongue to the surface of the scissors and licked it clean.

"Go down and bring that body back," said the thing behind them, its possessed and resurrected body shambling into the chamber that had once been its own.

CHAPTER 6

EARTH

Yskatarina, gasping, was afloat in green phosphorescent water. Her head pounded and throbbed like a thundercloud. She thrashed and sank, kicked out, rose again. She had never been in deep water before. Through the mutable light she glimpsed a drifting shape, a white, terrified face: a woman, perhaps her own age or a little older. Yskatarina cried out to the woman.

"Help me!"

The woman's mouth moved as Yskatarina herself spoke, but there was nothing more than an echo, and it was then that Yskatarina realized it was her own reflection.

"We are in a room," the Animus said, soaring overhead. He swooped, Yskatarina lunged and was lifted to the top of a flight of steps. Water lapped gently against her feet with the rock of the machine.

The mirror filled one wall. Yskatarina's face appeared spectral, a glistening green. The Animus flew in a slow circle. The room was vast, hangar-sized, paneled with rotten wood. Far above there was a cold crystal glitter as a chandelier caught the sea-light. But the water, though chill, had not been icy, and a warm breath of air made its way through the cracks in the splintered wood.

"Where *are* we?"

"I do not know," the Animus said. "We fell a long way, down a chute—look. You can see the end of it up there." As it folded its wings, Yskatarina saw that one edge was ragged, like a fraying sleeve. Droplets of black ichor starred the boards beneath their feet.

"You're hurt!" she said, filled with dismay.

"It does not matter. Look there."

Yskatarina looked up and noticed a ragged hole in the paneled wall.

"There is also a doorway," the Animus said.

The door itself had long gone. Now there was only a second hole in the wall.

"Don't leave me!" Yskatarina swallowed a lump of panic.

"Do not worry." The Animus's eyes were luminous in the darkness. "There are stairs at the end."

Yskatarina clutched the Animus and was taken forward over chill, oily water. The place smelled stagnant, salty, and rank with weed and mold. Soon, however, her feet knocked against something solid.

"I will hoist you up," the Animus said. "You must feel your way up the stairs. There is a rail to your left. Hold on to it."

Groping, Yskatarina found the rail and the first step. She made her way shakily upward. The Animus followed. There was the sound of clicking talons on wet wood.

"Be careful. Many of these steps are fragile."

Yskatarina kept close to the rail and climbed.

"There is a door at the top," the Animus said.

"Is it closed?"

"Yes. Perhaps locked, but I see no bolt."

The night-sight of those lamp-eyes must be sharp. To Yskatarina, even accustomed as she was to the gloom of Nightshade, the blackness was complete. She reached out and touched a door. She could find no handle, no lock. The door was firmly shut.

"Wait," the Animus said. "I will try."

Yskatarina felt the Animus's body push past her, then a thud.

"Are you breaking down the door?"

"I am trying to do so," the Animus said after a pause. Again the thud, the sound of rending wood, and a gleam of light.

"Are you all right?"

"I am unharmed. The door is open."

Yskatarina's hand was taken in the Animus's spiny grasp and it pulled her through into a passageway. She stood on thick carpet, patterned with crimson dragons. Mirrors lined the walls, reflecting ornamental sconces. Most were unlit, but two still burned with an antique glow. The discrepancy between this interior and the alien outside of the great shell was alarming, but now that she looked more closely, there were signs of connection. Thin struts of bone ran along the edges of some of the panels, fanning out to form skeletal networks, faint as the marks left by weed torn from the face of a rock.

When she examined these patterns, Yskatarina could see that some of them were translucent; a white liquid fell and rose within. It was as though organic technology had grown across the surfaces of this older vessel, incorporating the structural integument of the ship into itself. Yskatarina's head ached anew, the thought struck her that perhaps this was no more than some lingering dream, experienced on the verges of death. The Eldritch Realm seemed suddenly very close. She shivered.

"If the lights are on, perhaps there is someone around," Yskatarina whispered.

"Perhaps. But perhaps not—I would have thought that Prince Cataract would keep to less damaged levels, if there are such." The Animus paused. "And I have heard of *things*."

"What kind of things?"

"Ghosts in the fortress, in the ruins . . . They spoke of specter-ships, deserted by passengers and crew. Plague boats, crewed by the rotting dead. Asylum craft, where the long-ago results of failed experiments were pushed out to sea, to drift over the horizon and away from guilt and shame."

Yskatarina did not know what to say. She had never heard the Animus speak in this manner and it alarmed her.

"You did not tell me this," she said. "You should have done so. If there is any trace of haunt-tech around the ruin—"

The Animus blinked his black-lens gaze and the impression was dispelled. "We need to find a safer place," he said.

They made their way through silent passageways, mirror-lined, lit erratically by shattered sconces. Carpets were thick and moldering beneath their feet, emitting wisps and puffs of decay. The heads of carved dragons reared out from the walls, the gilding upon their teeth chipped and faded, their eyes wild and blank.

"This is nothing more than a wreck," Yskatarina murmured. "Is this the Dragon-King itself, or some other vessel that it has absorbed?"

The Animus's eyes gleamed in the dim light. "Something is still generating power. This is too old a ship to be running under its own; it must be drawing from the great machine." The Animus broke off, and skittered down the corridor.

More doors led into a further maze of passages. Here were signs, with arrows, clearly leading somewhere, but Yskatarina did not recognize the language.

"What alphabet is that? Do you know?"

"I do not."

They proceeded up a staircase, with a banister of ebony. Traces of varnish still remained beneath a coating of mildew. At the top of the curve of the stair stood another mirror: green with age, filmed with salt stain. Yskatarina watched herself and the Animus climb the stair. Her own face was still ghost-pale; her hair, drying now, fanned out like dark fire.

The mirrored walls were deceptive. She kept glimpsing figures in the shadows, which darted away and proved to be herself or the Animus, their images flickering in the roll of the ship. But sometimes, she was not so certain. She felt eyes upon her that were not her own mirror-self, heard whispers.

"Animus? I'm sure there's someone close by."

"I see no one."

They reached the top of the staircase. Yskatarina looked back. The hallway below was empty.

"Where now?"

"If we can reach the deck," the Animus said, "maybe we can find out where we are."

"If it's safe," Yskatarina said. The ship seemed huge, yet it plunged and rolled nonetheless. She wondered what kind of sea the Dragon-King sailed through, what kind of storm.

"We will soon see," the Animus replied.

More passages lay ahead, in better repair than those below. At the end of the final corridor was a door. Yskatarina and the Animus looked at each other.

"There are no signs," the Animus said.

"Open it." Yskatarina wondered for a disquieting moment if it might lead beyond the ship. Would they open the door to find the howling, whirling interior of the Dragon-King? Or empty sea?

The Animus stepped forward and tugged at the door. It swept open at once, to a blast of humidity and heat. Yskatarina gasped, welcoming the sudden warmth after the dankness of the lower levels. Within, all was wan and green, like the growing-chamber in the Grandmothers' house.

"Plants!" the Animus said. They went through. Yskatarina saw peppers on the vine, the sour blue pods called k'oan, the tendrils of oquii, and others that she did not recognize. The air smelled wet; a thick slime filled long tanks.

"Hydroponics," Yskatarina murmured. "These have been tended recently." She touched a pruned spear of growth; picked up a pair of small black scissors in the shape of a crane's beak. "But this is huge," she added in wonder. "There are whole crops of vegetables." Corn waved gently before her, as if in an unfelt breeze. Rows of outsized pak choi, each leaf a meter or more in diameter, formed a thick forest around the edges of the room. She looked down at the floor, which seemed to be formed of a semitransparent plastic, to see the faint green fronds of rice below.

"Enough to feed a shipload." Yskatarina glanced about her, seeking faces in the greenery. "Then where are they? Are they watching? We have seen no one."

"I do not know the answers to any of these questions."

Yskatarina pushed aside the veils of vines. At the far end of the chamber, she found a series of pods. The place reminded her of Elaki's laboratory. It was not a happy memory. She half-expected Isti to scuttle out from behind the fronds.

"Growing-skins." The Animus leaned forward and sniffed. Yskatarina saw the lenses flutter. "This is nothing human."

Yskatarina stared at the skins, which pulsed with a veiny beat. "Then what's in there?"

Gently, the Animus prodded one of the skins. Something prickled against the surface from within.

"It smells of insect. This one—" The Animus's mandibles twitched. "Perhaps reptile."

"It's more than two feet long." Yskatarina took a careful step back. "I suggest we leave well enough alone. Let's see what else we can find."

She pushed the door at the far end of the chamber, but it was locked. Yskatarina and the Animus pulled and tugged, to no avail.

"We'll have to go out the way we came in," the Animus said. They returned to the other end of the chamber. But here, too, the door was tightly closed.

"This was not locked when we entered," the Animus said.

"Are you sure?"

"I am certain." The Animus pulled harder. He emitted a thin whistle of concern. "Perhaps the ceiling has panels? Or the floor?"

They searched the chamber, but there was no sign of any access: no hatches or entryways. The chamber was entirely sealed. At last Yskatarina and the Animus stood in the center of the room, surrounded by the drip of water and the smell of growth.

There was a rustle from the far end of the chamber, a soft splitting sound like a ripe fruit falling to the floor.

"What was that?"

Together they walked toward the source of the sound. It came again, a wet, heavy noise. When they reached the end of the chamber, Yskatarina saw that two of the growing-skins were dangling limp and empty on the growing-racks. There was a pungent organic odor that made her eyes water.

"Something has hatched," the Animus said softly.

"A child?"

"A child would not be able to move from the skin. Someone would have to be here to help it." The Animus paused. "That is, if it was a *human* child."

Greenery rustled from two separate directions. In the midst of the growing corn, something hissed and was answered.

"Where are they?" Yskatarina whispered.

"I can smell them," the Animus said. His mandibles fluttered once more. "They are half-human."

Yskatarina eyed it askance. "What's the other half?"

"I cannot tell. But it smells of predator."

"They are only just out of the skin. How dangerous can they be?"

Something darted through the greenery at Yskatarina's feet. She glimpsed a small, pale shape.

"It's probably frightened."

"Don't go near it." The Animus's claw seized Yskatarina by the arm and propelled her toward the doors at the other end of the chamber. There was a scuttling among the vines. They had almost reached the doors when the vines shook and trembled. Two things spilled out of the tendrils, crawling swiftly between Yskatarina, the Animus, and the doors. Human children, very small, with round black eyes and the jaws of a snake. Soft, gristly mouthparts opened and closed. Yskatarina could see the long fangs within. A fleshy tongue flickered between the needle teeth. The small hands, plastered flat to the floor, were webbed, but the infants had no legs or feet, only tapering pale tails.

The infants hissed, a noise more reminiscent of a rasping saw than a serpent. They shuffled forward with alarming speed; Yskatarina and the Animus leaped back. Beads of something clear and sticky oozed down the curve of the needle teeth.

"They are hungry," the Animus said.

An infant bolted forward and struck out at the Animus. Yskatarina shouted a warning. The Animus reached down and snatched the infant up by the tail. The tail parted company from the infant's body with a damp snap. The infant fell to the floor and hid under a growing-tank, squeaking and hissing. The Animus flung the slimy tail across the room. The second infant's teeth met in the plastic of Yskatarina's calf. She shouted, striking down at the infant in revulsion. The Animus forced a claw into the infant's mouth, behind the fangs, and pulled it away. He hurled the infant across the growing-chamber. The snake-child hit the wall with a sound like a sand-filled sack, and its skull shattered. It slid to the floor, with a greenish ichor leaking from its deflating head.

CHAPTER 7

EARTH

Dreams-of-War stood before the cabin's antiscribe, together with the kappa. Lunae hovered around them, peering over their shoulders at the flickering screen. Her guardian and the nurse were ignoring her presence, and it irked her.

"Is there any news?" Lunae asked.

"The main network speaks only of a fire. It suggests a domestic accident at Cloud Terrace."

"That is foolish," Dreams-of-War snapped. "Anyone watching will have seen that it was ire-palm."

"The network news comes from the Ruling Council of Fragrant Harbor," the kappa said, "and in this instance, the Council will do as it is instructed by Memnos. Even those who saw the destruction will get the message. It may be of advantage. Whoever set the blaze intended no trace to remain. Perhaps whoever set it will assume that we, too, are dead."

"But who is that?" Lunae asked. "The Kami?"

"Or the Grandmothers themselves?" the kappa suggested. Lunae stared at her. The nurse had dropped the fluttering, flustered demeanor that seemed to form her protective persona. Lunae barely recognized her.

"The Grandmothers? That's a thought," Dreams-of-War mused.

"They knew we were safely away They have connections. Someone would have had to have helped them leave the mansion."

"And then set the fire," Dreams-of-War said. "But if that is the case, I feel it is likely that the Grandmothers would contact us. And they have not done so."

"Not yet." The kappa stared back at the antiscribe.

"And neither has anyone else. I placed a Chain missive to Memnos soon after we boarded. That is now a day ago and I have heard nothing. Silence from Memnos is not a good thing. I feel as though we have been cast adrift on the tides." Dreams-of-War spoke angrily. "I have been told little enough by the Grandmothers as it is—only that we are to travel north and seek sanctuary. I was expecting more information. As usual, I did not get it."

"Do not worry, warrior. You know that we are heading for the Fire Islands, for the protection of my people. Once we are within the sea-space of the kappa, things will be different."

But from the look that Dreams-of-War bestowed upon her, Lunae thought the Martian was not reassured.

CHAPTER 8

EARTH

Finally, Yskatarina and the Animus managed to force open the door. Had Yskatarina's hands been flesh, they would surely have bled. The Animus's tough claws were scuffed and dulled. The tailless snake-child had retreated to the far end of the room, where it sat nursing the stump of its wound and staring at them with unblinking, reptilian resentment. Yskatarina kept glancing over her shoulder, but there was no sign of movement from within any of the remaining growing-skins.

"Do you think it was deliberate?" she asked the Animus in an undertone, as they worked on the door. "That someone locked us in with these things?"

"Two grown beings, against babies?" the Animus mused.

"There is a cruel kind of whimsy about it. I think someone is watching us. I think someone is *bored*."

The frame of the door gave way with a wrenching of wood, releasing a shower of beetles that scattered around Yskatarina's feet. Pale light flooded through into the growing-room.

The Animus glided past her and stopped. Something was standing in the passage.

It was another of the snake-children, but this one was older. It was the height of the Animus. It wore a long gray shift, hiding the tail on which it balanced. It regarded them gravely, from eyes like obsidian marbles, its small hands clasped before it. The protruding mouthparts worked in silent rhythm.

"I have come to take you to Prince Cataract," it said. Its voice was sibilant and hoarse, as if infrequently used.

"He knows we are here?" the Animus asked.

"Of course."

"We were locked in there," Yskatarina said, voice rising. She pointed to the growing-chamber. "Your siblings attacked us. Why?"

"They hatched. Yes, you were locked in."

"One of your siblings is dead," Yskatarina said.

"No matter," the snake-child said, serene. "It will provide food for the others when they hatch. And more can be grown. Come with me."

Yskatarina and the Animus followed it down corridors, until it came to a door. She saw a thick, split tongue flicker out, leaving a film of saliva across a complex lock.

The door opened. They stepped through into a high, narrow room. Portholes, just beneath the ceiling, let in a stormy sliver of moonlight. Yskatarina's feet ticked against metal.

In the sudden light, something at the end of the room shifted and glittered. The snake-child bowed low and glided smoothly away.

"Prince Cataract?"

"Why, you are from Nightshade," the thing said. She could not see it clearly, only an angular hulk. An equine head reared up, swaying on a too-thin neck. There was the oyster-shell gleam of a single eye. Teeth snapped in the long jaw. It was surrounded by a pile of—something. She stepped a little closer. She could see the dull shine of scales. Snakeskin? But the pattern did not look quite right. Perhaps the creature *shed* . . . She sensed an ancient, bewildered evil.

"Come here," the thing said. "It is a long time since I tasted the blood of Nightshade."

Yskatarina took a skittering step back. "You'd know about Nightshade and blood, wouldn't you? You were the Animus of the women known as the Grandmothers. My aunts."

"And so you are my niece, one might say. I hear that Yri and Yra are dead. Did you kill them?"

Yskatarina hesitated.

"It does not matter," Prince Cataract said. "We quarreled a long time ago now, irrevocably."

"Why?"

"I don't remember," the thing said, very bland.

"You are lying."

"Give me blood, and I will tell you. Or a small piece of flesh," the thing said, wheedling. "Only a drop . . . I live off fish and gulls and the snake-kin, these days. But they have ichor in their veins. It is not the same."

Yskatarina forced a laugh. "I have little enough spare flesh."

There was a whispering murmur in return, not quite mirth. "You may yet have more than I."

"What will you do for me, then, if I give you this—this taste?"

"I will tell you what you wish to know."

"About the vessel that brought you from Mars?" She tried not to sound too eager, but she thought she might have failed.

"What do you know about that vessel?"

"That my aunts, your bonded females, came to Earth via Mars, on a stolen haunt-ship. I am interested in that ship."

"You understand that I do not know all?"

"But do you know where the ship is hidden? With its records, with details of the *hito-bashira*?"

"Let me taste, and I will tell you."

"No. I need more than that."

"The *hito-bashira* is an ancient project. I know of it, of course. But I have told you enough, without blood."

The Animus made a small whickering noise, perhaps of protest or alarm. Yskatarina ignored him. "You will have to take it from my side."

She pulled the bodice free of its straps and rolled it up, then stepped grudgingly forward. She motioned to the Animus to keep close, for it occurred to her that the thing might try to exact vengeance for the deaths of its women. "Here."

Somehow, she expected Prince Cataract to be both hesitant and slow. He was not. The long head darted forward and struck. Lightning danced down her side, as though she had been stabbed with a thousand needles. She cried out. Her vision swam black. Then the head was weaving back again, preparing for another blow. The Animus came forward in a rush and dragged her to the comparative safety of the opposite wall. Yskatarina panted with shock and outrage. Her side burned. When she looked down, a spiral of scarlet drops marked the transparent surface of her legs, as though she stood on a thin column of blood. The thing in the chamber clicked and clattered its teeth.

"Now tell me what I came here to learn," Yskatarina said, above the racing of her heart.

The thing sank back into its pile of skin. "Very well."

CHAPTER 9

MARS

The Kami that occupied the former Matriarch was becoming accustomed to its new body. At first, the desiccated corpse had proved difficult to animate effectively, as the woman from Nightshade had warned. Limbs flailed, striking out in random directions without control. Had it not been for the assistance of the excissieres, it would have taken the former Matriarch several hours to descend from the room at the top of the Tower. As soon as she had managed to activate the replacement phial, however, the excissieres had taken immediate steps, driven by the unquestioning loyalty engrams that had been programmed into their kind for those who possessed the Matriarchal DNA.

Even now, understanding came and went, ebbing and flowing like some psychic tide. Mars, at least, was not so greatly changed. Accessing the former Matriarch's memories, the Kami recognized the old clan names of Caud, Winterstrike, and other places, and the Tower was the same. But the influence of Mars was waning. The rule of Earth was starting to slip from Memnos, and Nightshade's grip was stronger than it had ever been. The Kami rejoiced.

Using old codes, the former Matriarch summoned the records from their secret caches, undisturbed for a hundred years. Half-forgotten names flowed past her gaze: Yri and Yra, the sisters-in-skin who had journeyed to Earth, there to initiate a forbidden project. Embar Khair, the warrior who had traveled with them on the first of the haunt-ships. Embar Khair had returned. The ship and the sisters had not. There had been a horned woman, too: Essa? Impossible to know what had become of her.

An excissiere, moving with brisk efficiency, operated the controls of the Chain-connection. Shortly after, the Elder Elaki's face flowed across the antiscribe.

"You have not changed" was the first thing that Elaki said.

"Think again," the old Matriarch replied. Her voice was still rusty, the voice box partly withered. "I am Kami now."

Elaki grinned. "Does your revival make the Matriarch your predecessor, or your descendant? I have been wondering."

"In either case, she is dead. She fell to a pulp on the rocks."

"At some point, it would be helpful to have her reanimated, too. She must possess some useful information."

"The body may be too broken, but we will try. There are many ghosts rising now," the old Matriarch said. "Gaezelles, ram-horns, others."

"Frivolities, nothing more. You know my views on such sports."

"That once included this body."

Elaki gave a thin smile. "So it did. But you—your body, that is—was still Matriarch. The phial is keyed into your genetic line. It cannot be used by just anyone."

"You did not approve of genetic dead ends," the Matriarch said. "I remember what you said at this body's trial: that Nightshade sought perfection of form. And yet here you are seeking the help of something that was one of the Changed. Now, what of those 'frivolities'? Shall I send them back to the Eldritch Realm?"

"No, leave them. They are harmless enough. It is the others that we require before we can proceed. The armies. The Sown."

"Dragon's Teeth," the old Matriarch whispered from her decaying throat.

"Just so. You are to begin to raise them. Raise them now."

Behind Elaki's visage, the Kami that possessed the old Matriarch could see only darkness: the abyss that lay beyond Nightshade. It seemed to her that it was here that the Eldritch Realm itself must lie: Hades, Dis, the dimension of the dead to which all spirits flew. To those who lived long ago, it had been only fancy, a fairy tale against the end of life. But these days, after the emergence of haunt-tech, spirits were known to be real. And spirits could fly back again.

CHAPTER 10

EARTH

Wearily, her side still bleeding, Yskatarina undertook the flight back to the ruin. She clung tightly to the Animus, wishing never to let him go. All the same, she thought she must have fainted, for she woke to find herself on solid ground, with the Animus weaving over her. Wet wood was rough beneath her exposed skin.

"Where are we?" Yskatarina raised her head and saw that she was lying upon the veranda of the mansion.

"You must rest," the Animus said, anxious.

"No. Not yet." Yskatarina struggled to her feet, wincing with pain. She leaned a hand against a pillar of wood, breathing in the scent of salt and jasmine. The sea air should have been refreshing; instead, she felt stifled, weighed down by humidity and the lingering heat of the day. Her side burned and stung. "I'll need the medical kit. Band-stats, and a blood test. Those teeth must have been filthy."

The thought reminded her of something. Yskatarina smiled as she took a long sliver of ivory from an inner pocket of the robe. It was razor-sharp, bloody at the root. She thought she might have it polished, then mounted in silver, with perhaps a few sea-pearls for contrast, and wear it as an ornament. A souvenir. "At least he gave me what I needed."

Yskatarina gave a small, grim smile, remembering the pile of skin and the bones it sheltered. The Animus had been merciful enough in its first strike, in payment for the mouthful of Yskatarina's flesh. The snake-children had done the rest, creeping from the cracks and seams of the room to fall in silence upon the body of their creator.

She did not think anyone would greatly miss Prince Cataract, the creature that had once been an Animus of Nightshade. It had been too easy. But then, perhaps the prince had merely grown tired of being alive. As well as the tooth, she had taken a sample of the skin for analysis. She was looking forward, she found, to having the run of Elaki's laboratories when the time came. The first to go would be Isti . . . After Elaki herself, of course.

She thought back to Prince Cataract. How would she feel if the Animus decided that he wanted to go his own way? The thought was almost inconceivable, and swamped her with dismay.

"It was useful. We now know where the haunt-ship was hidden." Yskatarina hesitated. She moved to the rotting railing and leaned bone-and-plastic hands upon it. The missing fingers still irritated her. The hot damp night had drawn in now, and there was only an occasional flutter of lightning across the horizon to show that there was ocean there at all. She thought of the Dragon-King, submerging into the depths of the sea as she and the Animus spiraled upward, of the sad, vicious things it contained. She turned from the storm-dark, heading for the inner courtyard and the antiscribe.

"I have spoken to the boat, to Sek. Rule has changed in Memnos, so that is another task accomplished."

The Animus wove over her shoulder, neck snaking out in a series of popping vertebrae. "Do you trust Sek?"

"Sek is loyal to the Matriarchy, not to any particular Matriarch. If the Matriarch changes, then her loyalty changes with it. She is ours now, if she wants to keep her boat and its modifications. They have the girl on board," Yskatarina continued. "From now on, she, too, is mine."

The Animus's mandibles whispered across her neck.

"Perhaps you should not become too confident."

Yskatarina laughed. "Why not? Coming here, I realize how isolated Nightshade has become, how limited is Elaki's understanding. Put in a line to the contact. It is time we made the acquaintance of the *hito-bashira*."

CHAPTER 11

EARTH

Dreams-of-War woke. There was a chilly light in the east, and the wind blowing through the cracks of the porthole was cool. She was immediately aware of difference, of wrongness. It took her a moment, aided by the armor's feedback, to realize that this emerged from the salt-laden air, the wetness that created a faint sheen over the surface of the armor. She missed the desert air of Mars with a sudden pang, and as quickly suppressed it.

There was a sound from deep within the junk, a little cry. Across the cabin, Lunae lay curled and unmoving. The kappa's wide mouth was open, revealing a melon-pink interior and a thick sliver of tongue, but she made no noise other than an occasional rasping breath. Frowning, Dreams-of-War rose from the bed and padded to the door, cat-quiet as the armor's foot-servos went onto maximum. She opened the door and looked out. The passage was empty. The cry came again: thin, filled with a distant, desolate anguish.

Dreams-of-War looked back at Lunae in momentary hesitation. The problem of having a charge who could bilocate at will was beginning to be brought forcibly home to her. Lunae was long past the stage where she would automatically obey. Dreams-of-War could not help but respect this, yet it was disconcerting all the same. What if the girl took it into her head to undertake a major shift, and ended up in the middle of the ocean? She had not been properly trained in her talents. Hardly surprising, since no one knew quite what they were. And that, of course, included Lunae herself. *If she becomes a liability, what then?* Dreams-of-War was seized by a claw of resentment against the Grandmothers, who had told her so little. Were they truly dead? Still, she had heard nothing.

The cry came once more. It occurred to her that it might be some kind of distracting trick. She did not like being so hesitant. She thought of Lunae, snatched or slaughtered in her sleep while her guardian was lured off on some wild-goose chase. What if something happened to the kappa? Dreams-of-War imagined the kappa's wrinkled body, pierced and probed, and her mouth was suddenly lemon-dry. She had no empathy for the nurse, but all the same . . . Silently, Dreams-of-War cursed her recently acquired emotions. They were supposed to apply only to Lunae, but they appeared to be spreading. It was an inconvenience that Dreams-of-War could well live without. She quelled the rising flood of worry with as much ruthlessness as she could muster and applied herself to more immediate issues.

"Separate," she whispered, drawing the gutting knife from the armor's thigh. The armor crept from her skin, to stand unsteadily on the rocking floor of the cabin, until she was clad only in the underharness. "Remain. Protect."

Armed with the knife, Dreams-of-War locked the door behind her and made her way along the passage. The cries were coming at regular, breathy intervals from within the hold; it sounded like some small creature in torment. Dreams-of-War went down the stairway and found a passage leading through the hold. This part of the junk was damp, the walls and floor salt-slick beneath Dreams-of-War's bare feet. There was an unwholesome seaweed smell that reminded her of the Grandmothers' chamber. At the end of the corridor lay a hatch. She hastened to it and looked in through a crack.

A woman lay supine on a long, raised couch at the center of the room, facing the opposite wall. She was naked. Both of the woman's legs were missing beneath the groin; Dreams-of-War could see the pale knob of the joints, protruding and polished. The woman's arms were thin spines of bone, fleshless from the shoulder downward, interlaced with gold and jet. Something was crouched over her. Dreams-of-War saw faceted eyes in a visage half-human, half-insect, a molten black carapace, jointed arms pinning the woman's shoulders to the couch. A spiked spur the length and thickness of Dreams-of-War's forearm hammered between the woman's artificial legs, rotating like a screw.

Dreams-of-War had never seen anything like it; at least, nothing that was bigger than a beetle. Wasp or scorpion? Ant or crab? It was all of these, and more. It should have resembled a patchwork abortion: instead, it possessed a gaunt and unnatural wholeness, a glistening, sinister beauty.

Dreams-of-War had seen worse sights in battle, but this disgusted her. Her mouth filled with bile and she drew a short sharp breath. The woman's head rolled back. Dark hair fell in a shining sweep to the floor. The woman was grinning, but her eyes were as glazed as glass. The sounds came from deep within her throat. On her shoulder, Dreams-of-War caught sight of a curious symbol, etched into the flesh: a bristling gold-and-black star.

Slowly, the woman arched her spine and began to circle her hips. Dreams-of-War backed away, fled down the corridor, and did not look back. The sounds followed her all the way to the cabin. She assumed the armor like one shutting herself inside a box, confining and safe, and sank down onto the seat by the porthole. She remained there until the sun was up, staring out over the great clean sweep of the sea.

CHAPTER 12

EARTH

When Lunae awoke, Dreams-of-War was sitting on the porthole seat, armored knees drawn up against her chest and bristling like a porcupine.

"What time is it?" Lunae asked.

"Almost eight," Dreams-of-War said.

"Is everything all right?" The Martian's face looked pinched around the mouth and her eyes were gritty. Wisps of pale hair had come loose from her plait, giving Dreams-of-War an uncharacteristically disheveled appearance.

"Everything is fine," Dreams-of-War snapped.

"Where are we?"

"How should I know? The sea looks all the same; I have seen no land. Stay here, don't answer the door, and don't take it into your head to go wandering. I'm going to find Sek."

"Why? Is something wrong?" For Dreams-of-War was emanating a wire-taut sensation, a kind of psychic jangling.

In reply, her guardian turned on an armored heel and marched out.

Lunae crossed over to the porthole and looked through. Beyond the narrow line of deck and the railing, she could see nothing but ocean, stretching hazy and blue to the horizon's edge. Now that they were beyond Fragrant Harbor, the water had changed to a deep, rolling swell, flecked with foam. Lunae watched, enchanted, as each wave rolled up, green and clear as molten glass.

The junk lurched and swayed. Lunae kept waiting for sickness, but to her relief, it never came. She rested her elbows on the rim of the porthole and watched the sea churn. Then something passed across her vision: a kind of blurring. Lunae frowned, wondering if her vision was affected, and thinking with dread of the Kami. It came again: a sudden dimming of the view of deck and horizon, as if two pillars of heat had passed by. Lunae squinted upward and saw a strange thing.

A woman was hovering above the deck. She wore a short leather kilt. Above was a black metal bodice that reached down to her hips. Long dark hair, unbraided, swept to her waist. She was looking out to sea, so Lunae was able to see her profile: a pale, sharply etched face, with a sensuous mouth. The eyes were hidden behind round lenses, like the eyes of an insect. Her arms were nothing but bone and metal, the shoulders peaked like wings and the fingers skeletal and long, but her body ended at the hips. She had no thighs, no shins, no feet. Lunae stared as the woman moved away, and now she could see that the woman was supported, after all: by two transparent legs ending in spiked heels. Artificial toes tapped across the deck. Despite the height of her heels and the motion of the deck, the woman moved quickly and with assurance. She was soon gone up the steps that led to the upper levels of the junk.

When Dreams-of-War marched back in, Lunae told her of what she had seen. By this time, the kappa had also awoken and sat blinking.

"This woman," Dreams-of-War said, frowning, "what did she look like? Did you see her face?"

"Yes," said Lunae. "She was beautiful, with long black hair. But her face was cold and closed, all angles. She did not look like anyone I have ever seen before. There was a—a foreignness to her face, yet it reminded me of someone. And she had no arms, and no legs. They were glass, or plastic, and transparent. It didn't seem to hinder her in walking."

She was surprised to see an expression of distinct unease cross her Martian guardian's countenance.

"Do you know her?" Lunae asked.

"No," Dreams-of-War replied, too quickly. "But I have reason to believe that we are not the only passengers. Why should we be, after all?"

"There are many strange things in the north," the kappa said. She waddled closer to Lunae and patted her arm. "Do not worry. I am here. Dreams-of-War is here."

"And I'm grateful," Lunae said.

The Martian turned to the kappa. "Strange things? Have you seen this woman before?"

The kappa stared at her, bemused. "I have not. But you must know how common it is in the more primitive regions for children to come from the growing-bags without limbs."

Dreams-of-War looked at her with palpable disgust. "Why aren't such infants terminated?"

"Because it takes time and expense for poor folk to grow a child," the kappa said. "And some women do not regard that child as disposable." Lunae thought there was a hint of anger in the kappa's answer, but perhaps she was imagining it. The nurse's moon-face was as placid as ever.

"What about another kind of creature? A sort of gigantic dragonfly, with a hide like black armor? A scorpion's tail?"

The kappa's eyes grew wide with alarm. "I have never seen or heard of such a monstrosity, and I do not wish to."

Dreams-of-War acknowledged this with a nod. Turning to Lunae, she added, "Are you still feeling sick?"

"A little," Lunae answered quickly. She longed to go on deck and watch the waves. "If I could go outside . . ." She faked a grimace.

"I will make tea," the kappa said, and began to busy herself over the cabin's small iron stove.

"Come with me," Dreams-of-War said. "If you are going to be ill, best you are closer to the side." Her face wrinkled with distaste. The Martian did not, Lunae felt, approve of bodily functions. She wondered again whether the armor took care of elimination for Dreams-of-War, but it was not a subject that she felt able to broach.

She followed her guardian onto the deck. There was no land in sight, only the heaving sea under a clear, cerulean sky, but far on the horizon Lunae saw a smudge rising up from the water.

"What's that?"

"Smoke," Dreams-of-War said. "Hakodate, perhaps, or one of the more southerly volcanoes."

"Is Hakodate a rift-volcano?"

"No. The only rift still active is the one beneath the Shattered Lands—what was once known as the Western Continent. It is said that it was this rift that caused the fall of prehumans and precipitated the Drowning. There is only a fragment relating to it; it says that many folk died in the cataclysm and after, when the clouds of ash and smoke blotted out the sun. Diseases would have been rife. But geologists believe that the Drowning was already well under way at that time. The great rift of the volcano merely hastened matters."

"Do we know anything about the people of Earth at that time?" Lunae asked, scouring her memories.

"They were certainly nothing but savages—apes or some such, half-humans and men-remnants like the hyenae of Mars, all teeth and whiskers. But by then, Martians had developed spaceflight; we did what we could to salvage the remains of Earth." Dreams-of-War paused. "There were—experiments, at this time. A mingling of Martian and indigenous genes. Some of these experiments were perhaps unwise." Lunae could tell from the sour twist of her guardian's mouth that Dreams-of-War hated to admit any misstep on the part of her people. "It took centuries for rebuilding to take place. But there are many such remains of the things that lived before the rift and the floods: the tailed women of the western tribes, the Mottled Elders, the Hollow Children."

"I have seen none of these. Are there pictures?"

"Yes, but why should you have an interest in such creatures? You are an advanced being, a made-human from the civilized East. Relatively civilized," Dreams-of-War amended.

"There is a story that Fragrant Harbor dates from before the Drowning."

"Certainly, Fragrant Harbor is ancient," Dreams-of-War conceded. "But probably it was little more than a fishing village. When we reach the islands of the kappa, you will see the kind of thing I mean."

And with that, Lunae had to be content.

CHAPTER 13

EARTH

Yskatarina was certain that they were being watched. She had felt eyes upon them that morning, on deck, and she did not think that the crew alone were curious. Sek herself treated Yskatarina with a wary respect, but Yskatarina was confident that the captain's loyalties to the Matriarchy would hold.

The girl was, so Sek had assured her, confined to a cabin below with her nurse and her guardian. Yskatarina set eyes on the Martian warrior later in the day, as she stood conversing with Sek in the prow. A formidable figure, but perhaps no more than a hollow one; bound to the dictates of Memnos—rigid, unquestioning. She was not so stupid as to take this for granted, but Dreams-of-War appeared the typical Martian, and thus far, Yskatarina had not been disappointed by the race. Perhaps the earlier attempts to dispatch her had been unnecessary. And then there was Dreams-of-War's armor, a piece of haunt-tech that had traveled on the stolen ship . . . Prince Cataract had implied that the armor contained memories of that ship and its operation. Yskatarina intended to explore this at the earliest opportunity.

The nurse was a kappa, and as such, did not present a great threat, although after the previous assassination attempt, Yskatarina remained wary of the toad-women. Since the attempt to snatch the girl had ended in failure, she intended to try another tack, and perhaps it was better this way. She planned to intrigue Lunae, and then befriend her. The Martian would not interfere, if instructed not to do so by Memnos.

She rested bone-and-metal fingers on the railing of the ship and contemplated the churning sea. It was good to have a change of limbs once more. Her spare parts had finally been delivered, arriving via a scow the previous day. But she did not like this expanse of water; it seemed somehow unnatural. And she wondered what lived beneath those waters. She thought of the Dragon-King, gliding along the seabed. What might it be thinking? Did any vestige of consciousness or memory remain to it? Did it remember the cataclysmic rift that had shattered the world?

Prince Cataract had been elusive on the subject, but Yskatarina thought it more probable that he simply had not known. He had told her that the Grandmothers had raised the great machine from the seabed, deeming it a suitable place on which to hide. But he had not told her why they had quarrelled, and the idea continued to distress her. The Animus glided to the railing beside her, regarded her with dark lambent eyes. She reached out a hand to touch its claw. "I have put a call through to Nightshade. Elaki is waiting."

Yskatarina smiled to herself. One could tell that they were far from home. On Nightshade, the Animus would never have dared to describe Elaki thus, without any honorific.

"More respect," she murmured, teasing.

But the Animus said nothing, and not for the first time, Yskatarina wondered whether he truly possessed thoughts and ambitions that were separate from her own. Elaki had claimed that such a thing was not possible, and indeed, she had never questioned this before. But then, that was before they had come across Prince Cataract. And Elaki and Isti, too, seemed less closely linked than the Animus and herself. Abruptly, she turned away from the rail and the ocean's expanse.

"I'll talk to her, then," she muttered.

Elaki's voice crackled and spattered over the antiscribe like hot fat.

"Yskatarina? Where are you? Why have I not heard from you?"

"You *have* heard," Yskatarina said. "I've sent regular reports."

"I need to hear your voice," Elaki said with angry impatience.

So that you can tell whether or not I am lying to you, Yskatarina thought, and this was precisely why she had not wanted to speak to her aunt directly. She was filled with relief at the thought of the emotional loss that Memnos had given her, and terror that it would show.

"I contacted you," Yskatarina said. "I told you that the Matriarch gave me the whereabouts of the *hito-bashira*, and I made the necessary arrangements. The Matriarch, as I trust you know, is dead. Her predecessor has been reanimated, and has replaced her."

"I have spoken to the thing. I am pleased, Yskatarina, with what you have done."

A handful of weeks before, such a compliment would have elated Yskatarina for days. Now there was only a merciful numbness. She tried to infuse her voice with an appropriate degree of gratitude.

"Thank you, Aunt. Thank you. And other matters are proceeding well."

"Did you speak to the Mission?"

"I tried, but there was no response."

"Something is wrong at the Mission," Elaki fretted. "I have heard nothing since they sent word to me about the girl."

"Don't worry. I am no more than a handful of yards away from the *hito-bashira*."

"And you will kill her," Elaki stated. "I understand. You are seeking the best opportunity, even now."

"That is so," Yskatarina lied, as smoothly as she could manage. "That is so."

CHAPTER 14

EARTH

Toward noon the heat grew until the reek of weed and dead fish enveloped the junk. Lunae, whom Dreams-of-War suspected of having feigned sickness, grew pale in earnest and now asked to go below—a request to which Dreams-of-War readily agreed. Lunae's absence gave her the opportunity to seek out Sek. It had not escaped her attention that Lunae did not like Sek, and Dreams-of-War was not sure what to make of this. Her ward had met so few people, after all—an acquaintance limited to herself, the kappa, the Kami and the assassin (who could hardly be said to count), and the Grandmothers. Perhaps Lunae was simply nervous and defensive . . . but then again, perhaps not. There was something about Sek that made Dreams-of-War uneasy, something familiar. She resolved to question Lunae at the next opportunity. A fresh eye, she felt, was often helpful.

Neither had she been told where the Grandmothers had found the captain. Was she under contract to them? An independent operator? Dreams-of-War had tried to find out, but failed.

She located the captain at the helm. Sek squinted out to sea, paying no attention to her visitor. Dreams-of-War watched her for a moment. Where *did* Sek originate? She did not have the look of a Northerner, though Dreams-of-War knew that the vessel was registered in the Siberian Islands. There was something strange about her and yet familiar: an outworld feel that made Dreams-of-War's skin prickle beneath the sheltering cover of the armor. The captain had an almost Martian look to her. Sek seemed surrounded by sudden darkness: a star before the abyss of night. Dreams-of-War blinked. Sek was once more the salt-stained sailor in ragged red clothes, rough hands tracing the intricate fretwork of the helm.

"I should like to see where we are," Dreams-of-War said abruptly. "Are there charts?"

"Of course." Sek spoke mildly. She ran her palm across a nearby screen. "Here."

Dreams-of-War studied the map that unscrolled itself across the surface of the screen. There, at the far bottom corner, lay Fragrant Harbor: a tiny scattering of islands bisected by the wide waterways. Dreams-of-War touched a finger up the splintered coast to a skein of islands: the southern reach of Hakodate. They were heading for the port of Ischa. She looked through the porthole. The sea stretched before her, untroubled. Dreams-of-War walked to the other side of the cabin. Nothing but water until the far horizon.

"Why can't I see the coast?"

"Because we are too far out to sea," Sek said patiently.

"Why are we not following the coastline? Would it not be safer, given the chance of storms?"

"There are dark-ships that lurk in the inlets and islands. I deemed it best that we sail the open sea."

"Dark-ships? Do you mean pirates?"

"Of a kind. There are marauders all along this coast. They do not seek to enslave or steal; they seek to destroy. They speak of holy waters, of violation by the shipping trade. They come from nowhere, their ships materializing in clouds of mist. They use old, half-forgotten technologies. No one knows much about them. No one would wish to."

Dreams-of-War tapped impatient fingers on the surface of the screen. "Yesterday you spoke of Dragon-Kings. What of them?"

"How much do you know of the Dragon-Kings?"

"I believed them to be a myth. I have been doing some research. I now know that they are rare, dangerous, their origins unknown. I also know that they can rise up and cause even the greatest vessels to disappear."

Sek nodded. "Essentially accurate. They hunt alone, emerging from the deep seabed."

"And you said that you glimpsed one on the voyage here?"

"In the distance. A shell was seen. We lowered the sail, which can attract their attention—or so it is said. No one knows for certain. It came no closer."

Dreams-of-War frowned. "Where are we now? Are we anywhere near the place where you saw the Dragon-King?"

"The chart should show the junk's passage. And no, it was farther north."

When Dreams-of-War looked more closely, she saw that this was so. The junk appeared as a minute crimson dot, trailing slowly across the screen like a leaking droplet of blood, leaving a faint wake behind it. Yet she still did not understand why they were so far out to sea. The junk looped away from Fragrant Harbor. It had been Dreams-of-War's understanding that the junk was heading directly for the Fire Islands.

She glanced at Sek, whose face was turned to the sea. Sek appeared as serene as a stone.

"What are you looking for? Land? Or danger?"

"Both, or either," Sek replied absently. "Does your armor give you farsight?"

"It can," Dreams-of-War admitted. "But possibly no better than those binoculars."

"Look through them. Tell me what you see."

Dreams-of-War did so. After a moment, she found the faint line of the horizon and scanned it. The line—darker water, paler sky—was unbroken.

"I see no land. Yet we are supposed to be nearing the southern reaches of Hakodate and I can see no sign of it. I thought I saw smoke this morning. A volcano."

"There is a single peak surrounded by islets. The weather has been gentle. You see for yourself; the water is placid as milk and there has been little wind. We cannot have strayed off course."

"Perhaps your instruments are malfunctioning," Dreams-of-War suggested.

"The crew are checking them now. Did you come here merely to question me about our course?"

Dreams-of-War thought back to that dawn glimpse: the woman with artificial legs spread, the thing poised above her, drilling inward, and was glad that the armor concealed a shudder. "No. I have a question about a woman. I assume she is another passenger and not one of your crew."

"Ah." Sek smiled. "You mean Yskatarina Iye. The woman with the ornamental limbs."

"I did not see her onboard when we arrived."

"That is because she was not here at that point. She arrived by speed-scull in the night."

"Just so. This morning—" Dreams-of-War paused, reluctant to conjure once more the scene that she had witnessed. She chided herself for cowardice. "I saw her in one of the cabins. In sexual congress with a—thing."

"That is her companion."

Dreams-of-War stared at her. "You knew about this?"

"How not? It accompanied her on board; it belongs to her."

"But what is it?"

"I have been given to understand that it is a bio-artifact, at once a kind of artistic representation and the repository of her family's memories."

"I have never seen such a thing before," Dreams-of-War said.

"No? Yet it seemed to me that it is in part the same kind of technology as that armor you wear. Sentient, aware, capable of storing and interpreting information, old memories. Capable of acting independently." Sek looked at Dreams-of-War and a faint smile crossed her mouth, like a ghost's.

"I do not rely upon my armor for sexual gratification," Dreams-of-War said, cold as the sea.

Sek shrugged. "That is your affair. And what Yskatarina does with her creature is her own business."

"And her arms and legs? An accident? A birth defect?"

"I have not liked to ask. She had her prosthetic limbs shipped aboard shortly after her arrival. Sometimes they are metal, encrusted with ornamentation; she showed me a pair that end in claws like the feet of a great bird. They can be used for battle. Perhaps you should discuss it with her." Sek turned back to her contemplation of the horizon and reached out a hand for her binoculars.

"But where does she come from? Was she born on Earth?" *Were you?* Dreams-of-War almost said, but bit back the words.

"I do not know," Sek said blandly. "Perhaps she is from the North. There are many people there who come unwhole from the growing-skins, who are genetically affected by ancient disasters. I have seen others like Yskatarina. We all bear our wounds as best we may. It is not my business."

"I can see something," Dreams-of-War said. It was nothing more than a speck, coming fast across the sea. Thoughts of Dragon-Kings, of pirates, of unknown dangers raced through her head. Dreams-of-War touched the helmet control at her throat and in a second, her head was encased within the armor's hood.

"Sight," Dreams-of-War said. Her voice echoed within the confines of the helmet. The visor ratcheted up its magnification until Dreams-of-War could see the oncoming thing more clearly.

It was black and shining. Bands of jade light played along its sides, like a small traveling storm. Something much larger was carried within it: a hunched shape. As she watched, the edges of the cloud split and broke apart, shattering into a thousand whirling fragments before reforming. It seemed to be a flock of something very small, bearing a thing the size of a human.

"What is *that?*" breathed Dreams-of-War.

Sek grasped the wiring of the helm.

"I do not know!" The words snapped back through the calm air. Dreams-of-War sprinted along the deck, heading for Lunae's cabin.

The cabin was a place of peace. Soft air drifted through the open window; light marbled the ceiling so that the cabin resembled an underwater sanctuary. Lunae was sitting on the bench, reading something on an antiscribe, and the kappa was occupying herself with a mess of tangled knitting.

"Bolt the porthole," Dreams-of-War ordered.

Lunae looked up in alarm. "What's happening?"

"We're under attack."

"From what?" The kappa was gaping at her.

"A cloud of *things*. Do you know what they might be?"

The kappa's eyes opened wide. "I have no idea."

Lunae was scrambling from the bench, her face fierce. For a moment, Dreams-of-War barely recognized her. "I can take care of it! Let me, Guardian."

"No!" Dreams-of-War said, swallowing a bolt of pride. "It's some kind of swarm; you can't grasp it as you did the assassin. Besides, it's too dangerous. We don't know what the consequences might be." She pictured Lunae ending up in the middle of the ocean. "We stay here, with the door locked. The crew will take care of it." She hated being left out of a fight.

They waited: Dreams-of-War poised by the door, blades bristling, the kappa holding tightly to Lunae's resisting hand. Dreams-of-War closed her eyes for a moment, to listen. There was something whirring overhead, a sound like an orthocopter, shouts, a deafening crashing crack. The junk shuddered.

"What was that?" the kappa quavered. "Is the mast down?"

"How should I know?" It was all Dreams-of-War could do not to throw open the door and run onto the deck. A second later, she did not have to.

The side of the cabin exploded inward in a shower of splinters. In the exposed gap appeared whirling blades, a mass of black propellers. The air was filled with something sparkling and hot. Dreams-of-War thrust her longest knife into the nearest row of blades. Metal shrieked on metal. The front part of the swarm swung up and over, headed downward. She glimpsed the passenger behind, riding on a cloud of knives.

"Armor!" she cried, intending to protect Lunae, but it was too late. The kappa, seizing Lunae by the hand, dragged her through the gap and was gone over the side of the junk before Dreams-of-War could utter a word of protest.

Cursing, Dreams-of-War caught the rider by the back of the hood and hauled it to its feet. It was wheezing, but it stamped and flailed, striking out at her. It spat out a sticky ochre stream that trickled down her armor, leaving molten metal in its wake. It reached no further than the armor's epidermis, but Dreams-of-War was outraged. She tore away the hood to find a reptilian face. A forked tongue snaked out from a mouth ringed with teeth. Dreams-of-War seized the tongue between finger and thumb, armorservos on maximum, and gave a short, sharp tug. The entire jaw tore away, leaving a bloody, gaping hole.

Dreams-of-War flung the jaw over the side in disgust and peered into the remains. A brain, definitely, but differently lobed than a human's. Dreams-of-War let the thing fall to the deck and rushed to the side of the boat. Sek was ducking beneath the sail, shouting out.

"Princess! See what it's brought . . ."

Dreams-of-War, hanging half over the rail, ignored her. There was no sign of either Lunae or the kappa, only the churning, foam-flecked sea and something rising from it.

CHAPTER 15

EARTH

The kappa moved with such uncharacteristic swiftness that Lunae had been taken aback. As they hurtled through the gaping hole in the cabin wall, toward the railing, she tried to pull free, but the kappa held her hand tightly in a clammy grip. She tried to shift time, but something constricted her throat and brain, sending wire-hot pain through her synapses. She remembered the sudden sparkling of the air——but then they were over the side of the junk and falling.

The kappa dived like an arrow, clutching Lunae to her breast. They hit the water with a great rush of sound, and then were down under the waves. Lunae was dazzled by light and water. It was like being encased in shining green stone, fading to darkness as they sank. The breath had been knocked out of her. She thought her lungs would burst, her head explode, but the kappa's grip was like an iron band. She saw the kappa's mouth gape open, skeins of air stream forth. A slitted fan opened at the kappa's throat, but Lunae was choking on water. The kappa kicked out. They began to rise toward the light, broke out through the surface of the sea. Lunae took a rasping breath of clean air. Her eyes burned with salt. She saw a tiny red square, far behind them: the junk, sailing swiftly on. The kappa's mouth was open, her face appalled, her gaze fixed on a point just beyond Lunae's shoulder.

"I don't——" she started to say. Lunae squirmed around.

Something was coming up behind them: an immense length of curving shell. Spokes rose from it, fanning out into gleaming silver-black petals. Water streamed past as Lunae and the kappa were caught in the lattice of the spokes. Lunae reached out and clung to them; they felt like wet bone. The kappa's eyes were wide—with fear, awe, realization. Bubbles poured from her gills like a collar of pearls.

Lunae, still clutching the lattice, lay gasping on the curve of the shell. It was, she noted distantly, warm, like damp ceramic. She raised her head and looked down its vast length. More spokes were sailing up from the gaping joints of the shell, forming a webbed network. The shell now bore a fan behind it: the spokes unfurling like someone opening a great, many-fingered fist. Each one was at least twice the length of the mast of the junk. Lunae had never known that something so big existed beneath the waves.

"What is it?"

"It is a Dragon-King," the kappa breathed. The webbed lattice did, Lunae thought, look very much like the ruff of an imperial dragon, but there was a grinding sound deep within, an engine-hum.

"It's a machine!"

She saw the kappa nod. But then the joint below them began to open. Lunae glimpsed a thousand-foot mesh of gears, coils, flickering lights as the lattice started to withdraw. She tried to hang on, but the wet struts moved easily and swiftly through her hands. The portion of shell on which they lay curved more sharply yet. Lunae and the kappa started to slide toward the open joint. Lunae, panicking, tried to hold on and could not. The bone strut retracted fully. Her hands scrabbled briefly on the surface of the shell, and then she was slipping down toward the joint. Her last glimpse was of the shell arching above her, blotting out the stormy sky, and then, frantic, she thought to reach inside her mind and twist time.

CHAPTER 16

EARTH

Dreams-of-War watched, frozen, as the Dragon-King rose up from the sea. It was perhaps a half-mile or more from the junk, but it towered up from the churning waves like an island. Six black necks spanned out from either end of its carapace, terminating in flat spatulate heads that probed the air. Water poured down the sides of its shell. She could see the joints that separated the segments begin to split open. Spines emerged from within.

She heard Sek cry, "Turn! Turn the ship around!"

Ponderously, lurching on a heaving sea, the junk began to spin. Dreams-of-War grasped Sek by a tattooed arm.

"Send out a boat! We have to find Lunae."

Sek turned on her, face snarling, voice calm. "We cannot. The junk is listing; there is a hole in the hull. That thing launched a bolt of fire; we have only just brought it under control. You see what awaits us on the horizon, what demon. My ship cries out in anguish; I can spare no time."

"You do not have to. Issue me a dinghy, a raft—anything. I will set out upon a tea tray, if I must."

"Can you not see?" Sek pointed to the horizon, and the thing that rose up against a green boiling cloud.

"My ward—"

"She is with her nurse. I saw them go over the side. The kappa can breathe beneath the waves. It will be in its element."

"Lunae is a made-human, not a mutated sea-breathing thing. What if she drowns?"

"The kappa will keep her safe. My concern is for my ship. The demon is waiting."

"That is no demon," Dreams-of-War said. "What you call a Dragon-King is an antiquated sea-schemer—a weather-control device. Old Martian tech. I recognized the thing immediately."

"Whatever the case, it's dangerous. It could swallow this vessel whole." Sek grabbed a passing crewwoman, issued urgent orders. "See?"

Curdled cloud occupied the whole of the eastern horizon. Dreams-of-War had never seen such a sight, not even during the worst of all Dust Seasons of the Crater Plain. The jade clouds towered hundreds of feet above the sea, anvil heads forming and collapsing within seconds. Lightning flashed, green as the eye of a god.

"It is starting its work, that is all," Dreams-of-War said. "It is summoning a storm. Who knows why? Its programming is probably damaged."

"And in a moment, the seabed will move beneath us and this vessel will go down. I need to speak with the ship." A moment later, Sek was gone below.

Dreams-of-War hung over the side, desperately searching for sight of Lunae, but the sea was a heaving mass of cold. From behind her, a voice said, "I may be able to help, should you wish."

Dreams-of-War turned. The woman named Yskatarina Iye stood behind her, balancing on serrated metal legs. Above the rising wind, Dreams-of-War could hear the faint whirring of the servomechanisms, keeping her supported and upright. Yskatarina's pale face peered forth from a voluminous bundle of garments. Black metal glinted between sheaves of wool and velvet; something stirred beneath Yskatarina's cloak. The woman's face was remote and cold. Dreams-of-War forced herself to remain where she was and not to step back.

"How?" Dreams-of-War asked. "And more to the point, why?"

Yskatarina spread a protective hand across her breast, caressing something within the gathered cloak. "We are fellow passengers, and I sorrow for your loss. My companion can help you." There was no shame in her face, Dreams-of-War noted with disgust, only a distant, reflective wistfulness. "I can send him out, to scan the sea."

"Thank you," Dreams-of-War said, startled into courtesy by this unexpected offer. "But Sek told me that the thing is very old, containing the memories of your family. I'm surprised you'd risk it. And why should I trust you?"

Yskatarina Iye laughed. "Perhaps you should not. And my companion is not so easily destroyed. Maybe you will have a chance to see what he can do. Come with me."

"I think not."

Yskatarina spread artificial hands. "You have other options, perhaps?"

Dreams-of-War was silent.

"At least let me make a few suggestions. Come."

With misgivings, Dreams-of-War followed Yskatarina down the swaying steps and into the cabin.

The room was bare except for a slablike bed and a long metal chest. Slats of wood were piled against the walls, and there was a strong smell of the sea. The place felt damp. The memory of Yskatarina Iye, legs splayed, face contorted, rose uncomfortably to mind. Dreams-of-War felt her own skin growing hot beneath the armor.

"You travel light," Dreams-of-War said.

"I had it sent on," Yskatarina said, following Dreams-of-War's gaze toward the chest. "It contains my limbs, my garments." She drew aside her robes. The creature uncoiled itself; the black glittering eyes fixed on Dreams-of-War. Long fingers flexed and curled, twice the length of a human's and multijointed. Now that Dreams-of-War could study the thing at greater leisure, she saw that the long head was more skull-like than insectoid, terminating in a narrow mandibular mouth. Protuberances, like thin coiled horns, emerged from either side of the skull. Facedown and horizontal, the thing would resemble a thin, horned scorpion. The tip of its tail bristled with unknown armory. It was covered in a slick black-and-iron hide. Wing points showed above its narrow shoulders.

The creature slid downward until balanced on the coiled tip of its tail. It crossed its limbs over its narrow breast and hissed. Dreams-of-War glimpsed a long tongue inside its convoluted mouth. There was no sign of the drill-like phallus.

"Isn't he beautiful?" Yskatarina said softly.

"What *is* it?"

"He is a bio-organism, manufactured in the first of the lunar laboratories, before the moon was blighted," Yskatarina said smoothly. Her smile became condescending. "But I suppose you have encountered few male beings."

"Obviously not. Hyenae, and awts," Dreams-of-War said with disdain. *Nor do I wish to make the acquaintance of another.*

She could not help wondering about the nature of that lunar laboratory. It must be old, for the lunar colonies had fallen two hundred years ago, overrun by stone-plague. Besides, Yskatarina's creature went beyond mere practicalities, was surely sculpted into perversity. She had never heard of such things being made on the moon. A toy, perhaps, from a day when sexual behavior was still the norm? Or was Yskatarina simply lying and the thing originated somewhere else entirely? Dreams-of-War repressed a shudder.

"They have their uses, believe me," Yskatarina said.

"I'm sure."

Yskatarina's face was reflective. She looked Dreams-of-War up and down. "Perhaps if you relinquished that armor, we could show you."

"I have no intention of removing my armor. You said you would help me."

The memory of the Dragon-King boiling up out of the ocean flickered at the forefront of Dreams-of-War's brain. What was the great machine doing now? Were they about to be consumed? She thought of Lunae floating down through turmoil and weed, and momentarily despaired. "Best that I go, I think."

"Wait one moment. I overheard your conversation with Sek," Yskatarina said. "The kappa took your ward?"

"Yes. They went over the side before I could stop them."

"If she is in the water with a kappa, even under such circumstances, it is likely that she will be safe. How much do you know about the kappa?"

"I have never thought to inquire."

Yskatarina gave a brief, dry smile. "No, I suppose you did not. But they are water-breathing, after all. My companion can carry a person upon his back, to search the sea." Yskatarina's manner was earnest. "He is very strong, but the armor will weigh him down unless you remove it."

"No!"

"Then reduce it to its minimum setting. It will be easier that way."

"I shall not."

But the woman had a point. What other means of locating Lunae did she have? She could not set forth in one of the sculls, not on this heaving sea. Dreams-of-War hesitated. The prospect of a trap loomed large. She had no reason to trust Yskatarina, or her sinister creature. She could, perhaps, remain on board and wait, but Dreams-of-War was loath to take this particular course. Action, of whatever kind, was the only viable solution.

"Very well," Dreams-of-War said, with poor grace. "Armor!"

Liquid flowed across her skin, redefining itself until it was only a thin epidermal covering.

The creature reached out a spidery limb and drew a finger down Dreams-of-War's breastbone. Dreams-of-War leaped back. "Never touch me!"

The creature's mandibles opened in wet anticipation. She could see the probing tongue within. A chill trickle was snaking its way down her body, where the thing had touched her, but she was covered by the armor. She must be imagining things, she thought.

She followed Yskatarina and the creature onto the deck.

The creature opened spiny gossamer wings. Its head went back, as if in exultation. Dreams-of-War wondered if it relished the sudden freedom. Impossible to know what went on in its mind, if anything.

"Climb on," Yskatarina Iye said.

Dreams-of-War once more hesitated. She pictured herself falling from the back of the thing, spinning down into the waves. If the creature had designs upon her life, she would make sure that she took it with her.

She placed her feet on either side of the thing's tail, and put her hands on its shoulders. The touch sent a shudder through her. Revolting, to be so close to another being.

"Armor!" Her fingers stretched, elongated, and wrapped around the creature's shoulders, securing Dreams-of-War to its back. Yskatarina Iye watched with some amusement.

"He won't let you fall," Yskatarina said.

"I've made sure of that," Dreams-of-War informed her.

The creature spread its wings and they were up in a rush. Dreams-of-War did not even have time to gasp. The thing's body moved beneath her, sinuous and strong.

Dreams-of-War stared grimly ahead. The junk fell behind, and then there was only the sea.

THE TEMPLE

CHAPTER 1

ELSEWHERE

The ocean, the storm, and the Dragon-King were gone. Lunae and the kappa, drenched with seawater, stood on dry land before an empty reach.

Here, everything was drawn in shades of black and gray, silver and shadow, as far as a ridge of mountains that ran around the perimeter of the horizon. The mountains themselves were red and jagged. Even from this distance, Lunae could see every rock and crag, delineated in a sharp, cold light. Yet there was no sign of sun or moon. The sky stretched above them, an opalescent lid upon the bowl of the world. Lunae looked for the outlines of the Chain and found them, but they were contorted and shattered. She could see a black light flicker in the heavens, as though a maw had been snapped by some immense force and left the gateway to the Eldritch Realm exposed. The sight filled her with horror; she had to look away.

Reeds rustled at their feet, in a wind that could not be felt. A river, perhaps ten feet or so in width, slid between deep banks of black earth, but it looked more like oil than water, sluggish and slow.

"Where is this place?" the kappa whispered.

"I don't know. But I think I've been here before. I think this was where I took the assassin." Lunae looked around, dry-mouthed and wary, but there was no one to be seen, only the grass and the reeds. "Can you breathe?"

"Yes, without difficulty." The kappa turned to face Lunae, eyes round with panic. "Where have you brought us?"

"Kappa, I told you, I do not know. I don't even know if this is Earth. Do you think we could be on Mars? Those summits are red."

The kappa stumped down to the river, sliding a little on the dense, packed earth, and dipped a cautious forefinger in. She snatched it back. "It burns! This place is poisoned. I can feel it. The earth, the water—all is wrong." She stumbled with difficulty back up the bank. "Still, we are no longer on the cursed vessel. That is one good thing." She wrung thick fingers. "Can you take us back, to a place of safety?"

Lunae looked at her nurse. "But I have no idea how to navigate through time. I haven't been able to learn. I can move forward and back a little way, enough to snatch someone from the world or get out of trouble, but you have to understand that I don't really know what I'm doing. I don't even know what I *am*, or how I'm able to do what I do. A *hito-bashira*, so they tell me, but what is that? And you? Do you know anything about me? I sometimes feel, kappa, that this placidity of yours is nothing more than a disguise." She gestured around her. "There is nothing and no one here. No one to overhear, no one to report back to the Grandmothers—if they still live—or anyone else. If you know anything, tell me now."

The kappa stared at her, once more seeming unhuman, unknown, the eyes aglow in the moon of her face.

"I will tell you this. It is as much as I or you know: that you were created by the Grandmothers."

"I know that. But why? And what is a *hito-bashira*?"

"A *hito-bashira*, a woman-who-holds-back-the-flood, is a person who is not tied to time, but one who can move through it at will, as you do."

"But that's the principle behind haunt-tech, isn't it? That spirit and flesh are not one and can be separated?"

"Spirits can be summoned through time, but no spirit can exist without a living body. I think you are a combination: a living person whose spirit behaves as though it were free of the time stream, and who can move yourself and others through it."

"But what does it mean—hold back the flood? And are there others like me?"

"I believe that it means that there will be a certain event, in which your ability to alter time will prove crucial. I do not know the form that this event will take. The Grandmothers did not discuss it with me. I know only what I overheard them say, and they were careful when they spoke in front of me."

"What did they say?"

"That you would know what to do when the barrier was breached and the time came," the kappa said. "As for sisters—yes, there were others, but as you know, they died. I do not think there are any other beings like you, Lunae. Whatever your kind might be, it is unstable. The flesh does not withstand it so well."

"How did they die?" Lunae asked.

"One withered in the skin. When the time came to open it, so the Grandmothers told me, something small and shrunken and ancient fell forth. Another passed through time upon emergence, flickering past their sight until there was nothing left but a bag of bones. Another—disappeared, after weeks of growth. And one would not grow at all, but remained as an infant for a few days, before the opposite process occurred. She shrank back into a fetal state over the course of a week, becoming smaller and smaller until there was nothing there, only a droplet of blood like the eye of a demon. I have told you all that I know. Truly. My purpose in the household was to nurture you, and I have done this to the best of my ability."

Lunae smiled at the kappa, thinking how strange it was to be undergoing this conversation here, on this unknown plain, between these alien crags. "Your ability has been great."

The kappa sighed. "I do not know if I have succeeded. Here we stand, in a place that seems to be no place at all. We have lost your guardian; the world we know is gone. I confess, I do not know what we should do next."

"I can try to take us out of time again," Lunae offered, but something within her shrank at the notion.

"It is so unpredictable. Unless it is truly necessary"—*Unless we are once more attacked*, Lunae could see the kappa refrain from saying—"you should hold back."

"I agree. We can't stay here. I think we should start walking and see what we can find."

"In that case, we should follow the river."

Lunae looked dubiously at the glistening water.

"If it is, indeed, a real river, and not merely a toxic drain."

"Even a toxic drain must lead somewhere." The kappa turned and began waddling along the stony bank.

CHAPTER 2

EARTH

Dreams-of-War and Yskatarina's companion flew across the water. She looked down on a turgid swell. Glancing to either side, she saw the creature's wings reach out in a graceful sweep of black lace wire, seemingly too fragile to ride the churning winds. Pulses of information, of a complexity that the armor was unable to analyze, snapped along the synapses of the creature's spidery limbs and ran along the interiors of the horns. Some kind of broadcasting equipment, or sonar. But Dreams-of-War also detected a kind of exultation running through the thing—an emotion that was familiar and yet entirely unhuman.

"You will not understand me, passenger," the thing warned. Its voice hummed and buzzed inside her mind like a distant hive.

"I do not intend to try," Dreams-of-War replied.

"You should approve of me," the creature said, very sly. "Am I not a made-thing, like all higher forms of life?"

"You are clearly one of the Changed."

"Parts of me lived and died as men," the thing informed her.

"As men? Or humans?"

"The former."

"I am unfamiliar with male things," Dreams-of-War said curtly. The creature wheeled, wings breaking the crest of a vast curl of wave. "There are few of them left."

"Have you ever met a man, girl of Mars?" The voice was sidling, filled with mockery.

"As I told your mistress"—unfortunate term, but she had spoken too quickly—"I am familiar with men-remnants. There are a handful in the amusement circuses in Caud. They keep them for sport. And there are those that live in the hills: hyenae, vulpen, awts—mutations all. But they are the brute form, with little intellect left."

"Amusement parks," the creature voice said with wonder. "Yes, I have been to Mars. It does not surprise me."

Was there mockery in that inner echo? Almost certainly.

"Why should humanity bother with outmoded and antique dualities, or with the complications of outworn instincts? We are all made-beings now, with no need of mating, of sex, of the desires and emotions that are thereby entailed. Pleasure can be attained through devices."

"Do you attain it so?"

"That is none of your business!" Dreams-of-War snapped. "But, in point of fact, I do not bother. I consider pleasure to be overrated. Loyalty and power are all that matter." But again, that maternal rip and twang whenever she thought of Lunae . . . *Loyalty*, she thought. *It is all loyalty, all duty. There is no need to think of love.*

"Indeed," the thing agreed with a mild peacefulness. "We are all made. Now, take note and care. We are close to the storm's heart."

Dreams-of-War looked toward the far horizon. The storm crackled with green fire along its edge. There was no longer any sign of the Dragon-King.

"That machine should have been destroyed," Dreams-of-War snapped. "Such things are dangerous, running on ancient programming. And what is it *doing* here? There are some in the Small Sea, but I recall no attempt by Mars to reform this world after the Drowning."

"Perhaps not. But it seems attempts were made, nevertheless," the creature said. "I believe that the storm is a byproduct of its weather-control operations."

"Can lightning affect you?" Dreams-of-War asked. She was not exactly afraid, riding upon the body of this creation, but she could not help but wonder what might befall her should the creature be struck down.

"Of course," the creature said, surprised. "I am enduring, not indestructible."

"It was kind, then, of Yskatarina to lend you to me," Dreams-of-War said grudgingly, but she wondered what Yskatarina's motives really were. Kindness surely did not enter into them. "Could her family build another, if you are destroyed?"

"Perhaps," the creature said. "Look downward. Can you see it?"

Dreams-of-War peered ahead. They were approaching a great roil of water, a canopy of sea-spouts rising up from the waves, drawn on the wind. The green fire flashed between them, casting the sea beneath into pools of grassy light. Dreams-of-War had a sudden longing for desert, for the bleak endlessness of sand.

"I see the storm," she said.

"No, not the storm. The machine."

Focus ratcheted in as the armor undertook visual adjustment, and now Dreams-of-War could see the Dragon-King below. The weather-forming machine had split, its parts separating so that she could see within it. Its interior was studded with wrecks: a metal vortex of captured shipping, contorted and welded to the lattice. At the heart of it, half-consumed, lay a liner bigger than any she had ever seen. Its prow rose up as an immense double arch: It had clearly been some kind of hydrofoil. It was perhaps a mile or more in length.

"What is that ship?" Dreams-of-War demanded. "Where does it come from?" She did not know of any city-state that had possessed such a large vessel.

"It is from the far past."

"What? They had no such vessels then, surely. Are we going down to the machine?" Dreams-of-War asked. But surely this was far from where Lunae had fallen into the water, and if she had somehow been drawn into this huge device . . . Dreams-of-War, with woe, realized that she would not know where to start looking. No matter, she told herself. The armor would know, since it had imprinted Lunae.

But the creature said swiftly, "No. We must not; it is too dangerous."

"Unstable, you mean?"

"In a manner of speaking." The thing turned, gliding at the edges of the storm. "I have scanned the waves all this while. There is no sign of your companions. And below, I can sense, there are small swarms of creatures, but they are not human."

"Are you sure? Then what are they?"

"Made-creatures. The creations of the one who piloted this vessel. The girl is not among them."

"Then Lunae is drowned," Dreams-of-War whispered, and felt herself grow cold. The armor had detected no trace.

"Do not give up hope just yet." The creature arced above a wave, dived down through icy spray.

"Wait!" Dreams-of-War cried, but the creature was already flying swiftly back to the junk. "Wait, I—" But the sea was speeding beneath them.

CHAPTER 3

EARTH

In the light cast by the lamp, the Animus's hide gleamed bloodred. It lay coiled before the antiscribe, the lenses flickering before its eyes. Yskatarina watched as information unskeined itself, unraveling from the faceted eyes of the Animus down into the antiscribe's lenses. She knew that it was only illusion, a whimsical by-product of the download process, but it seemed strange all the same, to see these numbers and letters drifting through the air like moths.

"There was no sign of her? You are certain?"

"There was no sign. I tasted her DNA from a hair she shed on the deck. I would be able to sense her if she had been anywhere within the radius of my sonar."

Yskatarina shook her head, pacing the confines of the cabin. "The thing that attacked us was one of Prince Cataract's creatures, I am sure."

"You think it was aiming at you and me, rather than the girl?"

"I believe Prince Cataract's children are seeking revenge." She paused. "He was not the kindest parent, perhaps, but all they knew, and they were male, and bred for war and vengeance, too, perhaps. And now Lunae is lost. If she has drowned . . . Well, Elaki will be pleased. But not I." Yskatarina slapped her palm down on the table. "I still do not understand why she is so important to Elaki. We have to keep looking for her. I will speak to Sek."

"Yet something good has come out of this, at least. We have more understanding of that piece of armor."

"You are sure that you have all the specifications?" Yskatarina asked. "That armor is the key to the ship, I'm sure of it. Prince Cataract suggested as much, and I have spoken to the former

Matriarch. The Kami has accessed some of its memories. Embar Khair went with the Grandmothers when they traveled from Memnos to Earth. She was the one who flew the ship. Two pieces of early haunt-tech, both connected. Understand that armor, and we understand the ship."

"I answered you before," the Animus murmured. "I have it all."

"And she suspected nothing?" Yskatarina paused. "More to the point, the *armor* suspected nothing? I would not be surprised if the Martian failed to see her hand in front of her face on a clear day."

"I do not know what the Martian may have thought. I cannot see inside her head."

Yskatarina sighed. There were times when the Animus was overliteral, or perhaps it was just that his thoughts ran upon a different track. "But the armor?"

"I do not know. I don't think so. I was careful."

"It should not have been able to tell," Yskatarina mused. "It is an old piece of tech."

The Animus turned back to the antiscribe. In silence, Yskatarina watched the codes ratchet down into nothingness.

"It is done," the Animus said.

"Good." Her eyes met those of the Animus. "Nothing of this goes back to Nightshade. I am working for myself now. For *us*."

"Do you miss it?" the Animus asked. "Your loyalty and love for her?" There was a curious sadness in his artificial voice and it struck Yskatarina as strange, then, that out of all those whom she had known, it sometimes seemed that the Animus was the one who most completely understood what it was to love.

"No," she said slowly. "I do not miss it. Memnos has freed me from her." She touched a hand to the Animus's claw. "All of these elements—the Martian's armor, Prince Cataract, the Dragon-King—all are links in the chain that will get us to a place of power. Trust me."

The Animus stared at her. "You want Nightshade."

"Yes," Yskatarina said, very softly. "I have become sick of being controlled by others. I want Nightshade. And then I want more."

CHAPTER 4

ELSEWHERE

The plain was littered with chasms and boulders, obliging Lunae and the kappa to follow the lower banks of the river. They made slow progress and at last the kappa sank down onto a nearby rock.

"I can go no farther. My feet hurt."

Lunae sat disconsolately beside her. "So do mine." She had tucked the skirts of her robe up under the sash, but already the hem had become ragged and frayed, torn on the sharp stones.

"And there is nothing to eat," the kappa said after a pause.

"Or drink."

They looked at each other.

"Lunae, I think you are going to have to move us once again. I know why you're reluctant. Believe me, I share it. But even so . . ."

They sat in silence for a few minutes.

"We ought to try to rest," Lunae said at last. The kappa looked as miserable, footsore, and hungry as she herself felt. The kappa nodded.

"I suppose so."

Together, they scraped aside the loose stones, revealing a thick layer of earth, then wrapped themselves in their garments as best they could and lay down, back to back. Lunae lay awake for what seemed to be hours, worrying about the kappa, Dreams-of-War, herself. At last she fell into an uneasy doze, plagued by strange half-waking dreams in which the Grandmothers, separate now, stood over her and berated her in their echoing voices.

Then she was fully awake. The strange twilight glow was unchanged, but she could hear voices, carried on the wind that was now blowing over the rocks and striking her face with a hot sift of sand.

Free us. Free us. We would be free . . .

The words were unchanging and desperate.

"Who are you?" Lunae whispered. "Where are you?"

But there was no answer, only the wind-borne voices, speaking now in a multiplicity of tongues. The kappa rolled over, to lie blinking and alarmed amid the stones.

"Lunae! What is it?"

"I can hear voices." She seized the kappa by the arm.

But the kappa was staring. "What is *that?*"

Away to the left, a patch of earth was beginning to move, congealing until it formed a globule of black liquid, shot with blood red. It began to rise, gathering the thin soil into itself and liquefying it. Lunae helped the kappa to her feet and they started to back away, but more areas of soil were assuming form. A face appeared at the crest of the first shape; distorted into a silent howl.

The kappa said suddenly, "Look!"

Something was floating above the horizon, catching the unseen light like a diamond.

"What is it?"

It was gliding swiftly over the rocks: a teardrop in the sky.

"It's a wet-ship," the kappa said.

Lunae began to wave frantically. A forest of shapes was emerging around them, the voices crying out once more, pleading and begging. And now the wet-ship was drifting downward, pulsing gently, to land beside them.

The woman who stepped from the wet-ship was, at first, transparent: Lunae could see the rocks through her body. She wore a long, loose shift colored ruby, like the sail of the junk. Her face was oval, her eyes blue. Russet hair was piled upon her head between a pair of coiled horns.

"Who are you?" Lunae breathed.

As she walked swiftly forward, the woman became more solid. The translucence faded. Her lips were moving, but no sound emerged. Then, her voice suddenly came into phase, a blurring glide of speech that resolved itself into Lunae's own tongue.

"I am Essa," the woman said. She glanced at the forms emerging from the soil. "And we must leave. Now, before they assume their whole form. They won't be able to sustain it for long, but it will be long enough."

The kappa bustled up behind her, agitated.

"Tersus Rhee," the horned woman said, turning.

The kappa rocked back. "You know my name?"

"You have a name?" Lunae said, startled.

"Come," Essa said. Skirting the forms, she took Lunae and the kappa by the hands. Her skin felt cool and smooth, not quite human. Lunae hung back. "Quickly," Essa said sharply. "It will not take them long."

The forms were towering now, six feet in height and more. The tortured faces dangled from thin necks and the columns of their bloodshot bodies were starting to grow limbs.

"But what are they?"

"The last remnants of bio-tech. There are not many left. Be thankful." Swiftly, Essa led them to the wet-ship.

"I'm taking you to a place of safety. Relative safety, at least. Go in. Just touch it."

Lunae put out a hand. The wet-ship slid up her arm. There was a gasping, drowning moment as the surface slipped across her face, and then she was inside. The kappa and Essa followed. Reaching down, Lunae ran an experimental hand over the floor. Her fingers passed across it, and came away with a wet sheen.

There were no visible controls within the water-pod, only a low curving seat.

"There are no straps? No means of containment?" The kappa was visibly nervous. Lunae could not blame her.

"None are needed. Sit."

Lunae did so. Again, she touched the side of the pod. Again, her hand was moistened. "How do you get it to hold together?" Lunae asked in fascination. She had heard of such things on Earth, but never seen them.

"It is an old technology. I cannot answer your question, for I do not know," Essa said, and reached out to stroke a glistening wing. The craft rose, faltered, then dipped over the plain, leaving the half-formed beings far behind.

"Where are we?" the kappa asked.

"Mars. Or what is left of it."

"Mars?"

Essa stroked the side of the ship and it moved into a steep glide, sliding down the hazy air toward a chasm.

Lunae had a sudden glimpse into the heart of the chasm. A bristling mass like a great sea urchin lay below, nestling between the cliff walls. Shadows wreathed its spines. It moved gently, in and out, as though impelled by breath. A face swam up from the cobwebby depths, mouthing something in fear or anger. Next moment, it was gone, like a ghost in sunlight. Lunae jerked back. Essa showed no sign that anything unusual had occurred. She touched a wing. The craft veered, then sailed out toward the curve of the world and the red range.

CHAPTER 5

EARTH

So," Yskatarina said. "You did not find them. I am sorry."

"Do not be sorry yet," Dreams-of-War told her. "For they *will* be found."

The creature had been folded up in a huddle of legs and wings in a corner when she had next come to see Yskatarina. Dreams-of-War turned her back on it. She could still feel its presence, like a spider, sticky and itching. She had no desire to be in the same room as the thing for a moment longer than she had to. And she did not feel much happier about Yskatarina.

"Can we talk outside?" she said abruptly to Yskatarina.

Yskatarina bowed her sleek head. "Of course. I have spoken to Sek. The Dragon-King has dived. The storm has gone with it; the air on deck will be fresher."

Dreams-of-War thought of Yskatarina seducing the creature, or perhaps the one who had been seduced, and shuddered. She was thankful to close the cabin door behind her.

When she stepped onto the deck, she saw that Yskatarina had been correct. The storm had passed; the horizon lay in an untroubled line. The air was warm and humid, covering her armor with a mist of droplets. Sek's crew worked to repair the fallen sails, which spilled over the deck like blood. Dreams-of-War remembered the swarm and its passenger.

"Your creature," she began. Yskatarina turned to her, serene and smiling.

"He was of help, I hope?"

"It did its best," Dreams-of-War informed her sourly. "I am grateful. But the thing that attacked us—what might that have been, do you think? Did you see it?"

Yskatarina was smiling still. "I saw it. But I do not know what it could have been."

"You are certain? You have no theories?" The Memnos Matriarchy had long ago tried to introduce Dreams-of-War to the concept of subtlety; she would be the first to agree that they had failed to instill it. A pity that such methods could not be installed with the same facility as emotions.

"I assure you, I have none. But there are many strange things in this part of old Earth. Many fragments and remnants of lost cultures and species. Most of them seem to war with one another."

"Your companion," Dreams-of-War mused. "Do other families, other clans of Earth, possess beings like this one?"

"Perhaps. I could not say." Yskatarina turned to face her. Her limbs, which were today fashioned of wrought metal, flashed in the sunlight. "There is a great deal that you do not know about Earth. There is much that *we* do not yet know. The lunar laboratories were extensive as well as ancient, and there are all manner of rumors regarding their production lines before the stone-plague petrified the folk. They manufactured for every aspect of life in the solar system—pleasure, pain, industry, war."

Interesting list order, Dreams-of-War thought. And if anywhere could be said to have been the originator of genetic modification lines, it was not the moon, but Mars and Nightshade. "The history of this world is well documented," she said, taken aback.

"By Martians."

"Of course. By who else?"

Yskatarina smiled again. "You must understand that the Martian story is not the whole story. There are other accounts, secret histories of how the world came into being, how societies have formed."

"Naturally," Dreams-of-War replied. "There will always be myths and legends, stories of origin."

"That is not quite what I meant." Yskatarina leaned back upon the rail. "Let me digress. What of your own history, the story of Mars? The history of your own sect?"

"This is well-known," Dreams-of-War said, pleased to have a chance to boast a little after the discomfiture of her flight.

"The manuscripts date back many thousands of years. They tell of a time in our far past, when the cities of the plain were connected by great canals, where the Riders went out to subdue unruly men-remnants. They tell of the distant origins of my own people, the Royal Warriors of the Age of Children and the Lost Epoch."

"I have heard of the Martian canals," Yskatarina said. "I have visited Mars, for a short while, and glimpsed the canals only from the air. But I should like to study them more closely."

"No traces of those ancient cities or their waterways remain," Dreams-of-War told her. "They were lost in the dust storms that ravaged the planet during the Lost Epoch. What you see on Mars today—the Grand Channel, for example—is a re-creation of those great structures. But these are themselves antique, dating back to the period before the colonization of Earth."

"What would you say if I told you that there is a legend that it was not you Martians who colonized this world, but the other way around? Men and women of Earth who traveled to Mars in distant antiquity, before the Drowning, and set up settlements? Who, over the course of a millennium, created an atmosphere and terraformed the planet until what had been barren, freezing desert became the lands of seas and plains and cities that you know today? That there were no great canals, only ancient stories, which were later held up as truth?"

Dreams-of-War smiled. "I would say that a conquered people need to recover their pride as best they may, and that a comforting lie is as good a way to accomplish this as any."

Yskatarina inclined her head. "You are entitled to your opinion. I tell you merely as a matter of curiosity."

"It is an intriguing myth," Dreams-of-War conceded, for the sake of courtesy.

"I need to speak with Sek," Yskatarina said after a pause, "so that my companion may tell her what he has seen."

"Do you wish me to be present?" Dreams-of-War asked.

"There is no need. My companion will tell her everything that must be known." Yskatarina flicked a finger. The creature emerged on deck, facedown now and bouncing on insect limbs. The tail coiled above its head, flickering and caressing the horns.

"Come," Yskatarina instructed it. She bent, locking the door of the cabin. To Dreams-of-War she added, "We will speak later."

Dreams-of-War watched as the creature, obedient as a plainshound, followed her along the deck.

Its mistress, indeed, Dreams-of-War thought with revulsion. But Yskatarina interested her. There was something about the woman, a foreign scent, a demeanor different from any that Dreams-of-War had yet encountered. She looked back at Yskatarina's cabin, then along the deck. The figures of Yskatarina and her companion were moving toward the prow: Yskatarina stalking on elegant metal legs, the creature scuttling behind like a spider's shadow. Dreams-of-War decided to take her chance. Swiftly, she activated the hand-tools of the armor and picked the lock, then ducked through the doorway into Yskatarina's cabin.

She did not know what to look for, and what if there was nothing? In the chest she discovered Yskatarina's spare limbs, stacked neatly in pairs. Some were ornate: gleaming black metal ornamented with pearls, a substance that resembled carved garnet, intricate plastic cages.

Her next investigation proved more fruitful. Within the chest was a narrow box, chased with a lacquered phoenix. It would not open.

"Assist me," Dreams-of-War commanded her armor. It obliged with a narrow, pointed spire that, when inserted into the keyhole, caused the lid of the box to click up. Inside, neatly packed, were star-charts. "Tell me if you hear someone coming," Dreams-of-War said to the armor. She fished the first of the charts from the box and unscrolled it.

It was a map of the solar system: familiar, unremarkable. Here was Earth, with the Chain clearly marked in silver etching. Here was Mars—Dreams-of-War suppressed a sudden nostalgic pang— and the made-worlds surrounding Io-Beneath and the Belt. And here, out beyond the ancient boundaries, was the planet of Nightshade, depicted by a black sphere and a golden star. The star was many-pointed, a bristling mass, identical to the symbol on Yskatarina's shoulder.

Dreams-of-War flicked through the rest of the charts. Planetary maps, trade routes, nothing out of the ordinary. She put them back in the box and closed the lid, then sat back on her heels. If Yskatarina was from Nightshade, then what did this mean?

"Someone comes," the armor said into her ear. Dreams-of-War thrust the box back into its place and slid out into the passage, locking the door behind her. She could hear footsteps approaching along the deck, an arachnid rustle. Quickly, Dreams-of-War dodged along the passage and around the comer. Yskatarina seemed to be humming to herself, or perhaps it was the creature speaking in some speech of its own.

Dreams-of-War hastened back to her own ruined cabin and sat down with the sea wind whistling around her. Lunae's absence was palpable. With difficulty, she turned her thoughts back to the matter in hand.

Nightshade. She had heard all the rumors. The planet had been founded long ago by a religious sect, commonly supposed to be mad, who believed in sustaining the creation of male forms and who sought the creation of a perfect being. Dreams-of-War thought of Yskatarina's creature with distaste. The world was closed to ordinary traffic. The lab clans insisted upon it, and it was a condition of keeping the end of the Chain secure. But secure from what? Dreams-of-War asked herself, as so many had asked before her. Nothing had been known to cross the great chasm of space between the systems, unless one counted the Kami.

Dreams-of-War scowled. If Yskatarina was a member of a Nightshade clan, then what was she doing all the way here on Earth, on the same boat as Lunae? And Yskatarina felt *wrong,* as if she did not belong here on this world. This was not simply her own instinct, Dreams-of-War realized now, but that of the armor: a sensitivity of semisentient haunt-tech, relying on cues that were unavailable to human senses.

Dreams-of-War's first inclination was to return to Yskatarina's cabin and beat the truth out of her, but after a moment of temptation, she dismissed this as a useful course of action. She was not afraid of Yskatarina's creature, she told herself, but she did not know of what it might be capable. She sat glowering out to sea, until the sun dropped over the horizon and the sea sank into a twilight haze.

Later, she went to stand at the prow of the junk as it limped through the waves. At last, she thought, they were approaching land. Memories of the desert nagged at her, combined with the guilty, frustrated ache of Lunae's loss. The emotion had become so all-encompassing that she had almost ceased to notice it.

The islands rose up from the horizon like the humps of a sea-serpent, sharply arched. Dreams-of-War thought of the Dragon-King and grew colder yet.

"This place we're going to," she said to Yskatarina, who had come to join her on the deck. "What is it called? We are not heading for Ischa—that is farther north."

"According to Sek, these are the southernmost points of the Fire Islands," Yskatarina replied. "We're putting in to repair the damage to the ship. This harbor is known as Toke'ui. You will see many of the kappa there. I do not know what they call it."

"I see no smoke," Dreams-of-War said. Remembering the discrepancies in the navigation charts, she was starting to wonder whether this had not been Sek's destination all along. But if so, why?

"This part of the archipelago is not volcanic. That is more the nature of the northern islands, which border on the Great Rift. We are too far south to see many volcanoes yet."

"I will not be traveling north," Dreams-of-War said. "I shall seek the help of the kappa from Toke'ui."

Yskatarina glanced at her, askance. "I did not like to say so before, but you realize that in all likelihood your ward and her nurse are dead?"

"I will not believe it."

"Will not—or are too afraid? What becomes of you, if your mistresses learn that you have let the girl slip from your care?"

Dreams-of-War glared at her, but Yskatarina had spoken neutrally, with no hint of a threat.

"Nothing will 'become' of me. I shall hunt down that which attacked us and return to Mars, that is all."

"Memnos will not punish you?"

"Why should they?" Dreams-of-War braced armored hands on the rail and leaned out into the sea wind. But privately she was by no means certain. She remembered the honeycomb of cells beneath the Memnos Tower and what they contained. She pictured the Matriarch squatting at the center of those cells like a wasp queen, exuding poison. The thought reminded her uncomfortably of the Grandmothers. Warriors had disappeared before, never to be seen again, mourned with the full rites and mealy-mouthed sanctimony, when everyone had suspected the truth. But these were the secrets of Memnos and not for the ears of Yskatarina.

"You are fortunate," Yskatarina murmured. Dreams-of-War looked at her. Yskatarina was gazing blandly out to sea, yet there were undertones, swift currents beneath the placid surface. Dreams-of-War wondered how the clans of Nightshade might deal with those who failed. It crossed her mind that now might be a good moment to challenge Yskatarina, but an unfamiliar caution held her back. The creature stalked behind its mistress, upright now, arms folded in a tight knot.

"Look," Yskatarina said. "You can see Toke'ui."

"Where?"

"The black smudge at the edges of the shore. See it?"

"You have good eyesight," Dreams-of-War remarked.

Yskatarina merely smiled.

They reached the small port as twilight was falling, the gloss of lamps casting out across the still water. Dreams-of-War watched as ripples and wakes made their way out from the long harbor wall, heading for the junk. It was a moment before she recognized the round heads of kappa, perhaps twenty or so, as swift in the water as seals.

"They will bring us in," Yskatarina informed her.

"You seem to know a lot about the manner in which things are done," Dreams-of-War remarked. "Have you traveled this way before?"

"Perhaps," Yskatarina said, but did not amplify.

"You have family in the region, maybe?" Dreams-of-War probed.

"Something like that." Yskatarina turned away from the rail. "We will dock shortly I must prepare."

When she had returned to her cabin, Dreams-of-War went in search of Sek. She found the captain on the bridge, inscribing coordinates into the sail monitor.

"Captain, I need information. How is it best to contact the kappa? Shall I speak to them when they board?"

"There's an office at the end of the dock. The harbormistress works there. But it is late; she may have gone. In that case, you will have to wait until morning."

"Do you believe that they could have saved Lunae?"

"The kappa are easily underestimated," Sek said. "They are a strange, secret people. It's said that they have access to ruined palaces beneath the waves, tall columns of buildings many storys high, that are home to shark-monkeys and porpoise; long-drowned temples to lost gods. The kappa have been persecuted relentlessly throughout their history. They have ways of keeping safe."

Seething with anticipatory frustration, Dreams-of-War went back down to the deck and stood in the prow. The port was clearly visible: a muddle of tumbled houses heading up the hill, lit erratically by lamps. Along the shore, several lights were flickering, as if about to go out. A smell of mingled soap and fat drifted out across the water.

A *poor place*, thought Dreams-of-War, but this came as little surprise. Most of Earth was in a similar condition. She was sure that they preferred it that way. The Memnos Matriarch's words echoed from some half-forgotten conversation: *"The people of Earth are lazy, slack-willed. They do not understand discipline."*

Dreams-of-War longed suddenly for Mars: for stone and metal, for sleek hard lines against sand. She began to doubt that the kappa would be able to proffer anything resembling aid. An image came to her, of Lunae tossing within the embrace of the waves, eyes open and hair streaming through the water like bloodstained weed. She gripped the rail more tightly and willed the junk into port.

CHAPTER 6

ELSEWHERE

Essa took the wet-ship low over the red range, skimming between serrated peaks and through bands of light and shadow. Yet there was no sign of a sun in the pallid sky, only the vast, shattered construct of what remained of the Chain's maw.

"Where is the sun?" Lunae asked. "And where are we going?"

"The Illuminant gives this world its light now. All the land worlds of the solar system have undergone such—remodeling, transformation, shattering. As for your destination, we are going to visit someone."

The ram-horned woman stroked the wall into a shower of droplets that sailed through the air and fell against Lunae's face. "The crevasse is beneath us now. That's where we are headed."

Lunae looked down and saw a rent in the red land.

"I can't see the bottom," she said. "How deep is it?"

"No one knows. No one has ever measured it."

"Have they not tried to fly to the bottom?"

"This is the only craft we have. I do not want to risk it."

Lunae pictured the vehicle disintegrating into gentle rain, and shivered. Essa once more stroked the wall. The craft swerved and dived, heading for the chasm.

"Let us not test it, in that case!" the kappa said in alarm. Essa smiled.

"We are not about to do so. The person we are going to see lives in the chasm, not far from the lip."

The craft took them down, gliding over spongy rock. But as it drew closer to the ground, Lunae could see that it was not stone at all, but banks of lichen and fungus, shading into bloodier colors in the shadows of the crevasse. The walls looked as rich and soft as velvet.

"This is what gives the red range its name," Essa said. "Mars has become covered with lichen like this. There are entire forests of huge fungi . . ."

Lunae thought of Dreams-of-War with a twinge of anguish. Her guardian would never, she felt, take her to see the plains and forests of their own day, now.

The kappa frowned. "This was not the case in my time."

"Perhaps it seeded when Mars underwent the Blight."

"The Blight?" Lunae could cope with the height, the ravine, the racing craft, but the distances of history left her feeling fragile and dizzied.

"The splintering of the Chain," Essa replied. "See where the temple lies?"

Lunae peered through the shimmering wall of the craft to see a narrow ledge jutting out from the side of the ravine. They were descending swiftly now, the shadows of the surrounding peaks casting darkness over the land.

"Who is the temple dedicated to?" the kappa asked, leaning forward.

"It is no longer known. Perhaps the one who lives there may know, but if so, she has not told me." Essa touched the wall of the craft, sending it gliding toward the platform. As they drew near, Lunae could see that the platform was carved out of the fungus: a great jutting ridge of it, the underside of the bracket grooved with runnels, through which the little craft could easily have slipped.

The kappa said, surprising Lunae, "Does it ever spore?"

"Every so often. We have to keep inside, then. The chasm is filled with the dust when the brackets emit their charge of spores, and it saturates the lungs beneath even the finest masking."

The craft swooped toward the platform, landing in a puff of dust. Lunae and the kappa climbed forth, to stand on the spongy surface. The columns of the temple rose up before them: worn, weathered stone stained by ancient rain, mottled as if spattered with acid. The stone was the color of roses, of the dust of other worlds. The air smelled like the inside of a cupboard: hot and dry, with a mushroom mustiness. There was no wind.

Lunae watched as Essa placed both hands on the side of the craft. It melted down into a smooth lake, shining in the last of the light and creating an oily film over the velvet of the fungus.

"Won't it dry up?" the kappa asked nervously.

Essa smiled, made a gesture of negation. "It is not quite like water. You have no need to worry. Now, let us go within."

CHAPTER 7

EARTH

The kappa of Toke'ui crowded around the dock, securing the junk with ropes. Sek stood with both hands on the prow, eyes closed.

"What is she doing?" Dreams-of-War said to Yskatarina.

"She listens to the ship," Yskatarina replied.

"It speaks to her?" She remembered Lunae's talk of voices when they had first arrived.

"So she says."

"But this is surely a filament vessel, not haunt-tech. How can it possess sentience?"

"I don't know," Yskatarina murmured. "Perhaps when she told me of it, she spoke in metaphor."

But Lunae had meant it literally, Dreams-of-War was certain. What would be comprised of haunt-tech, in a vessel such as this? The most likely possibility was the navigation system. But what if Sek had some other agenda that she was pursuing? Did that connect with the goals of Yskatarina, or not? If Yskatarina had summoned the swarm-assassin . . . And she also wondered whether this was the original destination, as ordered by the Grandmothers, or somewhere else. And if somewhere else, then why? Dreams-of-War was sure that they had started to change course before Lunae had gone missing. The situation was as murky as the waters of the harbor below.

"By the way, I meant to ask if you have traveled much in space?" Dreams-of-War said, as casually as she could manage. "You said that you have visited Mars."

"I have been off-world once or twice. I have visited some of the worlds; I have been to the Crater Plain, where I believe you yourself come from." Yskatarina spoke smoothly, and did not look at the Martian.

"How do you know that?"

"The Martian clans are not so extensive or so great in their complexity that I cannot recognize an accent," Yskatarina said. "I know a little of the origins of the Warrior Clans of Memnos."

"I thought perhaps a woman of your means might have traveled farther," Dreams-of-War remarked.

"To Io-Beneath, perhaps, or Europa? Or do you just mean farther up the Chain?"

"It costs money to make such voyages," Dreams-of-War said, "but you have riches, clearly. If I had that kind of wealth, I would wish to journey as far as I could, to the very ends of the Chain, perhaps even as far as Nightshade."

Yskatarina laughed. "You would not be permitted to visit Nightshade. The lab clans do not admit outsiders; you must know that."

Dreams-of-War shrugged. "I was not sure if they made exceptions."

"They make no exceptions. Believe me."

Yskatarina's voice was light, dancing like the reflection of the lamps on the water, but Dreams-of-War wondered once more about the currents that ran below.

"I know little of Nightshade," she said, probing.

"No one does," Yskatarina replied, still lightly "It is a dark, closed world."

"I've heard rumors that they run programs, to crossbreed, to mix human genes with those of ancient animals, to produce a perfect being. Do you think they have had any success?" Dreams-of-War said, carefully casual.

"I have no idea. It's out-world rumor, probably nothing more. Interesting, though." Yskatarina sounded sincere, but Dreams-of-War was not deceived. "Look, they have secured the junk."

"I need to go ashore," Dreams-of-War said. "I have questions that must be answered."

Yskatarina nodded. "Very well. I will see you later. Good luck with your questions."

Impatiently, Dreams-of-War left the ship and brushed past the throng of kappa that congregated along the dock, which was no more than a mass of roughly cut blocks of stone, slippery with seaweed and water. She felt the treads of the armor alter against the soles of her feet, to provide her with a better grip, but even so, she nearly fell. Humiliated, Dreams-of-War glanced around to see who might be watching. The kappa were all gazing at her, gleaming eyes betraying nothing. Dreams-of-War strode angrily on. At the end of the dock she was forced to press through a knot of the creatures that huddled, murmuring in low liquid voices, before a small metal gate.

"Let me through!" Dreams-of-War said, and her voice sounded harsher and more panicky than she would have liked. Half a dozen mild eyes stared at her incuriously, but the kappa did not move. "Out of my way!" She was grateful for the armor, which kept out the touch of their thick clammy bodies, but she was still forced to make contact. Repelled, she stumbled out of the gate into the street.

Here it was silent, and there was no one in sight. Dreams-of-War stalked through soft darkness, illuminated periodically by glowing lamps. She recalled the dry burn of the moss-lamps of the clan house with a distant, half-realized nostalgia.

A tumble of tenements rose above her, climbing upward from the street, ascending in layers. Small windows curved out at the level of Dreams-of-War's feet; she reached down and touched them with brief curiosity. They were smooth and warm to the touch. She recognized some kind of plastic; they must be very old. Certain of the windows were partially buried in the packed earth, as though the buildings had sunk beneath their own weight. Dreams-of-War looked up. The upper reaches of the tenements were equally unusual: wood and thick laminated paper. So many of the trees of Earth were under the floodwaters, sad rotting stumps. Had they imported the wood from some lunar forest? She thought of Tsukiyomi on Luna, last remaining outpost after the stone-plague: the acres of fir beneath sparkling domes, the air electric with resin and quietness, studded with entrances to the underground labyrinth of the laboratories. But imported wood was surely a province of the very wealthy. Perhaps the kappa had taken over the mansions of the rich and the dead . . .

Along the upper storys, faux metal gleamed in the lights from the bay. Dreams-of-War reached the end of the street and looked around her. No sign of the harbor office and no one to ask . . . Dreams-of-War quietly seethed. Then she spotted a narrow alley, leading between two of the tall houses. A light shone at its end.

Dreams-of-War stepped into the alley. It smelled pungent, of rotting fish and something else, something spicier that she was unable to identify. There was nothing to remind her of the air of Mars, odor constantly betraying the absence of home. Dreams-of-War found the source of the light and halted. A low building, made of driftwood, the cracks crammed with dried weed, was stuffed in between the neighboring buildings. Not promising. Dreams-of-War banged imperiously upon the door.

After a moment, it opened. An anxious, moonlike face peered forth.

"Yes? What is it?"

"I'm looking for the harbormistress."

"Come in."

Dreams-of-War followed the shuffling figure into a room so low that she could not stand upright.

"Sit, sit." It was a kappa, indistinguishable from all others. Perhaps the armor might be able to tell them apart. She did not like the idea of being surrounded by a horde of identical creatures: too much room for ambivalence, error, deceit. Could Lunae's nurse be trusted? Dreams-of-War was no longer certain and, now that she considered the issue, she was not sure that she had ever been.

"You are not from Earth," the kappa said.

"Obviously not. I am a Martian warrior."

"Indeed, you have an Arian air," the kappa remarked whimsically. It seemed to be clad in sackcloth; it had a strong, shellfish smell. Dreams-of-War decided to breathe through her mouth.

"Doubtless so. I have come because of a difficulty. My ship was attacked, and—"

"You have come in on the junk belonging to Ayadatarahime Sek? Yes, we heard about it."

"Do you know what attacked us?"

The kappa shrugged. Folds of flesh slid up its bared arms, formed tight rolls of fat, slid away once more. "A being riding a swarm-host."

"A swarm-host?" Dreams-of-War frowned. "What's that?"

"Some form of nanotech. I don't know how they make it behave as it does." The kappa gave an indifferent shrug.

"Do you know where they come from?"

"Death-dealers are commonly owned by the war-madams, of whom there are many, but only one person commands swarm-technology in these waters, and that is Prince Cataract."

"Who is she? He," Dreams-of-War corrected.

"He is a warlord. No one knows where his base is to be found, but he has a private army of snake-kin and other made-beings."

"Do they often prey upon shipping?"

"No. He is not a bandit. It is unusual."

"Do you have any idea why this thing attacked us?"

"I do not know. What became of this thing?"

"I killed it. It was not human. I pulled its face away. There was some kind of rudimentary brain inside the skull."

"And what was the ship carrying?"

"I was in charge of my ward. She is just a young girl, nothing more. She went overboard with the kappa who is her nurse. Someone spoke of sea palaces. If there is any hope that the kappa took her to a place of safety, I must know."

"This kappa. What was her name?"

Dreams-of-War bridled. "I have no idea. Do you have names?"

She thought that the kappa smiled, but it was hard to tell from the broad, lipless mouth. Perhaps the kappa snarled.

"Of course, just as you do. It would be helpful if we knew which clan she comes from. Everyone has their secret harbors, their holds and sanctuaries. I could not tell you where they all lie. We have our tribes and factions. Just as you do."

"This particular kappa was employed by folk in Fragrant Harbor. Everyone calls them the Grandmothers; they lived in a mansion called Cloud Terrace, at the summit of the Peak, which has since been destroyed."

"I know of them. I will make inquiries. I think I may know already whom you mean. In which case—well. We shall see. Return to your ship; do not linger. There are those here who have no love for the people of Mars. I will send word to the ship when I have it. It is unlikely to be before morning."

"Very well," Dreams-of-War said, though she did not like it. "I will do as you suggest."

She left the dank room with relief, feeling cramped and tainted.

There are those here who have no love for the people of Mars. What was that supposed to mean? The ingratitude of the people of Earth was a continual irritant to Dreams-of-War, like a grain of sand between the armor's heel and her skin. There was no reason for such hatred. No doubt it was attributable solely to resentment of those who were congenitally superior, Dreams-of-War reminded herself, and instantly felt better.

She returned to the junk without incident. The decks were empty. She passed Yskatarina's cabin, but the door was firmly shut and there was no sound from within.

Much later, Dreams-of-War snapped from sleep. She did not know what had awoken her, but the armor was bristling and prickling like a wild creature. It would, she thought, make a mess of the mattress. There was a sound coming from outside the ship, in the direction of the dock: a thin, high keening. It did not sound like either kappa or human. There was a hiss from the armor: a single word.

"Excissieres."

Dreams-of-War was up off the bed and onto her feet before the sibilance had faded.

"Memnos's executioners? Here? Why have they come? Can you hear them? Are they broadcasting?"

"They've come to take you in," Yskatarina's voice said from the shadows. Dreams-of-War turned.

"You!"

"My companion picked up their frequency just now. They arrived by drop-boat a short time ago. Memnos has sent them."

"And you came to tell me this because—?"

"I can help you, if you'll let me."

"Always so helpful. Why?"

"I don't have any love for Memnos. It would take too long to explain why." The creature crackled in the corner of the room, sinking down into a bony knot of limbs. "That makes us allies, of a kind. You've failed, have you not? You've lost the girl, and they're going to bring you back." Without the customary lenses, Yskatarina's eyes were huge in the darkness, bearing a faint luminescence.

"You're from Nightshade, aren't you? I thought they did good business with Memnos. I'm wearing part of it."

Yskatarina betrayed no surprise, did not ask her how she knew. "I suggest we make a move," she said.

"I'm not going anywhere with you." Yskatarina was surely not Kami, for she did not shift and blur, but she was of Nightshade, and that was bad enough. Yet Dreams-of-War was unwilling to face a squadron of excissieres.

"They are coming!" the armor said urgently.

Yskatarina shrugged. "Have it your own way. But I can get you out of here. All that I am proposing is a temporary alliance, nothing more."

"Where are we to go, then?" Dreams-of-War asked.

"I have a plan. Follow me."

CHAPTER 8

ELSEWHERE

Within, the cavern was cool and strangely bright. Lunae could not tell where the light was coming from, but it fell all around her as softly as rain. The walls were covered with carvings, but they were so old that nothing more than a trace of the reliefs remained. Then she looked again, and thought that perhaps the patterns were only fungal infestations, or the rivulets carved by water. The floor, however, was smooth and hard, marble-veined. At the far end of the cavern stood a statue, but when she looked at it again, it was just an outcrop of stone.

Essa, ignoring her surroundings, glided forward.

"Where is this person?" the kappa demanded, sibilant voice hissing in echo from the walls of the temple.

"She will be down among the fumes," Essa said. She paused for a moment to pat the rough russet hair between her horns back into place, then vanished into the wall. Lunae, startled, followed and found a slitted opening. A breath of heavy air came from it: resinous and strong, forest-fragrant, followed by the sudden, salt-laden scent of the sea. Lunae stepped into it and followed Essa downward.

The light here was somehow faded and stained, but still enough by which to see. Lunae trod upon metal steps, sending echoes up against the walls. The scent changed and grew stronger: old roses, an amberous pungency. Soon, the air itself began to thicken, until Lunae descended through a sultry haze. Behind her, the kappa began to wheeze.

At the base of the steps, Lunae found herself in a small, round chamber filled with fumes. The smoke was so heavy that it was difficult to see. Her eyes watered.

"Come forward," she heard Essa say.

Stumbling a little, Lunae did so. A figure swam out of the smoke, seated at a tripod brazier. Essa grasped her hand and again there was that odd sensation of unhuman fingers against her own. But when she looked down, Essa's supple hand seemed wholly usual. For Lunae, however, the betraying sensation could not be overlooked. She snatched her hand away.

"What are you? Are you Kami?"

"Not Kami. She is a haunt." The figure seated at the tripod spoke.

"A haunt?"

"A spirit in a shell of flesh."

"Isn't that what everyone is?"

"You know that the Kami possess others? They seek bodies for their convenience. But unless the possession is undertaken in early childhood, or lasts over a long period so that spirit and body have a chance to settle into phase, the new flesh retains a memory of its original physical host. That is why so many of them look one way and feel another. But Essa is born out of the land itself: nanotech, inhabited by a spirit from the far past."

"And who, in that case," the kappa said, still wheezing, "are you?"

Lunae went to crouch by the figure, looking up into her face. But the hood that the seated woman wore was enveloping, and her features were concealed within. The voice was remote and distorted by a curious buzz of static: a product of voice-technology or a deliberate device to hide identity? There was something familiar about the figure, all the same.

"You should not fear Essa," the form continued. "She does not share the ambitions of the Kami. This is why we have brought you here."

"We?"

"It hasn't been easy to bring you through time," the woman said. "To take advantage of the snatched moments when you shifted the temporal fabric, drifted free within the stream of time and could be ensnared."

"Like a fish on a hook?"

"Like a fish in a net. I did not think we would succeed."

"But why?"

"Because you are the *hito-bashira*, the woman-who-will-hold-back-the-flood."

Lunae said, "I have grown tired of asking what this means."

"Then it is time you knew Your world and your time face an invasion, one which has already begun."

The kappa frowned. "From the Kami?"

"Just so. You may believe the Kami to be alien, but they are not—though it is not quite true to say that they are human anymore."

"Then what are they?"

"Ghosts?" the kappa whispered.

"In a way—but not ghosts from the past, like Essa. They are the spirits of the future living, the last conscious remnant of humanity within the solar system. They come from a day when nothing remains of humanity in its ancient home except for disembodied semihuman consciousnesses. In your own day, Nightshade has found a way to summon these disembodied consciousnesses back through the Eldritch Realm, to harness their knowledge, their power."

"Haunt-tech," Lunae said.

"But there is a great irony. Humanity has achieved its greatest degree of knowledge of consciousness at the very end of human history, when nothing remains of the great worlds except ruin or flood, and there is no other life and little means of sustaining it except the eking out of an existence underground. The consciousnesses that are the Kami cling to the walls of their craters, thousands of them, like spectral bats. Until Nightshade summoned them, they were trapped in formlessness, but now they seek new bodies to inhabit, and Nightshade has helped them to find them—in the past, in other bodies."

"And do those people ask to be possessed?"

"Would you?"

"If I wanted knowledge, perhaps. But I would have to want it very badly, I think."

"But what is their aim?" the kappa asked. "To change history? Or just to provide themselves with bodies?"

"They may wish to change history, but the outcome would always be the same. Nothing can save a dying sun. No, the last of humanity want a last chance at life: possessing the bodies of the living, holding sway over the worlds. Do not think that they will be generous mistresses. They are no longer human. Some seek power, but most just want the amusements of the flesh. Wars and combat, sexuality, perhaps—and on a grand scale. If their invasion goes ahead, the system will become their playground."

"And how do you know this?"

"Because I have seen it happen," the voice said. The blurring was growing fainter now, the true voice coming through. It was the voice that Lunae heard every day within the confines of her head, or coming from her own lips. She sat back on her heels, staring.

"Yes," the oracle said. "Yes, of course you know me." She put back the hood to reveal the woman Lunae had seen within her dreams: her own self. "Do you wish to see what a world under the Kami would be like?" her self continued, "for I can show you."

Lunae swallowed hard. "Show me, then."

Her older self reached out and took her hands. Lunae closed her eyes, but her older self said sharply, "Keep them open!"

Lunae stared ahead as the walls of the cavern began to blur. She could feel her older self's hands clasping her own, but then the sensation faded and next moment, she was skimming across water. Her own voice said into her ear, "This is Earth, shortly after the Kami invasion. We are not really here; I am weaving this out of memory You are about to see Fragrant Harbor. Or what is left of it."

Land appeared on the horizon and Lunae recognized the Peak. Seconds later, they were diving down toward High Kowloon. Many of the tenements lay in ruins, burned and stripped of their carefully cultivated exterior vegetation, which now lay in steaming heaps in the street. "It is much hotter now," her own voice said. "The Kami like the heat. They have spent too long in the cold."

Lunae's consciousness skimmed through the streets. At a junction, she saw a makeshift edifice: a series of poles, joined by crossbars. From the poles hung the bodies of kappa. They appeared curiously deflated, as though their bodies had been sucked dry of flesh from within. But as they drew closer, Lunae saw that one of the kappa was still alive. Its skin had dried into a mass of cracks. Beneath it a pool of thick fluid had accumulated. It blinked bewildered bloodshot eyes. A group of women stood below it, prodding at it with sharpened stakes.

"What are they doing to it?" Lunae silently cried.

"The Kami are obsessed with physicality in all its manifestations. And because they are disembodied consciousnesses, they have little real understanding of pain. It fascinates them. They like to experiment. They move from body to body, wearing them out and leaving them behind."

They flew on, leaving the tormented kappa behind, but there were other scenes. Lunae watched in horror as half-formed infants were methodically torn from growing-bags and dissected. She saw a woman chased to the end of a typhoon shelter and ripped to pieces. The women doing these things all had the same out-of-phase appearance.

But on the slopes of the lower Peak, Lunae saw a group of peculiar beings: heavy and armored, like lumbering half-human turtles. The faces that squatted beneath their lowering brows were tight and gnarled, with small glistening eyes. They carried Martian weapons: shot-bolts and scissors, but the weapons seemed part of their bodies rather than separate tools. But they, too, were blurred and hazy, moving in and out of direct vision.

"What are they?" Lunae whispered.

"They are the Sown. In your day, they lie within the Martian soil, bio-tech prototypes, waiting to be called forth. The Kami have called them and inhabit them now. They are the vanguard of the Earth invasion and they swarm across Mars, also."

"This is a dreadful sight," Lunae said.

"It is hell," her older self agreed. "The Kami have brought hell to this system. Have you seen enough?"

"Oh yes."

"Then close your eyes and open them again."

Lunae did so. She was back in the Martian cavern, holding her older self's hands in her own.

CHAPTER 9

EARTH

Yskatarina's companion rustled behind them through the village of the kappa. All was quiet, the high-piled houses walled in behind night and salt air. The lamps were burning down to a misty dimness. From up in the crags Dreams-of-War heard something cry out, perhaps a hunting seabird. Yet despite the stillness, she could not help feeling that the town was awake and listening, that the kappa were only pretending to sleep. She thought of thick bodies, motionless as lumps, waiting to rise up in toad-silence and strike. The armor drew in upon her, sliding close over her skin. She listened ceaselessly for the excissieres, but there was no sound. It meant nothing, of course. The excissieres were huntresses of astonishing skill, and preferred to play a little before the strike. The thought raised the hair at the nape of Dreams-of-War's neck.

"Do you know where we are going?"

Ahead, she saw Yskatarina nod. "But it will not be easy," the woman from Nightshade said.

Dreams-of-War bristled. "I am not accustomed to 'easy.'"

Yskatarina smiled. "Just as well."

The creature unfolded its wings with a rattle and took off, circling up through the narrow cracks between the houses.

"Where is it heading?" Dreams-of-War said in some alarm. She had visions of the thing triggering alarms, rousing the town—assuming, once again, that they slept. "What if the excissieres see it?"

"That's the point," Yskatarina said with barely restrained patience. "It's gone to keep an eye on them, and if they come too close, it'll draw them off."

Dreams-of-War eyed her askance. "What if they harm it?"

"They will not. It knows how to hide." Yskatarina spoke with confidence, but Dreams-of-War had seen an excissiere shoot a dactylate out of the Martian sky at dusk with nothing more than a slingshot.

It was not just the excissieres who concerned her. There was also Sek, in the Grandmothers' pay, who had been carrying the Grandmothers' most precious possession, yet with no guards on the junk . . . Where was Sek, and what might she be doing now? Not to mention Yskatarina, and why Memnos might be after her. Assuming it was even true, and she was not leading Dreams-of-War into a trap . . . But in that case, why not simply let the scissor-women catch up with her?

"We are looking for something," Yskatarina said. She put out a hand, bringing Dreams-of-War to an abrupt halt. "Wait." Her eyes were closed, her face dreaming. "Ah, I have it." Dreams-of-War saw her smile.

"What are you doing?" Dreams-of-War demanded.

"I'll show you."

Yskatarina stepped into a sliver of a passage, picked her way with exaggerated delicacy over mounds of discarded fish heads.

"There is nothing down here, surely? Or do you seek a place to hide?"

Yskatarina glanced over her shoulder. "I am not accustomed to hiding."

She said nothing more. Dreams-of-War, seething, followed.

The armor bristled and prickled as they went, relaying information to Dreams-of-War's weary, paranoid cortex. Yskatarina walked with surety through a labyrinth paved with fish refuse and shit, as though she knew exactly where she was headed. In some instances, the passages were so narrow that Dreams-of-War was obliged to turn sideways to enter them. Yskatarina's secrecy was beginning to grate even more severely upon her. She felt constricted, confined, and when she glanced upward, she could no longer see the stars, only a haze across the sky. After the burning Martian nights and the clear desert air, this place felt rank, dank, and hostile. Occasionally, Yskatarina's creature passed overhead like a great rattling bat.

"That thing of yours will attract attention," Dreams-of-War hissed. "Someone will see."

"It has its own safeguards," Yskatarina replied, infuriatingly calm. "Do not worry."

But Dreams-of-War could already feel a glaze of sweat frosting her skin underneath the armor. Who, exactly, had Memnos sent? She thought of the excissieres, bearing their scissors before them. Or the rarer cenulae, perhaps, seducing you with nets of sound and song, holding you in a trance before you complied with whatever they might desire you to do. Humiliation would be a part of it, she was sure: the warrior's greatest fear.

The sooty, stinking passageway grew even narrower. To calm herself, Dreams-of-War thought of her heroines, the women from the old stories: Teoris of the Plain, who had captured a thousand men when the brutes still roamed freely about Mars; Dei of the Olympian Heights, living with animals and speaking their speech. None of these woman had, to the best of Dreams-of-War's knowledge, ended up in an alien maze that reeked of fisher-women's offal. It was the indignity of the whole affair that rankled, rather than a fear of Memnos. Or so Dreams-of-War told herself.

"Your creature will tell us if they are near?" she said to Yskatarina.

The woman looked absently back. "Who?"

"The excissieres. Or the kappa. Or whoever else doesn't like us and might even now be in pursuit."

Yskatarina nodded. "It will tell me. Ah!" She stopped, and began scuffling again in the fish refuse. Dreams-of-War eyed her with distaste.

"What are you doing?"

"My companion tells me it is here." Yskatarina stood to reveal a web of dark fire set into the stones of the passage.

"What is that?"

"A door."

Dreams-of-War stared at the glittering square. "That is no technology of the kappa. They have surely progressed no further than the wheel and the village pump."

Yskatarina smiled. "Perhaps so. Yet here is a haunt-lock, nonetheless."

Her creature rocketed down to join them in a clatter of wings. It placed its mouthparts to the fiery web, and whispered.

"And it is doing what, exactly?"

"Opening the door."

"Where did it get the incantation runes?"

"From something old and dead."

The haunt-lock flared up. A crackle of scarlet spread outward, like flame applied to charcoal. A moment later, a hole appeared in the floor of the passage. Dreams-of-War peered cautiously inward.

"Are you sure this is a door? I can't see a thing."

Yskatarina stepped onto the hole and stood there, ostensibly floating on air. "It is not open space. This is an elevator." She reached out a hand. The creature sidled close to her. "Come."

Ignoring the hand, Dreams-of-War moved to stand beside them. The surface was glassy beneath her feet. Then they were hurtling downward, coming to a halt far below the earth.

Dreams-of-War peered dubiously into the darkness.

"Where are we?"

Yskatarina appeared pleased, almost smug. She said nothing. Her face wavered through the halo of light that emanated from nodules along her creature's abdomen.

"Well?" Dreams-of-War folded her arms. "I shall go no farther until I know where we are going and what manner of place this is. This *cannot* be the doing of the kappa."

Yskatarina's creature, wings folded, skittered up the wall and glided along the ceiling of the passage.

"If this place is what I think it is, then it is old," Yskatarina said.

"Old? You mean, this may be an early Martian installation?" But this black light technology did not look quite like anything that Dreams-of-War had seen before. Ancient haunt-tech? The feel was the same—the same queasy *otherness*, the sad itch in the head, the heaviness of the heart—but there was no such thing as a homegrown version of haunt-tech on Earth. Therefore, this had to have come from elsewhere.

"No," Yskatarina said with amused patience.

"But what *is* this? What is the function of this place? It feels like haunt-tech, but there was surely none such on old Earth,

even if what you say"—she swallowed a bolt of disdain—"about
the Martians is partially true." She would not concede all of it.
She was reluctant to accept even this much.

"Perhaps" was all that Yskatarina said. "If I am right, we will
soon see."

Yskatarina was clearly following her companion, but how did
the thing know where to go? Its spidery form bustled unerringly
around corners, down passageways, through arches. This place
must be vast, Dreams-of-War thought with unease, extending
right under the hill. Already they must have walked more than a
mile. And what of oreagraphs, spy-eyes, weir-wards? Why were
they being permitted to wander around like this? And, most
pressing of all, where were the excissieres?

Moreover, the sense of haunt-tech was growing: ghosts
whispering inside her skull, as neural echoes bounced forward
and back; a sweaty quivering of the spine; the chill trickle
of alien presence throughout her veins . . . Dreams-of-War at last
acknowledged to herself that she did not merely fear the Kami,
but hated them. And yet she wore the weapon that they had
supplied: the mesh between armor and ghost, the inhabited shell
that kept her safe and on which she had so come to rely . . .

Yskatarina paused before a wall formed of interlocking
plates, curved and overlapping like the shell of a pangolin. Her
companion's chitinous mandibles moved slowly over the surface.

"What is it doing?"

"Tasting for weir-sequences," Yskatarina said.

The lights winked out. The curve slid open. Yskatarina
and Dreams-of-War stepped through into a cavern. The place
smelled of electricity and age. Something lay at the center of the
cavern: dark and glassy, with viridian shadows rippling across its
membranes. The sense of haunt-tech grew to a screaming pitch
inside Dreams-of-War's body and mind. She did not recall ever
feeling its presence so strongly before, even inside the Chain.

"It's a ship," Dreams-of-War whispered. "How did it get
here?" Her voice seemed to echo around the chamber, hollow
and small.

Yskatarina placed both palms against the vessel's sleek flank.
"Ah. Quiet, now. But it will wake."

Dreams-of-War's armor was beginning to filter back technical specifications, storing details of metal and manufacture, skeins of eso-technic information. It grew clammy against her skin, as though absorbing the negative energies of haunt-tech and feeding them back across her body. She felt as though she inhabited the armor with a thousand ghosts. Her skin began to crawl.

I remember this, the armor said. *I remember you.*

Finally, suspicion began to dawn. Dreams-of-War stepped back, unable to bear the sensation any longer, but it was too late. The hand of her armor elongated and flowed out to weld to the side of the ship. Her arm was suddenly encased in a loose-flowing sleeve as the armor softened.

"What—? Return to me!"

But the armor, for the first time in their mutual life together, did not obey. Instead, it continued to flow, gliding up the side of the ship in a thick coat of moving metal. Dreams-of-War stood dismayed, clad only in her underharness. She turned on Yskatarina, but the woman was no longer there.

"Open it!" she heard Yskatarina cry.

An oval hole sprang apart the side of the ship, releasing a green fungal light. Dreams-of-War darted forward, growling, but was encased in sharp arms. Yskatarina's creature, clasping her from behind, plucked her up off the floor as if she were featherlight, and threw her to the ground. Dreams-of-War sprawled across the floor as the ship began to move. Rolling over and throwing her arms over her head, she saw the creature disappear through the hole, which closed. The ship was powering up, sending shudders throughout the cavern. Dust and shattered stone showered down on Dreams-of-War.

"Come back!" She could still see the armor, a bulky lump smeared across the top of the ship. The face of Embar Khair appeared briefly from the mass: eye closed, mouth open in distended horror. Then the roof of the cavern began to split apart. The ship was too high and too smooth for her to scale. Dreams-of-War scrambled up from the floor and ran to the sides of the cavern, where she cowered behind an outcrop of rock and shielded her face. The ship glowed, bright as a great jade eye.

Then the roof of the cavern gave way. A mass of masonry tumbled inward: shards of tile, a carved dragon, a splintering fall of wood. Above the sea-rush of the craft, Dreams-of-War heard a thin, unhuman wailing. Then sound broke over her like a tide, stunning her, and the ship was no more than a star in the riven heavens, fading fast. Then the edge of the cavern gave way. Moments later, Dreams-of-War was buried beneath a torrent of falling stone.

CHAPTER 10

ELSEWHERE

Lunae's hands were trembling. She said, "How do you come to be here?"

"I have lived on."

Lunae gaped at her. "Lived on? For how long?"

"Between this day, and the day on which I failed in my task. The day on which I failed to be the *hito-bashira*, failed to hold back the flood. As you have now seen, the Kami took sway over the system, ruled it, turned it into hell, sent more emissaries out into the Abyss to engineer other hells on other worlds. And now the end of times is here. They will go across the Abyss relatively soon, leaving one last little redoubt behind them."

"I've glimpsed the end of Mars," Essa said. "It goes out in fire, as befits a Martial world."

"They have ruled for all this time? For millennia? And they let you live?"

"They had no choice. I—we—cannot die, Lunae. Instead, we jump, just at the moment of the last of life. We spin time, like a weaving. We have a degree of mastery over it, and yet it still bends us to its constraints. And that is why Essa and I are going to send you back, to the days before the invasion, to fulfill your role as *hito-bashira*. To Mars in your own day."

"If all this is so," the kappa said, "why can't you escape from this place yourself?"

"The Kami bound me into time. I can only watch, or snare my earlier self, and then only when she unties herself from the time-stream. Lunae the Younger is much more powerful than I, but untrained. She has not had the time to learn what I have learned, and I no longer have her abilities."

"But what must I do? Will I not be destined—*was* I not destined—to fail again?"

"I cannot say." Her own older face grew sad. "I do not know, after all this time, what I was meant to accomplish. It may be that all this is for nothing and you will fail again. But we have to try."

"Can you at least give me a date?"

"All I can say for certain is that the event will take place at the Memnos Tower and you must go there. Nightshade had a machine there, a haunt-engine. I was discovered, and taken." She paused. "You have to understand that on the day of the invasion, time was erratic. I cannot give you an exact day—and by the time you return, the day may have changed, anyway. Time is so fluid where you and I are concerned. However, do not trust anyone but your immediate companions. Do not trust the Matriarchy, or the woman known as Yskatarina Iye. Yskatarina is of Nightshade, and in your day, Memnos is ruled by one of the Kami in an inhabited body."

"And this person"—here the kappa gestured toward Essa—"where does she fit in?"

"I am of Mars," Essa said. "I endure."

"And she is to be trusted?" the kappa asked.

"As greatly as anyone can be," Lunae the Elder said with a trace of sadness. "When you return, try to find Essa, if you can. She will be able to tell you more; she will be in that time-stream."

"You said you could send us back." Lunae shifted from one foot to the other. The small chamber was suddenly stifling, pressing in upon her with the weight of claustrophobia. "I ask you to do so."

"And so we will," Lunae the Elder said. "But you must make the first move." She gave a faint smile, as if remembering. "I envy you your recent memories, little-self. I should like to see a sea once more . . . Take my hand." She reached out to both Lunae and the kappa.

"I wish you luck," Essa said. She seemed to be fading back into the smoke, her features indistinct and blurring.

"Now *shift*," Lunae the Elder told her.

There was a familiar sensation inside Lunae's mind, much more powerful than any that she had ever experienced: the relationship of pindrop to thunderclap. She cried out, echoed by the kappa. The last thing she saw was the face of her elder self, eyes filled with tears, as the red world spun below and fell away.

CHAPTER 11

EARTH

Dreams-of-War awoke to find herself moving. She tried to sit up, but could not. She squinted around her, seeing curved walls and a low ceiling. Her arms were tied, as were her ankles, but she was not gagged. Dreams-of-War spoke.

"Where am I? Where am I being taken?"

No one answered. She tugged at the bonds, twisting in order to break free, but they were secure. Their edges were sharp, biting into her flesh at wrists and ankles. She could feel the motion of a vehicle beneath her, something riding and bouncing on pockets of air. There was a strong smell of raw meat, filling the enclosed space. Dreams-of-War was suddenly conscious of hunger. Her mouth filled with saliva. She turned her head to one side and spat.

A sudden surge of acceleration hammered her against the wall. Dreams-of-War raised her head as far as she could, and squinted along the length of her body. Beneath a rough layer of sacking, she was naked except for the underharness. The memory of her armor being whisked into space on the back of the ancient ship was a sharp and piercing pang. Dreams-of-War lay stiffly back on the couch to which she was strapped.

Loss of armor meant loss of her status as a warrior. She had often considered that she might be taking the armor too much for granted, and now that dependency had led to this: the armor's loss, in a moment of misjudgment, and her own helplessness. Moreover, there was the knowledge that someone had handled her while she lay naked and unconscious. She wondered with fury what other liberties they might have taken. If anyone had attempted anything extreme, it was likely that they would have lost fingers . . .

That thought reminded her that she was not entirely without weapons. There were her teeth and nails: surgically enhanced with a small but effective range of toxins. There were the retractable barbs that Memnos had implanted into the sides of her tongue, the inlay that circled her scalp, the vaginal modifications. But none of it was as good as the armor, and unless she could free her hands, little of it was of any use to her, either.

The vehicle was slowing. Soon it drew to a halt. Dreams-of-War heard voices, low and murmuring. Kappa? Memnos's excissieres? She could not repress a shudder at the thought. The clicking of ceremonial dispatching scissors suddenly seemed alarmingly loud, echoing within the confines of her paranoid mind. But she was beginning to wonder if the excissieres had even been real, or an excuse conjured by Yskatarina to lure her down to the ship.

From her limited viewpoint, this did not look like a Matriarchy vehicle, but then again, it was unlikely to belong to the kappa. Dreams-of-War ground sharpened teeth. And what of Lunae?

The back of the vehicle swung open. A dismal artificial light flooded in, making Dreams-of-War blink.

"Princess?" a voice said. "You awake?"

Dreams-of-War recognized it immediately. Sek. Her heart leaped within her for a lunatic moment, before the realization came that it was probably Sek who had sold her out in the first place. Next moment, her suspicions were confirmed. Sek said, quite without expression, to someone beyond, "You've done well. This is, indeed, the woman. Her armor is missing, I see. That should make things all the more interesting. Take her to the combat ground."

Dreams-of-War snapped at Sek's hand, missed. "You betrayed me!"

"I have to follow my orders," Sek said with a shrug. She did not seem greatly perturbed. "Memnos owns my boat; I do what I am told to do, nothing more."

"But why should Memnos betray me?" Dreams-of-War demanded.

"There is a new Matriarch now. I'm sorry, princess." But Sek sounded entirely unapologetic. "I follow the orders of the Matriarch alone. They said they would grant you to me as payment."

"Yskatarina. She's from Nightshade, isn't she? Tell me the truth! And who is the new Matriarch? What happened to the current one?" Dreams-of-War was too angry to reflect that she was not in the best position to begin making demands, but Sek only shrugged again.

"I do not know about Yskatarina. I do not ask such questions; it is not within the terms of our contract. As for the Matriarch, I know only that she carries the seals of authority. I am of Memnos origin, like yourself. You know what that means."

"You are lying. Yskatarina has documents pertaining to Nightshade in her possession. I know where she comes from. You took us to a place other than our original destination. Was this all a ruse, to gain control of the ship? Has everything been because of a need for my ghost-armor?"

"I do not lie," Sek said, apparently unaffronted. "Yskatarina told me nothing, save where to voyage and what—or whom—to carry with me."

"Your boat. It uses haunt-tech."

"I purchased the navigation system from Memnos. I paid dearly for it, too, but it has been worth it."

"And what of now? Why have I been brought here? What is going to happen to me?" Dreams-of-War tried to keep a rising panic from her voice.

"Why, I have already said it. You are to be taken to a combat ground, where you'll fight."

"'Fight'? Fight what?"

Above her, Sek gave a distant smile. "You will see."

Remember, Dreams-of-War reminded herself later, alone in a small cramped cell. *Remember what you used to be, so little time ago, a few years, no more. You have not always had your armor to rely upon.* And what had the armor truly done for her, along with the spirit that animated it? Nothing more than possession, if one considered it in a certain light. *There was a time when it was only I and none other to aid me . . .*

Sek's people had released her from her bonds, at least, and now she sat up and inspected the scars that covered her from shoulder to hip. Here: an arrow-wound from a skirmish out near Yslingen Fort. Those dappled, silvery bands: scar tissue from an electric flail, wielded by a war-madam whose name she could no longer recall. This notch: a hyenae's tooth from a later engagement, knocked out by its contact with her rib. And then she had earned her armor and there were no more scars.

She sat up with sudden resolution. *I will just have to return to what I was.* But resolution ebbed, draining away from her like water. Dreams-of-War, to her horror, was by no means sure that going back was even possible anymore.

The faint light had long since died behind the cracks of the shuttered window when they next came for Dreams-of-War. Sek, accompanied by another woman, stood warily in the doorway, bearing shields and a prod that snapped and crackled with blue fire. Dreams-of-War studied the stranger. She did not look like either warrior or sailor, though she wore the latter's salt-stained crimson. Her face was flat and closed, pinched in upon itself as though her features were suffering from permanent cold. The tilted eyes spoke of the north, but her hands, encased in fingerless red leather mittens, were as thick and shapeless as a kappa's own. *A hybrid?* thought Dreams-of-War, and dismissed the notion with revulsion.

"Here," Sek said. "These are for you."

It was familiar fighting garb: a kilt, boots, underharness.

"This is Martian gear," Dreams-of-War stated, shaking out the kilt. It was almost identical to the one she had worn as a girl: standard battle wear, with a narrow metal waist-strip that was now bare of insignia. If she was to fight, she would be doing so anonymously. No doubt, Dreams-of-War thought with bitterness, it was no more than she deserved.

"Of course." The sour-faced woman spoke with impatience. "You are a Martian warrior. This is what they have come to see."

"Who?"

"Your audience."

"This is an arenic fight? Gladiatorial?"

Sek laughed. "A little grandiose, perhaps. Though, obviously, it is an arranged form of combat. Get ready; I am sure you are anxious to begin."

Sek was, in fact, right. Dreams-of-War was burning for action of any description. She was not, she thought, well-suited to enforced contemplation.

"Very well." She put on the boots and the kilt, then bound up her breasts while the women watched impassively.

"Hold out your hands," Sek said. "Yes, straight in front of you, like that. Good."

When she steps close to me, I will strike, Dreams-of-War thought. Her mouth was suddenly dry. The spines along her tongue slid forth, prickling her gums. Mucus welled up from the floor of her mouth, coating the soft parts with a protective, hardening saliva. Claw-implants twinged at the tips of her fingers.

But Sek was taking no chances. She raised the prod and touched a button. Azure fire flicked out and wrapped itself with barbed-wire pain around Dreams-of-War's wrists. She tried to pull free, but the flame sizzled and hissed, singeing her skin until she forced her hands to relax within its fiery grip. Then it subsided, to a sharp ache and a band of bright blue.

"Follow me," the woman accompanying Sek said.

Dreams-of-War did so, stumbling a little. Sek kept well out of the way. They stepped out into a filthy passage, luminous with opalescent mold.

"Where are we?" Dreams-of-War asked.

Over her shoulder, Sek said, "This is a very ancient place. It dates back to before the Drowning, before the eruptions. It was buried for millennia; it is known only to a few."

"Is it a temple? A palace?"

"No one knows."

The passage ended in a thick metal door rimmed with rust. Sek pushed it open and Dreams-of-War followed her out into an echoing space. The ceiling was low and made of some kind of artificial stone. Columns of similar material ran at regular intervals into the farther reaches of the chamber.

"Those markings. What are they?"

"Letters, in some lost tongue, or numerals, or symbols only. Again, no one knows what they mean."

There were also marks on the floor: thin yellow lines and white squares.

"It is believed they have ritual content," Sek informed her.

"This audience," Dreams-of-War said, impatient. "Where are they?"

The next moment, her question was answered.

People streamed through the metal doors that stood at intervals along the chamber. Most were human women, though some were kappa and some, she was sure, were the Changed. There were a few whom Dreams-of-War was unable to place: faces that were out of proportion to their bodies, arms that ended in clubbed fists rather than hands, eyes set too deeply into the skull. She could have sworn that a handful of them were male. Perhaps these, too, were crossbreeds. It was forbidden, not to mention difficult, but there were all manner of backwoods genetics operations in these distant districts, impossible to regulate. She stared at them as they formed loose lines, stood unsmiling and silent, but she could feel their avidity.

"Here," Sek said. She gave Dreams-of-War a shove between her bare shoulder blades. The blue flame sizzled around her wrists and disappeared. "This is your weapon."

It was a gutting knife with a scale handle. It fitted Dreams-of-War's palm as though made for it.

"What am I to fight? These folk? I thought they were here to watch." There were at least two hundred of them, too many with which to do battle. Dreams-of-War resolved to kill as many as she could before she herself escaped. She would not countenance the possibility of being vanquished; that was the first lesson that she had learned as a warrior.

"No, you are correct. They are the audience."

"Then whom am I to fight?"

"Wait."

Dreams-of-War could hear a low humming note echoing throughout the chamber. Minutes later, a glide-car appeared, swiveling on low-slung motors so that its back was toward the audience, and sending spirals of dust up from the floor. The vehicle was large, with a high back. As it drew to a halt, something within the enclosed section thudded against the wall. The glide-car rocked on its jets. The crowd sent up a low murmur of pleased anticipation. Sek gave Dreams-of-War another shove.

"Go."

Dreams-of-War moved forward into a crouch, with the gutting knife drawn. A hatch slid open in the back of the glide-car, to reveal a cage. Something stirred heavily within. The cage door rattled up. Two beings leaped out and sprang to either side of the chamber, dodging behind pillars. Dreams-of-War had a fleeting, confused impression of striped skins, gaping mouths, hot yellow eyes, and human hands. The crowd howled. Dreams-of-War glanced from right to left and back again. There was no way out.

The change-tigers closed in, one on each side.

THE CRATER PLAIN

CHAPTER 1

MARS

A t first, Lunae thought that the long voyage back in time had been no more than an illusion. The place in which they now stood was also small, dark, and filled with smoke. It took her a moment to realize that the smoke was coming from a fire, blazing a little distance from the entrance to a cave. Snatches of muttered conversation came from the direction of the flames: harsh voices, abrupt words. The cave was filled with a pungent smell, a bloody, overwhelming odor.

"Someone is cooking meat," the kappa hissed, picking herself up from a bone-strewn floor.

"Is that what it is?" Lunae had never smelled anything like it before. Cautiously, she stepped to the lip of the cave and peered out.

Two slender crescents hung low over the horizon, against a sparkle of stars. After a moment, Lunae recognized familiar constellations, angled differently through clear sharp air. A blue star shone in the heavens between two ragged peaks.

"There," the kappa said in her ear. "Earth!"

There was rough sandstone under Lunae's hand, red in the light of the fire. And huddled around the blaze were three figures: squat, maned, licking short-clawed fingers.

"Hyenae."

Very quietly, Lunae and the kappa made their way back into the recesses of the cave.

"What are we to do?"

"Perhaps there's a way out at the back of the cave," Lunae said. But investigation proved fruitless. The cavern ended in a

243

smooth wall of rock. The only exit lay past the hyenae, whose home this all-too-clearly was.

The kappa nudged her. "If worse comes to worst, you must bend time for us."

Lunae shivered. "I wish never to bend time again. Look where it's got us."

"Yes, but now we are back on Mars, in what I fervently hope to be the present day. And it is thanks to your gift. Or," the kappa amended, "what your gift is to become."

"I don't want to take the risk."

The kappa sighed. "Then we must find another way out."

Lunae returned to the entrance of the cavern. The hyenae still sat, bickering over snatched scraps of gory meat. The smell of the meat, and of their bodies, was so strong that she hoped they would not be able to detect either herself or the kappa. But at some point they would surely return to the cave, when the night became dangerous and colder, and there was nowhere within it to hide. She could almost feel eyes on her back . . . The sensation was so overwhelming that Lunae whipped around.

There was, indeed, an eye, yellow as a lion's, peering out at her from within the wall.

Lunae sprang away and cannoned uncomfortably into the kappa.

"What is it?"

"Look!"

The kappa stared. The eye rolled around, angry and alarmed.

"Someone is in there. They've walled them up!"

A breath of sound, nothing more. Lunae, after a moment's hesitation, put her ear to the wall. The kappa was already beginning to scrabble at its base, where a small pile of stones had been accumulated.

"Help me, Lunae."

"We must be quieter!" She cast an anxious glance at the cave mouth. The hyenae were still there, but their meal was almost over. A mound of bones, glistening with saliva in the firelight, had grown behind them. Lunae clawed at the stones, placing each one gently on the ground. The kappa's broad hands paddled away, scraping stone and mortar both. The mortar released a clear, gummy substance that clung to Lunae's hands and stank. Soon, bound feet were revealed, then legs. The prisoner was not, Lunae noted, wearing armor. More space was cleared and the prisoner writhed downward, angling her body through the newly made hole and struggling clear. The kappa hacked at the bonds on wrists and ankles with a rock, freeing her.

There was a high-pitched yell from the mouth of the cavern. Lunae turned to see a hyenae bounding toward them on all fours, jaws gaping. The teeth were like a baboon's; claws rasped on the rocky floor.

The prisoner tore a filthy gag from her mouth, gave a yell of her own and rushed forward. Lunae snatched up a rock and threw it at the hyenae. The kappa emitted a warbling cry like a trapped frog. Her tongue lashed forth to catch the hyenae underneath the ear. It fell, with a bloody puncture staining the matted mane. Two more entered the cavern, fanning outward. The prisoner kicked up, catching one of the hyenae in the groin. It reeled back, whimpering. The second creature grasped Lunae around the waist and lifted her up, spinning to avoid the kappa's tongue.

The prisoner cried out in Martian, a long and hissing string of syllables. Something—fire-blackened, stained, unnatural—rose up in a liquid column from the floor. It fell upon the hyenae that held Lunae and flowed smoothly about his head and shoulders. Lunae, abruptly released, dropped to the floor. Muffled cries came from within the enveloping mass, but soon were stifled. The mass glided away, to rest at the warrior's feet. The hyenae lay where it had fallen, tongue lolling, quite dead.

Lunae stared at the corpses in fascinated horror. When she next looked up, the prisoner was encased in armor that resembled that worn by Dreams-of-War, except that this was ochre and fawn instead of burnished green. There was a faint facial resemblance, but Lunae could not tell if this might be due to genetics, or simply Martian arrogance. Besides, this woman had red hair.

"Who are you?" the kappa gasped.

"I am a warrior!" The voice could have been that of Dreams-of-War: arrogant, irritated. "Who are *you*?" the warrior demanded.

Improvising hastily, Lunae said, "We have come in search of a—kinswoman of yours. We last saw her on Earth. Perhaps she has returned to Mars." As far as she knew, this was far from the truth, but she felt compelled to offer some explanation for their presence.

The warrior frowned. "It was as though you appeared out of the air."

"Not so. We wandered the region and found ourselves in the hands of these creatures. Perhaps you lost consciousness for a moment," the kappa remarked smoothly.

"Perhaps," the warrior said reluctantly, clearly unconvinced. "And yourself?"

The warrior's face became a rictus of anger and disdain.

"I was captured." Having spent months in the company of Dreams-of-War, Lunae could tell what this admission cost her. "They knocked me unconscious and stripped me of the armor. They prize such things, though they do not understand how to use them. They fight and snap and bicker endlessly, trying to coerce our technology to do their bidding. They never succeed."

"But they didn't kill you."

"No. I was with others, who are now dead. The hyenae are not wholly unintelligent. They walled me up, to make sure that I was secure, until they wished to eat me."

"I am surprised," the kappa said with care, "that a meal was all they had in mind for you. I know the reputation of males."

The warrior snorted. "It would have been the worse for them had they tried. I have internal modifications, like all members of the warrior clans."

A short, contemplative silence ensued.

"What manner of creature are you?" the warrior asked at last, scowling at the kappa.

"I am a kappa, from the northern regions of Earth. I am the nurse of this girl."

"You are an amphibian or some such?"

"An amphibian, yes."

The warrior's scowl deepened. "You will not find it easy in this part of Mars. This is the Isidis Reach, the southern part of the Crater Plain. We are far from the Small Sea or the lake lands."

"I will have to manage," the kappa said with a sigh.

"What is your name?" Lunae asked.

The warrior drew herself up with a familiar show of pride. "I am named Knowledge-of-Pain."

"I think I have heard that name before."

"Naturally. I am infamous."

"I think it may have been spoken by my guardian, a woman of Mars—the person we have come here to find."

"Her name?"

"Dreams-of-War."

The warrior gave a slow nod. "I know her. She and I grew up in the clan house together. We do not make bonds, as you know, but she and I are not wholly antagonistic, except insofar as is natural. I had heard that she was sent to Earth. I don't know anything of her return."

"Do you know the ones who sent her?"

"Of course. They are the Memnos Matriarchy, who govern us all. They will know what has become of her." The warrior paused. "How did you become separated?"

"It's a long story." Lunae was thinking of the words of her future-self: *Do not trust the Matriarchy.*

The warrior nodded. "Very well. As you can see, it is dark, and I am hungry. I have had no food for three days. They would not remove the gag, in case I summoned my armor."

"There may be roots or berries, perhaps," the kappa ventured. Knowledge-of-Pain gave a hiss of disapproval and rolled the body of a hyenae over with her toe.

"Nonsense. There is plenty of meat." She plucked a knife from some inner fold of the armor and tossed it at the kappa's feet. "Start gutting."

CHAPTER 2

EARTH

Dreams-of-War ran backward until she was up against one of the stone pillars. The crowd kept up its muted sound, almost a low growl. It did not sound like anything that should come from a human throat, and perhaps, Dreams-of-War grimly reflected, it did not. The change-tigers were prowling, playing, paying little attention to her. They bore a faint resemblance to the hyenae of the Martian mountains: of similar height, but less bulky, products of ancient and whimsical engineering, crude soldiers for another age. Dreams-of-War had to admit, however, that they were impressive. Upright, the rib cage was massive; she could see the complex weave of bone beneath short, shaved fur. The legs bent forward at the knee, like a human's, but the jaws and skull were long. They moved with blurred speed, almost faster than she could track, occasionally dropping to all fours and bounding. One of them pranced up to her, tail coiling, jaws agape.

"Get away from me," Dreams-of-War hissed, and struck out with the gutting knife.

"Oh no," the tiger said, low and purring. "That would be no fun at all."

Some kind of mechanism whirred and clicked in its throat, permitting speech. Its eyes were noon-bright, filled with amusement. It batted Dreams-of-War with a casual clawed hand, a blur of stripes. She dodged away, shifting aside from the feint, but the next blow sent her sprawling. The change-tiger turned and loped away. Dreams-of-War scrambled to her feet.

The second tiger was sitting in a neat heap between two pillars, energetically licking a hind foot. Dreams-of-War stole a glance at the crowd. Sek stood, arms folded, with the dour woman at her side. The faces of the crowd were impassive, and Dreams-of-War realized with a shock that this was not some frenzied audience baying for blood. This was just an ordinary night out for them. The muted howling was the equivalent of polite applause. They did not really care who killed what, as long as killing was done and they got to see some blood at the end of the evening, to puncture the tedium of their everyday lives. And if by chance she killed the change-tigers, what then? They would only capture more, and the same scenario would be replayed until Dreams-of-War was torn to pieces or the crowd became bored.

But what option did she have? Flight was next to impossible and so was strategy, of which Dreams-of-War was not in any case enamored. No, it would have to be direct battle, she decided with relief. She uttered a yell and rushed forward.

One of the change-tigers, still coiled in a knot to wash, glanced up with mild yellow surprise, and rose languidly to its feet. It towered above her, perhaps seven feet or more. Telling herself that it was no different from the hyenae, Dreams-of-War feinted, darted aside as the tiger swiped, stabbed again, leaped aside. She fought with grim determination; the tiger had not even begun. It grinned at her, tolerant, a human adult confronting an angry child. Dreams-of-War fought as though the whole of her concentration had become focused upon this single foe, as if the odds against her had caused her to grow desperate. She fought as though there was not a second beast, sidling up behind her, discernible from scent and shadows and the growing, expectant hush of the crowd.

Ghostly claws, like some monstrous shadow puppet, appeared on the pillar before her, cast by the flickering light. The beast before her grinned again, made a small, mock pounce. Dreams-of-War dodged, and without looking, stabbed back in a sweeping arc with the gutting knife.

The change-tiger was too close to avoid the blow. Dreams-of-War felt hot, wet satisfaction, as thick as the blood that spattered her bare spine. She ripped upward with the gutting knife, almost losing her grip on its handle. She did not glance back to see what had become of it; she saw the shadow go down. The beast before her uttered a wailing snarl and dived forward. Dreams-of-War stepped with precision into the widening pool of blood and slid, fetching up with her back against the pillar.

The tiger turned and threw itself upon her. She did not think it cared any longer if it lived or died. In all the old stories, the cunning warrior-maiden would have turned the tale around: spoken softly to the tiger, offered it inducements to flight, fled with it into the mountains, away from the people who exploited it. But Dreams-of-War knew she did not possess the necessary guile. She brought up the gutting knife as it leaped. It speared itself, burying her in a tide of blood and torn skin and fur. She felt its final hot breath wash across her face, stinking of old meat. It winked at her as it died: a last cat-joke.

The crowd surged forward with a howl. Dreams-of-War thrust the corpse away, sprang to her feet, and ran for the nearest door. If the crowd were in the way, she thought as she ran, so much the worse for them.

Behind her, a terrible baying filled the air. At first, she wondered if it might be one of the tigers, not dead as hoped, but a swift look back told her that it was the normally languid Sek: head thrown back, eyes tightly shut, mouth open in an animal howl. Dreams-of-War decided not to waste time on what this might mean. Thrusting the scattering crowd out of her way, she kicked open the door and was through.

Hours later, Dreams-of-War stood on the edge of a headland, staring out across the ocean. It was not long since dawn and the maw of the Chain glittered in the west, catching the light of the rising sun like a skein of captured stars. Dreams-of-War chafed cold, scraped hands and cursed beneath her breath, but inwardly, she exulted. She had thrown off her pursuers at some point in the night, running through the tangle of forest behind the combat ground.

Sek's howls still echoed in her head. Dreams-of-War frowned. *Memnos has a new Matriarch now.*

What did that imply? Nothing good, surely. At least she no longer had to suffer Yskatarina's creature's crawling presence.

Somewhere out there was Lunae, floating in those green waves, tossed by the world's tide. Dreams-of-War's exultation faltered and faded. Whatever her current state of freedom, she had failed, and Lunae's loss bit at her, sharper than a tiger's tooth. She did not like feeling so helpless. Instinct told her to go on searching, but Dreams-of-War knew that in this case, instinct lied.

You do not mourn the dead. They are gone, and will not thank you.

The Martian way was to remove all traces of the person: warrior's insignia melted down, images destroyed, the name never mentioned, even to oneself. There were, of course, exceptions, relating principally to armor and weapons, but that was a legacy of haunt-tech rather than any ingrained stoicism in the face of mortality. If the spirits of the dead can be used as a source of power, then that power must be contained and limited. Dreams-of-War knew that it was not so superstitiously simple as that, but she still could not help but believe.

Lunae is gone. You mourn a memory. Your emotions are a product of your modification, nothing more.

She squinted into the sun, imagining that the flash and glare of its light was scouring her mind clean, leaving behind only what was necessary. And then she turned and began walking along the cliff, heading west, as the Chain spun into shadow overhead.

It was close to dusk before she realized that she was being followed. She had made her way along the headland, following the coast, hoping to come across some village from which a boat or flyer could be procured. Dreams-of-War had little compunction about stealing from the locals. As far as she was concerned, the planet was Martian property. Once she had transport, she planned to return to one of the cities—not Fragrant Harbor, as they would be watching out for her there, but one of the other coastal centers. There was nothing, however—no villages or settlements, just the endless coast and a thundering sea rising up against the cliffs in clouds of spray. The only sign of habitation was the gradual turn of the Chain's maw, thousands of miles above her head. Dreams-of-War trudged on into a steamy afternoon, longing for Martian cold.

Apart from the gulls and the flies, she saw only one other living creature: a small, doe-eyed beast that stood tremulously at the edge of a clearing. It stared at her with dreaming innocence, to which Dreams-of-War swiftly put paid with a throw of the gutting knife. The animal fell without a sound, to lie twitching on the forest floor. Dreams-of-War stripped it of its skin and ate it raw, saving a leg for later. The forest grew more densely here, and she was forced to slash and hack her way through the vegetation, becoming so absorbed in her task that at first she failed to notice the new sound that had snaked its way through the cries of birds and the hum of insects. When she noticed it, however, she froze.

It was a steady, throbbing pulse, reverberating from the trees and seeming to deaden the air. Dreams-of-War's head rang with it, but not so painfully that she did not discern the other sound that lay beneath it: the quick snickety echo of scissors. She turned, snarling, with the knife at the ready, but it was already too late.

Excissieres burst into the clearing, clad in waxy armor that slid over their skin in a multiple patterning of scales, eyes bright behind black visors, the sharp blades of their scissors clicking and hissing. Both bore prominent and unmistakable insignia. The Memnos Matriarchy had found her.

CHAPTER 3

MARS

Lunae tried not to think of their meal as flesh that had, however far back in genetic history, been human, but it was hard. The kappa seemed to have no such difficulties, and Knowledge-of-Pain wolfed down the scraps and sinews without bothering to cook them over the fire.

"Good," she said when she had finished. "And it is a cold night. The rest of the meat will keep. We can butcher it, divide it into parts for the journey."

"The journey?" Lunae questioned.

Knowledge-of-Pain stared at her. "To the Memnos Tower. That is where you wish to travel, I thought? To seek Dreams-of-War?"

"Are you intending to guide us?" the kappa said.

"I am intending to return there in any event. It is where I am based. It is the base of all members of the warrior clans when they have left the clan houses. I thought you would know this."

"In one tower?" Dreams-of-War had given Lunae the impression that there were many warriors within the Memnos Matriarchy.

"In the complexes, not the Tower itself. And many are in temporary residence in Winterstrike and the cities. Besides, I do not wish to insult you, but how would a girl and an amphibian fare on their own? Already you have met the hyenae, and there are worse, by far, roaming the Crater Plain, especially this close to the beginning of winter. All manner of things hunt now, to store food for the colder months."

Lunae could not imagine what that must be like. The night was already chill, forcing her to huddle close to the hyenae's blaze, and she could tell that the kappa was shivering. Her future-self had told her not to trust the Matriarchy. What, then, of this offer of aid? But they could not roam Mars alone, searching fruitlessly for answers, and her future-self had told her that if the flood was to be held back, it was at Memnos. Yet it was also at Memnos that her future-self had been captured . . . Lunae swallowed fear.

"You come from a warmer climate?" Knowledge-of-Pain asked.

"Warm and humid."

"You will find little of that here. Mars is a cold world, good for the flesh and the spirit both."

"I see no virtue in cold," the kappa remarked, disconsolately.

Knowledge-of-Pain laughed. It reminded Lunae of the hyenae's bark. "And I none in warmth. It must make you soft, vulnerable, overly secure."

"Perhaps the cold merely numbs," the kappa said.

"And what's wrong with that?" Knowledge-of-Pain asked, frowning once more.

They slept close to the fire, with the armor keeping watch. Lunae woke once in the night to see it standing above her. It had retained its human shape and was a mercurial gray in the light of the moons. Its face swam out of the liquid depths: the visage of a proud and angry woman, no longer young, with a hooked blade of nose and arched eyebrows. The face came and went, emerging from shadow. It was, indeed, like watching a ghost. Lunae regarded it for a few minutes before lapsing back into sleep.

They awoke to a chilly dawn and a thin band of light above the horizon. Shortly afterward, the Martian day grew on, light spreading over the red rocks and casting solid-seeming shadows over the ridges of earth and stone. Lunae lay blinking in the new light, watching as Knowledge-of-Pain opened her eyes and rose immediately to her feet. The kappa lay like a boulder on the other side of the fire.

"First we eat. Then we move," the warrior said.

She turned, summoning the armor with a flick of her hand. Her back was a mass of scar tissue. Lunae could not help gasping.

"What?"

"Your back . . ."

"What of it? Old wounds. Vulpen in the hills, wanted my spine as a trophy. He did not get it," she added needlessly. "Instead, I removed his own backbone and had it gilded. It hangs on the wall of my chamber."

There seemed little to say to this. Lunae crawled closer to the fire and gnawed reluctantly on a scrap of cold flesh. The kappa woke with a faint cry.

"Will it get any warmer?" Lunae asked.

Knowledge-of-Pain gave her a strange look. "Haven't you noticed? At this time of the year, the weather is always the same, unless we get a storm up from the south. Cold at dawn, then milder throughout the day, but never less than ground frost. Have you finished? Good. Then we douse the fire and take the rest of the meat."

Lunae and the kappa worked in silence, carving chunks of flesh from the corpses of the hyenae.

"I'd prefer vegetables," Lunae remarked after a time.

"And I fish." The kappa sighed.

Knowledge-of-Pain produced packs of loose webbing in which to carry the meat. It dripped.

"How long will it take us to reach the Memnos Tower?" Lunae asked.

"Perhaps three days."

"And there's no way except on foot?"

Knowledge-of-Pain shot her a disdainful glance. "Of course, Mars has flyers, but what does a warrior need of such technology? Walking is good for the spirit."

"We are in a hurry, however. We are anxious about our companion."

"Dreams-of-War is a warrior. There is no reason to be concerned. Either she has died fighting or she is safe." Knowledge-of-Pain's expression left no doubt as to what was the most desirable option.

"Nevertheless . . ."

"In any event, I have no means of summoning a flyer," Knowledge-of-Pain went on. "The possibility of rescue softens the soul."

Lunae refrained from asking about the armor. Knowledge-of-Pain was beginning to bristle, rather in the manner of her absent clanswoman. With the meat safely, if messily, stowed, they set off down the slope.

After the rigors of their recent spin through time, Lunae could not help feeling relieved at being in one place and one age—one, moreover, in which she had been made. Despite the threats of the Crater Plain, she enjoyed the first morning of the journey: the chill, the frost that crackled beneath her feet, the clear skies across which the occasional dactylate raptor glided, leather-winged and bronze-scaled, like flying statues. The Crater Plain stretched out before them and there was a periodic glint of water in the distance, a sign of the Grand Channel. The landscape was studded with ruins: the remains of ancient fortresses, dating, so Knowledge-of-Pain informed her, from the Rune Memory Wars.

Lunae did not find herself to be well informed about Martian history, a fact that appeared to horrify Knowledge-of-Pain. She launched into an immediate monologue, covering the building of the canals, the Beast Time, the Age of Children, the thousand-year rule of the Isidis Monarchy, and innumerable other periods of interest. Lunae listened, half from courtesy, half from genuine interest. The kappa grumbled along behind.

". . . Of course, our own history does not resemble your own. Some believe otherwise, but it is my own view that Mars has only ever possessed one gender, unlike the splitting that occurred on Earth—it is thought, due to changes in the genetic structure from the adverse effects of solar radiation, or viral infection."

"But there are male creatures on Mars," Lunae protested. "The hyenae, others . . ."

"Stray mutations, nothing more. Kept for purposes of amusement or the hunts," Knowledge-of-Pain announced firmly.

"I wonder that there seem to have been so many of them on Earth."

"They were phased out swiftly enough," Knowledge-of-Pain said. "What is the point of having two kinds of humans, after all?"

"But there are many kinds of humans and protohumans," Lunae said.

"And most of them are a single gender. A degree of purity is thus maintained."

The kappa was frowning. "How, then, do creatures like the hyenae breed?"

"There are females, but few of them, and without intelligence. They live in caverns, where they pup. They never see the light of day." Knowledge-of-Pain dropped to a crouch and ran a hand over the loose, stony earth. "Tracks."

"More hyenae?"

"Perhaps. Or more likely, mirror-men."

"What are they?"

"Other dwellers of the plain. If we meet one, you will find out." Knowledge-of-Pain grimaced. "I do not like to talk about them." She rose and strode onward.

CHAPTER 4

MARS

Dreams-of-War struck out with the gutting knife. The blade glanced over the excissiere's side, adding a real lesion to the flickering images that crossed the woman's flesh. The excissiere snarled, lashing a war-whip. It caught Dreams-of-War across the thigh. She fell into a roll, came up again. The excissiere bent, slashing with her scissors. Dreams-of-War's teeth met in her forearm, releasing a mouthful of toxicity into the excissiere's bloodstream. The scissor-woman dropped, twitching in the dusty earth. Dreams-of-War tried to rise and could not. There was the whistle of a second war-whip, then only the hot dark.

When she next returned to consciousness, she knew immediately that she was on Mars. The knowledge came to her with a great glad rush, swiftly followed by dismay. If she was, indeed, on her home world, that could only mean one thing: capture and disgrace. The armor's lack was a palpable sensation; she felt as though she had been stripped of her skin. She raised her aching head and looked around.

Her limbs were free, but the flesh was striped and mottled with slashes and bruising. The second excissiere must have held back, since she was whole and not in a thousand tiny pieces, but the skin over her ribs still burned with the ritual scissor-strikes, and the lash of the war-whip had raised a great weal across her shoulders. The torn flesh had been dressed with oil and held together with clamps.

She lay upon a metal bed: a traditional piece of clan furniture, with a waving headboard decorated by horned skulls. When she swung herself from the bed, her bare feet scraped softly upon the coldness of an iron floor. There was a window in the wall, a tall, narrow opening through which an occasional gust of wind whipped. Dreams-of-War got to her feet and went unsteadily to the window. Bracing her hands against metal walls, she peered through.

Olympus rose in the distance, a snow-tipped, perfect cone towering up against the sky. She could see a russet patch of forest spreading around its foot, the ruin of the Tellur Fortress snaking up between the trees. Familiarity, memories, home. She knew exactly where she was. She knew this view, had spent hours or more crouched in a window seat during the days of her warrior induction after leaving the clan house, gazing out across that great cone, those distant forests beyond the Crater Plain. That view had been different only in that it had been seen from lower down. She was in the Tower of the Memnos Matriarchy.

Dreams-of-War stood by the window for a long time, gazing out across the plain. She told herself that she should move, act, plan—but something kept her there beside the window, drinking in the view like wine. At last she dragged herself away and crossed to the door. It was, unsurprisingly, locked. Dreams-of-War picked and scratched at the edges with her nails, more for the sake of it than out of any genuine hope, and returned to sit on the bed and take stock.

She still retained most of her internal armory, which was a promising sign. If they had not stripped her of everything, then it seemed feasible that she would be permitted to make a showing for herself in a hunt. That did not hold much chance of survival, but at least it might give her the opportunity to salvage some dignity. Things, Dreams-of-War considered, were looking up. At least, if she did not think too closely about Lunae.

The day dragged on. Dreams-of-War, after a compulsory session of banging on the door and berating her captors, felt that honor was partially satisfied. She went to perch on the windowsill, to stare out across the falling dusk. The air was colder yet. She realized with dismay that she had lost track of the year on Mars, but it was bound to be one of the long winter months. Summer at these latitudes was mercifully brief. Dreams-of-War breathed chill air and thought with a shudder of the humid reek of Fragrant Harbor. It all seemed suddenly so distant, nothing more than a dream. Only Lunae seemed real.

Earth rose. A small moon crept over the horizon and lay in the east like a droplet above the edge of the world. High on Olympus a light flickered. The ruin of the Tellur Fortress was a patch of shadow against the slope. The air became suddenly electric and anticipatory. There was the whisper of a haunt-lock being disengaged. Dreams-of-War waited, holding her breath. The door of the room swung open.

Four women entered. One was Yskatarina Iye, whose eyes slid over Dreams-of-War with careful indifference. There was no sign of her companion. She was followed by two excissieres, both in full armor, scissors at the ready.

The fourth person was one of the Changed, moving with unsteady concentration. Her head wobbled back and forth as though seeking balance, and occasionally she blurred in and out of phase. She smelled of death. Dreams-of-War thought: *She has been reanimated. She is a Kami.* The being wore the robes of a Matriarch. Dreams-of-War surged up from the windowsill and launched herself at Yskatarina's throat.

"Where is the previous Matriarch? *And where is my armor?*"

The excissieres hauled her unceremoniously back and pushed her onto the bed. Dreams-of-War sat quivering with fury, a pair of glassy blades at her throat.

"The armor is safe," the Matriarch said, voice creaking from her throat.

The armor. Not: *your* armor. *Well,* Dreams-of-War thought, biting back rage, *it will never be mine again, but no matter. I'll still kill her.*

Yskatarina nudged the Matriarch. "You told me that you would make a decision."

"I am aware of that," the Matriarch said. She blurred again. "And it has been made. There is a form, which all hunts must follow. You know this, I assume?"

Yskatarina inclined her head. "Of course. But I protest." She stared at the Matriarch. "I should not have trusted Sek to do the job. I want her killed now, without ceremony."

The Matriarch gave a thin crescent smile, displaying a row of sharp teeth. She gestured to the excissieres and they stepped forward, brandishing scissors. Yskatarina slid back in alarm.

"But the excissieres still answer to me. And I should like to see a hunt, even through a far-viewer. This body remembers it." The Matriarch's dull eyes filled with a sudden, dreadful eagerness.

Dreams-of-War could see from Yskatarina's face how little she liked this, but then she seemed to acquiesce.

"Very well, then. As long as she dies."

"I am to engage in a hunt?" Dreams-of-War queried.

The Matriarch stared into the twilight, but Yskatarina answered, "Just so."

"First the change-tigers, now this. And what has become of my armor? Am I to use it for the hunt?"

"No. The armor of Embar Khair is safe, though you may not recognize it when you see it again," Yskatarina informed her. "You will be hunted in what I understand to be the traditional manner, by excissieres."

The Matriarch turned, and without another word, lurched from the chamber. Yskatarina stared after her in what appeared to be some consternation, then added with a trace of irony, "I'm sure it will be an honorable death." She, too, departed, followed by the excissieres. The door was locked behind her, leaving Dreams-of-War to seethe in silence.

They came for her after twilight: two excissieres, bearing hunting gear. Desperate to be free of the confines of the room, Dreams-of-War swiftly put it on and strode to the door.

"You are anxious for this to be over with," one of the excissieres said with a razor smile.

"Of course. I am a warrior."

"The hunt is in traditional form. You will be given a three-hour start. At midnight, the hunters will set forth and will search until they find you. You will fight, and die."

"I am aware of the format," Dreams-of-War said with hauteur.

"It is expected that you will put up a suitable defense."

"Of course." She longed to be outside the Tower, into the clear night air. And if Yskatarina Iye was close by, then what did that imply about her armor?

The excissieres led her down the stairs of the Tower. Memories assailed her. The last time she had trod these worn iron steps had been when she left Mars to travel to Earth. Then, her armor-shod feet had rung on ancient metal, and Embar Khair had whispered inside her mind. Now, her leather boots made little sound, as though she were already no more than a ghost in this world. Was this what it was like to be dead? Dreams-of-War wondered. Did Embar Khair feel this way, perhaps, trapped in the ghost-armor, a prisoner in the shell? Living no life except that which was granted to her through someone else's eyes? For the first time in her life, Dreams-of-War felt truly afraid. She halted abruptly on the stair, causing the excissiere behind her to stumble and curse.

"What are you doing?"

"A thought, nothing more." Through the slitted window of the Tower, an affectation from the days when Mars was at war with itself and the bow-women prowled, she could see a single glowing star. Was that Earth? Venus? From this angle, she could not tell. There was the snagging touch of scissors between her shoulder blades.

"Move. Do you wish to live to see the hunt?"

Dreams-of-War acquiesced with a nod of the head. She continued down the staircase until they reached the stone vault of the hall. This place must be wreathed in ghosts, she thought, even without haunt-tech. In the Lost Epoch, the bones of warriors had gone to make the walls, embedded into plaster and girdled with Isidis adamantine. The practice had been discontinued thirteen centuries before—or so the Matriarchy claimed—but the bones remained, fragmentary now, hard as the stone that contained them. *And so are we, the living. Hard as Mars itself, tough as our world-cradle, little difference between us. I am about to die*, Dreams-of-War reflected. *My bones will make Mars.* There was a certain comfort in the notion.

The excissiere was hauling open the oldest door: a narrow plate of sheet metal, thinner and taller than any Dreams-of-War had ever known. Almost as though the door had been made for something not human, a curiously twisted opening that one had to angle oneself through to pass. As the excissiere opened it, the door emitted a ringing note like a bell, to signal the beginning of the hunt.

"Your weapon," the excissiere said. She handed Dreams-of-War a knife-flame. The blade flickered in the twilight, a sliver of gleam.

"Go," the excissiere said, but Dreams-of-War was already through the door.

CHAPTER 5

MARS

oward late afternoon, they reached the banks of the Grand Channel. Ramparts of crumbling crimson stone tumbled down to the water, frosted with a thin glitter of ice in the shadows. The canal was perhaps a quarter of a mile wide, big enough to take the great barges that Lunae had seen on the image-viewer, traveling to and fro along the curve of the world. Knowledge-of-Pain frowned.

"The canal is low."

"Where does the water come from?" the kappa asked.

"From the poles. It's channeled down the Ninth Meridian, all the way to the Small Sea." She climbed to the summit of the rampart and stood, looking out across the plain. The frown remained.

"What's wrong?" Lunae asked, clambering up to stand beside the warrior. Up here, the air was even colder, a cruel drift of wind across the plain.

"Look."

A tower stood beyond spires and pillars of rock, so twisted and convoluted that at first Lunae thought it was no more than the rock itself. Even from this distance, she could tell that it must be huge, rising out of the floor of the plain in a mottled sequence of red and black, all blood and bruises.

"That is the Tower of the Memnos Matriarchy," Knowledge-of-Pain informed her.

Smoke was emanating from the summit of the Tower, smudging the clear sky.

"Is it on fire?"

Knowledge-of-Pain shook her head. "No. The smoke signals the beginning of a hunt. Once the sun goes down, some transgressor will be sent out into the wilds, to fight for life and fail."

Lunae stared at her in horror. "They'll hunt the person down?"

"It's the ancient way." Knowledge-of-Pain seemed unconcerned. "You have similar things on your world."

Lunae was silent. After all, Earth was hardly a haven of peace . . . "What do you have to do, to be hunted so?"

Knowledge-of-Pain shrugged. "It depends on the whim of the Matriarchs. Offenses may be slight, or major."

"Do you know if you've offended them? Is there a—rule list, or some such?"

"Of course not." Knowledge-of-Pain gave a feral grin. "It all adds to the excitement of being. The Matriarchs reflect its unpredictability. Memnos is a mirror of life."

Cruelty, suffering, and woe, Lunae thought, but did not say. *What of beauty, of gentleness?* She looked from Knowledge-of-Pain's sharp profile to the sharper silhouette of the Tower, and reflected that there was little point in voicing her doubts. Mars and the Martians were all of a piece.

"We follow the canal," Knowledge-of-Pain said now. "It runs past the Tower; it is the straightest way."

"What of the hunt?"

Knowledge-of-Pain looked blank. "What of them? They are occupied with their own ends and aims. They will not bother us." She began climbing back down the ramparts, sidling, surefooted. The kappa hung back.

"We cannot trust her."

"But do you think that she really knows what's going on?"

"Whether she does or not, we cannot simply stroll into Memnos and ask for clarification. Remember what your future-self said."

"I have never forgotten it. And there has been no sign of Essa."

The kappa sighed. "I do not even understand what Essa is."

"My future-self said that things would be decided at Memnos. She said I had to go there."

"Maybe we can trick Knowledge-of-Pain in some way," the kappa said. "Lose her, perhaps."

"I think that might be difficult."

The warrior was waiting impatiently at the bottom of the ramparts. Lunae took a last look at the Tower, like a fire-twisted arrow in the distance, and slid down to join her.

"Who are the huntresses?" she asked. "Other warriors?"

"Yes. They are the most extreme of us, the most evolved. They are excissieres, the killing-women—nothing more, nothing less."

The kappa snorted. "I would not call that *evolved*."

"You are not asked to do so," Knowledge-of-Pain snapped. "What can you know of power? The huntresses live for the chase, just as in the most ancient texts of the time before all time. The bow-women of the Martian forests are legend."

Lunae and the kappa followed her to a gap in the ramparts, leading to a narrow walkway.

"This is the towpath. We follow it."

The kappa frowned. "I have seen images of barges. What could be used to tow something so large?"

But Knowledge-of-Pain was already striding ahead out of earshot. It was not long, however, before they found out.

The barge was moving swiftly, at first no more than a black square in the distance, but rapidly resolving into a curling hull, ribs of ridged wood, a cabin formed of metal arches upon the deck. It was perhaps a couple of hundred feet in length, at once sinister and whimsical. Fretwork decorated its sides, like cobwebs. But it was the thing that pulled it that made Lunae stare, openmouthed.

The creature was attached to a chain, leading the barge along close to the bank. It was the size of a beast she had seen pictured in an ancient image book: a pachydermic genetic cross. Its hide was a mottled jade-and-black, stretched over prominent bones that gave it the look of a huge moving skeleton. Its eyes were as dull and mild as the surface of a weedy pond. Its back was covered in overlapping scales. It padded, splayfooted, along the towpath, bony jaws moving in rhythmic counterpoint.

"What is that?" Lunae breathed.

"A water-beast," Knowledge-of-Pain informed her indifferently. "They use them throughout the canal network."

"I don't see anyone on the barge."

"That is because no one is there. The water-beast guards the barge, from both land and canal-side."

"Does it have intelligence?" the kappa asked doubtfully. "It does not look as though it does."

"Of course not. It is programmed, nothing more."

The barge glided on, keeping pace with them.

"It's slowing down," Lunae said.

"The beasts appear to like company. No one knows why."

"But it hasn't even glanced at us."

Knowledge-of-Pain shrugged. "Who is to say why they do what they do?"

Lunae studied the creature for a while, but it did nothing remarkable and eventually she grew tired of looking at it. It became part of the landscape: the glowing sky, the crimson and ochre rocks, the padding skeletal leviathan. Lunae sank into a kind of trance, still slightly nauseated from the meat she had eaten.

They had been walking for perhaps an hour alongside the barge before the sun started to sink down over the horizon. A moon hung low in the west, like a chewed bone. The shadows lengthened, until even the kappa appeared as a tall, slender figure, gliding over the waterglow. The air grew colder and Lunae's mouth tasted of metal every time she took a breath. Knowledge-of-Pain said, without pausing, "Soon, we will halt and make a fire. Best we keep away from the canal when true darkness falls. Things live in it, which are drawn up by the moons."

"What kind of things?"

"Just things."

A long, trembling note rang out across the plain and faded into silence. Knowledge-of-Pain's head went up.

"The hunt's begun."

Lunae could not help thinking about the woman who must, even now, be sprinting for her life across the stony ground. Did she care that she was about to die? Did she regret what she had done to bring her to this pass? Or was she as cold as all these Martian women seemed to be, without any real feelings beyond duty and rage? It was at once admirable and unnatural. Lunae drew closer to the kappa, another unnatural being, and yet somehow closer in her humanness, despite her amphibian form. The sun vanished. Twilight drew on.

CHAPTER 6

MARS

D reams-of-War moved swiftly across the plain, heading for the hills. The cone of Olympus quivered on the horizon, catching the light from the sinking sun and glowing like a beacon of rose-and-white ice. Dreams-of-War fixed her gaze on its distant promise and ran on, pausing only to reach down and snatch a handful of fragrant grass from the edges of a dewpond. When she reached the edge of the rocks, where the ground became littered with boulders and the going was no longer so easy, she slowed, then halted. She doubled up, panting, clutching at her chest, as if winded. Let whoever might be watching from afar think that her time on Earth had lessened her fitness. With her other hand, working swiftly, she twisted off a strap of leather from the back of her harness and looped it into a snare. She hung this from a point of rock above a sage bush, and ran on, paying close attention to her harness, where it rubbed and chafed.

For the next half hour she dodged around boulders, through a narrow canyon that smelled of herbs and death, and back to where she had set the snare, taking a different route through the stones.

The snare was snaking about, turning and writhing. Dreams-of-War reached back between her shoulder blades and found what she sought: a round nub of metal attached to the harness. It was a tracking device. She tore it free, then bent to the snare. Within it, caught by the neck, was a plains hare, its great dark eyes frantic in the growing light of a little moon. Dreams-of-War reached down and grasped it firmly behind its ears, then, with difficulty, secured the tracking device with a leather thong around the struggling creature's throat. When she released it, the hare shot off into the shadows, zigzagging away up into the canyon. Dreams-of-War rose from her crouch and took the steepest route up the rock face.

This was, she was now sure, the place where she had confronted the four hyenae all those years ago. She could almost smell the charred odors of human flesh, fire, sweat. And above all these scents was the rank-blood and rotten-meat signature of the Earthbones, which lay concealed and congealing beneath the treacherous soil.

She looked up into the starlit sky, wondering if Yskatarina's stolen ship was somewhere in orbit. Yskatarina would surely not have risked bringing the armor back to Mars, Dreams-of-War thought, for she must know that Dreams-of-War would stop at nothing to retrieve it.

She turned, looking back toward the Memnos Tower for the first time. It was shrouded in darkness now, but she could still see the dying glare of the torch that blazed at its summit, signaling the hunt. They would have started out by now, would be heading across the plain. She wondered where the hare might be. Wherever, it would not deceive them for long. This was as good a place as any to make a stand. Dreams-of-War strode along the canyon, and began to make her preparations.

She worked quickly, listening to the wind all the while for signs of approaching pursuit. The huntresses would be expecting a trap of some kind. Dreams-of-War had no way of knowing how much they were aware of the nature of this particular piece of terrain, but it was the only advantage that she currently possessed and she intended to make full use of it. She had stripped herself of everything but the knife-belt, and was now engaged in covering every remaining inch of flesh with a mixture of ash, earth, and water from the nearest small pool. She bound her hair into a tight knot, smothering it with mud. The night was freezing, but she had long since learned to ignore the cold. Then she retreated into the shadows, to watch and wait.

Pursuit was not long in arriving. She heard them coming along the pass, scented them on the wind above the moldering smell of the Earthbones and the rankness of her own mud-smeared skin. Dreams-of-War closed her eyes against any betraying gleam and crouched lower between the rocks. There were three of them, moving swiftly and silently, with only the occasional snap of brushweed under foot or the roll of a pebble to indicate their presence. Dreams-of-War held her breath.

Finally, they were visible: shadows in the double moonlight, gliding past the walls of the canyon. She knew that they had spotted her. A shadow paused, raised the great bow, notched an arrow . . . It was then that Dreams-of-War broke cover, mimicking panic, bolting up from the rocks and dashing through the scrub toward the only apparent exit: the cavern mouth. An arrow sang past her, whizzing into the bushes, and she heard the huntress's whistle, sending sonar trails out against the canyon wall. But Dreams-of-War was into the cavern and down, dodging past the first mouth of the Earthbones.

Her intention was that the mud and ash would disguise her scent long enough to enable her to dodge past the initial maw, but it became immediately apparent that the plan was not flawless. Perhaps she had not covered herself adequately, or perhaps the Earthbones was more sensitive than she had given it credit for. The walls of the cavern began to grind inward, a thousand needle spines curling out from the surface and stiffening as they scented her. Dreams-of-War dodged between the spines, throwing herself to the floor, rose again on a patch of ground that was in the middle of the second mouth. Here, the spines were longer, and barbed. But there was a sudden wailing shriek from behind her, followed by shouts. The air filled with a raw iron odor. Dreams-of-War silently rejoiced.

The first mouth had, it seemed, claimed a victim from the huntresses. That left two to go.

As she dived through the twists and turns of the second mouth, the spines caught her skin, snagging it. She tore herself free, snatching at a spine and wrenching it from the wall. The Earthbones shuddered and heaved. The floor buckled; Dreams-of-War went down. A further short shower of arrows, notched and fired at random, struck the wall, releasing an acrid stream of liquid that smelled more mineral than animal. The floor rocked like a ship at sea. Dreams-of-War slithered forward, out of the maw and into the sultry, dank realm that led down to the third mouth and the gut.

"Come back!" The call came from behind. "You will die in the maw, digested slowly. But we will make it a quicker death . . ."

Dreams-of-War did not answer. Instead, choosing her position with care, she paused at the lips of the third mouth and began hacking swiftly at the curling spines with the gutting knife. The spines thrashed and coiled, lashing out with barbed tips that bit deep into Dreams-of-War's flesh, sending lightning along the wounds made by the excissieres. Behind her, the padding feet of the huntresses drew closer.

Ducking between the spines, Dreams-of-War made a deep vertical cut in the wall of the lip. It drew back, flattening out against the earth. Now she could see the threads of the Earthbones, running red-veined through the soil. Moonlight flooded through as the breathing vent opened, and in another second Dreams-of-War was swarming up the side of the third maw, using the spines as a ladder. She was already forcing herself through the vent into the cold night air, emerging from the ground in a witch-haze of smoke, as the third mouth turned back upon the huntresses. Dreams-of-War listened to their brief cries with a grim satisfaction, before all fell silent. At her feet, the vent closed once more with a wet snap.

Dreams-of-War strode away down the canyon, and did not look back. With the Earthbones evaded and her pursuers dead, she was now free to plan. When she reached the end of the canyon, she squatted at the edge of a spring sink, gazing out across the shallow water. Rust-red reeds swayed in the breeze, cracking the ice that lay across the sink. Dreams-of-War welcomed the cold.

There were, to her mind, only two true choices. She could remain out here in the wilds, battling hyenae and other men-remnants, for an indefinite period. The notion held a certain appeal. Dreams-of-War was sick of people, particularly her own kind. But thoughts of Lunae kept intruding, weakening her. To restore her spirits, she drew more closely to the fire of anger: a rage that was directed purely at Yskatarina and the Memnos Matriarchy. That, then, was the second choice: to return to the Tower and extract vengeance. To Dreams-of-War's mind, this was by far the most alluring option. Besides, the Memnos Tower seemed to present the greatest opportunity for gaining information.

She splashed the cold water over her face and stood, scenting the air. She was now to the east of the Tower, perhaps a day's walk. Taking a roundabout route through the canyons, she set off.

The horned woman stepped out of nowhere. One moment, Dreams-of-War was walking through an empty canyon, the next, the woman was standing in front of her.

It was immediately apparent to Dreams-of-War that she was not real, nor yet a hallucination, like the herd of gaezelles that she had encountered before. The woman was slightly transparent. Coiled horns grew up from her head, lending her a top-heavy appearance. Her feet, which resembled hooves, were small. She tapered to a point, like a jar. Dreams-of-War had seen her like before, on the stele that decorated the interior of the Memnos Tower: an ancient people, whose name had long since been forgotten.

"You are from the past," Dreams-of-War said. "Are you a ghost?"

"I am Essa. I am a message," the ram-horned woman said. "From a hundred years ago. I have been programmed into the soil. I have come to find you. It has not been easy."

"A hologram, then?"

The ram-horned woman smiled. Her eyes, Dreams-of-War noted, were intensely blue, the color of the skies of Earth.

"'Ghost' is better. I programmed myself in many permutations."

"Why do you appear to me now, then?" The armor had spoken of someone called Essa, she remembered now.

"Because once we prepared for this day—the old Matriarch and I, and she whose armor you wore, and the twinned women Yri and Yra. We set things in motion. Some of us died, for a time. And now I am back, and learning. Haunt-tech is feeding back upon itself, sending information out and retrieving it from the tech in the land. It was through this I found out about your return and the hunt. Moreover, a ghost is running Memnos. Did you know this?"

"I had noticed. How did that happen?"

"The Matriarch had her reanimated. Once, she was my mistress, but now she is governed by Nightshade. She is Martian no longer, but the excissieres listen to her, because she holds the Matriarch's phial. And the warriors obey her because she controls the excissieres."

Dreams-of-War snorted. "It's time for some changes at Memnos."

"Come with me." The ram-horned woman turned and began to walk. Warily, Dreams-of-War followed the woman along the canyon. She seemed to be solidifying, growing harder and sharper-edged with each step she took. Dreams-of-War wondered whether the programming was more detailed the farther one went into the rocks. It seemed likely. Even without the armor, she could sense the programming: a hum in the air, the flickering of the shadows. Lost technology: an ancient by-product of terraforming, perhaps nano-driven, in which the very soil could speak. It made her wonder how this might be used against the Matriarchy. And it was homegrown Martian, which gave her a little pride. Haunt-tech was not the only technology that could be useful.

"Where are we going?"

"To find my ship. And your armor."

CHAPTER 7

MARS

Lunae was awoken by the armor.

"Someone approaches!" it said.

Lunae sat upright, quivering. The kappa stirred. Knowledge-of-Pain was already on her feet and stepping across the smoldering fire to the armor, which flowed smoothly over her body. Next moment, an arrow-bolt shot past Lunae's head and embedded itself in the side of the barge. Knowledge-of-Pain cursed. The kappa, moving with startling speed, grabbed Lunae by the hand and pulled her down the rampart to the towpath. Other bolts were coming through the dark, hissing into the waters of the canal. Something gave a mournful cry, rose from the depths, and sank once more. The kappa and Lunae sprang for the side of the barge and fell sprawling onto the deck. Then, keeping low, they made for the protection afforded by the other side of the cabin. No one was in sight.

"Who are they?" the kappa gasped. "Is that the hunt?"

"Knowledge-of-Pain said that they had no interest in us!"

"But Knowledge-of-Pain is of Memnos," the kappa muttered.

"She's been away for some time, evidently. I don't know what to think," Lunae said. A terrible squalling broke through the hissing darkness. Gripping the metal edging of the cabin, Lunae peered across the deck. The tow-beast was plunging at the end of its chain, causing the barge to rock up and down. A bolt stood out from a crack between the bone plates.

"The poor thing's been hit," the kappa said.

"What's happened to Knowledge-of-Pain? Do you think we should try and make a break for it? Swim across the canal? Are they even shooting at us?" She paused. "I could take us through time—but I just don't know, kappa. What if this is my moment of failure?"

"I do not know. As for swimming, the warrior said that there are creatures in the canal," the kappa replied. "I might be successful, but you might not. There is nowhere else to go. We are trapped."

They could hear shouting, but could not distinguish the words. Lunae fretted, wondering whether she should take the risk and move them forward. Just an hour or so might be enough . . . But she thought of her future-self and the memory was enough to stop her. The barge continued to plunge, then the deck was doused in a sudden wave, drenching the kappa and Lunae. The prow of the barge veered sharply around, heading for the opposite bank of the canal.

"The tow-beast's gone in," Lunae cried, spitting bitter water.

From the bank came a cry of rage. Once more Lunae peered around the casing of the cabin, this time to see that they were already far from shore. The tow-beast was swimming as swiftly as an arrow, the chain stretched taut between the boat and its throat. A figure sprinted along the towpath, armor rippling. There was a hiss of arrows. Knowledge-of-Pain gave a sharp cry, but ran on.

The kappa threw herself to the boards and shuffled to the side of the boat.

"This is a war-arrow," she called back. "Only warriors use these bows. And the tow-beast is heading downstream, toward the Memnos Tower."

Lunae stared at her in dismay. The barge sailed on, moving swiftly.

Soon even the running form of Knowledge-of-Pain was no more than a distant shadow on the bank. The tow-beast arrowed through the oily waters of the canal like a fish, its lumbering land form forgotten. Occasionally its sinuous spine broke the water, the long tail rippling in sea-serpent configuration.

"When will it stop?" the kappa asked at last, sitting disconsolately on the deck, with her back to the casing. "It has been swimming for more than two hours. Do you think it will ever stop? Or will it take us to the very pole?"

"Perhaps when it's light we'll be able to swim for it," Lunae said. She looked at the heaving black water and shuddered. "Maybe the creatures are nocturnal."

"Perhaps." The kappa sounded doubtful.

"The attackers will surely catch up to us at some point, too." Lunae stood, hastily. "It's heading for the bank."

The tow-beast was slowing as it changed direction, and now they could see that a lock was opening up ahead.

"It's taking us in," Lunae said. The Tower of Memnos clawed upward, filling the sky. Smoke drifted against the brightness of the stars. The tow-beast clambered out of the water in a bulky mass of bones, to stand shuddering upon the bank. The barge sank slowly down, stretching the chain. In the side of the Tower, a gate swung open and figures poured forth.

"Lunae," the kappa's voice was urgent. "We have to go."

Lunae nodded. They were now close enough to the sides of the lock to swing down over the side of the barge and cling to the rust-stained struts. Below, the barge sank, and then was gone through the lock gate. The tow-beast padded forward, where it was greeted with faint cries, like the voices of birds. Lunae and the kappa gripped the struts and turned their faces to the wall.

"What if they see us?"

"They will have to come looking," the kappa said. The lock gate closed with a muffled clang. They were alone.

They waited until the sounds of voices had disappeared, then clambered up the wall of the lock. A narrow ledge led up toward the Tower. There was no way back; the gates of the Tower were closed behind them. They were within the complex of Memnos.

Lunae and the kappa sidled around the edges of the Tower. Voices floated down from the slit windows, but outside, all was silent. They ran behind a towering pyramid of barrels, then through a storeroom and out into a courtyard, covered by the shadows cast by the Tower itself. The kappa seized Lunae and drew her back behind the barrels, a hand over the girl's mouth. They watched as a squadron of excissieres came by, weapons at the ready. The women's faces were fierce and blank, wounds gliding over their skin. They looked like the walking slain. There were, perhaps, a dozen of them.

Lunae crouched down behind the barrels.

"We can't stay here. They'll find us. Maybe this was how I was captured."

The kappa gave her a little shake. "That was a different time line. Your future-self said so. What is to come, is not set in stone."

"Even so."

"Let's see what we can find."

They made their way around the perimeter of the courtyard, keeping to the shadows. More excissieres ran by: a pair, this time, wearing black armor. Their faces were set in a snarl.

"They all look so angry," Lunae whispered.

"Martians are always angry," the kappa replied. "All the time."

"I can hear something." Lunae stopped.

"What is it?"

There was an itching inside her mind, a prickle of Eldritch energy. Lunae shook her head, trying to clear it.

"Lunae? Are you all right?"

"Something's calling to me."

"What's the matter?"

"Look!"

There was a ghost standing before them. She could see the barrels through its body. It wore a familiar armor. Half of its face was missing.

"Embar Khair! The armor must be close by."

The ghost raised a mailed hand and beckoned, then drifted backward across the courtyard. Lunae and the kappa followed, around a corner into a great open space.

A ship rested on a landing pad, raised some distance from the Martian earth. From this distance, it looked like a scorpion, crouching above the red soil, tail curved above its spine, all dark glitter and menace. Lunae supposed that it could have been beautiful, but it was too ancient, too alien, for her to feel anything but afraid. The ghost of Embar Khair gestured: *come*.

Then the ship itself moved and the ghost began to fade. Lunae blinked and drew back. There was a creeping glide across the surface of the ship, as though the skin of the ship had begun to crawl. Lunae felt her own spine shiver in response. A single droplet, green and glistening, fell to the dusty earth. Lunae and the kappa backed away. The droplet elongated, became a writhing serpent that angled itself through the dust, so swiftly that she barely had time to dodge out of the way. The kappa cried out. And then the snake was upon Lunae, rising out of the dust, neck arched, eyeless and striking. She gave a muffled cry, but the snake struck her wrist as gently as a drop of rain. A moment later, her hand was coated in a jade glove. She looked down at a dissociated fragment of armor.

The hand pulled at her skin, gripping it, tugging. It was trying to draw her in the direction of the ship, and at first she resisted. But the hand reached out, raising Lunae's arm, the fingers pointed and quivering. She took a reluctant step forward. The kappa tried to drag her back, but the pull of the ship was as strong as a magnet. The skin of the ship shivered, rippling like grass in the wind. Lunae took another step, led by the insistent hand. The tail of the ship sprang into life, hammering down into the earth like a pile-driver. Lunae dodged, ducked, tried to turn and run, but the hand exerted a magnetic pressure upon her, drawing her forward. Again the tail struck out, pounding down into the dirt.

"Kappa! Run!"

The ground shook. A column of dust rose up, obscuring the moving skin of the ship. Lunae doubled up over the unnatural hand, coughing and choking, but then something was rising out of the dust: a pillar with a half-formed head at its summit. It bowed over her, embedding her in a watery coolness. She felt another consciousness slide over her own, just as the armor encased her.

WINTERSTRIKE

CHAPTER 1

MARS

The armor of Embar Khair, carrying Lunae with it, marched toward the ship.

"Wait!" Lunae cried. "Turn back! It's attacking us. It—" but the armor paid no attention to its passenger. It strode onward. The scorpion-sting of the ship once more quivered and plunged, sending shivers and reverberations throughout the armor's shell.

"Kappa!" But she was unable to look back. The armor moved swiftly, diving and twisting through the cloud of dust. Lunae felt shock waves travel across her joints. She did not like being at the mercy of the armor. Its strength was horrifying; the shell moved with forces that seemed far beyond what the human body could normally bear. She remembered its weight from the moment when it had imprinted upon her. Yet Dreams-of-War had welcomed it. Were Martians so different? The armor was bearing her beneath the body of the ship, reaching up to run a hand across the slick surface.

"Ship! Be still. There is no danger," said the disembodied voice. "What are you *doing*?"

The armor did not reply, but she could hear Embar Khair talking to itself, or perhaps to a throng of others, inside the armor's helmet.

The babel grew, a hissing susurrus of inner sound, like the waves on some distant shore. There was a wet click. The side of the ship peeled back, revealing a walkway.

"Upward!" Embar Khair said inside Lunae's mind. It marched her up the walkway and into the ship.

Within, it was dark and quiet. Skeleton-ribs lined each wall, curving inward. The armor had to duck as they moved forward.

"Wait," Lunae said, desperate. "What are you doing? My nurse is back there, she—"

"The duty of my former occupant was to protect you. That duty remains. She who stole me is absent. The ship prefers a living pilot."

"But where are we going? We cannot leave the kappa!"

"To find she who owns me, where else?" The armor evinced a distant surprise.

"You mean, Dreams-of-War?"

The armor said nothing. It raised a hand and beckoned. Struts angled down from the ceiling, sealing the armor in a standing web.

"Prepare yourself."

For what? Lunae was about to ask, but in the next moment, she was suddenly and horribly aware of the mind of the ship. It touched her mind—sly and sidling, somehow harsh and spined, like the scorpion discovered, too late, in the toe of a shoe. It felt ancient, powerful, and perverse. She could not withstand it. She thought of the kappa in despair.

"Tell it to lift."

Lunae would have disobeyed, but the thought of lifting was enough. The ship swayed on its struts. She could feel the dust rising up around it, was aware of cold air. Then they were up and soaring through the Martian sky.

Voices whispered inside Lunae's head: the ship, the armor— it was hard to differentiate them after a while. Linked to the ship, she could see several dimensions at once: the wheeling heavens above, the Martian terrain below, fed back to her with a bewildering onrush of information. Gradually, she realized that the ship spoke in different tongues, some in languages that she could not understand. She did not think that all the voices were even female.

"Who are these people?" she asked aloud, when the whispers of conflicting advice became too great to heed. It reminded her disquietingly of Sek's boat.

"They are the pilots of past ships," the armor said. "Those who flew spacecraft in and out of Nightshade. They were brought back from the Eldritch Realm to provide the knowledge base of this craft. A mass of downloaded souls."

And what, Lunae could not help but wonder, had the ship in mind for her? She longed for Dreams-of-War.

"The one who wore you," she said to the armor. "You said you could find her."

"The ship is scanning the land, even now, for the signature of her being. It will not be long."

"She *is* still alive, isn't she?"

"I would know if she were not," the armor said, with such confidence that Lunae had to believe it. But what about the poor kappa? She thought with horror of the excissieres. The ship swooped downward, crossing a ragged lip of rock. The plains lay before them, rolling to the edge of the world and a rising moon.

"She is near," the armor said, very softly.

The landscape scrolled out before Lunae's linked gaze. She saw a chasm between the rocks, sharply black in the dying sunlight. A tall, pale figure stood at the entrance, and there was something beside it, something flickering and insubstantial.

"What is that?" Lunae asked.

"A ghost."

The ship flew downward, alighting in a puff of dust. Lunae was at the door and opening it before the ship had settled, then was out and running. And as she did so, she saw that the ghost was Essa.

"Lunae!" Dreams-of-War strode forward, held out her hands, let them fall before Lunae could fling her arms around her. "You're alive." She sounded astonished. "I'm—relieved."

"Guardian," Lunae said. "So am I." She stared in horror at the lacerated wounds that covered her guardian's body. Few places remained unbruised or untorn.

"What happened to you?"

"Little of note." Dreams-of-War gave her a razor-edged grin. "Where is the kappa?"

"At the Memnos Tower." Lunae felt her smile fade. "The ship brought me here." She turned to Essa. "I didn't expect to see *you.*"

The ghost looked puzzled. "You are the *hito-bashira.*" She smiled. "I have waited a hundred years for you, and you know who I am. How so?"

"We've met," Lunae said, "but not in this day and age."

She turned to Dreams-of-War. "You should take this back." She gestured to the armor and saw her guardian's face contract with disbelief, relief, a sudden joy, and something else. Unease? She could not tell. But this time, Dreams-of-War held out her hands without hesitation. The armor flowed from Lunae, up and over. Dreams-of-War was again the martial, bristling figure that Lunae remembered so well.

"I need to gain information. I will be back," the ramhorned ghost said, and began to face back into the interface of the rock.

"Wait!" Lunae cried, but Essa was already gone.

"Lunae. Come with me." Dreams-of-War made for the ship. Lunae followed.

CHAPTER 2

MARS

Yskatarina stood at the base of the Memnos Tower, listening into the darkness. She could hear nothing.

"Animus? What's happening?"

"Someone is coming," the Animus said.

"Do you know who?"

"They are shod in metal. They have a human weight."

"Excissieres?" Yskatarina said.

"Perhaps the Matriarch has sent them."

"I do not have much faith in the Matriarch," Yskatarina said. "Kami or not."

"I think she is mad."

"Not surprisingly." She stepped forward as the excissieres reached the bottom of the stairs. The Animus melted back into the shadows.

"The Matriarch wants to see you," one of the women said.

"Very well."

"Your creature? Is it here?" The excissiere sniffed the air suspiciously.

"No," Yskatarina lied. "I told it to stay beyond the perimeter of the Tower. Have you located the ship?"

"It has not left Martian orbit; we are certain of that. But it continues to baffle the sensors."

"It should not," Yskatarina said. "The tech we gave you should be able to detect it."

"But the ship is old," the second excissiere said. "It uses frequencies to which our equipment is not attuned."

"The ship must be found," Yskatarina said in agitation. "It is a great prize. I cannot let it slip away."

"It will be found," the excissiere said. "The raven-ships are out looking for it, even now." She shifted impatiently. "Do not keep the Matriarch waiting."

Yskatarina, acquiescing, followed her up the stairs. With every step that she took away from the Animus, it felt as though a link between them was being stretched, an almost physical ache. Eventually, they reached the top of the Tower.

"In there," the excissiere said. Yskatarina stepped through the door and halted.

The study of the former Matriarch had changed. The furniture was gone, leaving bare stone walls and floor. Wires and tubes ran from the center of the room, channeling down through the floor, pulsing with pallid fluid. Yskatarina was immediately reminded of the Grandmothers' chamber; this was the same kind of tech, keeping the desiccated corpse of the former Matriarch sufficiently intact to permit her spirit to animate it. The results were mixed. The body moved in a series of twitches and jerks, the jaw unhinged and gaping. Yskatarina wondered how long the ghost had to spend hooked up to this apparatus each day. The long head swung up to stare blearily at Yskatarina. The excissieres stood close behind her. She could feel their breath on her neck, like the edge of a blade.

"Send them away," Yskatarina said to the Matriarch's ghost, without looking behind her.

The ghost gave a soft, whistling exhalation. "Why should I?"

"Because they will not like what we are about to say."

The long head dipped and nodded. Yskatarina saw the knobbed line of vertebrae, now bound together with skeins of slimy wire.

"Go," the ancient voice said. Yskatarina waited until the excissieres had clattered from the chamber, then she closed the door.

"I wonder that you bother with that body," she said. "We could arrange for you to inhabit a new one."

"I could take another body, if I so chose. This one is—interesting."

"It's a mummified corpse. It's falling apart."

"Still, its decay intrigues me. When it finally falls apart, then I shall move on. And it gives me such power. The lightest word from me," the thing went on, "and the excissieres will come running. They will cut you to ribbons and I will mount your limbs on decorative plaques in this chamber. And there is also your creature."

Yskatarina grew cold and still.

"If you harm him—"

"No one has harmed him yet," the Matriarch said. "And no one will do so. At least, not until the arrival of your aunt Elaki."

CHAPTER 3

MARS

Dreams-of-War was silent once Lunae had finished telling her what had befallen them. She sat frowning, encased in the armor, on the deck of the stolen ship. Phobos rose up through the porthole, casting a thin light across the floor. The ship remained on the floor of the canyon; Dreams-of-War did not want to risk orbit just yet. Lunae, racked with fatigue, sat beside her.

"The Kami are the ghosts of the future? Returning to the past to possess the living?"

"This is what I was told by my future-self," Lunae said. "And what I saw—Earth is become a hell. Mars was a wasteland. My self spoke of other worlds, names I did not know."

"And the Kami control Nightshade now?"

"I believe so."

"It would make a certain degree of sense. Nightshade has always been apart from the rest of the system, first as a renegade colony, now as a powerhouse. It sits at the system's edge, draining it of life and wealth. It is a vampire planet."

"And it gave the system haunt-tech."

"If haunt-tech is not an old discovery," Dreams-of-War said, "but a discovery that comes from the far future, it explains how it seemed to emerge from nowhere. It is a scientific anomaly, an unexpected direction. For thousands of years, the physical sciences held sway. And then, quite suddenly, via Nightshade, the Kami appear. They have no bodies; they tell tales of a place where the dead go—the Eldritch Realm. Superstition is revealed as truth. Ghosts are a reality. Consciousness can be separated

288

from form. Séance is a viable form of scientific methodology and technical development. Once, this would have been seen as delusion." She blinked. "A strange thought."

"And now the Kami are to invade, and I am to be the one who holds them back." Lunae rubbed eyes that were reddened by the Martian dust. "The trouble is, I have no idea how to go about it."

"What did your future-self have to say on the matter?"

"My future-self said that she had failed. Essa was there—the horned ghost with whom you were speaking. They told me that there would be a time when I could act, but she could tell me little about it. She implied that time could be changed. And this makes me most reluctant to shift time." She looked at Dreams-of-War. "What if I do the wrong thing?"

"There is no way of knowing what the right thing might be," Dreams-of-War said. "And there is another issue. That woman, Yskatarina, is here. She is of Nightshade; she and the reanimated Matriarch control Memnos now."

"And the kappa is still at Memnos. If anything has happened to her—"

"Don't worry," Dreams-of-War said, but it was clear to Lunae that she did not believe this. "We will save her, if that's what you wish." She looked around her at the ship. "Do you know what is happening at Memnos?"

"Memnos has been broadcasting," the ship said with startling abruptness. "The woman from Nightshade is raising an army."

The approach of twilight saw Dreams-of-War standing at a crack in the cliff face: the entrance to the eastern tunnels. Lunae remained with the ship. Dreams-of-War approached the entrance cautiously, expecting guards, but no one seemed to be there. Dreams-of-War slipped inside.

The tunnels were old, dating back to the foundations of the Matriarchy and perhaps before. Dreams-of-War walked on smooth, bare stone, mottled with the droppings of the small dactylates that lived high in the cavern roof. She could hear them now, twittering and rustling, and this was a good sign. She would not put it past the Matriarchy to flood the tunnels with gas. But this was only the beginning.

She walked for perhaps an hour or more, trying to remember the twists and turns of the labyrinth. It had been years since she had trodden these paths, and the network was deliberately disorienting. Dreams-of-War had argued with Lunae of the wisdom of attempting to rescue the kappa in the face of everything else that was going on. It would, the Martian argued, be simpler to leave the nurse to her fate, rather than risk capture. The kappa herself would not expect them to place themselves in danger on her behalf. Dreams-of-War thought that she had convinced the girl, for Lunae had fallen silent and contemplative at last.

"Moreover, remember what the Grandmothers told you," Dreams-of-War said, pressing home the message.

"The Grandmothers are dead," Lunae murmured. "But yes, I remember."

Satisfied, Dreams-of-War had gone to the ship's interface to inspect the monitoring relays. When she returned, Lunae had gone.

Heart pounding, Dreams-of-War made sure that the girl was nowhere on the ship, then raced outside. Lunae was halfway down the canyon, walking quickly.

"Where are you going?" Dreams-of-War cried. Lunae looked at her, quite calm.

"To rescue my nurse," she said, as if none of the previous conversation had taken place. Recognizing defeat, Dreams-of-War had marched Lunae back to the ship and gone in her stead. But the incident had finally made her realize something. In the span of time over which they had been apart, Lunae had become an adult, however willful. If the situation had not been so desperate, Dreams-of-War would have stood back and given in. She could control a child. She would not control a woman who, to all appearances, was not even so very far from her own age. And that thought, too, was disturbing: When would Lunae stop aging?

Another long hour, and she stood beneath the foundations of the Matriarchy, before the iron doors that led into the cellar chambers. Here, the walls radiated an icy chill and the stone felt damp to the touch, rimed with the remnants of cobwebs. Dreams-of-War doubted that even spiders lived down here these days. The doors were tightly shut, the ancient locking mechanism blackened with soot and age. Last time these doors had been opened, to the best of her knowledge, had been when she herself had forced them from the other side. It was easy to believe that they had not been opened since. She could feel the Tower rising above her, sense the weight of it. The holding chambers were deep underground, banded by weir-wards generated by the Tower's black light matrix. If the kappa still lived, which Dreams-of-War doubted, she would be kept down here.

"Armor," she said. The fingers of Embar Khair's battle-dress snaked out, spreading into hand-tools. Dreams-of-War tried to stifle the sense of relief that being back in the armor had granted her, and failed. She had managed without it, she told herself. She had fought change-tigers and excissieres, had survived the Earthbones and the Crater Plain. But resuming the armor had felt like coming home. *Never mind Lunae's own aging*, Dreams-of-War thought. *I myself have grown old. Old and soft.*

The doors slid open. Ahead lay the sparkle of weir-wards, and beyond that, the holding cells.

CHAPTER 4

MARS

Yskatarina stood with the Matriarch at the summit of the Memnos Tower.

"Your aunt Elaki is here. All the way from Nightshade, to oversee the army," the Matriarch murmured. "The engine is being prepared."

Two excissieres now walked with Yskatarina wherever she went, and did not let her out of their sight. Failure gnawed at her. She had not found Lunae, did not know why the girl was so important to Elaki, although the Matriarch had now explained to her what Elaki planned to do. She did not know where the Animus was being kept. On the previous night, she had tried to creep from her chamber and search, but the doors were firmly bolted. After some minutes of fruitless scratching at the locks, the door had opened to reveal one of the scissor-women: arms folded, holographic wounds chasing across flesh, and a dreadful eagerness in her eyes. Yskatarina had stepped quickly back into the room.

Even now, the excissieres were making the final adjustments to the haunt-engine in the basement of the Memnos Tower. When all was ready, the Matriarch would give the word and the engine would be switched on. Already, the black light matrix was linked up to the broadcasting facilities of the Tower, connecting with dormant nanomemories across the Crater Plain and the Olympian slopes, sending ancient signals out to the ghosts that lay latent in the Martian soil and that would be summoned to feed the haunt-engine.

Yskatarina was biding her time. The Animus would, she knew, be working to free himself and come to her. She had to have faith. She had gambled and, for the moment, failed. One question was, however, besetting her. Did Elaki know of her earlier modification? Was her aunt aware that Yskatarina was no longer bound by that mortifying love? The previous Matriarch had been instructed to keep no records, just in case, and Yskatarina could not believe that she had discussed it with her reanimated successor. If the current Matriarch did not have knowledge of Yskatarina's changed state, then it might be possible to deceive Elaki.

It was one of the few cards remaining to Yskatarina, and she intended to use it.

CHAPTER 5

MARS

Within the confines of the ship, Lunae soon became bored. The ship itself was willing to talk to her, but for most of the time its speech was such a mad jumble that Lunae at last asked it to be silent. She prowled restlessly about the deck, trying to access the databanks, but much of them were written in an alphabet that she did not understand. At last she activated the screens and sat gazing out across the floor of the canyon.

After a few minutes, movement captured her attention. Something was walking along the canyon. Frowning, Lunae peered at the screen. For a startled moment, she thought it was Essa. There was something familiar about the movement, about the gliding walk, but then she saw that this being was different, and not alone.

They were rising up out of the ground. There were many of them, perhaps fifty or so: red-legged gaezelles, women with speckled skin and tails. They came to cluster around the sides of the ship, staring at it in wonder from great golden eyes.

"Ship?" Lunae asked with some alarm. "What do they want?"

"We do not know," the ship said after a pause.

The creatures made no attempt to touch the ship. Their hands remained by their sides, or held up in front of them in the manner of paws. They milled around for a few minutes, whispering to one another. Lunae could hear them over the monitor, but their speech made no sense, and perhaps it was not even words. Then they turned and began to ran, moving swiftly away down the canyon, as if summoned. Lunae watched them until they had disappeared. None of them looked back.

"More are rising," the ship said. It was by now quite dark. The ship lay at the bottom of the canyon, as if it had fallen down a well.

"More?" Lunae said. She peered into the blackness. "I can't see anything."

"We will not put on the lights," the ship said. "It will draw them forth like moths. They like the light. There is little enough of it in the Eldritch Realms."

"But aren't they ghosts?" Lunae said. "Phantoms?"

"These are animated ghosts," the ship said. "These are solid."

As if to punctuate its words, something heavy slammed against the side of the vessel, causing it to rock. Lunae leaped up.

"What was that?"

"I do not know."

"Put the lights on! They're already here—I want to see what that was."

A moment's pause, and then the canyon was flooded with light.

The things were everywhere: massive armored shapes, moving with heavy purpose. They were a world away from the delicate gaezelles. Beneath the armored helms, their faces were stripped down to gaunt bone, and in the next moment, Lunae saw that they were not covered in armor at all, but thick hide. She had seen them before, overrunning Fragrant Harbor.

"What are they?"

"They are the Sown," the ship said. "Who once were known as Dragon's Teeth. Armies seeded into the earth, to lie dormant until needed."

The creatures were swarming around the ship. She could hear their tread above her. The ship swayed.

"They're attacking us! Can they get in?"

Through the viewscreen, she saw the scorpion-tail of the craft spin across and strike. A swath was cut through the Sown. They fell without a sound, severed limbs tumbling to the earth. They oozed black fluid, like mud. Lunae breathed again, but the ghosts were once more rising, gestated by the soil itself. A rhythmic thundering assailed the sides of the ship.

"They're trying to break in," Lunae said.

"There are too many of them," the ship said.

"Then take off."

The ship shifted, engines powering. A moment later, it rose, lurching into the Martian sky. The Sown fell from its sides like leaves. Lunae ran to the viewscreen and watched as they drifted down toward the mouth of the canyon. A needle shape appeared on the ship's monitor, moving fast and closing in.

"Memnos has found us," said the ship.

CHAPTER 6

MARS

Dreams-of-War set the armor to maximum protection and stepped into the passage that led to the holding cells. She held out a hand. The black light matrix sizzled, sending sparks cascading across the surface of the armor. Even through the protective casing, the workings of the matrix stung her skin, passing through metal and bone alike into the Eldritch Realm. But if she held her hand there for long enough, the armor would be able to create a feedback loop within the matrix. Hopefully, without attracting too much attention from the excissieres . . .

Bone and blood, a sensation of binding tightness, as though her nerves were a screw, linking her with the Eldritch Realm. And then the black light matrix hissed once and fell silent. She could feel energy elsewhere, somewhere at the back of her head, but the way before her was silent. She strode forward toward the holding cells.

The first cell was empty of all but a few chewed bones. She could not tell what they might have been. The second cell, too, was bare, and the third, and the fourth. The kappa was nowhere to be found. Dreams-of-War ground her teeth in frustration. It seemed increasingly probable that the nurse had met her end, after all. Lunae would be disappointed, but this was the nature of things. Dreams-of-War herself was merely aggrieved at the realization of a wasted journey.

Then, as she came to the last cell of all, something flung itself at the encasing field.

"Kappa?" Dreams-of-War cried. She stepped forward, the lights of the armor sparkling off a shadowed shape. But it was not the kappa. It was Yskatarina's creature.

Dreams-of-War sprang back.

"What are you doing here?"

"They have imprisoned me," the thing hissed. "My mistress is betrayed. Nightshade comes."

"What do you mean, Nightshade comes?" Dreams-of-War asked. She spared little thought for Yskatarina. *Betrayed* sounded good enough to her.

"The Elder Elaki is here, to oversee the final phase. Her ship orbits. Excissieres are installing the engine."

"Final phase? You mean, the Kami?"

"Memnos raises ancient armies from the Martian soil. Elaki will summon the flood of future souls, to inhabit the bodies of the Sown. Once they have subdued Mars, they will move on to Earth, and other bodies. Set me free," the thing pleaded. "Let me go to my mistress."

"An excellent idea," Dreams-of-War spoke coldly. "To bring succor to she who stole my armor and sold me to the arena. Further help to her surely features large in my plans. And how did they come to cage you? Did you not fight?"

"They threatened Yskatarina," the creature said. "I would have fought my way to her, but it was not politic. She needs Memnos. She wanted to negotiate. Now, I do not know what is happening. But you should know that my mistress has no love for her aunt. What the Elder Elaki intends, my mistress will try to prevent."

"You're lying."

"I can help you." The thing rustled and rattled against the walls of the holding cell. "Excissieres are on their way. Listen."

Dreams-of-War realized that it spoke the truth. The sound of metal-shod feet was approaching. Activating the armor, she cut a hole in the shield of the holding cell. The creature surged out like an uncaged bat. Three excissieres charged around the corner, scissors snicking. Dreams-of-War threw the gutting knife and caught one in the throat. The woman sprawled to the floor. The creature shot forward, a sheet of ire-palm gushing from its throat. There was a sticky hiss, the smell of melting flesh. The excissieres dissolved before Dreams-of-War's eyes.

"The Grandmothers," she said. "It was you."

"Yskatarina wanted them gone," the thing said. It crouched over the remains of the excissieres, eyes glowing. It spoke, Dreams-of-War thought, with a strange innocence, as if it did not know that it was a wicked thing. And perhaps it did not. It seemed to care about nothing except Yskatarina, its world. Dreams-of-War had lost any hope of finding the kappa. It struck her that the removal of the Matriarch might be a good next step. She was loath to rely on the help of Yskatarina's companion, but then again . . .

"Let's go," Dreams-of-War said.

CHAPTER 7

MARS

More needles danced across the screen, moving in fast.

"Can you evade them?" Lunae asked. She did not like being at the mercy of the ship, and the vessel was once again starting to talk to itself: a swift and rapid mumble, only half-intelligible. An image appeared before her, hanging in the air and connected by a sequence of lines: the attacking ships, in three-dimensional representation. The central vessel was amber-black, a black light matrix flickering across its sides. It bore a needle-pointed star on its side.

"What's that?"

"That is the craft of the Elder Elaki," the ship said. It twisted, shooting downward and arrowing along a canyon.

"Do you have weapons?"

"None that will be of use."

The walls of the canyon shot past with barely a hairsbreadth between the sides of the ship and the rock. Lunae was thrown to one side. Looking up, she saw that the amber-black craft had altered course.

"It travels to Memnos," the ship said.

Lunae experienced a moment of relief before she saw that the other ships were splitting in formation. Most were still following. The ship was filled with a sudden blast of indigo light, sizzling out across the system banks.

"We are struck," the ship said, with such soft gentleness that Lunae at first thought she had imagined it. But the craft was plummeting now, the dark surface of Mars coming up fast beneath them, the viewscreen showing the point of impact in merciless detail—

—and in panic, Lunae shifted time, before even thinking about it. The next minute, the ship was gliding bumpily along the desert floor, hammering the dust into great red clouds. There was daylight outside, walls rising up to meet them . . . Lunae cried out, but the ship had already stopped.

"Where are we?"

Silence.

"Ship?"

But the voices were still. A sparkle of indigo shimmered across the system banks and then the ship was quiet. The viewscreens died, one by one. Lunae waited. She could hear nothing. After a few moments, she hauled herself to her feet, walked unsteadily across to the doors, and pressed her hand to the code pad. The door fell open in a musty hiss of air. The ship was canted to one side, with a long drop beneath the opening. Lunae hesitated, then jumped down, landing heavily in the dust. She looked around her.

Red walls rose up before the nose of the ship. The city was a crown of towers, walkways hanging between them and glittering in the harsh sunlight. The air smelled of dust and water. Close by ran the high banks of the Great Channel. Lunae recognized it from her lessons: It was the city known as Winterstrike, first city of the Crater Plain.

She heard the voices of the ghost herd before she saw them. They clustered, murmuring, behind the tail of the ship. Lunae turned, alarmed, to see the gaezelles waiting for her, red-legged and golden-eyed.

The ghost herd flowed around Lunae, surrounding her. She tried to push them away, finding to her surprise that they were solid. Their breath smelled of grass and sagebrush. They made no attempt to touch her, and when she, panicking, moved back, they moved with her. Their eyes were mild. A figure appeared in their midst: a woman with coiled horns.

"Essa!"

"They will not harm you," Essa said. "They seek to keep you safe, on my instructions."

"Safe?" Lunae faltered. "How?"

"My kind herded the gaezelles, once. As for now, the streets of Winterstrike are haunted. The Sown arise and are attacking. Darkness falls from the system's edge. It's time."

Time.

"When is this?" Lunae asked. "I changed time, to bring me here." The memory came in a cold rush of dismay. What if this had been the wrong thing to do, the forerunner of failure? She thought of herself and Essa, enduring down thousands of years. What would they find to say to each other, during all that time?

Essa said, "It is the afternoon of the day on which Mars may, or may not fall. You must leave the city, return to Memnos. The Tower is where the flood will rise."

"But have I done the right thing?"

Essa only stared. "I do not know."

The gaezelles drifted alongside. Lunae could hear them murmuring among themselves, wondered again if they possessed proper speech. They seemed to converse in fragments, quickly losing interest.

The walls of Winterstrike were a solid, ruby stone, unlike the bloodshot walls of the Nightshade mission. Lunae thought of Dreams-of-War and the kappa and fought back agitation. As the ghost herd came near, taking Lunae with it, she saw that the great metal gates of Winterstrike lay open. The clan houses lay beyond: towering constructions of metal and basalt. All that Dreams-of-War had told her of Mars flooded obligingly back. Each house bore an insignia, hanging before it. The streets were filled with steam-cars and land-boats, all abandoned, without any discernible care.

Then they turned the corner. A crowd of women were racing toward them, screaming in horror. The gaezelles closed around Lunae, jostling her into an alleyway. She was pushed and pulled up a flight of steps to a balcony. The gaezelles milled into the rooms beyond, but Lunae hung back. The balcony afforded an excellent view of the street. She was looking down on the heads of the crowd. Many of them were bleeding from ragged wounds. Close after them came a knot of the Sown, lumbering shapes wielding scissors that were part of their flesh: heavy pincer arms, weapons skittering out from their sides. They were identical to the creatures that her future-self had shown her in Fragrant Harbor.

"They will become the Kami when the flood is summoned through," Essa said beside her. "We have to go."

They had been seen. Two of the Sown broke ranks and clambered after them, but the fragile staircase broke beneath their weight, sending them tumbling back into the street. They roared with rage and struck about them. A woman crumpled to the ground, her torso severed from her legs. The crowd were being methodically butchered. The air reeked of death and blood.

"Hurry!" Essa tugged at Lunae's arm, drawing her through a pair of ornamental doors and into the depths of a mansion. There was no sign of any inhabitants.

"They have fled," Essa said over her shoulder, "or perhaps they hide in the cellars." She pulled Lunae down a staircase.

"Don't they have guards?" But Lunae did not think that much could withstand the Sown.

"They would have raised their armies and fought, but Memnos has sabotaged the weir-wards of their mansions. If they are wise, they have left Winterstrike for the sanctuary of the hills. Folk would rather face awts and vulpen than the armies of earth. You have seen why."

"And if they catch up with us?" Lunae said. "With me?"

"They will tear us all to pieces. They are not like the gaezelles, who once existed in life and lived out their time on the Crater Plain. The Sown are souls who were destined for war, but never born. Their forms lay dormant in the soil, like seeds—much harder to raise, but Nightshade can do it now. Their spirits boil with anger. Now their time has come and they cannot be held back. Ultimately, they will be aimed at Earth and then the lesser worlds. The ships are waiting on the other side of the city. Nightshade will commandeer the Chain for the invasion."

They hurried through deserted streets. The cries of the crowd faded and died. Other spirits slunk forth. Some were little more than air, but many were solid flesh. Lunae saw creatures that were formed of bones, covered only by tight red skin, beings that stalked on disjointed legs but had the serene faces of human women. Sometimes they chattered and laughed, speaking either to the air or to that which she was unable to see, but most moved silently, with unknown purpose. Of them, none resembled the Sown. But Lunae thought she could hear the army behind, the march of iron-shod feet.

Then the fortress lay before them, nestling at the heart of the crater: a mass of red metal spires, rising in fretwork lace against the darkening sky. During the Lost Epoch, Knowledge-of-Pain had said, one of the towers had been shattered. The stump still strutted up, never mended. Light flared within it.

"There's someone up there."

"I told you. Folk have taken shelter there."

But the light did not look natural to Lunae: a flickering, wan mist that wreathed around the stump of the spire. She hesitated, but the gaezelles moved her gently onward.

"We go around," the ram-horned woman said.

As Lunae and the herd approached the lip of the crater, something fell shrieking from the spire and bounded up the walls. It fell upon the nearest gaezelle, which uttered a piercing cry and fell bloodily to the ground. The thing surged forward, mouth gaping. Lunae glimpsed teeth within teeth: a humanoid shape moving on all fours, with a stump of a tail. It had no eyes, only a wide, batlike snout and a pair of fanned ears. The gaezelles closed around her in a protective mass of reanimated flesh.

"Awt," the horned woman whispered.

"A ghost?" The gaezelles were pressing her forward, but at the edges of the herd there were shrieks and squeals. The odor of blood was strong in the air.

"Living flesh. As soon as the city gates were opened, the men-remnants came through."

A red limb was flung at Lunae's feet. But before she had time to respond, Essa and the herd were pressing her toward the city gate. She needed no urging. She hurried through the shadows, trying to ignore the cries behind her, and stumbled out into the expanse of the plain.

CHAPTER 8

MARS

Dreams-of-War, accompanied by the hovering form of Yskatarina's companion, raced up the stairs of the Memnos Tower. They encountered resistance only once, in the form of a single excissiere, and she was swiftly cut down. But it was clear that something was occurring in the base of the Tower. They could hear a thrumming, a note that traveled up Dreams-of-War's spine and raised the hair on the back of her neck.

On the third level, a figure stumbled out of the shadows, a stout woman clad in crimson. Dreams-of-War saw a sour moon-face that lolled and rolled on a snapped neck.

"Matriarch?"

"She—" the Matriarch said, through twisted vocal chords. But then she started to fade—no true raised ghost, after all, but a shadow only, the spirit recalled, with all its fleeting memories of form and flesh.

"Haunt-tech," Dreams-of-War said. "That noise below us. It's a haunt-engine."

But the sounds from the basement were themselves drowned out by a greater roar from outside the Tower.

"What's that?" Dreams-of-War hurried to a slit window. An amber-black ship was setting down on the banks of the canal, bristling with weaponry, the star of Nightshade prominent upon its side. Amassed ranks of excissieres stood waiting, explaining the lack of their presence in the Tower.

"The Elder Elaki comes," the Animus said. But Dreams-of-War was already halfway up the next flight of stairs.

By the time they reached the landing of the seventh level, spirits were swarming from the walls of the Tower. The filmy forms of dead excissieres flocked past them, mouths agape. Warriors wearing kilts and armor, or naked save for their battle scars, milled about the stairs. Outside, the Elder Elaki's vessel could be heard, powering down.

"They'll be at the summit," Dreams-of-War shouted. As she stepped onto the landing, however, the armor began to melt from her body, forming an iridescent green pool along the floor. "What are you doing? Stop!"

"I cannot." Embar Khair's shattered face rose from the ichor. "It summons me."

"What, the haunt-engine?"

But Embar Khair's face was already transforming. In the next moment, the armor rose up, resumed its form, and strode down the stairs. "Wait!" But the armor had gone. Dreams-of-War was once more left in her underharness with the gutting knife, still slick with the blood of the excissiere. She swore.

"You will have to do without it," the creature advised, unnecessarily.

"I have done so before," Dreams-of-War snapped. She angled her way through the ranks of spirits, ran up more flights. At last, they reached the final landing. Ghosts watched from the shadows: older things, creatures that were half-human and male, crouched, waiting with a pale-eyed gaze. Dreams-of-War paid no attention to them, for the double iron doors that led to the Matriarch's chamber were gliding open.

A shambling figure shuffled forth: the Matriarch, with Yskatarina at her elbow. Excissieres stood behind them. Dreams-of-War saw Yskatarina's eyes widen with an unholy joy as she caught sight of her companion. It flew to her, wrapped her in its spined embrace.

"Take them," a voice commanded from below. Dreams-of-War looked down. A figure stood beneath her on the stairs: black-robed, with a tall hat.

Yskatarina's voice echoed down the stairwell. "Aunt Elaki!"

CHAPTER 9

MARS

Yskatarina watched as Dreams-of-War paused, caught between the Matriarch and the Elder Elaki. Yskatarina permitted herself a moment of grim satisfaction. Dreams-of-War had proved irritatingly difficult to kill. But Dreams-of-War was a nuisance, not the primary threat. That stood farther down the stairs, in the form of Elaki herself.

Yskatarina's courage almost failed her at the sight of her aunt, and if it had not been for the presence of the Animus, she would have faltered when she said, with as convincing a pretense at joy as she could manage, "Aunt! You are here!"

"Yskatarina." Elaki's voice was as grating as ever. Isti, Yskatarina was unsurprised to see, hovered at Elaki's heels like a conjured familiar. "This warrior. The woman in the Grandmothers' employ. You told me she was to die. *And where is the girl?*"

"The warrior was supposed to die. There was a hunt. It failed. Blame whoever occupies the Matriarch, not me." The hollow in her head might still be present, but old habits died hard in the face of Elaki's icy disapproval. "The girl is here, on Mars." Best not to tell Elaki what had happened just yet.

"Then kill the warrior now. Your creature may do it"—Elaki clearly regarded this as a concession—"in the time that is still remaining to it. And why is the girl still alive?"

"I'm taking care of it," Yskatarina lied. *Bide your time. Wait.* Besides, she had no argument with the demise of Dreams-of-War. The Animus uncoiled itself from her body and whipped around. Its mandibles opened. Dreams-of-War danced back, but the bolt of ire-palm was already sizzling out.

It did not, however, strike Dreams-of-War. She threw herself to the floor and rolled. The ire-palm shot overhead, leaving a mottled stain upon the wall of the Tower.

"There!" Yskatarina shrieked. The Animus wheeled, but Dreams-of-War was already up on her feet. She leaped onto the balustrade of the stairs and threw herself from the edge as another bolt of ire-palm gushed toward her.

Elaki frowned. Yskatarina rushed to the balustrade and looked down. Dreams-of-War's spinning shape was already as small as a broken doll. No one could survive such a drop, unarmored.

"Get down there!" Elaki shook a nearby excissiere by the shoulder. "I want you to make sure she dies."

"The haunt-engine is running, Aunt." Yskatarina hastened to distract Elaki's attention from the Animus's failure.

"I can see that." Elaki grasped her firmly by the arm and led her through to the window. Yskatarina looked out across the plain. From the banks of the Grand Channel onward, the Sown were rising from the ground, rank upon rank. She could see the great armored heads moving from side to side, the tight multiple limbs, similar to those of the Animus but more massive, beginning to unfold. Far on the horizon, a line was crawling.

"They march on Winterstrike and the spaceports," the Matriarch said. She gestured upward. The Chain glinted. "It opens. For Earth."

CHAPTER 10

MARS

Dreams-of-War had had little thought of anything other than escape, but on the long way down, it struck her forcibly that this had not been the best way to go about it. The round circle that was the hall of the Memnos Tower was growing with terrifying speed. Dreams-of-War flung out an arm, grabbing at one of the lower balustrades. Her hand slipped, then held, with a wrench that came close to pulling her arm from its socket. Dreams-of-War hauled herself over the balustrade, to stand on a lower landing.

Two storys above, she caught a glimpse of Embar Khair's armor, moving swiftly downward amid a flock of spirits.

"Armor!" Dreams-of-War cried. She struggled up the stairs to meet it. "Wait!"

The armor's face worked; it reached out a tentative hand toward her—but then it was turning away and walking on, called by the lure of the haunt-engine. Higher up the stairwell, she could hear pounding feet: the excissieres, presumably. Dreams-of-War ducked through a door, flinging it closed behind her. It was a warrior's chamber. A battlesword hung on the wall; Dreams-of-War seized it. Behind her, the door was kicked open. Yskatarina stood in the entrance, the Animus at her shoulder.

"I have decided to finish you myself," Yskatarina said. She drew a long knife from her belt. The Animus soared up to float above them in the chamber.

"You are a half-person," Dreams-of-War said with deliberate scorn. "What harm can you do me?"

Yskatarina grinned. "You might be surprised."

She charged. Dreams-of-War swung the sword in an arc, but Yskatarina easily dodged out of the way. Her speed turned her into a blur. Dreams-of-War once more lashed out; again, Yskatarina was not where she had been, but already across the other side of the chamber. A long bloody slash had appeared across Dreams-of-War's breast, from a knife so sharp that she had barely felt it. She wheeled around. Yskatarina stood at her shoulder. Dreams-of-War looked into her eyes and thought: *She is quite mad.*

"A half-person?" Yskatarina said softly. "Then what does that make *you*?"

Dreams-of-War lunged. Yskatarina was away and turning. Again, a wound appeared, this time along Dreams-of-War's forearm. She feinted, struck, feinted again, and skewered Yskatarina through the shoulder. Yskatarina, hissing, pulled away. Dreams-of-War looked down to see an oozing hole beneath her underharness, where Yskatarina's blade had entered.

"My aunt has offered me a bargain," Yskatarina said in conversational tones. "If I kill you, she will let the Animus live."

"This is foolish." Dreams-of-War spoke through gritted teeth. "You do not trust her. Your creature told me so."

Yskatarina grinned again. "I did not believe her, and neither did my Animus. I kill you because I want to." She lunged. Dreams-of-War twisted away and threw the sword upward with all her strength. Black, sticky rain spattered downward. Yskatarina shrieked, an eerie, unhuman cry. The Animus made no sound. It spun, then crashed to the floor where it lay twitching. The sword had pierced its exoskeleton, where a heart should be. Ire-palm flickered wanly across the floor.

Yskatarina fell to her knees. Dreams-of-War kicked her hard in the jaw; she fell, sprawling, but next moment, with a whine of mechanisms, she was once more standing. The Martian grasped the knife by the blade and twisted it from Yskatarina's hands. Yskatarina turned, but the knife tore through her breast. A torrent of blood gushed forth. Yskatarina, however, was still upright. She swung to face Dreams-of-War. Her eyes were welling up, and at first, bewildered, Dreams-of-War thought that she wept. But it was the glitter of a black light matrix that filled Yskatarina's gaze.

The blood still fountained from her breast; one hand reached upward, groping, and sealed off the wound.

"We are not so easy to kill," the Animus said from the floor, with a hiss that might have been a laugh. And it seemed to Dreams-of-War that the voice was no longer the artificially modulated tones of the Animus itself, but Yskatarina's own.

"Animus?" Yskatarina faltered. Her voice was a rasping murmur. Something was uncoiling behind her eyes. "I remember—"

"I, too," the Animus whispered. "You and I are one."

"What?" Dreams-of-War snarled, but she was beginning to suspect that she already knew. "You're both Kami, aren't you? The vanguard. And so is that aunt of yours."

Yskatarina, eyes full of black light, metal hand sealing the gaping wound in her chest, spoke with difficulty.

"I remember . . . At last, I remember. Elaki brought me back. Do you know what it is like, to cling to the walls of a world, ethereal, incorporeal, with the Eldritch Realm waiting only a moment away? Our ancestors betrayed us. When they strove for the mind-body separation, they thought to liberate us from the flesh. They sought to make us immortal. Instead, they turned us into living ghosts with only the dark to cling to. I sought true death, for all of us. Elaki, as she was then, disagreed. She fled back, to possess the woman who summoned her."

"But you and the Animus—you're the same soul?"

Blood oozed between Yskatarina's metal fingers; she tottered. *Surely*, Dreams-of-War thought, *she cannot stand for much longer, reanimated or not. Give her a moment, then strike, and we'll see who is far from the Eldritch Realm then.*

"She split me," Yskatarina said. She fell to her knees. "We were old rivals, in the realms of the last night. When she summoned a Kami to possess her niece, she brought me back, and only then knew me for an enemy. She could not kill me, for then her niece's body would die also, but more important, it would serve nothing—I would flee back to the Eldritch Realm and plot against her. So she separated me, sent me deep into this body's mind and that of the Animus, kept me separate, so that I would be powerful and yet under her control." The bitterness was palpable.

"No wonder you hate her," Dreams-of-War said.

"No wonder." She thought Yskatarina might have tried to laugh. "And what is Lunae to you?"

"Lunae is the enemy of all of us," the Animus said, for Yskatarina's voice was now no more than a husk. It crawled to its mistress, its other self, and curled around her as she sank to the floor.

"But if you hate Elaki—"

"I want to bring my people here, then send them into the Realm," the Animus said, and Yskatarina's mouth moved in a silent echo. Dreams-of-War was reminded of the Grandmothers, and filed that thought away for later. "But I've no love for you or your kind. I will not help you, if that's what you are hinting."

"I never hint," Dreams-of-War said. "I do not agree with the prospect of bringing the Kami here. I do not believe you. And your ability to help anyone is in serious question." She looked down at them. Yskatarina knelt on metal legs, hand still clutching at her breast, and the blood pooling with the dark ichor of the Animus. If she struck off their heads—but would that make any difference to a reanimated far-future ghost? And Yskatarina was, at least, giving her answers . . .

But Dreams-of-War did not believe in either intrigue or mercy. She sliced through the throats of both Yskatarina and the Animus, severing nerve and sinew.

There was a bolt-bow hanging on the chamber wall. She took that, too. Then she strode through the door of the chamber, locking it behind her. Later, she thought, she would come back and check that they stayed slain. Once she had dealt with Elaki.

CHAPTER 11

MARS

The gaezelles moved swiftly. Lunae was soon out of breath and stumbling to keep up. The hard Martian ground beneath her feet was uneven, strewn with boulders and stones. The herd flowed smoothly around ancient pits and craters, up and down the hills and hollows of the plain. Lunae, panting, could see the Memnos Tower in the double moonlight. Its summit was a blaze of light, casting the crawling shadows of the plain into sharp relief.

"Those are more of the Sown," Lunae gasped.

"We have to head for the canal," Essa said.

"Why?"

"Look at the ground. There."

Lunae did so. A little way ahead, the earth was broken into long, regular furrows.

"They've risen from here," she whispered.

"And they may not have finished rising. If another phalanx rises up and finds us in their midst . . . We must reach the canal. The banks, at least, will be safe from the emerging Sown. But not from excissieres."

"Do you have weapons?"

"The gaezelles will distract them." The horned woman spoke serenely enough, but Lunae remembered the havoc wreaked by the awt, and grew cold.

A short time later, they reached the banks of the canal. It was as Lunae remembered it: flowing slow as oil between the high ridges. The hooves of the gaezelles clattered on worn, ancient stone, but it was easier to run. Lunae was, however, having to pause more frequently for breath. She felt like the kappa, permanently wheezing—and what had happened to the nurse? To Dreams-of-War? She took a deep breath and carried on. The profile of the Memnos Tower became sharper in the growing gray light. Dawn was not far away.

The gaezelles slowed and paused as they came to the gates of the lock. They had met no excissieres, no resistance along the banks of the canal, and now Lunae could see why. The Sown filled the plain before the Tower of Memnos. She could not have slipped a blade between them. They stood with their skull-faces turned to the blaze at the summit of the Tower. Lunae could not tell what was causing the light; it did not look natural. It was filled with sparks and dark spaces, which seemed somehow solid.

"What is that?"

"Haunt-tech," Essa said. To Lunae's dismay, she seemed to be growing fainter. Her voice was a murmur on the wind and the ranks of the Sown were visible through her body. The gaezelles, too, were growing less clearly delineated. Their flesh was filled with shadows, their eyes with light. They whispered among themselves in palpable dismay.

"What's happening?" Lunae asked, but the horned woman was now no more than a shade, and the gaezelles themselves were twisting into spirals of pale and red, like colored smoke.

"Lunae, I—" Essa said, and was gone.

The smoke drifted up into the air and was sucked in the direction of the Tower. Lunae stood, staring at the ranks of the Sown in dismay. Then there was a rattle of rock and another phalanx sprang out of the soil.

It's feeding from them, Lunae thought. *The Tower has taken the gaezelles, used the energy to feed the Sown.*

"Essa?" she whispered, but there was no reply.

The new phalanx lay behind her. If they spotted her, then her only means of escape would be the canal or a time shift, and she was afraid of what the latter might bring. The only thing to do was to go on. Lunae slipped into the shadows beneath the bank and continued walking swiftly toward the Tower.

CHAPTER 12

MARS

The moment Dreams-of-War stepped through the door, she was forced to dodge back again behind a column. The Elder Elaki and the Matriarch were coming down the stairs, surrounded by excissieres. Dreams-of-War waited until they had passed, then followed.

Avoiding the main staircase, she took the side stairs that led down the Tower. *There must be a way actually to kill these things*, she thought as she ran. Her limbs ached, the war-whip weal across her shoulders stung and burned, and the edges of her numerous cuts were starting to fray once more with blood.

Yskatarina had implied that the Kami were only a moment away from the Eldritch Realm, and if they could be dispatched there, they would need to be summoned back again through a haunt-tech interface before they could return. But how to slay them? If they were living ghosts, inhabiting flesh as one might put on a suit of clothes—or was it that simple? She thought of the faces trapped in the cellars of the Mission, of the possessed woman in the meat market. How connected were the Kami to their borrowed bodies? Could the tie be severed voluntarily? If she was simply to kill Elaki, strike off her head from behind, what would the inhabiting consciousness be capable of once it was released into the air? Anything? Nothing? Could they move from body to body? *Useless to theorize*, Dreams-of-War decided as she reached the small door that led into the main hallway. *Just kill as many as you can and see what happens.*

She paused before the door, placing an ear to it to listen. If she had been in possession of the armor—but Embar Khair's battledress was marching down to the basement, drawn by the magnet of the haunt-engine. Cautiously, she opened the door. The hallway was empty. But she could hear voices and the strike of metal-shod feet on stone. Once again, Dreams-of-War went in pursuit.

At the bottom of the basement steps, before the beginning of the weir-wards that marked the entrance to the holding cells, she caught up with Elaki's entourage. The excissieres were massed at the back of the hallway: a solid phalanx of bristling armor and clattering weapons. Ahead stood Elaki and the Matriarch. They were standing before a set of iron doors, some twenty feet or more in height. These led to the labyrinth of passages that ran beneath the Crater Plain. But before the passages lay a cavern.

"Open the doors," she heard the Matriarch say in its rusty, wheezing voice. An excissiere stepped forward and placed a palm on the side panel. The doors hissed apart. There was a blinding moment of black light, and the haunt-engine lay exposed.

The engine was massive, reaching out to the walls of the cavern chamber. From the back of the crowd of excissieres, Dreams-of-War gazed, aghast. She could not, at first, work out how they had gotten it into the Tower, but as the thing shifted and coiled, she realized that they had not. It had been grown down from Memnos's own black light matrix, and it was still growing. Spirals and sparks of light arced out from the twisting burn of its core, seeking purchase on the stones of the cavern wall. When a spiral touched the stone, it stuck, merging, transmitting pulses down the light-line into the core. It was drawing on the latent tech of the planet, sapping information, learning.

The Elder Elaki strode forward, accompanied by the Matriarch.

"It is working," she said. She put out a black-gloved hand and held it just short of the haunt-engine. Sparks cracked out and were repelled again, as if by the touch of Elaki's hand. Dreams-of-War watched, mesmerized, as Elaki circled the engine, hands outheld.

"How big will it become?" Dreams-of-War heard the Matriarch say.

"It will encompass the Tower," Elaki replied without turning her head. She continued to stroke the energy coming from the haunt-engine, like someone soothing a pet. "The matrix down here will spread and merge, seek information buried in the walls of the Tower. Already it has brought forth many of the ghosts that are embedded here. They go to feed it."

My *armor*, thought Dreams-of-War. What had happened to the animating spirit of Embar Khair? Had it been sucked into the vampire-drain of the haunt-engine, leaving the armor empty? Or had the armor itself melted away into a pool of nanoenergy? Dreams-of-War reached for the stolen bow that now hung at her side.

"It grows," the Matriarch said. The echo of her whispering voice filled the chamber. Dreams-of-War raised the bow and notched the bolt, feeling it quiver, aiming at the figure of the Elder Elaki.

Can you kill these future ghosts? We shall see.

Her sight was directed on Elaki, but it was becoming hard to see. The air around the black light matrix sparkled, and Elaki appeared as through a haze. But Dreams-of-War had trained on men-remnants in the half-light and she had good aim. She raised the bow to fire.

CHAPTER 13

MARS

Yskatarina, headless, reached out and clasped the spined claw of the Animus. Her detached and splintered consciousness drifted above her shattered body, tied by a thread.

"How badly are you hurt?" She thought the words.

"I am wounded." The Animus twisted across the sword. "But I will live. I am already healing."

And with her fading sight, Yskatarina saw that the flow of ichor was slowing, the space between the Animus's chitinous plates was starting to close and sinews regrowing to reattach its head.

"I will not," she whispered. "I cannot heal this. You have to take me inside you." As she thought the words, Yskatarina was conscious of a vast relief. A handful of human years, and an eon before that.

"It will be as before," the Animus said softly. "It will be better. Do you remember now the walls of the world? The crater lip of Nightshade? We had no body then. But now, we will."

"I remember. It was a nightmare. Another life, another self. It will be strange, to return to being a single form."

"I tell you, it *will* be better. At least we will *have* a form."

"Yes, it will be better. Take me. And we will go and look for Elaki."

CHAPTER 14

MARS

Just as Dreams-of-War was about to fire, she was struck from behind in a tangle of spiny black limbs. Together, Dreams-of-War and the Animus fell from the steps into the midst of the excissieres. They hit the floor of the cavern in a tangle of limbs and bowstring. Any illusions that Dreams-of-War might have entertained about the Animus's state of health were now dispelled. The strength that she had earlier discerned during their flight over the sea was back in full force. The thing was hissing, snaking around, spines ripping through her flesh. It was like wrestling with a giant scorpion. Excissieres milled about them, reaching out. The Animus's tail lashed forth and brought two of them sprawling. The tail snaked up and over, striking down at Dreams-of-War's face. She rolled, pinning the creature beneath her. The sense of the Eldritch was redoubled when she looked into its black lens gaze and saw Yskatarina looking back at her.

"That body is dead," the Animus spat. "And we are back together again."

"Congratulations." Dreams-of-War stabbed a thumb into one of the lenses. It shifted beneath her touch, then snapped back again, taking Dreams-of-War's thumb with it. The severed digit vanished into the depths of the Animus's eye. Dreams-of-War swore in mingled pain and fury.

"What is happening?" she heard the Elder Elaki cry. There was a commotion among the excissieres. They parted. Dreams-of-War had a brief glimpse of black robes as Elaki strode through. The Animus's tail was thrashing about behind her. She felt the side of the sting graze her shoulder, twisted to one side. Seizing the razor-sharp bowstring, she wrapped it around the Animus's wasp neck and pulled it tight. It lacerated her bloodied hands, but the Animus's head again parted company from its body. Dreams-of-War leaped to her feet and kicked the head into the haunt-engine just as an excissiere's scissors plunged into her side. Dreams-of-War doubled up, but as she did so, she saw the still-twitching tail of the Animus beneath her. She grasped it, dragging the body upward, and thrust the sting into Elaki's abdomen.

The sting went through the Elder's robes with ease. Elaki's mouth gaped open. Her hands drifted up, slowly, slowly, to clasp the tail.

"Out . . ." she said.

But the neurotoxins were already taking effect. Reeling back, Dreams-of-War saw black glitter spark through Elaki's veins, lighting her from within. Her eyes fell shut, opened again a moment later. And once more Dreams-of-War saw Yskatarina looking back at her from someone else's eyes.

"I'm here," she heard Elaki say, and then the Elder dropped to the floor. The excissieres stared in mute shock. No one moved. A spinning shape flowed from the Elder's open eyes, bicolored silver and black, and was sucked into the haunt-engine.

"Not wise," Dreams-of-War heard someone say. She could not think who it might be. "Kill her. Throw the body to the Sown, to feed upon."

Dreams-of-War looked up and saw the swaying shape of the Matriarch standing before her. But the cavern and all it contained were overlaid by somewhere else: a vast caldera of night, filled with stars so small that Dreams-of-War could have reached out and grasped them in her hand. She was standing on the edges of the Eldritch Realm, on the lip of death.

"Dreams-of-War!"

The voice was very distant. *This*, she thought, *cannot possibly be important*.

"Dreams-of-War, listen to me. Open your eyes."

She forced herself to do so. The Matriarch was still standing in front of her, but it, too, had no head. A little trickle of blood, nothing more, seeped from the severed tendons and arteries of its neck. Then it crashed to the floor. Dust, the color of old iron, gushed out. The kappa stood behind, a sword clasped in thick fingers.

"You!"

"I have been biding my time," the kappa said mildly. "Not a good idea to die, right now. You'd enter the Realm in very bad company."

Stepping to Dreams-of-War's side, she strapped a torn strip of cloth over the wound in the Martian's side. Cold antitoxins flooded through, making Dreams-of-War gasp. "Now your hand," the nurse commanded. Numbly, Dreams-of-War raised her injured hand to the attention of the kappa. The Eldritch Realm was receding, a dark line at the limits of vision. And now that it was going, she saw that the excissieres were standing in a silent crowd, rigid and unmoving.

"Why aren't they doing something?"

"They have no leader, I suspect. The Matriarch is dead." The kappa nodded toward the fallen figure of the old creature, now decaying into ash. "Whatever inhabited it is gone into the engine—I saw it. They're controlled by the key in that perfume locket. It's tied into their DNA. You're of the Memnos line, aren't you? I'd suggest taking it, once I've attended to your hand."

Dreams-of-War stood watching as the kappa bound her wound and then, stooping, picked up the little phial.

"Here," the kappa said, unstoppering it. She sprayed a mist of perfume onto Dreams-of-War's skin, making Dreams-of-War cough. It stung for a moment, then seeped out through the chamber. The excissieres stirred into life. As one, they turned and looked in the direction of Dreams-of-War. She heard the snick of scissors. She had an army, but behind them, the haunt-engine was still growing.

CHAPTER 15

MARS

Lunae watched as a flood of excissieres poured through the gates of the Tower. The dawn light was glowing rose and white above the distant Olympian cone. Certain that the excissieres were coming to join the ranks of the Sown, Lunae shrank back against the bank of the canal. But the sounds from the foot of the Tower suggested otherwise: shrieks of fury, and the clash of battle. Unable to resist curiosity, Lunae slid up over the top of the bank again and looked out. Excissieres and the first rank of the Sown were fighting.

The Sown surged forward, leaving the plain empty before Lunae. Stumbling along the bank of the canal, she ran, skirting the army. The Sown paid no attention to her, but as the light grew, she could see that the excissieres were falling. The Sown moved inexorably onward, surrounding the Tower. Soon, Lunae reached the edges of the lock. The Tower reared up above her. Black light poured out of the slit windows, vying with the dawn. Lunae stood in a glittering twilight. Sparks poured from the chitinous carapaces of the Sown, running into the ground, which churned and boiled as the mass of the Sown passed across it.

Then, running up onto the edge of the bank, Lunae saw a woman. Her pale hair streamed out behind her. She wore body harness, carried a bow. Beside her, struggling to keep up, was a familiar squat figure. Lunae almost cried out, but the Sown were too close. She clambered up the lock gate, clinging to wet splintered wood, and dropped down to the other side. She landed painfully on her hands and knees. The fall knocked the breath out of her and it took a moment for her to haul herself to her feet. When she did so, Dreams-of-War and the kappa had vanished. Gasping, Lunae continued along the bank and looked down.

A glimpse of long blond hair and white skin, like a candleflame through the shadows. The Sown were cutting their way through a line of excissieres. The scissor-women went down as easily as the gaezelles had done. The Sown, trudging forward, caught up with Dreams-of-War and the kappa and surrounded them.

"Dreams-of-War!" Lunae shouted. The Martian whipped around.

"Lunae! Stay on the bank! Don't—" She struck out. There was a sword's gleam. Two of the Sown fell. Black light was still pouring out of the Tower and then, as abruptly as if someone had flicked a switch, it stopped. The Sown turned. In the skull-faces of those nearest to her, just a step down now from the edge of the bank, Lunae saw life stop for an instant, and another consciousness flood through. The Kami had come, conjured through time. She had failed to stop the Flood.

She paused in indecision at the top of the bank. If she acted now, would it be the right time? If she moved herself through time, what would it accomplish? She might find herself in the very midst of the Sown, about to be cut down. Her future-self had said she could not die, would move forward at the moment of death . . . But it was not herself that she was worried about.

One of the Sown, perhaps swifter or stronger than the rest, wheeled around from its temporary interruption. A great arm came down upon the kappa's head.

Lunae did not know whether or not she cried out. There was no more room for indecision. Instead, she shifted.

She intended, in that split second, to move only the kappa and herself. But as she made the shift, she felt the presence of the Kami, rank upon rank. The shift attracted their attention. In the smallest space between times, she felt them turn. And she could feel the haunt-engine, too: a great pulsing beat at the edge of the world, a gateway to the Eldritch Realm.

She also saw the scene below her with anguished clarity: Dreams-of-War bloody, bandaged, half-naked; the kappa, a second away from death at the Sown's fist, the red Tower, the army . . . Lunae, still in that space between times, turned her full concentration upon the haunt-engine. She could see it, now, as though she stood in two places at once. It filled the Memnos Tower: a gate of black light. Beyond it, she could see what must be the Eldritch Realm itself, a whirling, spinning mass of darkness and light and something in between that she could not describe. A stream of sparks arced out from the mass, half-resolving into faces before fading into smoke and pouring into the haunt-engine.

Before, she had taken the chrysalis through time, and then the kappa. She knew that she could shift solid objects. But that had only been under her own power. The power of the haunt-engine, designed like a smaller version of the Chain, to bring spirits through time, was far greater. Lunae reached out with shifting senses and touched the edges of the black light matrix. It surged through her like a released sea. She looked down into the abyss of the Eldritch Realm itself: the million layers and nations of the dead. Into that realm she shifted the haunt-engine. She felt Mars turn beneath her feet—a terrible sensation. A weight of bodies and souls moved in behind her, drawn in the engine's wake, and finally the gateway itself collapsed inward.

She knew where to take them. She had been there before. This time, it was not the toxic, fungal mountains of Mars, but the very end of the world: the gray plain. She drew everything behind her, skirting the Eldritch Realm, which flashed fast by. She glimpsed things that she could not comprehend; in those glimpses, she saw that the Realm itself was alive. Something was coming to join her, spiraling up from the chaos below: the tiniest spark of light. She did not have time to study it. With a great effort, she set her thoughts on the plain. Then the Realm was falling behind, beyond—and Mars lay below.

She was once more standing on the plain, but it was darker now, and colder. The grass beneath her feet was crisp with frost. The only light came from the Memnos Tower itself, as though shadows cast shadows.

"Lunae!" Dreams-of-War's voice came out of the dark like an arrow. She sensed a mass of bodies shifting all around her: the Sown, groaning into consciousness.

"Dreams-of-War! Where are you?"

But there was some light, she saw—a tiny spark, no larger than a firefly. It danced above the heads of the Sown, spreading what at first Lunae took to be light in its wake. But then she saw that it was not light at all, but fire. She thought of the thing that she had brought from the Eldritch Realm.

A hard wet hand clamped itself to her arm.

"Lunae! What have you done?" Dreams-of-War hissed.

"I took us through," Lunae said, but as she spoke, she remembered Essa speaking of the end of Mars.

And of firestorms.

"Where's the kappa?"

"I am here," the nurse said, seeming to bustle out of the darkness.

Dreams-of-War was staring at the spark, which spun frantically above the dazed heads of the Sown.

"It's looking for a *body*."

The thing was crying out, in a high, thin voice like a wasp. Dreams-of-War gaped at it. "*Yskatarina?*"

There was nothing to contain the spark, torn from the Realm. The haunt-engine was dead, the Tower quite dark now. But the coarse grass had caught, blazing up like burning hair. Lunae saw each one of the Sown burst like a pitch torch, fire streaming from beneath the chitinous helm-heads. She heard the Kami shrieking, fleeing their borrowed bodies—but there was nowhere to go. Next moment, she looked up into a firewall. A blast of heat struck her, so intense that it felt cold. Lunae snatched Dreams-of-War and the kappa up and out.

The Eldritch Realm once more lay before them, but this time it seemed a calm and ordered place: a sea of night, filled with stars and sparks, each gliding around its appointed sphere. The Realm spoke to her.

"Are you disembodied?" It did not sound greatly disturbed, merely somewhat puzzled, as though the smallest cog in its mechanism had developed a minute perturbation.

"I don't know."

The Realm made a minuscule adjustment, turning in upon itself, leaving room for Lunae to take them back to the place they had left—to the Martian morning and the rising sun.

EPILOGUE

They stood in the Martian dawn, staring down into the newest crater of the plain. Where the Memnos Tower had stood for thousands of years, where the Sown had risen and the Kami poured back through time, there was now only a gaping hole, a wound in the red earth.

"No matter." Dreams-of-War, latest Matriarch of Mars, spoke briskly. She stood in only her underharness, unweaponed. But not, Lunae suspected, for long. "I've never liked that place. Too much intrigue. I don't like intrigue. Now that I have the Matriarch's phial, I shall return to the clan house and recruit from the women of Winterstrike. We will live as we once lived, out on the plains and mountains, doing what we do best."

"And what of Earth?" the kappa said, mild as ever. "Who will govern our world, now that Memnos is gone?"

"I don't know." Dreams-of-War gave her a blank look. "You kappa are pretty much running its industries and services, as far as I can see. Sort something out."

"That is your only piece of advice, Matriarch?"

"Why should I care?"

"Why, indeed?" the kappa said after a moment. She turned to Lunae. "And you?"

Lunae thought back to Fragrant Harbor, to the smoldering ire-palmed ruin that had once been her only home. Then she looked at the crater, now starting to flood as the canal seeped forth into it.

"Do you really understand what you are?" the kappa asked.

Dreams-of-War scowled. "What is she, then?"

"She is the first of the Kami, really. A person who can move through time. Perhaps the only one—though we do not know what has become of the Mission on Earth, whether any remain there."

"Well, I can't think of her as Kami," Dreams-of-War spoke firmly.

"Yet she is." The kappa gave a grim smile. "And what if Lunae's existence causes the kind of future we have just prevented to unscroll again?"

Dreams-of-War made a dismissive gesture.

"Don't trouble me with paradoxes. I have decided not to believe in them."

"The kappa is right," Lunae said. "And I know what I want to do."

"Then what is that?"

"I told you, back at Cloud Terrace. I want to travel as far as I can. First to Nightshade, to look for answers. And then— perhaps—beyond. If I can shape time, perhaps I can shape space, too. Who knows what I may be able to do? Who knows where I might be able to go?"

"Who knows?" the kappa agreed, and they followed her gaze upward, to where the Chain was slowly turning.

ABOUT THE AUTHOR

Liz Williams is the daughter of a stage magician and a Gothic novelist, and currently lives in Brighton, England. She received a PhD in philosophy of science from Cambridge, and her career since has ranged from reading tarot cards on Brighton pier to teaching in Central Asia. She has had short fiction published in *Asimov's*, *Interzone*, *The Third Alternative*, and *Visionary Tongue*, among other publications, and is coeditor of the recent anthology *Fabulous Brighton*. She is also the current secretary of the Milford UK SF Writers' Workshop. *Banner of Souls* is her fifth novel. She is currently working on her sixth.